Gwyneth Stevens Book II:

THE
ENCHANTRESS

By

Mandy M. Roth

Romantic Paranormal Suspense

New Concepts   Georgia

Be sure to check out our website for the very best in fiction at fantastic prices!

When you visit our webpage, you can:

* Read excerpts of currently available books
* View cover art of upcoming books and current releases
* Find out more about the talented artists who capture the magic of the writer's imagination on the covers
* Order books from our backlist
* Find out the latest NCP and author news--including any upcoming book signings by your favorite NCP author
* Read author bios and reviews of our books
* Get NCP submission guidelines
* And so much more!

We offer a 20% discount on all new Trade Paperback releases ordered from our website!

Be sure to visit our webpage to find the best deals in e-books and paperbacks! To find out about our new releases as soon as they are available, please be sure to sign up for our newsletter (http://www.newconceptspublishing.com/newsletter.htm) or join our reader group (http://groups.yahoo.com/group/new_concepts_pub/join)!

The newsletter is available by double opt in only and our customer information is *never* shared!

Visit our webpage at:
www.newconceptspublishing.com

New Concepts Publishing, Inc.
5202 Humphreys Rd.
Lake Park, GA 31636

ISBN 1-58608-719-3
© copyright 2004, Mandy M. Roth

Cover art (c) copyright 2004, Eliza Black

NCP books are available at special quantity discounts for bulk purchases for sales promotions, premiums, fund raising, or educational use. For details, write, email, or phone New Concepts Publishing, Inc., 5202 Humphreys Rd., Lake Park, GA 31636; Ph. 229-257-0367, Fax 229-219-1097; orders@newconceptspublishing.com.

First NCP Paperback Printing: December 2005

Dedication:

To all of you who embraced Gwen and her many flaws, thank you for seeing the "bigger picture." To the other M, it's okay to turn the lights on. To Jaycee, thanks for letting me bounce the entire series off you and for still talking to me afterwards. To my brother, Kris, for not only encouraging my creativity when we were young (and yes, the fib I told you about the muscle cream being toothpaste counts as creativity--sorry you had to get your stomach pumped), but for also being supportive at this stage of the game. To Andrea, my editor, you never once make me compromise, regardless how bizarre I get and there's a lot to be said for that.

Chapter 1

I stared at the giant hole in the ground and stood silent. I'm not sure there is a good word to use when you think that someone's fallen off the deep edge--in an *'in love'* kind of way. Pointing it out almost seems cruel, especially when you're who they're in love with.

I couldn't believe I'd let Caleb talk me into this. We'd been dating for a couple of months now. It felt more like a lifetime, after all this wasn't my first go round with him. I'd been betrothed to him over two hundred years ago. Yeah, I know, that definitely takes the prize for the world's longest engagement.

Standing on the edge of the missing earth, I peered into the hole. It was huge. You could easily park at least two cars in it. "I thought you said you were making a tiny Koi pond," I said, looking down at Caleb. He stood in the bottom of the hole holding a yellow-handled shovel, pitching dirt up and over his head. His muscles hardened with each movement he made, and his back seemed to ripple as the sun glistened off his sweat. This was being done strictly for my benefit and I wasn't about to start complaining. Although, I would've preferred to have those muscles sweaty and taut above me. He could have dug the hole without any physical labor on his part whatsoever.

Caleb and I are both faeries. I don't mean faeries in the little pixie way with wings that grant wishes and hang with boys from Never-Never Land--I mean faeries as in tall, or at least Caleb was tall, slender, long haired, and pale skinned.

If Caleb really wanted to, he could have used his magical power to remove the soil from the ground and be done in a matter of minutes. No, he'd insisted on taking the hard way. He'd been digging the darn hole now for the last two weeks. I knew he wouldn't dare risk someone seeing him use magic, even though we were in the middle of nowhere. Not one single deer on the property would notice a little shift in the wind, or care, but Caleb wasn't one to take chances. He was conservative by nature and it suited him.

Someone had to balance us out.

Standing shoulder deep in a hole with a shovel in his hand made Caleb feel as though he had a purpose. His chosen profession was bounty hunter to the supernatural. If any sort of spook, undead, or out of the ordinary criminal was on the loose, Caleb was the man they called. Bounty hunting is extremely dangerous, but pays well. He loved his job and had been forced to cut his hours back to stick around and baby-sit me.

There had been several attempts on my life a little over two months ago. Vicious and smelly trolls had attacked me a couple of times. One of the nasty varmints managed to sink its ragged, rotted teeth into my shoulder. Apparently, a troll's bite is venomous and packs a hell of punch. It would have killed me if Caleb hadn't shown up when he did. I still wanted to launch a campaign to get trolls listed as one of the world's most deadly creatures, but that would mean exposing humans to the reality of their existence--no thanks.

The day we became reacquainted, Caleb had been tracking the trolls into this realm. He was curious as to why they were coming here at all. They weren't known for leaving their rat infested swamplands often. When he saw them attacking me he figured it out real quick. They'd been sent to kill me. The acting head of *Si*, (pronounced *shee*) Sorcha, had ordered my death.

Hey, I could be as much of a pain in the butt as the next gal but wanting me dead seemed a bit extreme. I am biased, I know, but still….

Turns out Sorcha had her reasons. One of which was to kill me before her son and I could meet--again. As far as Sorcha knew, I was just a reborn faerie out to trap her son in a loveless marriage.

Yeah, reborn, I know, crazy life, huh! It was a huge shocker for me too. It was still a little hard for me to deal with and I'd found out about two months ago. From what they tell me, I once lived for over a hundred years on this earth, never looking a day over twenty, and now I was back. The only major difference, physically speaking, was that my eyes had been violet before and now they were navy blue. But that was neither here nor there, and since my other life was close to two hundred years ago, I saw little point in dwelling on it.

Being hunted down by Sorcha's henchmen threw me for a loop. I had no idea that she even existed, let alone had it in for me. Did I forget to mention that Sorcha is Caleb's mother? Oops! Sorcha hated me from the day I was betrothed to Caleb, in my previous life. Hating someone for close to four hundred years was a long time to hold a grudge. I had to hand it to her, she was persistent. Bottling up all that hate for so many centuries could not be healthy.

I looked down at Caleb digging in the hole and was unable to figure out how I'd been so lucky to get him. He was a vision of beauty--his six foot four frame was well defined, thin, but not too thin, and his long shiny-blond hair hung to his waist. It was smooth and straight. I was so envious of his hair. I had to laugh at the fact that my boyfriend had better hair than me. Don't get me wrong, I'd been blessed all right, but I unfortunately didn't get to be a blonde bombshell. Genetics dealt me long wavy hair that was black as night.

Yeah, Caleb was beautiful, a little *too* beautiful. It didn't matter-- every bit of him was man, you can trust me on that. I know this because we had sex the first day we met. No, I don't normally run around having sex with strangers, but he wasn't a stranger. We'd been together for a hundred years once, so that had to qualify for something.

Sometimes, I even confuse myself.

"Are you going to be doing that all day?" I asked, missing his touch. He'd been consumed with getting the old farmhouse fixed up. It was his new mission. He was one of those people that always needed to be doing something constructive or they'd go mad. I was the complete opposite. I could sit for hours on a rock, observing the wonders that nature had to offer, and never once feel guilty about it.

Caleb glanced up at me with dirt smeared on his forehead and cheek. I snickered as he wiped his dirt stained hand across his cheek effectively blackening out the side of his face. "I'm sorry. I just want to get this filled with cement, before the weather gets too bad. I'm pushing it enough as it is doing it this late in the year. I want you to have this, Gwen. Let me do this for you, then we can sit out here, listen to the water roll over the rocks and maybe," he wagged his eyebrows and gave me a half-cocked smile, "we could do a little something else out here as well."

How could I argue with that? Caleb's forest green eyes looked at me with such love, I wanted to jump down into the hole and kiss him, but getting out would be an issue for me. Standing at only five foot five made it hard to get in and out of there without the aid of a ladder. He was making it seven feet deep, because the Koi needed it deep to survive the harsh winter. I personally think he did it just to tease me about how short I am.

When Caleb decided to help me fix up the farmhouse, we'd picked up a bunch of remodeling books and magazines. We sat together, cuddled in our bed flipping through the pages, picking things out that we liked. I'd stopped at a picture of an attractive white home, with a large man-made water garden in front of it. The magnificently colored pond lilies and large multi-colored fish caught my eye. It looked so peaceful, so serene. The next day I woke to find Caleb missing from the bed. I went searching for him, and found him out behind the house digging a hole in the ground. He had the magazine opened to the page with the water garden. My heart melted.

"Well, baby, do you at least want some lunch?" He hadn't eaten breakfast and it was pushing two o'clock. I didn't want him to get run down. He had to work this weekend. I hated the idea of Caleb leaving me to head off to wherever it was he went. His job was dangerous and I worried sick about him the entire time he was gone.

"Gwen, I'm fine, *a ghrá*, don't worry about me. I'm just about done for the day." He tossed more dirt over his head. I hated this. I knew that he was doing this for me, but I wanted to see him. I wanted to spend time with him before he had to leave.

We'd only been "back" together for two months, but already I felt attached to him. My body ached when he was away from me. I missed his smell--he always smelled so fresh and clean, like the morning air after a rainfall. I had often wondered if they could bottle the smell of him and mass-produce it. Women would dig it--I'm sure.

The wind around us picked up. It sent dried leaves scattering about the yard. Caleb didn't seem to notice or care about the weather cooling down, he still ran around with no shirt on and a pair of jeans most of the time. It was forever summer to him. I often wondered if he was running a core body temperature that was twenty degrees hotter than most. He had that California beach-babe thing going and I couldn't help but love it.

I, on the other hand, had packed my shorts away for the season and pulled out my winter clothes. I was always cold lately. I pulled the sleeves of my Cappuccino-colored acrylic sweater down and over my hands. I had a knit shirt underneath it, but I was still chilly. Great, I hoped I wasn't getting a cold. I hadn't really ever had one before, but I'd seen my friends and coworkers fighting them off. All the phlegm, hacking, and headaches, no thanks I'd pass.

Caleb glanced up at me. "Gwen?"

He was always so concerned about me. He was convinced that his mother would never stop trying to sabotage our relationship. I didn't worry about that too much. I figured my father would look out for us. He was, after all, the King--and no Caleb and I are not related. Sorcha, Caleb's mother only stepped in to lead the Dark Realm in the absence of my father.

Under normal circumstances, Sorcha was just the head sorceress for my father. He took her on for this duty when he saw that she had a young son, Caleb. Instantly, my father arranged a marriage between the two of us. I was only days old and he'd only seen me once. Not a good way to start out I know, but things had changed this time around, they were better--he was better.

Caleb gave me another questioning look.

"I'm fine. I swallowed some dust or something, really," I said, trying to sound as convincing as possible. I didn't want him to feel like he had to stay home with me. Caleb enjoyed his job and I didn't want to take that from him. Besides, James and Caradoc were coming up to stay with me for the weekend. It would be great. They'd turned into two of my closest friends in a relatively short period of time. They were both vampires, but that didn't faze me a bit.

I'd slept with their Master, Pallo, about two months ago. Yep, same time I began seeing Caleb. Walking in and meeting Pallo had changed my life forever. He had been what jogged my memory of my life before. I had been in love with him hundreds of years ago when he was still human. I'd even left Caleb for him, well not for him but for another vampire. Yeah, I know, I was totally screwed up in the head. What do you expect? I am, after all, the daughter of the King of the Dark Realm. I'm bound to have some hang-ups. Okay, maybe a lot of hang-ups!

The phone rang and I headed into the house to grab it. I ran through the kitchen door, almost knocking a can of paint over. It seemed like Caleb was tackling a project in every room of the house. He was now in the process of putting another coat of white paint on the kitchen cabinets. I had to admit, they looked great, like they were brand new. I just wished that he'd finish one project before moving on to the next.

Men.

I snatched the phone off the wall. "Hello?" I said, a little out of breath.

"Gwen? Are you all right?"

"Ken!" I was happy to hear his voice. Ken was my boss, and my ex-fiancé. There was a time not long ago, when the sound of his voice made me nauseous--that was when I was still operating under the assumption he'd cheated on me. I had gotten over that, now I just missed him. He'd been distancing himself from me. I could hardly blame him. Things in my life were pretty screwed up right now. "Yeah, I'm good. How about you? How are you doing?"

"Good, I'm doing good. I finally got all moved into my new place. It's nice, I like it," he said, his voice low. He was keeping his emotions out of this, I could tell. I also noticed how Ken didn't offer to show me his new place. I knew his new little sweetie, Beth, had been the Realtor who helped him find it. I'd had issues with Beth from the moment he told me about her. She was the Realtor who'd taken us house hunting when we were engaged. How convenient for her that Ken's apartment had been destroyed by hellhounds and that his fiancée had left him.

"Sounds nice...how *is* Beth doing?" I hit myself on the forehead. Why in the world did I bring her into this? Ken had every right to be dating other people, I was, but it didn't lessen the pain any.

I pictured his athletic body wrapped around hers and it made me sick. I could see Beth running her fingers through Ken's dark blond hair. Last time I'd seen him he had finally let it grow out from the tight cut he had always worn. It looked good on him. I bet Beth really liked it too.

"Beth's fine, but that's not what I called about," he said, voice flat.

"Well, what did you call about, Ken? It's obvious you really don't want to be speaking to me, so what gives?"

"I just needed to call you and let you know, that you don't need to come back in." He was getting at something I was sure I wouldn't like.

"I told you I'd be back in on Monday." I'd been his personal assistant for two years. I was his right-hand girl. He never did anything without my knowledge. I knew that my taking personal time, and telecommuting from home had put a burden on him, but everything was still getting done.

"No, Gwen, I don't think that's a good idea."

I stood there playing with the phone cord and my stomach tightened. "Ken, are you letting me go?"

"Yes," he said, his voice void of any emotion.

My cheeks flushed. I wasn't hurt. I was pissed. "Well, thanks for having the balls to tell me over the phone instead of in person. I really appreciate hearing it this way. You should have sent me a letter so you wouldn't have had to speak to me at all. But, I'm probably not worth the price of a stamp, so…" I was furious with him. I didn't care about the job, that wasn't it at all, and I didn't need the money. I'd saved enough over the last few years to get by. I cared about how hard he was pushing me away.

"Gwen, don't be…."

I cut him off. "What don't be what? Don't be mad that someone I care about hates me, or don't be mad that I still care about you?" I put my hand over my mouth. Did I really just tell him that I still cared for him? What the hell was I thinking? I had Caleb now and Ken had Beth.

Ken fell silent on the other end. I didn't really expect him to say anything, although, a *just kidding, you're not fired* would have been nice. Seconds ticked by before I gave into the impulse to hang up. There wasn't really anything left for me to offer that would be considered polite, so it was better this way.

If you can't say anything nice….

Walking over to the fridge, I took out the pitcher of lemonade. I wanted a glass of wine but the lemonade would have to do. I set the pitcher on the counter and grabbed two glasses down from the shelf. As I walked back towards the freezer to get ice the phone rang again. I knew it was Ken calling me back. I didn't want to talk to him. The machine could get it. I grabbed a handful of ice out of the icebox and dropped it into the glasses. The plunking sound was a nice distraction from the nagging feeling of loss threatening to consume me.

The phone had just stopped ringing when Caleb walked in the back door. My voice greeted the caller, from the answering machine in the hallway. When the machine beeped, I looked up at Caleb. Suddenly, I wanted him to be digging out in his hole again. Not in here listening to Ken's call.

I heard Ken's voice on the machine and cringed. "Gwen, don't do this. I'm sorry. I'm having a hard time with everything still. I just need some time. You're not fired, I'm sorry, I just thought…I don't know what I thought, pick up please…I know you're there, Gwen? I still have feelings for you, too…Maybe you should take a few more weeks off…I can't do this right now. I love you too much to watch you with someone…" The machine beeped and stopped recording.

Caleb stood very still. I never really got the expression about hearing a pin drop until that moment. The anger on his face was evident. "What the hell was that about?"

I tried to avoid eye contact with him. I didn't want to hurt him, but I didn't want to lie to him either. "I love you," was the best I could come up with.

Reaching out, he took my hand in his. His hand was rough from all of the manual labor he'd been doing. It didn't matter to me that he wasn't as smooth as he'd once been, I'd take him anyway, so long as he was with me.

"Gwen, don't do this, please," he said, his hand tightened around mine. I looked up at his face. The moment I saw his green eyes, I couldn't help myself--I cried.

Prior to finding out about my past, I was normal--well as normal as a faerie living among humans could get. I didn't have multiple men at one time. I hadn't even had sex for six months before I met Caleb. Ken had been the last man I'd been with and we'd been engaged. Since I began to remember bits and snippets of my past I began to have uncontrollable desires and I didn't like the new me one bit.

Caleb pulled me close to him. His body was sweaty but still smelled wonderful. I took a deep breath in and let his scent calm me as he held me tight against his chest. He was warm and lately I'd been cold all the time. I let my head rest against him and he stroked the back of my head gently.

"Marry me, Gwen, marry me and this will all stop, I promise."

I kept my head buried in his chest. How could he be so sure, how could he know that I wouldn't leave him again for another man? That's exactly what I'd done to him my last time on this earth. I couldn't even think about committing to him, then destroying him like that again. I had a hard enough time liking myself lately. Doing that to Caleb would kill me, I was sure of that.

"I can't," I said, between sobs. His hands tightened in my hair-- he was just this side of pulling it.

"You mean you won't." The hurt in his voice was evident. I wanted to comfort him, but I was crying too hard. I wasn't going to be much good in the consoling department when I was sobbing like a baby. I tried to pull away but Caleb held me tight. "I'm sorry. I didn't mean to get you all upset. I'm sorry."

"I love you, Caleb. I love you so much, but I can't hurt you again! This is all so fast...too fast." I yearned for reassurance that he wasn't mad and that everything would be all right. I couldn't imagine my life without him. He had become everything to me, my friend, my lover, my life. I wondered if we'd been this way before, and if so why did I leave him? I wasn't sure I'd ever know the answer to that.

He kissed the top of my head. "I love you, too, Gwen. I love you, too."

Sliding my arms around his back, I hugged him tight. He was so warm, so loving, so different from any other man I'd ever had in my life. He touched my forehead lightly with the back of his hand. "Gwen, you're ice cold. Are you all right?"

I smiled and the tears began to dry on my face. It was a little like having one of those facial masks drying on you only without the luxury of being able to peel it off, and as far as I know any exfoliating qualities. I did my best to wipe my cheeks before pulling Caleb's face down to mine to kiss his lips. The salt from my tears pressed into both of our mouths. I pushed my tongue in, diving, digging for his. When I found it, it was warm and wrapped itself smoothly around mine.

My body burned to be with him, to have him hold my naked body in his arms. I knew he had to get cleaned up and get ready to go, but that didn't change the fact that I still wanted to lie with him before he left. I loved him so much and didn't want to think about the possibility of the last time we talked ending in a fight. His job was dangerous and there was always a very real chance he wouldn't come home. I'd thought I'd lost him once already and that was more than enough not to want to go through it again.

"Gwen, I'm calling Mark, I can't go in with you like this." He walked around me and headed out in the hall to use the phone. Mark was his partner. I'd never actually met him. I'd heard Caleb talk about him a few times but that was it. I asked about him once, but Caleb just told me that in their line of work, the less people knew about them the better. I wasn't sure I agreed with that. I mean, he was putting his life in this guy's hands. Didn't I have the right to at least meet him? Caleb didn't seem to agree with me on that one.

I didn't want Caleb to stay home on account of me. He loved what he did. I could always see a spark in his eye when he returned home after hunting down some crazy creature. He loved to tell me all about his adventures. I usually sat there with an aching pit at the bottom of my stomach every time he went into detail about being in danger, but I kept a smile on my face all the same. Caleb was a thrill seeker--that much was plain to see.

"Caleb!" I called after him. He turned around and looked at me. "Hey, I'm fine, you go. Besides you'll ruin my weekend movie marathon."

James would be stopping at the video store before he and Caradoc came. James and I had taken to watching movies. We'd become our own two man critiquing team. Two fangs up or down. It wasn't the best rating system, but it worked. Besides, James may be the only person more jaded than me. I couldn't be sure, but maybe. Last week's marathon had been an ode to the eighties. We'd spent the weekend watching teen flicks that dealt with serious issues, like paying your paper carrier on time, turning sixteen, and spending a weekend in detention.

It was very stimulating.

Caradoc, one of the most serious vamps I'd ever met, refused to sit with us and stare aimlessly at the television screen. He always wandered off into the woods or brought a few books to read. I'm sure he thought James and I were childish. Even though I'd just turned twenty-five, Caradoc still had me by about three hundred years or so, give or take a little.

James, on the other hand, was a "smidge" younger than him. He kept his hair cut short, and bleached it blond. I had to laugh every time I saw him spreading hair gel through it to spike it up. I think, no I know, he owns every black t-shirt ever made, and he rarely incorporates color.

Caleb walked over to me and touched my head with the back of his hand again. "Gwen, you're really cool, what's going on? Are you still taking your pills?"

The pills he referred to were my birth control pills that a *Si* doctor, Dr. Brown, had prescribed for me. The word *Si*, means elf, faerie, or magical creature. I had to hunt around for a doctor who specialized in this. Going to a normal doctor would have been too risky. Ordinary everyday people didn't know that faeries, vampires, and other creatures of the night were real, and it had to stay that way.

I had no idea what was in the pills, but they were the equivalent of taking three normal birth control pills at one time. I had to take them twice a day because I was a *Si* and was in the reproductive prime of my life. No one knew how long I would remain fertile, it could be hundreds of years, or it could just be a few weeks. It could end tomorrow and revisit me again in a hundred years.

There was no rhyme or reason to it all and it made it hard to prevent unplanned pregnancies.

Caleb and I had agreed not to have a baby right now. I could have already been swollen with child right now if I didn't take the pills religiously. We were perfect matches, and in the life of a faerie, you only got a few of those--if you were lucky. A match, or life-mate, was someone whose essence was complementary to you, thus possibly producing a healthy offspring. My female *Si* body would be very selective on whom it would allow to impregnate me. I never actually got a list of prerequisites for the guy to possess, so I wasn't sure who all fit the bill. Two possibilities existed so far, Caleb was the only sure thing. He wanted to marry me and have a family, I knew that, but he also respected me enough not to push it, most of the time.

"Yeah, I'm still taking the pills, so no, I'm not pregnant."

Staring down at my stomach, he looked disappointed. My gestation rate was a bit more accelerated than a human's was, so if I were to become pregnant I would show in a matter of weeks. I'd still have to carry the baby for almost a year, allowing it to soak up magical powers from me, but I'd be huge by four months. I felt bad for letting him down, but this was my body, and right now, I did not want to have a baby.

He glanced up at me and knew I'd caught him fixating on my stomach. A slight smile played across his face. "I was just...."

"You were just hoping I decided to surprise you. Well I didn't, sorry." I hated being like this with him. "Look, I'm sorry, but do you really think I want to get pregnant, watch you head out that door hunting some lethal demon, only to never come back through it? Do you think I want to raise our baby by myself? Is that it? God, Caleb, get real, you can't expect me to do that, you can't expect me to say, hey let's do it, gee we've only been a couple for two months but let's start a family anyways. Oh, then after I have a perfect little version of you I can sit around and spend the rest of my life mourning the man I loved and lost every time I look into his eyes." I was rambling and I knew it. "I'm not cut out to be a mother. Take a good look at me, Caleb! I can't even take care of myself. I'm a mess and you know it!"

My temper flared. I had a nasty one and he knew it. He was always saying how much like my father I was. I wouldn't really know since the man didn't raise me. Two wonderfully loving humans raised me, not the King of the Dark Realm. I'd have to take Caleb's word on issues involving my father.

Caleb reached out to touch me. I pulled away from him. "Gwen,
I didn't mean that, and if you don't like what I do why didn't you
just say something? I'll stop, I'll quit right now if it will make you
feel better about us. I'll do anything you want. You just have to tell
me what the hell it is you want. I'm not like some 'people' we
know, I don't read minds."

Rolling my eyes, I sighed, feeling extremely defeated. I didn't
want him to quit his job. He loved what he did and I'd never ask
him to give it up. In truth, I didn't know what I wanted anymore. I
just knew that I didn't want to fight about this again. "Forget it,
I'm fine. Go, you need to get cleaned up."

"Just this once, I'll make an exception about magic." Warm air
surrounded us both. It wrapped itself around me and I closed my
eyes just for a moment to bask in the felling of Caleb's power.
When I opened them again, he was clean.

He reached out and grabbed me around my waist. Before I could
protest, he'd picked me up in his arms, and I grinned from ear to
ear. He could always make me smile no matter what. It was a gift
few possessed. He carried me up the stairs and to our bedroom.
We had taken over the master bedroom and he was in the middle
of tearing down the wallpaper. The walls looked like something
had been clawing at them, shreds of paper hung loosely to the
floor. I laughed at the state of the room as he tossed me down on
the bed gently.

Sliding his hands up and under my sweater, he traced his fingers
lightly over my silk bra. My nipples hardened under the weight of
his gentle touch. Moaning, I rubbed my body against his, needing
to feel every inch of him. Quickly, he removed my pants and
underwear before sliding back over me.

He bent down and captured my mouth with his. I loved kissing
him, I loved tasting him--I couldn't get enough of him. His scent
was manly, woodsy, rugged. Faeries came by their smell honestly.
I tended to smell like a touch of lavender, and Caleb smelled like
the fresh morning dew, earth, man. It could be traced back to the
first faeries that were in charge of watching over all things in
nature.

Caleb slid his fingers under my bra strap, gently caressing my
breast. Reaching down, I tugged on the button to undo his jeans. I
undid it and slid my hand down the front of his pants. I don't think
the man owned a pair of underwear. I asked him about it once and
he joked that he was always ready for me this way. I had to laugh,
he was right. I touched him, running my fingers over his velvety

smooth cock. I always loved the fact it took no time at all to be ready for sex.

"I can't get enough of you," I said, nipping at his mouth. He pushed me back gently and laughed.

"No, you can't get enough sex period. It's the nymph in you. All Fey women have ties to nymphs, yours is stronger due to the royal blood running through your veins."

"Mmm, would that make me a...?"

I stroked his shaft faster and he grabbed my hand, pulling me away from him gently. "Yes, Gwen...that's exactly what it makes you."

"Then what's that make you?" I asked, trying to take hold of him again. He shifted slightly and I grabbed him tight.

Caleb lifted my shirt and sweater over my head, exposing my stomach and chest to him. "That's easy...a fool for loving you."

I continued caressing the length of him--feeling him growing harder in my hand. He was so hot. It felt good against my cold hand. I wanted to bring him to me, and enjoy every bit of him before he left for the weekend. He seemed to be thinking the same thing as me.

Caleb always liked me to lay back and let him see me. I didn't bother questioning him about it anymore. I just did it. He traced the mounds of my breasts and ran the tips of his fingers down my rib cage. I pulled my arms in, trying to avoid being tickled any further. Grabbing my wrists, he put his entire body over mine, leaving my hands pinned above my head. A feral look came over him and I froze under the weight of his stare.

In every other aspect of his life, Caleb was gentle, easy going. In the bedroom he often let another side come through. A side where he told me what was going to happen. A side where he used my body in a way that left me breathless, sated and in awe of him. A side that made me wonder how much of his calm exterior was real. Killing things for a living had to harden a man to point and Caleb had been doing it for centuries. Did I really know him at all? I liked to think I did.

I'm not sure if it was the faerie in him or not, but Caleb didn't have sex, he became it. His hands were twice the size of mine, giving him an unfair advantage in the bedroom. I was no match for him physically and he knew it. He held both my wrists together with just one of his hands and used his free one to trace tiny circles down my side, teasing me, tickling me, making me pant with need. My body burned for his. I wanted him to take me, to make love to me, and not be gentle.

"Caleb…."

He nuzzled his face into my neck. I felt the tiniest start of a beard. It still surprised me. He was able to grow one but it would take a long time. He seemed to think I'd like him with facial hair. Maybe I would.

"Yes?" he asked, as he licked the side of my neck.

"Please, Caleb!"

A throaty laugh escaped him. It was so unlike his normal laugh that it made me take pause. "Please, what?"

I couldn't take it anymore. He was going to make me say it even if it killed me. I gave in. "I want you inside me."

"What do you want me to do inside of you?"

"Caleb."

He nipped lightly at my neck while grinding his lower half against my body. I jerked my arms, attempting to free my wrists from his grasp. It was pointless. I bit at his earlobe and caught it between my teeth. He made a small purring noise in my ear. It sent my body into a state of frenzy. I tugged harder on his earlobe, before sliding my tongue over it and moaning. "Take me, please. Caleb, I want it hard, and I want it now."

Amused by my need, he laughed softly. "How hard do you want it, Gwen?"

I tossed my head back, unable to take this anymore. "I want your cock buried so deep inside me that I can't think, can't talk, can't move."

He pulled his face up from my neck and stared down at me. His green eyes began to glow, signifying his ability to get me pregnant. It was like built in birth control.

"Caleb, your eyes."

His eyelids fluttered, drawing attention to his thick lashes. "It's getting too hard for me to control both of us. Your powers are growing each day and combined with mine, it takes too much of my energy. Energy I'd rather use to fuck you."

"Caleb!"

He shrugged, his eyebrows lifted. "That's what you want me to do to you right now, isn't it?"

As crude as it sounded, it was exactly what I wanted him to do to me. I wanted it hard, rough, now--I wanted fucked. "Yes."

"Say that you'll marry me, Gwen, and I'll give you what you want."

"Caleb."

"*An bpósfaidh tú mé?*--will you marry me?" Hearing Caleb utter those words in Gaelic made my chest tight and my body ache for him. When Pallo spoke, his accent was always prensent, faint, but always there. Caleb was different. He sounded like he grew up in the mid-west most of the time, but could slip into old habits at a moment's notice.

"Marry me, Gwen." He slid his fingers into my hot channel and found how very much I wanted him. He held them there and continued to taunt me. He dipped one in deeper, moving it around, caressing me, and then pulled it back quickly, teasing me.

"Marry me, Gwen, and I'll give you this and so much more for all eternity."

Could I see myself spending forever with him? Yes, surprisingly enough, I could. But the thought of hurting him was still there, just under the surface. My fear must have shown in my eyes.

"Once we're bound, it will get easier." He closed his eyes for a moment, not wanting to look at me while he talked about such a sensitive issue. "Not craving Pallo's touch will get easier. I promise. You'll have my will power, the full weight of my magic and control residing in you...you'll have my love."

"It's too soon."

He shook his head. "We love each other, how can it be too soon?"

I struggled against his hold and he tightened his grip. "Why is this so important to you?"

"Because I love you with ever fiber of my being. Because we've been in this place before and I let you slip through my fingers. I don't want to do that again. I won't do that again." Without warning, his lips crashed down on mine. The feel of his tongue parting my lips made my breath catch. I wanted to run my hands through his silky hair but he refused to relinquish control. My bottom lip grew numb and I stared into Caleb's eyes, wondering what he was doing. The fire in his green eyes shone bright as his power, his magic moved through me.

I felt the need he carried for me. And how thankful he was to have me in his life. But most of all, I felt his fear of losing me. He'd stripped himself bare for me, allowing me to see into his soul. He would love me for all eternity.

Caleb pulled away from our kiss, taking his power with him. "Still want me to fuck you?"

The remark didn't catch me off guard this time. I gave him a wicked smile and licked my lower lip. "Yes."

He shifted a bit above me and I felt the head of his cock teetering on the edge of my opening. I tried to push my hips up to force him to enter me. It didn't work. There was no way I was moving until Caleb was damn good and ready to let me up.

"Marry me."

"Yes, Caleb, I'll marry you." My response took me by surprise. Why in the hell had I said yes to him?

The look on his face said it all. He was shocked by my response and then elated. Smiling down at me, he made my heart soar. He plunged his fingers into me and I cried out. He smeared my juices on his shaft, and thrust into me in one fluid movement. I screamed out, bucking against his hips in an attempt to take all of him within me. He strained, trying to keep from hurting me. He knew his size sometimes made sex uncomfortable for me but today I didn't care. No, I wanted all of him in me now. I bit at his chin and he slammed his body into mine.

We shared a magical moment together as his lips crashed into mine. His powers, part of his core, entered me, and mine him. Heat washed up and through me. It was the way that faeries sanctified their bond--reaffirmed their commitment to one another. Humans used diamond rings. Faeries used raw power. I had a piece of Caleb now, and he me. When we officially wed, we would surrender our powers to each other fully, and they would merge forever.

As our powers joined, an orgasm ripped through my body. I screamed out as he continued to pump all of his power and all of his cock into me. Too much, too fast. Yelling stop entered my mind. But at that very moment, Caleb changed his stroke ever so slightly, sending another orgasm through me. I contracted around him as he pumped in and out of me. My eyes burned and I hissed as another orgasm tore through me. Then it was his turn to cry out as he emptied his seed into me.

Chapter 2

We spent the rest of the afternoon making love. Just the way I wanted to end the day. Finally, I had to push Caleb out of the bed to go clean up. He didn't want to, but I knew he would lose himself in his work once he was away from me. I dressed and headed downstairs to fix him something to eat before he took off.

I decided on heating up some pasta primavera for him. I had made that for dinner the other night, it would work well now. I pulled it out and put it in the new microwave. I loved having a microwave at the house now. I had one at my old apartment. It was trashed along with everything else I owned when my place had been raided by hellhounds. Ken's place had gotten hit worse than mine so I really didn't have room to complain. Insurance had replaced almost everything I owned so I didn't worry about it. I was just psyched that nobody got hurt, my stuff was all replaceable, but people's lives weren't.

"Mmm, that smells good," Caleb said, walking up behind me. I turned and looked at him. He was dressed in a pair of loose fitting black jeans and a matching t-shirt. He had on his boots and was in the process of putting his belt on. He looked like he was ready to jump on his motorcycle and ride off into the sunset.

He looked great. I wanted to have another round in the bedroom but I knew that he had to get on the road.

I fixed us both a plate and we sat down at the table. I studied his face for answers as to how it was possible to love someone so much, yet be reluctant to commit to them. What was my problem?

"Hey!" Caleb said. I jumped a little because he surprised me. He smiled. "Don't go getting yourself into any trouble while I'm gone."

I smiled back. Every time he left me he said the same thing, and I gave my standard response. "Don't you go getting yourself killed while I'm here."

"When should we tell everyone?" he asked. I knew *whom* in particular he had in mind--Pallo. He wanted me to tell Pallo that I had agreed to marry him, and I knew why. Caleb lived in constant fear that I'd leave him for Pallo. I tried to reassure him that he had my heart but he wasn't buying it.

"Soon, but I'll pick the right time, not you," I said to him, knowing that if I left it up to him he'd write it in the sky.

He seemed pleased. Come to think of it, so was I. I couldn't remember the last time I was this excited. Leaning forward, I kissed him softly. The doorbell rang. I pulled back from Caleb and glanced up at the clock above the stove. It was eight--that meant the boys were here. Caleb rose from his seat and put his plate in the sink. I stood up, rinsed his plate to put it in the dishwasher that *he* had installed. I heard James and Caradoc's voices in the front hall. I wiped my hands on the dishtowel and headed out to greet them.

When I saw James standing there, I stopped in my tracks. His hair was bright blue, honest to God blue. Did I mention it was blue? My mouth fell open.

In typical James fashion, he laughed. "Like it that much, do you?"

I didn't know what to say. "It's, *umm*, different." That was the best I could come up with. Cut a girl some slack, his hair was blue for crying out loud!

"That's what I was goin' for. I brought some for you, too," he said, holding up a brown bag. I just stared at him. I had no plans to dye my hair blue. I didn't know what to say. Turns out, I didn't have to say a word. Caleb handled it for me.

"James," he said sternly.

James gave him a devilish grin. "I was just takin' a piss, geesh, you two--party poopers. I swear sometimes that you're older than I am."

Refraining from making fun of the fact that a two hundred plus year old British vampire just used the term party pooper is hard to do. Trust me on this one.

"I am older than you," Caleb said dryly. As of late, I'd gotten the impression that Caleb was becoming more and more annoyed with James lately. When James first began to visit, Caleb seemed fine. Now, he was coming off as being, well--jealous. That was silly. I had no interest in James *that* way. He was one of my closest friends.

I walked over to James and took the brown bag from his hand. There were several DVDs in it and two boxes of temporary hair dye. They were both pink, flaming flamingo pink to be exact. Pulling one of the boxes out, I looked at the back of it. It said that it only lasted for a few hair washings, *neat*.

"Cool," I said, and looked up at James, my eyes wide. "Let's do it."

Caleb shot me a look of astonishment. "You're not serious, Gwen? You're not going to listen to this idiot, are you? He's not shut his *gob* once since he walked in the door."

James perked up. "Hey, who you callin' a gob?"

I glanced at James sideways. "It means mouth and I think Caleb may be onto something!"

James winked and grinned from ear to ear. "I got it, love. But thanks for takin' the time to help me out...just in case."

"The very fact that you felt a need to translate for the *eejit* should tell you not to let him go dying your hair." Caleb looked past me at James and smiled. "Yes, I called you an idiot, just in case you needed it in dumb-ass terms."

James just tipped his head and did a slow blink. It was strange to see James take the mature approach. Okay, it was down right spooky.

"It's just temporary, Caleb, besides it'll be cool. Maybe it will help me feel a little better, you know perk me up a bit." I pulled some of my hair out in front of me. It hung all the way to the top of my rear end. I did need a change, nothing permanent though-- this was perfect.

Caleb pulled me aside. "Gwen, are you sure you're feeling all right? I mean I don't want to take off and come home to find you full of tattoos and pierced from head to toe."

"What, you wouldn't love me covered in tattoos?" I asked, toying with him. I had no intention on marking my body. People were always saying *think before you do it, you have to live with it for the rest of your life*. Being a faerie made me immortal, so that's a really long time to have something stuck on your body. I stood on my tiptoes and kissed him softly on the lips. "Go, you're late enough already."

He smiled and turned to grab his bags. "Always shoving me out the door aren't you? You must really want to get rid of me?"

"You bet," I said, kissing him long and soft. He touched that piece of his power that resided in me now and moved it around. I could feel it deep within me. He was showing me that I was his now. I was shocked to find I loved knowing that.

"Guys?" James said, as he made a gagging gesture. I laughed, but Caleb looked ticked.

I bent down and tried to pick up one of his bags. It weighed a ton. I couldn't even get it off the floor. Caradoc was next to me in an instant, taking the bag from me. He was such a gentleman--an old school vampire. He didn't run around dying his hair blue or wear his hair short and spiked. Oh, and he had hair to chop off, it was long, curly, and naturally white-blond. It was gorgeous hair. He kept it pulled back most of the time, but that was fine, it showed off his green eyes. They were nowhere near as dark as Caleb's but they were vivid nonetheless.

Caradoc looked so serious in his black leather pants, boots, and white puffy shirt. Normally, I would question a man about deciding to wear a puffy white dress shirt, but Caradoc pulled it off without a hitch. It seemed tailor made for him. It was part of who he was.

We followed Caleb out to his truck. Caradoc handed him his bag and he tossed it into the back of his red Explorer. It was then I noticed the car parked next to it. It was a black Acura, four-door. I knew without asking that it was one of Pallo's fleet of cars. The man was rich beyond my wildest dreams and owned, at last count, fourteen cars. James was always bringing a different one when they came to visit. They could have just flown to see me, vampires can do that you know, but I didn't have a car anymore. Mine had been blown up by a sadistic bitch's little hellhound flunkies. And I was too cheap to buy another one. So, if we wanted to go anywhere as a group, while visiting, they had to bring a car along.

James came out and saw me looking at Pallo's car. "You like?"

I shrugged. Pallo's money didn't really impress me. I thought he was an arrogant prick. He was rude, he was crude, and I loved him deeply. I hated myself for that. I hated myself for loving him as much as I loved Caleb, maybe more. Caleb was a good man, he was kind to me, he never lied to me, and I knew he would gladly spend all eternity with me. Pallo on the other hand was the exact opposite. After we'd had sex, he'd come right out and told me that he wasn't making love to me, he was just "fucking" me. Then he punched me across the face. Somehow, his words managed to hurt worse than his fist.

"It's yours," James said. Unsure of what he was talking about, I looked at him puzzled. "Yeah, Pallo bought it for you. He said you shouldn't be up here by yourself without a vehicle."

The mention of Pallo's name grabbed Caleb's attention. His power rose quickly. Caleb was well aware of the fact that I still had feelings for Pallo and he wasn't happy about it. "She is not up here all alone and he knows it!" His anger prickled across my skin and headed directly for James.

James shrugged. "Stuff the magic! I'm just the messenger."

Stepping forward, I put myself between the two of them, afraid that Caleb would lash more power at James. "Hey, it's all right. I don't want the damn car. I don't want anything from him. And, how the hell would he know if I was alone or not? It's not like he's shown his face around here." I was angry, Pallo had promised my father he'd look after me and I had not seen him once since we left my father's castle. That was almost two months ago.

So far, there hadn't been any more attempts on my life, but Caleb was cautiously optimistic about that. Caleb had called Pallo the first time he had to take off on business, to keep an eye on me. Pallo refused to come. He sent Caradoc and James in his place. It was for the best, I know, but it still hurt.

"Guys," I said, looking at Caradoc and James. They nodded and walked into the house. The moment we were alone, I went to Caleb and put my hand out to him. "Don't do this, please. I don't want *his* damn car. I don't want anything from him."

Caleb put his head down. "Yeah, if only that were true."

There was no fooling him--he knew I wanted Pallo. I didn't want cars or gifts. I wanted Pallo. I wanted to have him by my side. I wanted to have both of them next to me. That would never happen.

"So, tell me again what you're doing this weekend?" I asked, changing the subject.

He must have thought that a change of topic was in order because he answered me. "I'm chasing down an Enchantress. She's been luring men to her and then controlling their minds. She managed to get several to commit suicide already. I think there's more to this than we know. I may be gone longer than I thought."

"What about the civies? Are they aware of the problem yet?" Civies was a polite way of discussing humans who didn't have a clue about the happenings of the world. These people believed that faeries and vampires existed only in books and movies. I wasn't planning to enlighten them. And a committee was in place to see to it that they didn't find out. That's how I'd met Ken, my ex. He descended from a long line of witches. He didn't practice the craft himself, but it did give him firsthand accounts of the paranormal. After completing law school, he was approached by the committee to work in the supernatural underground as a prosecutor. He accepted, of course, and needed help.

My friend Sharon was the one who'd gotten me a job with him, as his personal assistant. From the ways things were going with

Ken lately, I'd be looking in the classifieds soon. Hell, he'd already fired me once today.

"So, let me guess, you got called in to handle the situation before it gets out of hand and leaks out to the public," I said to Caleb as he tossed another one of his bags into his trunk.

"Gwen, you know that's the way it works. I hunt them down in order to avoid the police having to be involved. They're looking for a human, not a Siren. They would never dream of looking in the places I look, and most likely wouldn't know what to do if they happened across anything out of the norm."

Ah, that's why his bag weighed so much. The places he frequented required a lot of heavy artillery. "Okay, well, be careful, all right? Do you have your cell phone with you?" I leaned up and gave him a kiss. "*Gráim thú*--I love you," I said looking directly into his dark green eyes.

He smiled. Obviously pleased I was at least trying to learn one of the languages I'd spoken two hundred plus years ago. My choice of phrases were a bit dated, but Caleb was four hundred years old, he'd heard it all. "Trust me on this, Gwen I love you more. And, yes, I've got my phone," he said, pulling me towards him for another kiss.

I shook my head a little. I never knew if he was being serious or not when he started that, so I didn't touch it. The last thing I needed was a showdown to prove who loved who more. If I did fall prey to Caleb's line of questioning, then I'd be opening myself up wide to a verbal onslaught. No thanks, I'd pass. I was trying cut back on those.

"What are you going to do about Ken?" he asked.

I hadn't really given much thought to what I was going to do now. "I don't know. You heard what he said. He's revoked his dismissal, but still...I can't do it. I can't cause him problems and have a yo-yo relationship with him. I guess I'll head into town and clean my office out as soon as I get a chance. Looks like I'll be job hunting very soon."

He touched my cheek and caressed my skin lightly. "I'd rather you not look for another job. Can't you just stay home for a while? I'll handle things for you."

"Caleb, no, you don't need to be worried about covering my expenses. I'm fine, you know that."

"Gwen, *tá mo chroí istigh ionat--my heart is within you.* Everything I have...everything I am, is yours always, *go síoraí*--forever."

"We'll discuss it later, sweet talker, get going!" I kissed him once more before shoving him towards his truck. "I love you. Please be careful."

I watched Caleb climb in his truck and pull away slowly. Seeing him go was always hard. The fear of him never returning was very real and very warranted. I'd already thought I'd lost him once and it was too terrible to describe. I couldn't go through that again. There was no way I'd come out of it sane.

"You plannin' on standin' out here all night freezin' your *alans* off or are you going to come in?" James asked from the porch.

"Dare I ask what my *alans* are?"

James snickered softly. "*Alans*...you know, knickers, skivvies, smalls, your underwear. *Americans!*"

"Americans? It's not my fault you can't seem to learn to speak English. You've been here long enough. Hell, you might have been one of the founding fathers for all I know. You're like what, a billion?" I laughed softy and shot him a half smile.

"Sure, I've lived here for the greater part of a hundred years, but I've been speakin' English longer than you've been alive, that's the truth. I like to think of myself as a nice little blend. Besides, I've got you beat either way you look at it...across the pond or not."

My eyebrows rose slightly. "Which life would you be talking about, this one or my last, James?"

"You...always with the drama!"

I let out a loud laugh. "*Yeah*, Mr. Blue Hair!"

Stopping the witty banter, I looked down the lane and watched as Caleb's taillights disappeared. The cool October wind hit me in the face and a shiver ran through me. I tightened my arms around my body and headed back into the warmth of the house.

"He'll be fine," James said as I walked past him. I hoped he was right.

Chapter 3

James and I immediately headed for the upstairs bathroom to begin my transformation to a pink punk rocker. Caradoc thought we were nuts and decided to go for a walk. I'm sure the real reason he took off was to avoid being considered an accessory to my downfall--I couldn't blame him. He answered to a very scary judge--Pallo.

James brought a chair up from the kitchen and set it in the center of the bathroom. He then proceeded to display his little shop of pink horror. Two bottles of dye and a couple of packets of cream later, and we were just about ready.

"We need towels. I'll fetch us some." He left the boxes sitting on the edge of the sink while he ran down the hall to get some towels, leaving me to read the instructions--just like a man. It didn't matter that he'd been alive ten times longer than me, he still bailed on the directions. Typical.

The girl on the cover of the box was really cute in a *she's sexy but not overly sexy kind of way*. What I liked most about her was her short haircut. It was only about three inches long on the top and was closer than that in the back. My hair had hung to my butt ever since I could remember. There were pictures of me in the hallway at age two with long black hair. I can't be sure but I think I came out that way. It sure felt like it at least.

Glancing at the box cover, I was a bit envious of her. I had much the same problem as the vampires in my life. I was timeless. As wonderful as that was, it left little room for change. The proof in that was how long it was taking Caleb to grow facial hair. He actually had to concentrate on it. We were created to be one way, eternally young. Everyone likes a change sometimes. Even me. Pink and short would definitely be a change. I closed my eyes and shook my head. Silly, I knew I'd never cut it off. It would only grow back two days later. I'd be lucky if the dye held.

The bathroom door opened and I heard James enter. "Gwen?"

"Yeah?" I asked, turning towards him. His blue eyes were wide and his eyebrows were raised. "Did someone just declare you the winner of a clearinghouse sweepstakes? *Oooh*...let me see the check!"

"Huh? What did you do?" He walked closer to me and reached his hand out towards my head.

I hadn't done anything. I stood up to look in the mirror. It took a minute for my brain to register what I was seeing. My hair was identical to the girl on the cover of the box. All of my long black hair was gone, leaving me with a head of dark pink hair that was short--shorter than James' spiked hair. I had to admit it looked pretty good on me. It made the navy in my eyes stand out and it was fitting for my light complexion, but my hair, it was all gone. Closing my eyes, I shook my head in disbelief. What the hell had I done?

"*Ballocks*, Gwen, look!" I opened my eyes and saw my hair was back to normal. "Do it again."

I did and each time it changed from short and pink to long and black. I turned and looked at James with wide eyes, unsure what was going on. I glanced down at my shoulder in the mirror and visualized a sun tattooed on it. Suddenly it appeared. James gasped and clapped his hands together sounding remarkably like he was five years old.

"Cool," he said, making me drop his age to about three, but he was right it was cool. "You're a freakin' shifter."

A shifter--I'd read about those, they were creatures of magic that could change their appearance at will. I knew all elves and faeries possessed some degree of this magic, but I didn't realize I had this much. Saying that this was cool didn't quite cover it because this kicked ass. James and I stood in the bathroom trying to see what all I could do. We came to the conclusion that I could make myself look any way I could dream up. I even managed to make my hair appear to be live snakes. The Medusa thing was too freaky for me. James thought it was funny. *He would.*

The only drawback seemed to be the amount of energy it took for me to hold the illusion. My head had a steady, dull ache by the time we'd tried around twenty different looks, but we carried on with our experiments. We played in the bathroom until we heard Caradoc coming in downstairs. We looked at each other and squealed. Oh, this was going to be good. I made myself look completely bald.

"Oh, that's perfect!" James said, laughing hysterically.

"Shh!" I had to keep him quiet so Caradoc wouldn't hear. Heading out of the bathroom, I touched my head. It didn't feel bald to me. "Hey, did it go away?"

James touched it. "Nope, feels smooth--real."

"Are you sure? It still feels like my normal hair to me?"

"Gwen, do ya' really think I'd lie about your head feelin' bald? It's actually a bit unnerving to see."

"Good point."

Caradoc was at the base of the stairs with his back to us bringing in their blue ice cooler. They had to bring a cooler full of blood when they came, since I wasn't volunteering to feed them. "Caradoc, look what James did to me!" I ran down the stairs towards him. He set the cooler down and turned to me.

The look on his face was priceless. It was one of those moments when you wished you'd brought a camera. He looked horrified. No words came from his mouth. Never before had I seen this refined man look so lost. I couldn't do it to him anymore. The joke had been fun while it lasted. I shook my head and his eyes widened more. I turned to James. "It didn't work?"

"No, it worked, it's back to normal," he said, glancing at Caradoc and laughing. "I don't think that was any less of a shock to his system."

Caradoc walked up to me and put his long arm out to touch my hair. He let his fingers run through it--tugging on it gently, almost caressing it. He'd never stood this close to me before and I never realized just how tall he was. He suddenly seemed a lot more dangerous than I thought he was. Funny how you don't respect a person physically one moment, but as soon as you figure out they could take you in two seconds or less, you suddenly do.

I waited for him to yell at me for scaring him like that. He didn't. "Do it again," he said, and James laughed.

I repeated my performance for Caradoc, showing him everything that James and I had tried in the bathroom. An hour later, he stood before me silently. "A penny for your thoughts," I said fearing the worst.

He closed his eyes, sighing softly. "Gwyneth, you have no idea how powerful you are, do you?"

He must be joking. I was the mutt-faerie in the *Si* world. I hadn't been raised by anyone of magical descent. Two of the most caring humans ever put on this earth had raised me, but they were never able to teach me how to use my magic. Growing up, I tried to read as much as I could about faeries, but that didn't help me much. I always saw myself as a second rate elf. Could I have been wrong?

Chapter 4

James and I curled up under a blanket on the couch together. He lay at one end, while I laid at the other. I was surprised to see that Caradoc had joined us. He sat quietly in the chair with his feet propped up reading a book. I did a double take when I read the title--*Bram Stoker's Dracula*.

"He's kidding right?" I asked James as I nodded towards Caradoc.

James shrugged. "Ahh, that one's a clever-dick. He could most likely recite the damn thing to us, verbatim, by now--he's read it so much. Don't know why, though...it's not like he isn't livin' it."

The phrase *been there, done that* came to my mind. Having nothing more to offer, directed my attention to the television screen.

"Didn't we watch this one last week?"

"No, week before last." James smiled and shoved another handful of popcorn into his mouth. The first time I'd seen him eat, I almost fell over. I had no idea vampires could consume food. He laughed at my ignorance. Apparently, vampires could eat whatever they wanted. They craved blood and needed it to survive. Junk food was just a fringe benefit.

A shiver ran through me and I drew the blanket up around me. It slid back down a bit and I tugged on it again. This time it didn't move. Glancing down at James, I caught him pulling it towards him. I tugged and he followed suit. This continued, the two of us playfully aggravating one another. I wiggled a bit, trying to get comfortable and froze. Having James' body directly behind mine hadn't been an issue once in all the weeks we'd been doing it. Now, I could feel his clothed erection pushing against the back of my legs. He moved a smidge, and I got a "clear picture" of just what James was packin'.

He tugged on the blanket again, drawing my attention away from the "third party" on the couch with us. A devilish grin stretched across his face. Caradoc cleared his throat and we both looked over at him. His gaze was focused on James. And his look was anything but pleasant. "Perhaps it would be best if James moved from the sofa."

"We're good, Caradoc. There's plenty of room on here." I twisted a bit to better see him. This left the back of my legs pressed solidly against James' still hard member. I ignored it. Really, what else is a girl to do? Laugh and point? I think not. Well, not in this situation anyway. Besides, from my size calculation, it was James who'd have the last laugh anyways. I did have a new respect for the women he dated. Somehow, they managed to walk the next morning.

Caradoc's green gaze swept over me and his face softened a bit. I smiled. "You know...this folds out into a bed. We could all lay on it and watch the movie. You don't have to sit by yourself in the chair. We don't...scratch that...*I* don't bite."

"Hey, I take offense to that comment. Oh, wait you've got a point. I do bite, nibble, chomp and whatever else I can think to do. No worries though, I'll not be bittin' him anytime soon. He's bitter. Just look at that scowl."

"James, he is not bitter! He's refined...a gentleman." I tossed my hands in the air and shook my head. "Forget it! It'd be easier to describe color to the blind."

"Hey now! I'd watch yourself there. I'm likely to bite you if you keep it up." James pulled the blanket towards him and wrinkled his nose at me.

"You'd think after all these centuries, you'd be a little more mature," I said, laughing softly. Caradoc grunted and I focused my attention back on him. "So, wanna come hang out with us?"

His gaze locked on James, but he spoke to me. "I am *fine* here, but thank you for your kind offer."

I had one of those moments. The kind where you know something's wrong, but you just don't know what. The tension in the room dissipated before I had a chance to comment. Yanking the blanket away from James, I laughed softly and covered up.

James pushed gently on my back with his feet. He wiggled his toes and went for my sides. Giggling, I tried to push his feet away but his vampire strength out matched mine twenty to one. Caradoc cleared his throat and James pulled his foot away. We lay silent for a while, watching the movie. The weird feeling was back, but I didn't question them on it.

My stomach rumbled and I eyed the bowl of popcorn. It was on the coffee table, but more towards James' end. Leaning towards him, I put my hand in the bowl to get more popcorn. James must have had the same idea as me because he reached forward at the same time. My hand brushed over his and his hand stiffened. His pinky finger ran over the back of my hand softly, and I hesitated for a moment watching his face. His eyes never left the television screen.

It was an odd gesture. One I wasn't too sure I wanted to analyze further, so I focused on the film. James had a habit of renting movies that involved vampires. He liked to see the way Hollywood was portraying "his people." This particular movie was most definitely a B-movie. It starred a busty blonde who, surprisingly enough, had to run around in her skivvies and high heels to avoid the big-bad-vampire. She, of course, finds herself trapped and falls for his hypnotic powers and devilish good looks.

From the corner of my eye, I caught a glimpse of Caradoc peering over the top if his book at the movie. He shook his head in disgust. Looks like I wasn't the only one who found this flick tasteless. James was one hundred percent into it so I munched on my popcorn and watched it in silence. The longer I sat there, the worse I began to feel.

Out of the blue, I was cold again. Feeling like I was on the verge of going into a deep freeze was getting old fast. "I'm cold, guys. I'm going to go put some warmer clothes on."

James touched my leg tenderly. His hand felt warm. "You all right? I can get you another blanket."

"I'm fine," I said, reaching down and patting his hand. "I'll just toss something warmer on. I'll be right back. Take notes on the movie. I'd *really* hate to miss anything."

James caught my hand in his. A warm sensation ran up my arm. "Gwen, is somethin' a matter?"

"She said she is fine," Caradoc said, biting out each word.

I squeezed James' hand and smiled down at him. "I'm fine, Hon, really."

"Right then, give a call out if you need me...us."

Nodding, I pulled my hand from his and mourned the loss of the warmth he'd provided. Yeah, things were bad--a dead guy seemed warm to me.

I walked past Caradoc who was now back to memorizing another line from his autobiography and shook my head. *Crazy vamps.* I went up to my bedroom, and put a sweatshirt on over my sweater and shirt.

Satisfied, I headed down towards the basement, intent on checking the furnace. Caleb had sworn that he turned it on today, even though he'd put up such a fight about turning it on. He kept going on and on about the fact it was still sixty degrees outside. It didn't matter--I was cold and wanted heat. He buckled, or at least I thought he did.

James stood at the bottom of the steps and stared up at me. "Gwen, are sure you're all right?"

"I'm fine, why?"

He looked me over twice. "You expectin' a blizzard then?"

I headed down to the last step and stopped in front of James. Standing on the step put me eye level with him. It was nice, but a bit unnerving. His eyes were very, very blue. Why hadn't I noticed how deep they were before? Lost for a moment in his eyes, I was surprised when I felt his hand on my cheek. It seemed even warmer that it had earlier. That scared me. He jerked his hand back. "Caradoc!"

Caradoc appeared next to him out of thin air. This, thankfully, was something I was growing accustomed to. "What is the problem?"

"She's friggin' freezing. Touch her!"

Caradoc did. A shadow passed over his face and he nodded towards the door. "Gwen, stay here." The two of them headed for the front door, leaving me standing there dressed for winter. I knew that they went out there to discuss me. I didn't really care. I was hungry again. I'd already had a big plate of pasta, then popcorn and that normally would have filled me up but it didn't.

I headed out to the kitchen to get a snack. I settled on vanilla ice cream with bacon bits sprinkled on top. I'd never eaten them together before, but was craving something and that seemed to fit the bill. I heard Caradoc and James coming in the front door, they weren't speaking. I'm sure that they didn't want to concern me. I was getting used to that, too. James walked into the kitchen first. His gaze darted to what I was eating. He crinkled his nose up like he smelled a rotten egg.

"Yuck! Are you barkin' mad? That's disgustin', Gwen."

Smiling at him, I licked the spoon. It was good but didn't hit the spot. Caradoc came in next, carrying their blue cooler stocked full of blood. He set it on the countertop and opened the lid. James walked over, grabbed two glasses off the shelf and handed them to Caradoc, who then in turn filled them to the rim. Watching them drink blood out of my glasses used to creep me out. I would run them through the dishwasher twice after they left, but tonight it was doing the exact opposite. Watching them drink made me hungry. James set his glass down on the table. I swept my hand out and picked it up. After all, it couldn't be that bad, they drank it, right? Without thought, I slammed it. It was thick and cold and slid down my throat easily. It tasted so sweet and different than I thought it would be--it was delicious. I drained the glass and set it down on the table.

The room was quiet. For a moment, I thought I could actually hear the vampires hearts beating. *Silly, right?* James stood there looking at me as if I'd sprouted two heads. Caradoc didn't look much different. I shrugged, unsure what the big deal was. "What?"

A knowing look passed between them. Caradoc walked out into the hall and picked up the phone. I couldn't hear who he was talking to, I didn't care. I was drained, my body ached, and I was still colder than the damn vamps that were baby-sitting me.

I smiled softly at James, not wanting to alarm him. "Could you help me up to bed?"

He stood there staring at me. He bent his head down slightly, as if he was trying to figure out what was going on. I never asked him for help. I was independent and he knew it. I got sick of waiting for him to lend a hand, so I stood up to go it alone. Big mistake! My knees gave out, my body went limp and my side crashed into the table. James was next to me in an instant.

"Bloody hell!"

James lifted me into his arms effortlessly. His gelled blue hair never moved. "I love your individuality," I whispered, putting my head against his shoulder.

Chapter 5

"Come," a man wearing a hooded brown robe said to me as I walked past him. I tried to make out his face but all I saw was darkness under his hood. The room we stood in was large and circular--with a stone altar in the center of it. Visions of sacrificing virgins ran through my head, causing me to laugh. If they were after virgins then I was safe that was for sure!

The room was well lit but I could see no source of light. Many men spoke, but I saw only one. Shivers ran over my body as I listened to their voices pull together in unison. They chanted in harmony, saying words I could not understand. I still saw only one man, yet heard hundreds. Growing bolder, I walked closer to the hooded man. I reached out to touch him, and he dropped onto the stone floor on his knees, raising his hands up in the air.

"You are the vessel, you are the one," many voices said from this one entity. "The time is near, the time is near, the time is near...."

I was officially creeped out and had no desire to stand around while it continued on its multi-voiced spiel. My heart raced and the temperature in the room began to drop. It was so cold in there-- so *very* cold. I turned to run but was blocked by another man in a brown robe, identical to the other. I looked back to make sure that they weren't one and the same. The first man was still bent over on the ground.

"What do you want?" I was weirded out by them, but still curious. If I was about to die, I wanted to know what I was going to die for. He motioned to the wall. I glanced at it then back at him, waiting for the lemming to be a fountain of wisdom. "I don't get it."

"You are the vessel, you are the one," he said.

How original!

His hand rose towards the wall. I looked in that direction again and could vaguely make out some form of hieroglyphics. They faded away before I was able to get a better look at them. Not that it would have mattered. I didn't have a scientist in my back pocket or an ancient Egyptian decoder ring on me at the moment.

"Yeah, right then...it's been...err...fun." I turned to run but another appeared before me. I turned again--another appeared and another and another. They reached out to me, their hands touching my body, groping me, pulling me. They were like ice. I was like ice. I screamed out and pushed at them to get them away.

"Touch the vessel, the time is near, touch the vessel." Their chanting grew louder and louder, forcing me to cover my ears. "Gwyneth, Gwyneth, Gwyneth." They grabbed my face and jerked my head back. They began grabbing my breasts, pulling on my legs, and yanking on my hair. They weren't gentle. Being ripped apart in a dream was the last thing I wanted. I tried to wake myself up, but it didn't work.

"Shackle her and he will come."

Shackle me? Fear clutched hold of me. This was so real--too real. They lifted me high in the air.

"LEAVE ME ALONE!" I screamed out, waking with a start. I bolted upright in my bed, touching my face, my neck, anything I could get my hands on. I was okay. It was only a dream. But it seemed so real.

"Gwen," James said, his sudden appearance scared me. I jumped and he touched my cheek gently, soothing my fears. Quickly, I cupped my hand over his. He climbed into the bed next to me, and wrapped his arms around me. "It's okay. I've got you...I've got you." He rocked me gently and I slid my arms around his waist. "That's it--hold on to me, love. I'll not let anything happen to you."

The fact that James had a nurturing side should have surprised me. It didn't. I clung to him for dear life. "Hey," he said drawing back slightly to touch my face. When he wiped my cheeks with the pad of his thumb, I realized I was crying. I wanted to thank him for being so kind, but the words escaped me. Instead, I pulled on the back of his head and drew him to me. Our foreheads touched and I let out a small sob. Looking up through wet lashes, I locked gazes with him. At that moment I knew, that this vampire with a pension for mischief and odd hair colors had become my best friend. And I had never been more thankful for anything in my life. He knew me better than anyone else and not counting my last go round on earth, had only known me a short period of time.

A tickle started in the back of my mind, and I continued to stare into his dark blue eyes. It was odd, I felt as though we were connected on a level greater than either one of us could fathom. It was clear to see how much James cared for me, and I him. James treated me like an equal. Someone he could bounce ideas off of, joke with and still respect in a stressful situation. The best part of it all was that he didn't make demands on me like Pallo and Caleb. No, James accepted me for me--unconditionally.

"James...thank you," I whispered.

"Gwen, its okay, it's all right now. I've got you, you're fine." He pulled me closer to him, leaving my head resting on his chest. His fingers ran through my hair as he rocked me in his arms like a child. He whispered quietly against the top of my head, "I've got you, love. I'll always be here for you...and *yes*, what I offer is unconditional."

I hadn't remembered saying that aloud but I also didn't realize I was crying until after the fact so my opinion was worth squat. I gave into the shelter of James' large arms and tried to shake away the uneasy feeling from the nightmare.

The door to my room swung open. Startled, I looked up to see Pallo, James' master, and my ex-lover standing there. He looked so very ominous in his black silk shirt and black jeans. His dark brown hair broke up the monochromatic look he'd been going for, but did little in the way of softening his image. His eyes, which were normally a rich chocolate brown, were black holes. That happened to him when his demon pushed through and was never a good sign. I got the feeling this was about to become very ugly.

Pallo's icy gaze raked over James and me. A tick started in his jaw and he clenched his fists. James gave me a quick squeeze before moving me behind him on the bed. All I managed to catch was a blur before Pallo was on us. He snatched hold of my arm and yanked me clear of James. My feet barely touched the floor.

"*Ahh*...Pallo, stop!" I cried out, as he dug his nails deep into my arm.

James stood quickly, but Pallo was ready for him. He threw his hand up in the air, striking James hard across his chin. I heard it, hell I felt it--he hit him hard. I had a difficult time taking in everything that was going on. It was all happening so fast. Pallo made another move to strike James and I grabbed hold of his upper arm. "Pallo stop! Don't hurt him!"

He turned his attention to me and yanked me towards him. He snarled and the hair on the back of my neck stood on end. Knowing his demon was in control should have terrified me enough to keep my mouth shut--while it did scare the hell out of me, the thought of him hurting James scared me more. I tugged harder on him, and he in turn tightened his grip on my arm past the point of pain. "Ahh!"

James reached for him, and he let go of me long enough to deliver an awesome blow to James, sending him airborne.

"James!" I tried to pull my arm free from Pallo, causing him to tighten his grip on me even more. Pallo glared at me with his black swirling pits, and I struggled harder to get away.

"They summoned me here. They said you needed help. I leave everything and run here to find you in bed with *him*," he said, motioning to James on the floor. "Have you not had enough fun with your *little* Caleb, now you must seduce one of my own? I thought a fellow *Si* was just what you needed. If I had known you would go for a vampire I would have gotten back in line, although you may need ropes and a ticket taker soon with the amount of men you have ready to fuck you! You have not changed. Have you, *donnaccia?*" His fangs showed as he talked, and a sinister smile crept over his face.

That did for me. My fear switched to anger alarmingly fast. Who the hell did he think he was? He was pushing around the wrong girl. I didn't ask him to come here I didn't need him here. And, I didn't want him here! "Let go of me NOW! You've no right to be here and don't call me that ever again!"

"That is what you are and will always be, is it not? Are you not a whore, Gwyneth? Please enlighten me. I do so wish to hear your side of it," he said, sardonically.

Staring up at him, I knew he was and would always be bitter. He held me in so much contempt that it was amazing he spoke to me at all. I was able to look past it most of the time, but Pallo had a way of not letting me forget what he was--a vampire. Somehow, he seemed to take great pleasure in reminding me of the tragic events that unfolded hundreds of years ago. Part of him blamed me for what he now was, I was sure of it. If it had been within my power to erase his pain, I would have, but I seriously doubted he'd accept that from me.

The pain in my arm worsened. Tears streamed down my face. Pallo saw them and let go of my arm. He glanced down at his hand. It was covered in my blood. I watched, in a bizarre state of fascination, a drop of it fell to the floor. It was symbolic in so many ways. If I wouldn't have known better I could have sworn that I heard it hit the hardwood floor.

Pallo looked up at me and then to my arm again. Something registered in him. The part of him that was good and decent took hold. He staggered backwards and fell into the wall.

James came running to me. He grabbed me and tried to pull me towards the door. I dug my feet into the ground. He dragged me anyways. "James...no...ouch, stop," I said to him, he looked down at my arm, his eyes wide.

"Fuck, Pallo...look at her!"

"Don't draw his attention back to you. Go! I couldn't bear the thought of you being hurt over me."

"I'm not leaving you alone with him. If you'd been human he'd have torn your arm off!" Standing up to his master was not only foolish--it was deadly.

"Go, please...he's got a slight hold on himself and he's less likely to kill me than you."

James cocked an eyebrow. "Willin' to bet your life on that one, are you?"

"Yes."

"Right then, how's about I stand here for a moment--just to be on the safe side."

"Fine, if you want to get yourself killed, be my guest. Oooh, you're...you're...stubborn!"

He grinned and winked. "Be that as it may, I'm comfy here, love. And I'm not movin'."

Getting something through James' thick skull was next to impossible. I gave up and turned my attention to Pallo. He slid slowly down the wall, covering his face with his hands. If I didn't know better I would have said he was crying. Seeing his six foot tall, two hundred pound muscular frame there made my heart ache. He wasn't one to give in to the sentimental side of things--no he was a hard-ass and everyone knew it.

I glanced down at my arm, it was fine, except for four tiny half moon cuts that were now dripping with blood. I knew the marks were from Pallo's hand, and that was very sobering.

Pallo sat still on the floor, not making a sound. He had his elbows on his knees and his hands covering his face. I walked over to him and touched his arm lightly. It was so warm. I hadn't expected that. I tried to lift his chin to make him look at me but I couldn't get him to budge. He was strong as an ox because of the vampire in him and as stubborn as one too. No one would be able to get Pallo to do anything until he was damn well ready to do it.

I sat down next to him on the floor, putting my body close to his for his warmth. I never thought I'd see the day when I tried to warm myself off Pallo's cool vampire body. I leaned my head against him and could hear his heart beating fast. He was upset.

James began to walk towards us--I shook my head no. He looked a little hurt but nodded and walked out of the room. When he shut the door Pallo and I were left in total darkness. I put my head back against him and let him support all of my weight. His heart rate slowed as he began to relax.

He made no attempt to lift his head and look at me, he just sat silent in the dark. He truly had become the statue that the appearance of his skin led you to believe he could be--pale, almost white--marble-like.

We sat in the darkness. I was sure that Caradoc and James were close but they made no sound to give away their location. The dark, quiet room and the steady rhythm of Pallo's breathing lulled my body into a relaxed state. The nightmare had left me drained and the confrontation with Pallo hadn't helped. I was exhausted and regardless how Pallo had just acted, I felt comfortable near him. Relaxing, I found myself on the verge of sleep, in that place where my body was so calm, so at peace, as if I was already asleep, yet my mind was still aware of what was going on around me.

Suddenly, I heard the robed men chanting, "You are the vessel, you are the one." I tried to force my eyes open but they wouldn't budge. I knew I was just dreaming. I knew that it wasn't real, yet still I was afraid. I kept willing myself to open my eyes and wake up, I did not listen. I could be so bullheaded sometimes!

I found myself back in the circular room with the stone altar once more. No robed men had popped out at me--yet. I walked towards the stone altar. It was long--long enough for a person to lie on.

Great, it was just my size!

Tentatively, I reached my hand out and touched it. It was warm and soft. I looked closer at it. *Yes*, it was stone, yet it was soft to the touch. Puzzled, I pushed harder on it. Unable to make sense of my own dream, I gave up.

The temperature in the room plummeted again, and my teeth began to chatter. My fingers were going numb slowly. I looked down at them, they were blue, more importantly I was naked. I was dreaming about myself being naked in a freezing cold round room with a soft stone altar. I really needed to see a shrink.

Something brushed past my shoulder, touching my arm slightly. I froze. Fear gripped my body as my eyes wandered sideways. Pallo was with me. I get it now, I was really thinking about how much I would sacrifice to be with Pallo. It made perfect sense now. I stared at the likeness my mind was projecting of Pallo--it looked so real. I reached out, touching it gently. It was warm and smooth. I was surprised at my attention to detail. I'd even remembered the tiny freckles on his shoulders, and the two tiny scars below his nipple. He was naked as well and took my breath away. I knew how silky smooth his pale skin was in real life and couldn't help but wonder if I managed to get that right, too.

Pallo turned and looked down at me. His eyes were their normal deep penetrating brown--they were beautiful. I could look at him for hours, and for the first time since my bizarre dream had began, I didn't want it to end.

Never one to let a perfectly good sexual dream go to waste, I ran my fingers over his shoulders and down the front of his chest. He let out a small gasp. Man, I was too impressed with myself. I was doing a good job of recreating him. His left hand caught mine and he held it tight.

Wait, I didn't want him to do that.

I tried to force my mind to change that--to have him release me. It didn't work. Pallo pulled me to him and put his hands on my waist. Okay, I would give a little if that was what I'd be getting in return.

I could be as giving as the next girl.

I'd take sex with Pallo in a dream if I could get it. It wasn't as if he'd be handing it out in real life. He'd been avoiding me like the bubonic plague. And, since he thought I was a whore, it was best I not push the issue with him. Plus, there was another fringe benefit of having sex in a dream. It didn't count as cheating.

Whoopee for me! My night was really beginning to improve. This had to be the safest form of sex ever!

Pallo's strong hands lifted me quickly and he set me on the altar. It still felt warm and soft. I let him guide my body onto it, gently. He climbed up and laid himself over me. Our naked bodies pressed against each other, he felt so real, so warm--so alive. He bent his head down to kiss me and I welcomed him. He tasted sweet, like forbidden fruit.

I went at his mouth, nipping and tugging. I wanted him to push at me and be forceful. Instead, the Pallo in my dream was soft, kind, gentle. As our tongues found each other, the slickness between my thighs increased. I knew that if he dared touch me there he would feel the moisture moving downward--welcoming him.

Sliding my hands down his back, I traced tiny circles on the base of his backbone. I let my fingers play along the top edges of his apple shaped bottom. People paid big money for an ass like that. Pallo got his naturally.

He moaned in my ear softly, "*Mi manchi*--I miss you, Gwyneth."

Yes, this was a good dream indeed.

"I miss you, too," I said in a soft voice.

Pallo spread my legs gently with his knee. He ran a hand down my side, trailing over my breast and coming to a stop on my mound. I moaned as he spread my velvety folds and rubbed his fingers over my swollen clit. Each flicker, each pass made my legs shake, quiver with delight. He slid his long fingers into me, and I gasped. His brown eyes glazed over with lust, as he brought his lips close to mine. "*Baciami.*"

I had no clue what that meant, but I nodded my head all the same. His lips crashed into mine. We devoured each other, our tongues going made with need. Opening my legs more for him, I encouraged him to enter me. The feel of his hard body settling over me completely was almost too much. When the head of his cock found me, I cried out, digging my nails into his lower back. He hissed and tugged on my lower lip gently.

Wet, but tight, I left him no choice but to put some force behind his thrust. It felt so real, he felt so real--filling me up. "Pallo...."

His hand slid under my leg, lifting it slightly towards my head allowing him to enter me even further. I sucked my breath in as his hips pounded against me, driving his cock deeper into me. The sensation was so authentic, so perfect that I didn't want to wake. This was how it was supposed to be--the two of us making love, no fighting, no guilt, just passion. He hit the back of my cervix and I winced slightly.

Pallo pushed into me harder and faster, losing his rhythm. I grunted under him like a wild animal. He countered with primitive noises of his own. The robed men begin to chant over the sounds of our passion. Suddenly, they were all around us, enclosing us in a circle of their bodies. They lifted their arms high in the air and their chants grew louder. I tried to block them from my mind. I was not going to think about crazy robed monks while I was

Mandy M. Roth

dreaming of Pallo. They were just a figment of my imagination--a very annoying figment.

Pallo thrust himself into me over and over again. My body answered with swaying hips and tiny thrusts up of my own. My lower abdomen burned, tightened as waves of pleasure crashed over me. My orgasm was so intense, it left me clinging to Pallo, holding my breath and staring into his tender eyes as I rode it out.

The chanting grew louder. Pallo tossed his head back, still keeping himself inside of me. "*Oh dio mio!*" His neck muscles tightened and his breathing was erratic at best.

Confused, I pulled at the sides of his face, trying to get him to look at me. "Pallo, what's wrong?"

His head came back down. His brown curls fell loosely around his face. I looked up and into his beautiful black eyes, *what*?

Why the hell was I dreaming about him in his all out vampire-demon form?

He drove himself in me and the altar no longer felt soft, it felt every bit as solid as it looked. "No!" I screamed out, wanting to wake myself up. I didn't want to keep dreaming of Pallo like this. I wanted my gentle lover back, the man I'd give up everything for--my Pallo.

The chanting was overwhelming, Pallo slammed into me so hard I thought I would rip in two. I searched his face. The Pallo I loved wasn't there, only his demon was. He brought his head down quickly and struck my neck with his fangs. A cry broke free of my throat, as white-hot pain shot through my body. He pushed himself into me hard and finished inside of me, coming in jarring waves. I didn't want to enjoy it, not this way, not with the demon in him riding me, but I couldn't help myself. I came again, this orgasm was even fiercer than my last one. The weight of his body dropped onto me, I cried out. He was still inside of me--pulsating, every last drop of his demonic seed was deep in me now.

I pounded on his back, as he continued to feed off me, his cock still embedded deep within me. "Pallo! No, don't...let go...you're taking too much blood! Pallo, please come back to me...I need you...*I love you*, don't do this!"

Pallo pulled his head up quickly and looked into my face. "Gwyneth?"

Kicking my feet out, I jerked awake. It was only a dream, a nightmare really. I was still sitting on the floor in my bedroom next to Pallo. He was propped against the wall with his head down, sleeping. I touched his arm lightly, needing to know he was real. His head jerked up, his eyes were black and his fangs were showing. A tiny drop of blood was on his lip. It ran down his chin slowly and his tongue flickered out and over it.

He shook his head and came back to me. "Gwyneth?"

"Pallo?" I moved closer to him. "What's wrong?"

He glanced at me and then around the room. He shook his head and seemed to calm down. "Nothing, I am sorry, it was only a dream."

That caught my attention. I wasn't sure how to ask him if he had just dreamt about boning me. The guy hadn't even wanted to be in the same room with me for the last two months. Not a real good way to strike up a conversation. I decided that it was best I just let that one go. Putting my hands on the hardwood floor, I pushed myself up. Pallo was next to me and standing before I even got halfway to my feet. He put his hand on my upper back to help guide me. I had missed his touch but most of all I missed his friendship--I missed him.

I must have stood up too fast, because I felt faint. I held his arm for a minute to keep from falling. The room spun and he held me to him until it passed. He eased his grip on me slowly.

"Gwyneth?"

"I'm fine, really."

I made my way slowly to the door. When I opened it, light from the hallway flooded into the room. It was too bright, too much. I squinted, needing a minute for my eyes to adjust. I grabbed hold of the doorway, suddenly feeling very nauseous.

I dug my fingers into the wood, trying to maintain my upright position. I put my hand over my mouth and ran for the bathroom. I pushed the door open and dove down on the floor in front of the toilet, sweeping the hair dye James had brought with him onto the floor, before lifting the lid. It felt like all the contents of my stomach were about to fly out but none did. I just sat there staring in at the white bowl. The smell of water sitting in porcelain was potent. I could clearly make out all of the chemicals the water treatment plant used. It only made my stomach feel worse, but I did not get sick.

I heard water running behind me. I put my arm on the edge of the toilet and turned around slowly, I really didn't want to pass out head first in the toilet. It'd be my luck to go that way--death by way of toilet bowl, news at eleven.

Pallo was running a bath. I knew it was for me. I looked up at him and wanted to thank him, but I wasn't feeling very well at all.

I was a little concerned that if I opened my mouth everything but words would come out.

Maybe this was the flu that I'd heard my human friends discussing. They said that you felt chilled, then feverish. Nausea was common, along with body aches, and coughs. Yeah, that was it! I must have caught the flu. I didn't know I could catch human colds--news to me.

Putting all my weight on my arms, I pushed off the edge of the toilet, attempting to stand. I failed miserably. The strength in my arms gave out and I didn't fight it. Pallo's arms wrapped around me and he eased me down to the floor. He pulled my sweatshirt and sweater over my head and helped me out of my white undershirt. His fingers slid over my neck. I felt the tiniest bit of pain as he pressed down.

"Gwyneth?" he said, more to himself than me.

He pulled his finger away and came back with a tinge of red. I hadn't remembered cutting my neck on anything but the evening had been fairly eventful. I would be happy when it was over.

Pallo laid me back on the floor. I wore only a bra and my jeans now. I really didn't want him to be helping me. It didn't feel right. Not with tension that had been between us and especially not with Caleb in the picture. Pallo's presence always stirred things in me. Things that I could deny and bury deep when around Caleb. Sitting there half-dressed was hardly aiding with my already flawed character. I pushed at his hands as he tried to undo my pants. I knew that he was only trying to help, but I didn't care.

Go figure. I have a sex dream about him, have a chance to get naked with him for real and pass on it--that was *so* very me!

I touched Pallo's dark shirt, it was silk of course. I wanted to run my fingers under it and feel his muscular stomach. I didn't. Instead, I got hold of my wits and looked up at him. I could do this. I didn't need him to help me. *No*, I didn't want him to help me.

Pallo had said such hurtful things. He'd called me a *donnaccia*-- a whore--the minute he saw me with James. He didn't stop to ask what was going on. He immediately jumped to the wrong conclusion, again. Pallo had made such ugly comments about using me for sex that I found it hard to be around him without coming back to that. I'd tried to harden myself to him. If he undressed me, I would lose all of my willpower and I knew it. I didn't want to do that to Caleb, I couldn't do that to him--I wouldn't.

Pallo appeared slightly hurt but he understood. He stood up quickly. "I will get Caradoc."

I tried to sit up. My head was so loopy that I gave up and laid it back down. "No, not him. James...get James."

He hesitated. He didn't want James undressing me. It was obvious that he didn't trust James around me anymore since he found him comforting me earlier. I didn't know what the deal was with Caleb and Pallo but neither of them seemed too fond of my friendship with James. Too bad, I wanted him to help me not Pallo.

"James!" Pallo called out.

I don't think more than two or three seconds went past before there was a soft knock at the bathroom door. Pallo opened it. James crept in, no doubt sensing Pallo's hostility. I noticed for the first time that James was a little taller than Pallo, which put him at about six foot three or so. I couldn't believe I'd never bothered to notice that before. They were so very different. James' blue spiked hair was a sharp contrast to Pallo's long wavy brown hair. For vampires they were complete opposites, for men they were damn different, too. One was softhearted and good-natured. The other was cold and distant.

I smiled when I saw James. Even with his odd hair color choices, he was a sight for sore eyes. Pallo looked down at me and saw me grinning. He didn't look pleased as he walked out into the hall. And he did not shut the door. I didn't care if Pallo saw me naked. He'd seen everything I had to offer several times now. I just didn't want him to be the one undressing me.

James bent down beside me. He went out of his way to *not* notice that I didn't have a top on. I thought that was charming. James wasn't outwardly known for being a gentleman so this was a big step for him.

My head felt a little bit better, my stomach was still touch and go, but I thought it would be wise to try to sit up now. I did, it worked.

Yippee for me!

James looked as if he wanted to say something, but didn't. I reached my hand down to undo my pants, feeling like I was going to bust out of them. I must have eaten a whole lot for dinner. Maybe the glass of blood I slammed was making me bloated, I don't know. Vampires didn't put caloric and sodium amounts on their packaged blood, yet--bummer.

My jeans were cutting into my lower abdomen terribly. It was tender and hurt when I had to push my thumb in to undo my button.

"Gwen, you're getting chubby. It's about time you gained some weight. You needed more cushion on your arse. I like a girl with a shapely rear. Now, you lucked out in the ol' stacked department, but ya' really got the shaft when it came to the rump," James said, laughing.

I punched his pale arm. "Shut up! You know you'd have a steady girlfriend by now if you stop saying things like that. Did you ever think the way to a woman's heart, for you, is to keep your mouth shut? Oh, no I forgot, the women you date don't have enough sense to know you're speaking, let alone being an ass. What's the phrase you like to use for them? Ah, yeah, dead from the neck up."

I loved teasing James about his choice in women. He seemed to always be trying to date the super sleazy ones. It was a running joke between us. He didn't mind being razzed by me and I was fine with him doing it back.

He helped me get my jeans down my legs, and never once commented on my red silk panties. Good boy! He helped me stand.

"Turn around. I need to take my underwear off."

He did and I held onto his shoulder with one hand to keep my balance. I trusted James so much and I don't know why. I had always felt that way about him since the day we first met. I didn't have that kind of trust with Pallo. He'd betrayed me and I wasn't close to forgiving him for that.

It took everything in me not to get upset thinking about Pallo's deception again. It haunted me every day. I lived with the anger from that and the guilt for still loving him even though I had Caleb. I'd tried all the tricks in the book, but I couldn't forget Pallo or what he'd done.

I climbed into the tub. It was scalding hot. "Ouch!" I yanked my foot out, convinced I had second-degree burns already.

James put his hand in to check, still facing the other way. "Gwen, the water's a bit on the cool side."

I knew he wouldn't lie to me so I went ahead and climbed in. No, it still felt too hot. I wanted to jump and run but I acted like a big girl and stayed put. The heat rose up my spine and let my body relax in the big tub.

I glanced up at James still facing the other way and laughed. What a great guy! Whenever he did decide to settle down he'd make some vamp-gal a very lucky lady.

Taking a deep breath in, I tipped my head back in the tub. After soaking my hair thoroughly, I surfaced. Wiping my face, I looked up. "James, I've been having the strangest dreams."

"About me, I hope."

I snorted. "No really, they're odd and bit creepy. Gee, you're right, they could be about you!" I laughed and continued on, "I know that I'm dreaming while I'm there, but it feels so real. There're all this men in robes. I can't make out any of their faces, but I can hear them chanting again and again."

"What are they going on about?"

"They call me *the vessel, the one*, as Pallo takes me on this altar and...and he makes love to me on it." I bit my lower lip, waiting for a James to make a stupid comment. It didn't take long.

"Hey, if this is a sex dream, I want permission to sit down and hear all the juicy details." James laughed softly, as he turned to look at me.

"James!"

He shrugged and faced the opposite wall again. "Right, sorry, carry on. So, was it any good?"

"Was what any good?"

He laughed. "The sex, of course, was it any good?"

"Yes, it was fantastic, at first. Then he went all demonic on me and sort of killed the moment, if you know what I mean." I knew that James of all people could understand what I was talking about. He was a vampire so he knew the strings attached to that. He was also my friend so he knew my feelings for Pallo, and Pallo just happened to be his Master, so he knew him pretty well too.

"Gwen, kinky sex is all in the eye of the beholder. You found that creepy and I'm sitting here filing it away for a good long *thrapping* later tonight."

I had to laugh, he was right. Although the knowledge that James would be a one-handed-self-pleasuring-machine later in the night made my nausea return, there were some things I just didn't want to know about--James jacking off was one of them.

I finished cleaning up and rose slowly out of the tub. Bending down to undo the stopper and let the water out, I noticed that my belly looked even bigger now. I made a mental note to avoid slamming anymore O-positive and got out.

Chapter 6

James helped me back to my room. I had a hard time getting dressed. Packing on ten pounds in less than an hour will cause even the most prepared of girls to have clothing issues. I finally decided on a pair of blue jeans that laced up the front instead of buttoning. I grabbed a white tunic that tied in the front and put it on too. I debated on wearing a bra under it, and finally decided not to. My breasts were feeling a little sore.

I headed downstairs and expected to find that Pallo had left, but to my surprise he and Caradoc were closing all of the green wooden shutters on the house. We had to do that every time the guys came to stay with me, the basement of the farm house was a little less than cozy, it was small and smelled funny, and they couldn't very well sleep in an open room. If the curtain slipped a crack and allowed sunlight in, they would burst into flames. No, that simply wouldn't do.

I shrugged and went to find James. I found him in the kitchen making some scrambled eggs. They smelled delicious and I knew they were for me. I'd never seen Pallo or Caradoc eat and James wasn't too fond of breakfast foods. His tastes went more towards junk food.

I sat down at the table and poured myself a glass of orange juice. The smell of eggs made my mouth water. James had outdone himself, as usual. I glanced up at him, I just really loved being around him. I wanted to head into town and wished he could come with me. It would be fun to spend the day with him. He had a way about him. Carefree. Funny. Caring.

"Sometimes...well most of the time, I wish you weren't a vampire." As I said it, I knew it had come out all wrong.

He turned and cocked a dark eyebrow at me. He looked so silly with blue hair. I almost laughed. "What? You don't want to be around me?" he asked with a blank look on his face.

"No, what I mean is I wish you could come hang out with me today, that's all. The whole vampire-no-sun-thing kind of gets in the way...I wonder if we got you some of that baby sunscreen, the kind with the SPF of like a million, if that would work." Smiling at him, I waited for my eggs.

James' crisp blue gaze raked over me. He looked so serious. I wasn't sure if I liked that look on him. "You know, *Gwyneth*, I *am* a vampire and I am *not* one of your girlfriends. I do not think it is wise for us to be spending so much time together. It would be better if we cooled it for a while." He did not elaborate further, as if his statement had explained everything, all it did was leave me confused.

At first, I was hurt by the sudden change in his demeanor. He'd been so jovial with me less than an hour ago. Why the sudden need to pull back from me? We'd not had an argument, at least not one I was aware of anyway. I'm sure he was still catching some much flack from Pallo on our friendship but still. Then it hit me. He never called me Gwyneth. No, I got hot-cakes, sweet-lips, sugar-buns, love, and occasionally Gwen, but never Gwyneth, that was reserved only for Pallo.

In fact, the majority of his statement sounded exactly like something Pallo would say. James had been ordered by Pallo to distance himself from me! That was such a Pallo thing to do. My blood boiled. I would not accept any more interference from him. I'd had my limit.

"I'll be back in a minute," I said to James, pushing my seat away from the table and standing quickly. I headed towards the kitchen doorway.

"Gwen, don't go pissin' him off more. Leave it be. There are only a couple hours before daylight comes, let him sleep it off. When he gets up, you're free to have at him, and if we're lucky we'll get to listen in. I always love hearing you get your panties in a bunch." James got an odd look on his face, and then smiled.

"What the hell's so funny?"

He gaze slid down to my lower half and he chuckled. "I was just picturin' your red silkies bunched up, that's all."

I ignored him and headed outside to talk with Pallo. Stepping out and onto the porch made me second guess the whole tunic idea. I was cold enough as it was--being out at this time of the night, felt like winter. I rubbed my hands together and cupped them over my mouth to try to warm them. It didn't work.

I headed down the wooden steps and felt the frost on my bare feet. I picked up the pace a little. Running around to the side of the house, I saw Caradoc levitating high off the ground. Guess I did expect that, I mean he had to close the second story shutters somehow, right? Still, I was a little taken aback. I was going to call up to him when something caught my attention across the yard, near the edge of the woods. I turned and looked, expecting it to be a troll. We'd had a little infestation problem with trolls a couple months back. My eyes adjusted to the darkness and I realized that it was only Pallo standing at the edge of the woods with his back to me.

My feet were so cold they were burning. I looked at the amount of wet, cold grass I had to cover to get to him. I sucked in a big breath and made a run for it. Each step felt more like needles shooting through the soles of my feet and a lot less like grass. I had thought he would turn around. Vampires had amazing hearing and weren't sneaked up on often. I was close enough to touch him. Putting my cold hand out, I tapped his shoulder.

Pallo swung his arm around and I braced myself for impact but his hand stopped right next to my head. I let my breath out. He looked surprised to see me, guess it was possible to sneak up on them after all. Not smart, but at least possible. I was beginning to think they were invincible. It was nice to know they weren't perfect either.

"We need to talk," I said to him. I moved my legs back and forth a little, trying to get some body heat built up. It didn't work. I tried blowing on my hands again. That didn't help any. "Can we do this inside, please?"

"Gwyneth," he said as he let his hand touch my face gently, running it down my cheek slowly. I closed my eyes and leaned my face against his seemingly warm palm.

"Pallo." I took a step towards him and he stood his ground. The smell of vanilla with a hint of chamomile came to me. He owned expensive colognes, I'd seen them, but he knew I preferred him to smell sweeter, more like himself. I knew that he did this for me and it made my heart heavy. My body craved him, even though my mind said he was wrong.

My belly was still sensitive but it seemed to calm with just the touch of his hand. "I'm tired of fighting with you. I don't care anymore about what happened. I just want to stop this. Forbidding James from hanging out with me isn't going to solve anything. It's just going to tick me off more and we've had enough of that."

"Ah, I see. Did James tell you I did this?"

"No, he didn't have to. I know you and I know how you can get."

He nodded his head. "Yes, I am sure you would like to think you know me well. I must confess I did suggest that James try to curb your *new found* want for his friendship. We are all aware of your self-control, or lack there of. It is not wise for us to continue to taunt you with a man you have yet to fuck. Such a temptation could not possibly be left untouched by you. And as loyal as James is to me, he would still be foolish enough to test me on this. His attempt at playing the hero earlier proved as much."

That did it. I was pissed--again. Pallo had a way of bringing out my temper. "God, you know, you really have some nerve. You parade in here to 'save the day' and pick up the pieces, but you never bothered to come prior to this. I don't know what you want from me. You got sex, or excuse me...fucked. Someone who says that has no intention of being my friend, Pallo." I glared at him. "You never call...you don't even answer my calls. You expect me to field all my questions through James and Caradoc, then are surprised to find me getting close to him...*err*...them."

"Him?" He glanced back towards the house. "Would I be right to assume that James is the one you singled out?"

I'd had enough of him. I was freezing and he was being a jerk. "Yeah, you'd be right to assume that. I like James. There I admit it. He's my friend, in fact, he's moving up the chain fast. Soon he'll be campaigning for top spot on my buddy list. Hell, I'll do you one better--I consider him my best friend. Do you want me to lie to you and say we won't get any closer? I could. What the hell do you care, it's not like you've gone out of your way to give a damn about me?"

"Tell me, Gwyneth, what bothers you more? Is it the fact I am jealous of your and James' relationship, or the fact that you and I do not have one?"

His words cut deep, and I couldn't hide the hurt on my face. My lips were quivering but I didn't want to give him the satisfaction of seeing me cry. For some insane reason he seemed to get pleasure out of hurting me. Beating me down emotionally seemed to be his specialty--his forte. First, there were the comments he made after we'd slept together, and now there was this. I'd had enough of him. I tried to get us past this. He was the one who wouldn't let it go. Not me. If he wanted to spend another two hundred years being a bitter bloodsucker, he could do it by himself.

I looked up at the pre-dawn sky. "As much as I'd love to continue this little tit-for-tat with you, the sun is about to come up, and well, all the people without a heart, oops...I mean heartbeats, need to head in to avoid spontaneously combusting." His lips drew in as I continued on with my verbal assault. "I think it'd be for the best if you high-tailed it out of here by nightfall. You see, I don't need you here. I didn't ask you to come, and I don't want you here anymore. You can say all the hurtful and nasty things you want to me, I don't care. You win, Pallo, I give up. I'll even admit that I was a fool to have given a damn about you to start with! Get out of my life and get on with your death or whatever the hell it is that you call your pathetic existence!"

He tipped his head to the side. His face was unreadable. He was a pro at that look. "You believe what you say. You wish for me to leave?"

"Of course I do!"

I was so angry with him. I wanted to punch him in the gut--to slap his face and claw at his eyes. I wanted to make him hurt like he'd hurt me. I wanted to hold him close to me and tell him that I still loved him, that he had and would always have the biggest portion of my heart. Hey, I never said I was consistent. I just hoped he wasn't doing that mind scan thing he was completely capable of.

A little twinkle came to his brown eyes. Yep, he was doing it. He stepped closer to me, and touched my shoulder. "You are cold. Come," he said and led me back towards the house.

The walk back across the wet grass was even worse then the first trot out. My stomach grew fluttery again, our hands brushed past each other and it stopped. I stared at his profile as he walked next to me. He was so chiseled, such a work of art. His wide jaw with a tiny dimple on it set the tone for his body. He looked like he was a body builder. No doubt about it he was a fine specimen.

We climbed up the steps and went back into the house. Warm air, yes! Pallo stood in the doorway to the living room waiting for me to tell him what to do.

"I'll be right back. I need to get a sweater and some socks." I smiled at him and headed up the stairs. The knot in my stomach returned. Each step up I took made it grow tighter and tighter. I made it up about six steps and stopped to grip the railing tightly. It felt like someone was swirling a paintbrush around in a very small area of my belly. I tried to walk up another step but I couldn't do it, I couldn't get my body to cooperate.

Pallo's hand slid around my waist--he was suddenly next to me on the stairs. My stomach eased up rapidly, responding to his touch. He calmed my flu or whatever it was. Oh, pharmaceutical companies wouldn't like that getting out, that was for sure. Of course, people might have issues bringing home a dead guy to cure their ailments.

I put my arm around him and walked with him up the stairs. We reached the top and headed into the master bedroom. He tried to pull himself away from me. I held tight to him. "Just friends, just talking," I said to him softly. If he let go of me I knew that my stomach would be in knots again and I couldn't deal with that on top of being so damned cold.

"Gwyneth, I cannot be just friends with you, I know this now. I cannot be your *James*." He said this so calmly yet so full of passion. My body responded to the sound of his voice. I missed the way his words seemed to wrap themselves around me like an invisible cloak. I put my hand out to touch him. If we walked through that bedroom door together, it would not be as just friends. I had to know--I had to know how much he still meant to me, and I him.

"Come on," I said as I pulled on his hand.

"Gwyneth."

He could take the truth. I knew he could. "Pallo, I need to know. I need to know if I...if we can ever be...I need to know how I feel about you. This can't continue. Caleb's asked me to marry him."

Pallo looked at me, shocked, and followed me into the bedroom. He stopped at the foot of my bed and stared at it with disgust. "This is where you and Caleb sleep?"

I didn't know how to answer that, so I just nodded. He closed his eyes and tipped his head to the side. His curly brown hair fell below his chin and just missed hitting his shoulder. I wanted to walk up to him and put my fingers in his hair. I made my way towards him. He stood very still, almost rigid. It was hardly the welcome I wanted. Something tugged on my insides. A cool, foreign energy ran through me. I sucked in my breath, unsure of what was happening.

As quick as the energy came, it left, but not without lingering effects. I could hear his breathing. Normally, I needed to be very close to him to pick up on it. I think it had something to do with his being a vampire. My brow furrowed as I noticed yet another change. I could smell his desire for me and that was a first for me. This was scary, exhilarating, and a most welcome surprise.

Pallo keep up his suave exterior, showing no outward signs of interest, but I knew better. The only problem was that I had no clue how to break down the emotion walls he'd erected around himself. I wanted him to let them down, allowing me inside once more. It seemed only fair. I'd allowed him, this creature of night, into my heart and loved him with every ounce of it. I'd fallen victim to his lies, his betrayal, and as much as I wanted to hate him, I couldn't. If anything, I had to stop myself from begging him to leave with me, to run away and spend eternity together. Yes, I loved Caleb, but my love for Pallo was like nothing I'd ever experienced before. It was raw. It was real. It was terrifying.

Pallo looked up, his eyes narrowed on me, and I felt the slightest of tickles in the back of my mind. He was reading my thoughts again. I knew it. I had to avert my gaze to avoid begging him to take me. Being pathetic seemed too low, even for me. I'd spent years learning to block out others' thoughts, but here I stood, unable to keep the man I loved from reading my every desire. He carried so much anger inside him that I wasn't sure how he'd interpret my findings. Did he now know how much I loved him? How much I missed his dark humor, his fierce protectiveness and the way he made me feel? Did he know how much I craved his touch, even if it was nothing more than a bittersweet good-bye? Did he know the majority of the memories I had from my last life were of him--of how in love we'd been? Did he have any clue how quickly I'd throw everything with Caleb away for the promise of a future with him? As wrong as it was, it was still the truth.

Somewhere along the line, we'd made a mess of things, and I knew better then to expect a fairytale ending. Neither one of us could change history.

Glancing over at Pallo, I found him in the process of pulling his shirt off. He tossed it aside. A little silk puddle lay on the floor where it had landed. I stood in awe. He knew my bringing him in here was to be with him, if even for one last time, he knew and yet was still okay with that.

Reaching up, I untied my white tunic. I wore no bra under it, so when it flapped open my breasts were completely exposed to him. I reached down and pulled on the string of my jeans, loosening it, as I walked towards him. He met me half way and put his hands on my breasts, caressing them gently, causing my nipples to harden.

"I need this. I need you," I said softly up to him. He reached down and slid his pants off his legs. He was left standing in front of me completely nude. I was beginning to wonder if any male over the age of one hundred actually owned underwear and if they had classes specializing in seductive stripteases. *Supernatural Stripping--101?*

I let my jeans slide down my legs and stepped out of them. I stood before Pallo with my tunic open and a pair of tiny panties on. He grabbed hold of me quickly, wrapping his strong arms around me. He felt so warm to me, so good. He kissed my collarbone slowly and I tipped my head back for him. He kissed his way up my neck and to my mouth. A tiny moan escaped me. I let my hands run all over his back and shoulders, feeling how smooth and strong he was.

His hand slid down my breast and ran over my stomach. When his fingers skimmed over my tiny bulging abdomen, he stopped for a minute, and let his fingers dance along it.

I blushed. "Can you not play with my fat, it's kind of embarrassing."

"I think it is divine," he said, laughing softly as he backed our bodies up and laid himself down on the bed.

The sight of him laying there completely nude took my breath away, his ruddy cock stood at attention, ready for me, calling to me. I slid my panties down my legs and crawled over his body like a cat. A veil of long black hair covered my face and ran over his body. He reached up and pulled it back. I flickered my tongue over his marble member, extracting tiny moans of pleasure from him. Laughing softly, I drew him into my mouth. Pallo gasped as I moved my mouth all the way over him, deep throating him. He was almost too much for me and I had to draw back slightly. On my way up, I sucked hard, causing his hips to jerk. I pulled off him slowly, licked the tip of his cock and brought my hands up to fist him.

"*Ahh*...Gwyneth," he hissed.

Looking up from his groin, I met his eyes and held his gaze as I began sucking on him again. Knowing that he was watching me while I pleasured him made a torrent of cream flow between my thighs. I swirled my tongue against his shaft as I moved my mouth up and down. Saliva built up and pooled at the base of his cock. I rubbed my hands in it, stroking him faster and faster as I sucked him.

Pallo tightened his grip in my hair. "Slowly, *anima mia*."

I couldn't get enough of him. He tasted so sweet, so good. I stroked him harder and ran the head of his cock against the roof of my mouth, stimulating him further. He growled and grabbed hold of me. Instantly, I found myself being flipped onto my back. He trailed a line of kissed down my body, stopping only when he reached my sex.

"Pallo," I said, reaching for him. I needed to feel him in me, now.

He grabbed my wrists and moved his head down to the apex of my thighs. Once nestled before me, he looked up at me with a smile that held the promise of passion and pleasure. "No, I want to taste you."

"I need you." Begging was not beneath me, at least not in this situation.

He laughed softly. "Ah, yes, and I need to taste you. It would appear we have a problem."

"Problem? There's no problem! I want you in me, now! How is that a problem?" I really did not want to have this end in an argument like everything else we did.

He parted my folds and ran a finger along my slit, sending shivers up my spine. I moaned and he smiled. "You see, I will take no further pleasure from you, unless you allow me to please you."

I slammed my head back against the mattress and groaned. Here I thought I was stubborn. He had over two hundred years to perfect the art of resistance. I didn't. He inserted a finger into me and I writhed beneath his touch. My entire body lit with cool energy and I lost my train of thought. I'd wanted something, but what? Pallo's lips pressed against me. He licked his way around, tenderly, teasingly, leaving me whimpering. I reached for him and the moment my hands meet his shoulders, I knew exactly what I wanted--him.

"Yes, Pallo."

His eyebrows rose. "Yes Pallo what?"

"Yes Pallo, taste me...then fuck me." Hearing those words roll off my tongue should have embarrassed me. It didn't.

"Oh, I shall taste you, Gwyneth, but I will not fuck you." He drove another finger into my channel, fucking me hard and fast with them. "When I am done feasting upon you, *delizia*, I will make love to you."

My heart soared. Only Pallo could do that, make me so many promises with so few words. I could only hope he'd deliver on his pledge. If he did, would I be able to say good-bye to him once it was over?

Pallo continued to finger fuck me as he planted his full lips over my clit. He sucked gently on it, causing my legs to quake and quiver. Cream trickled out of my body, and Pallo moaned as he lapped it up. The thrusting, the licking, the muffled cries against my swollen bud, stimulated me to the brink of culmination. I jerked beneath him--trying to get away even though there was nowhere I'd rather be than with him. It was too much pleasure, too much Pallo. I screamed out and he licked harder, faster, cramming his fingers into me with supernatural speed. I came with a start and lifted slightly off the bed.

He didn't stop his oral siege. Bombarding my sense, he caused another wave of body numbing pleasure to crash into me. Animal noises tore from my throat as I shook my head back and forth, attempting to send the energy that was building within me anywhere but at him. I didn't want to hurt Pallo, and with my faerie powers so close to the edge of freedom, I feared for his safety. He, apparently, couldn't give a damn about my magic building, because he sucked harder on my clit, rolling it around with his tongue.

"Pallo!" I grabbed the sheets, clutching them for dear life as another orgasm hit me. Wet, slapping noises began as he continued to push his fingers into me. "No more...please, no more."

"Come for me again, *delizia*." The sound of his deep smooth voice did it. I came again, this time I laid there, barely moving as my entire body went numb from the combination of pleasure and power that now ran through me. Pallo withdrew his fingers from me, taking with him a line of my come. He put his fingers in his mouth and locked gazes with me.

Watching him lick my cream from his fingers was one of the most erotic things I'd ever witnessed. I wanted to reach for him, to take his face in my hands and pull him to me, but I was paralyzed out of fear of releasing my powers.

"Do not be afraid, *fata mia,* you will not harm me."

My power rippled just under the surface of my skin, demanding to be let loose, to be free. I went rigid with fear. The last time I'd lost control of my power while having sex with Pallo, I opened a mystical portal and let the world's craziest psycho vampiress in with her hellhound flunkies in tow. Gee, as much as I wanted a repeat performance of that horrible ordeal, I thought it best to pass.

Pallo chuckled and nuzzled his face back between my legs, giving me one long wet lick before moving slowly up my body. Working the full length of his muscular body over me, he left me no time to protest, not that I would have, as he spread my legs wide and thrust himself into me. His cock rammed to the hilt and I screamed out from a mix of pleasure and pain. I knew that he belonged there, between my legs and I think he did too, but I still had no idea what my magic was capable of. Hurting Pallo would destroy me.

"Ahhh...Pallo, no...off!" I pushed on his shoulders, trying to get him to stop.

He swayed his hips slightly as he pumped himself in and out of me. I growled and wrapped my legs around his waist. He felt so good, so right. The muscles in his arms went taut as he rode me. My hands began to tingle, as though they'd been submerged in ice water for an extended period, and I knew that I was a fraction of a second away from losing control.

Staring into Pallo's dark brown eyes, I pleaded silently with him to understand. To realize that I could never knowingly cause him harm. My eyes burned and I blinked them rapidly, trying to stop the pain. It eased, just in time for my power to let loose. Pallo's body jerked about me. As rigid as he went, I thought I'd hurt him. He locked his body tight to mine and spit forth his semen. My channel locked around him, milking him as he continued to come in me. My power moved through us. Pushing and pulling. It made our orgasms last and last. Each time I thought it was about to end, another wave of my power struck.

Pallo gasped for breath and kept his body tight to mine. He wrapped his arms around me and it took a moment for me to realize what was going on.

"Pallo...are we still on...the bed?" I panted, between bursts of his come and my clenching.

"Ahh," his voice sounded labored and he began to pump into me again, while still coming. "That is...hard to answer. You see," he thrust into me and I cried out. My magic continued to pour through us. "We are more above the bed...than anything else."

I wrapped my legs tighter around his waist, not wanting to let him go for so many reasons. "How far off the...ohhh...slow down a minute." He did and I took a deep breath. "How far off the bed are we?"

Pallo ran his hand down my back and cupped my ass. He didn't answer my question. Instead, he ran his finger around my anus, rimming it, teasing it. I tensed and he let out a manly laugh in my ear. "Fear not, you are not *yet* ready for that."

I no longer felt him coming in me, but he was as hard as when we began. I wanted to ask him about it, but he beat me to it.

"When one finds a treasure, they wish to enjoy the bounty, not take a little and leave. No, they return," he pushed into me harder, "again, and again until they are allowed to return no longer."

"Ahh...Pallo."

He pumped into me and held tight for a moment. "*Tesoro mio.*"

I stared into his brown eyes and prayed to every god I could think of to let us be together--to change the events that had played out, allowing us to be together, as it was once meant to be. He would have been my husband. We would have had at least one child, maybe more. And we'd have had each other. I'd given up my immortality for him, in my last life, and would have aged with him. Growing old gracefully and with the man I loved was what I wanted most.

"Do not dwell on what cannot be changed. Live the moment," Pallo whispered softly as he began moving steadily within me again.

I dug my nails into his back, clutching him and doing my best not to cause him pain. It was hard. He varied his stroke bringing me again. This was all too much. It had to end or I would die from pleasure. I felt us lift a bit higher off the bed. *Oh, God*, if I wasn't careful, I'd shoot Pallo through the ceiling.

I held tight to him and he laughed. "Worry not, *fata mia*. It is my doing. Your magic, your body, you, bring me such joy that I am unable to focus as I should."

I would have commented further but Pallo chose that moment to swivel his hips in rhythmic patterns, leaving his abdomen rubbing my clit and his cock hitting "that spot." Animal noises ripped from my throat as he pounded into me. Only his hands held me in place, suspended above the bed, with him buried deep. His lips met mine and I lost sense of everything but him. My legs shook. And I fought to keep them wrapped around his waist. Pallo held tighter to my ass, squeezing it, massaging it as we ate at each other's mouths--pushing me close, oh so close.

Pallo moaned, his mouth still pressed to mine and I gave into the looming orgasm. I cried out, my lips locked to his and clawed at his back. He came with a jolt and held himself stationary as he filled me with his come. My body continued to tingle and I moaned out again. Pallo withdrew from my core slowly. I was so wet, so full of our combined juices that I was sure I was a mess. He eased his kisses and pulled back just enough. Our lips still met, but barely.

He smiled. The feel under my lips seemed so familiar. He'd done this before. I was positive! During our time together, when he was still mortal, he'd been known to hold me after making love and smile while he kissed me. Was it really a memory of him or had I invented it to suit my needs?

Pallo smiled more and gave my ass a gentle squeeze. "You did not invent it, *fata mia*. You are correct. This is how it was for us...minus the floating of course."

I kissed his lips gently and laughed as I thought about what he'd said. "My dearest Pallo, surly you jest. *'Tis* one of the many reasons I love you."

Where the hell did that come from?

He stared down at me with the most peculiar look on his face. "Gwyneth?"

"Yeah...?" That sounded shaky, even to me.

Pallo twisted in the air. I yelped as he flipped me over and onto him. It was then that I saw we were a couple of inches off the bed. He eased us down and held me tight. Bringing his hands up, he cupped my face gently and stared into my eyes. "Does this happen with Caleb as well?"

I gulped. No part of me wanted to discuss what Caleb and I did behind closed doors. Why the hell would Pallo want to know about sex with Caleb? We'd just shared one of the best moments of my life and he wanted to discuss another man?

Sighing, he caressed my cheeks. "No, Gwyneth. I do not wish to know the details of what you and your faerie have done. I wish to know if you are remembering him as...."

"As well as you?" I asked, finishing his sentence for him. He nodded. "Yes, and no."

Pallo gave me a soft smile and I knew it cost him dearly to put on a happy face when discussing my relationship with Caleb. "You will need to be more specific."

Taking a deep breath in, I nodded. "Okay, yes I remember Caleb but not like this."

"What do you mean?"

Boy he wasn't going to let up! Nothing like putting a girl on the spot while she's naked and on top of you. "The only memories I have of Caleb, so far, are ones that directly involve you...I can remember a tiny, tiny bit of he and I together, while I was pregnant with *your* child, but that's all. Your face haunts my dreams. It's your laughter I hear when I think hard. I guess others memories will come in time, but so far, it's only you." I touched his hand softly and closed my eyes. "Please don't ask me anymore questions about him right now. I know how we are. This will end in a fight and I don't want that, Pallo. I want this to stay perfect."

"As do I, Gwyneth." He pulled me to him and I shifted my legs to straddle his waist. His hard shaft tucked under my body.

"You can't seriously be ready to go again?"

He smiled up at me and melted my heart. "You have this effect on me. You always have. It is you who are my addiction, Gwyneth. It is your face I see when I dream."

For once, I was speechless. I just stared into his chiseled face and memorized every line, every dimple. This would be our last time together and I wanted to etch his image into my mind.

"The night is not over," he said with a wolfish smile.

"No," I shook my head, "oh, no! I won't be able to walk."

"Then I will be assured you will not wander away." He slid his hand down to my lower stomach. He ran his fingers over me, seemingly drawn to my bulge.

Great, attracted to my newfound fat!

I pushed his hand away and slid up a bit to situate his cock under me. I positioned him just right and slid my body down slowly, easily onto him. I cried out as his girth pried me open--spreading me, teasing me. For a minute, I didn't know what to do next. It wasn't like I didn't have experience in the sex department. I just didn't know what to do about the way I was feeling. Sitting on Pallo, our bodies forming one, I knew that I would never stop loving him--that I had never stopped loving him.

Pallo reached up and touched my breasts, cupping them tight. They were tender and I winced a little. He eased the pressure he was applying to them. My nipples hardened in response to him. They were so symbolic of my entire body that I couldn't help but lean for his mouth--needing to taste him. His warm mouth met mine and I moved my body on his. The force of his cock buried deep in me was so glorious I cried out and increased my pace.

My knees hurt from rocking on him so hard. I lifted my legs, putting my feet flat on the bed next to his sides. He was still deep inside of me. I pushed off his chest and stood slightly with my legs, pulling myself off his hard shaft. When I had almost reached the tip of him I sat back down quickly.

Pallo cried out and grabbed my knees. I continued to raise and lower my entire body on him, each time Pallo made primitive noises and he grabbed at me with his hands. The feel of me sliding up and down on him made me cry out too. I ran my fingers down his tight abs, leaving scratch marks as I went. His jaw dropped open and from the look on his face, he was enjoying every minute of it as much as I was.

Pallo's body was hot and sweaty. I rode him hard and fast, pushing myself onto him, swallowing him up as if it would be the last time my body ever drank in his. My legs began to spasm and a tingling sensation moved up my body. It seemed to gravitate to my eyes. They grew hot. I hissed, and rapidly blinked, unsure what would cause them to feel this way. Then it hit me, the faerie in me caused my eyes to shift colors when my body was ready to create life. This only happened with a match, a mate. Caleb was my match now and in theory, that meant I couldn't mate with Pallo was well. My burning eyes begged to differ. Pallo couldn't have children. Vampires' reproducing was almost unheard of. I looked at Pallo and he seemed different through my eyes now-- even more beautiful than he already was.

Pallo glanced up at me. His hand came to my eyes. I slowed my pace just enough for him to touch them gently. At first, he seemed puzzled, but then pleased. "As...it once was...it is again."

I didn't know or care what he was talking about. All that mattered was him being here with me. I screamed out and rode him harder. He had his hands under my ass in an instant, squeezing it as I moved up and down in a squatted position on him. The tingling moved back down my body, leaving me moaning over and over again. My power built fast inside of me. This time I didn't fight it. I pushed it out at Pallo. He cried out and grabbed my hips, pulling me down on him firmly, as he ejaculated--filling me up with his come--it was so hot, so warm. His body twitched a little beneath me. I fell forward on him and he held me tight.

Every piece of me wanted to freeze this moment and never let it go. This was as close to perfection as my life got and I couldn't bear to think of losing it. I loved Pallo so much and didn't want to let him go. I wanted to hold him for all eternity. I was afraid to move, worried that he'd tell me I was a whore and that he'd acknowledge that he'd only used me again.

"No, Gwyneth, I did not use you. I have never used you," he said, his voice full of so much sincerity that my chest tightened. He brushed his hand across my cheek lightly. I felt the moisture under the touch of his skin and realized I was crying.

I held Pallo closer not wanting this to end. Knowing this would be the last time we would be together made it bittersweet. At least we'd ended it with a bang, right? Why was it so hard to let go of him?

I knew the answer to that--love. I was hopelessly in love with him.

He touched the back of my head, ran his fingers through my hair, and spoke softly, *"Ti amo--*I love you."

Chapter 7

Pallo looked towards the windows. We still had a little while until sunrise and I wanted to get out of the house and walk a bit. I could see the hesitation in his eyes.

"Just around the grounds...nothing more," I said.

"I would rather lie here and hold you."

I smiled and kissed his full lips gently. "I feel the same way, but my legs are cramping, my back hurts, my ankles are swelling and, well, I'm just a mess. I think a walk will do me good. I've been a bit under the weather and...."

He brought his lips to mine, silencing me. I lost myself in his kiss and whimpered when he took it away. He laughed softly, stroking my cheek. "Let us go and stretch your legs, *fata mia.*"

We dressed quickly and headed down the stairs. The tickling in my belly began to recede. Maybe, I was finally beginning to shake the flu bug.

We headed out the front door and down the steps to the yard. I chose to walk towards the woods I had found Pallo staring at earlier. He followed close behind me.

"Gwyneth?"

I walked at a slow pace as I answered him "Yes?"

"Are you going to marry Caleb?"

"I said yes to him and then we exchanged power." As soon as I said it, I had a gut wrenching pain in my abdomen. I bent forward and it passed quickly. A dull pain in my low back remained, but it wasn't something that I couldn't deal with. Pallo didn't seem to notice my discomfort.

"If that is what you desire, then I am happy for you."

I knew the minute he said it that he was lying. But there was nothing I could do to prove it. I'm not even sure why I said yes to begin with. I hadn't intended on marrying Caleb, but I think part of me knew that Pallo wasn't capable of committing. As much as I loved Pallo, I couldn't go through the rest of my life as nothing more than sex to him. He'd made it very clear once that that was all I was to him. As much as that hurt to hear, I was still pleased I'd repeated my "mistake" with him. He could think of me as nothing more then a notch on his bedpost for the rest of eternity but he'd always be so much more than that to me.

His confession of love in my bedroom had thrown me for a loop. Not so much so that I was willing to risk my future on him. He'd fooled me once before in the area of love. I couldn't handle having it happen again.

Caleb would treat me like a princess and never expect me to just be there for him sexually. He would be my life-long companion in every sense of the word. He'd never use me for sex and then discard me until he felt the urge to satisfy his needs again. No, he loved me with all of his heart. I knew this, yet I still felt uneasy about marrying him. I'd hoped that my romp with Pallo would push me one way or the other. It just served to confuse me more. Now, I had put my heart on the line with both men.

Glancing over at Pallo, I wondered how he felt about what we'd just done. As much as he hated to admit it, he and Caleb were friends and this was going to damage that severely. I wanted to be more concerned, I knew I should, but the pains in my back moved to my stomach and I suddenly felt flushed. I wasn't liking this human flu bug very much.

Something small and gray hurried past me in the pre-dawn darkness. I stopped and stared around for it. Then I caught sight of it. It was an adult rabbit. Something primitive rose in my body. I stayed focused on the rabbit. Its ears perked up. Lunging at it with amazing speed, I sunk my teeth into it. It twitched for a minute as my mouth filled with warm copper tasting liquid. My body felt better, warmer. Something grabbed hold of my shoulders and tore the dying rabbit from my face.

Pallo stood before me holding onto my shoulder firmly, staring at my face with a look of shock and horror--almost disgust. I could feel the rabbit's blood running down my face and slid my tongue out to lick it, as I heard myself laugh.

What the hell was I doing? I just attacked an innocent little bunny. *Oh my God*, I bit the thing practically in two. I should have felt sick to my stomach, I should have puked my guts out, but I didn't. Oddly enough, my stomach felt the best it had all day.

"Something's wrong with me, Pallo."

"I know."

Chapter 8

We entered the kitchen quietly. James was cleaning up his scrambled egg mess when he caught sight of me. "What in the bloody hell happened to you?" He threw Pallo an accusatory look.

I waved my hand in the air, hoping to avoid another ugly scene. "No, he didn't do anything, really. It was me. I, I…" I couldn't get the words out. I wasn't sure how one goes about saying that they'd just attacked an innocent little bunny and drained it dry.

"She fed," Pallo said those two words and the room fell silent. Caradoc had appeared near the hall entrance at some point in the conversation but did not ask any questions. Pallo had summed it up nicely.

Pallo led me to one of the kitchen chairs and I sat. He bent down in front of me and lifted his hand towards my neck. I didn't protest I just let him do his thing. He tipped my head to the side a little. "Have you seen Giovanni recently?"

Giovanni? I was shocked. Giovanni had been Pallo's master for over two hundred years. He was a gorgeous Italian vampire with long sleek black hair and hypnotically dark eyes. Oh, did I mention he and his cronies were the ones who killed me in my last life?

Yeah, I palled around with him all the time. *Not.*

Everyone claimed that at some point I loved Giovanni and that I'd been his companion for almost a hundred years. They also claimed that he was the "badest boy" in town. It was rather ironic considering that in my present life he'd already saved me once, and begged for my life to be spared another time. I'd even bargained with him for Pallo's freedom. Giovanni got to take a big bite out of my neck in the deal, and Pallo found himself a free man. All I got out the deal was bit, bruised and mixed emotions about a man I knew I should be terrified of--Giovanni.

He was over five hundred years old and everyone told me that his bite gave him enormous powers over me. The thought of anyone being able to bend my will terrified me and I couldn't believe Pallo had brought his name up. The last time I'd said Giovanni's name aloud he magically appeared. I didn't want to make that mistake again. We shared some sort of connection, one that transcended space and time. As much as I tried to instill the fear of God in myself when thinking of Giovanni, I couldn't. The tangled mess that had become my mind still seemed to think there was something redeemable about him. But I wasn't willing to bet my life on it just yet. Besides, I was conflicted enough already. I didn't need to add another dark and brooding vampire to the mix. Pallo was all I could deal with as it was.

I pushed Pallo's hand away from my neck. "Of course I haven't been around *him.*"

Pallo smiled slightly then looked nervously up at Caradoc. "She has a bite mark." Brushing my hair back, he showed the right side of my neck to Caradoc. James poked his head in around them and Pallo snarled at him. "Did you do this?"

James was stunned. "No, Master...I would never hurt Gwen."

"Don't call him master. I hate that. You're not his damn dog. And NO James has never bitten me. You on the other hand have!" I glared into his dark brown eyes daring him to contradict me. He scared the shit out of Caradoc and James, but I wasn't frightened of him. Well, not *that* frightened of him anyway. He stood up and stepped away from me. I'd struck him below the belt with my last comment. I was only half sorry I did it.

Caradoc leaned in closer and checked my "wound" with his fingers. He sniffed it. That was a little creepy, but I let it go. "Master..." He stopped and looked apologetically at me. "Pallo, it is only hours old and...."

"And what?" The anger in Pallo's voice was enough to make a normal person want to crawl under a table and hide. Good thing I'm not normal.

Caradoc took three steps back towards the hallway entrance, his face blank. I'd seen that look once before when I'd almost put a candlestick through his heart. If that was his "oh fuck," face then it was about to get ugly in here fast. "And the bite wound smells like it is yours. She carries your scent now...in more ways than one."

Pallo was on him in an instant. He had a hold of his throat with his left hand. Caradoc tried to free himself but Pallo's grip was too tight. James rushed over and tried to pry Pallo's hand from Caradoc's neck. Rising slowly out of the chair, I went towards them. I saw Pallo's right hand come up and shove James away, but I wasn't fast enough to react. James' body crashed into mine and we both went backwards. My mid-back cracked into the butcher-block counter top that Caleb had just put in. The back of my head smashed into the plate cupboard. Together we managed to bring the entire set of dishes crashing down on us. I screamed out and tried to cover my head. James had speed that no human possessed and was up and shielding my body from anything else in an instant.

"Are you okay?" James's face was so close to mine that I could feel his breath on my cheek and it felt warm. That meant that my body was getting cold again, damn. He pulled me to my feet. Pain shot up from my mid back, I was going to be really sore for awhile.

"Gwen," Pallo's voice was soft as he spoke. He never liked using my nickname. He was really trying to win "like me" points with me. "It was an accident. I did not realize you were there."

I glared at him. "You were being an asshole to these guys *again* and they didn't deserve it." I let go of James' hand and stormed towards Pallo. I pushed my finger into his chest and let just enough power roll off it to give him a harmless little jolt each time I came into contact with his perfect skin. "You do not come into my home and treat people this way. Are we clear on that? You are not the master of this house. I'm the one who's in charge here!" He stepped back from me and I followed him step for step. "And, while we're on the subject of me being pissed off with you, why in hell did you ignore my calls? Why did you refuse to come here? Do you really hate me that much? Its common knowledge that...what is it again, Pallo? Hmm...yes, that I'm nothing but a cheap whore...and I'm sure our romp between the sheets earlier did little in the way of disproving that, but still..." I smacked my forehead. It was an odd habit I had and couldn't seem to be able to break. "God, I'm so fucking stupid. I was so close to believing that you were capable of love. Hell, you're not even capable of being a decent human being to your own friends."

He tipped his head slightly, giving me a wry smile. "Perhaps that is because I am not a human being."

"Oh, stop using the 'dead-guy-walking' thing as a crutch. Call it was it is, Pallo--you being a dick!"

"Gwyneth."

"No, don't Gwyneth me! You have no idea how much I wanted to believe I'd been wrong about you, that you were capable of more than deception, hate and rage. Why am I so stupid? What we did upstairs will tear Caleb to pieces when he finds out about it. I hurt a good, honest man and for what...a chance to hear your sweet words of passion, your lies as you 'fucked' me." My emotions were out of whack, so much so that I was losing control over my own power. It spread like wild fire throughout me. I'd seen the ugliness, the carnage, I was capable of inflicting and no one here deserved that--not even Pallo.

"Get away from me!" I yelled.

He did the exact opposite--he reached for me. "Gwyneth, please...."

"NO!" Terrified of hurting him, I let my power roll into me. I bore the brunt of it. It warmed my body rapidly, too rapidly. Instantly, my skin burned and my head throbbed. Screaming out, I fell to the floor. James was at my side immediately, reaching for me.

"Don't touch me!" I didn't want to hurt him. I was afraid that I wouldn't be able to control it if he came into contact with my skin. I'd killed a man before with just my touch. I didn't want a repeat performance. Pallo kneeled next to me and from the look on his face he had no intention of listening to me

"Gwyneth, concentrate hard on calming yourself down. Think of something pleasant. Think of your *sweet* Caleb." I could not believe I had just heard Pallo encourage me to think of another man. I tried to pull an image of Caleb into my head but the only image that came to me was one of Pallo and me making love in a glorious room of yellow. I thought of his pushing himself deep within me. I thought of how my eyes burned when he made love to me, and how that, for a faerie, was a sign of finding a mate. A sign that together, our union could produce a child. My eyes had burned again during our most recent sexual encounter. It was so odd yet so similar to what had happened in that yellow bedroom over two months ago.

The ghost of my biological mother had arranged the perfect romantic getaway for Pallo and me. She'd recreated Pallo's bedroom of two hundred years ago in a mystical portal. It was a magical moment for me. I'd never felt such a bond with a person before. I'd never turned myself over to someone so completely.

I closed my eyes. Pallo touched my forehead with his cool hand. I sensed him reading me, scanning my thoughts to see if I was all right. I knew that he'd seen me thinking of him and not Caleb. He was my calming thought.

My power tried to rise and strike out. I still wasn't very good at controlling it. It made its way up enough to reach Pallo. He began to pull his hand back from me but stopped. He put his face on my cheek and let my magic ride over him slowly. For the first time, I saw what was in his mind, his inner most thoughts. He was remembering the night that we had first made love, too. I could sense how happy he was and how very long it had been since he'd felt anything but darkness. He replayed the night's events, when Talia the Keeper of Hounds had walked in on us at the very moment that our lovemaking had ended. I could feel his fear for my life. He knew full well what she was capable of and he knew what she would do to me if she learned how much I meant to him. How I was his world, his reason to continue existing.

Pallo's memories of that night continued to flood into me. His mind raced with ideas on how best to handle the situation with Talia. Then it hit him, he knew a way that might work, might get me out alive. He tried desperately to reach out with his mind to me. Talia struck me in the back with her whip at the same time and he lost his ability to focus. His body ached with mine--he felt my pain because he was my soul mate. He couldn't move to help me or show any sign of concern. He had to prevent Talia from knowing he was lying to her.

She had to believe that I meant nothing to him. It was the only chance he had to assure my safety. No part of him cared if Talia killed him, his only worry was me. Without me, he would lose his will to live anyway. Talia looked at him, her face full of suspicion. He had to do something to keep her from suspecting the truth. Pallo struggled with himself as he raised his hand to strike me. He knew about hellhounds, and he knew that they normally only attacked when they sensed fear or knew they were going to have a good fight. His hope was that he would strike me hard enough to knock me out. The hellhounds might leave me alone and move onto to a more lively target--him. He'd made me call for Giovanni already and he knew the master vampire would drop everything to come to me. The last thing Pallo wanted to do was see me tied to Giovanni again, but without him, I would not survive. Pallo knew what he had to do, he had to kill Talia, and he was ready to use whatever method he could to do it. He loved me so much that he was willing to sacrifice himself for me.

"*Dio mio!*" Pallo jerked his face away from me. He hadn't meant to share that with me, I could tell. I looked into his dark brown eyes. Everything that he'd said and done--all the ugly words, all the deceit, had been to protect me. He'd been more than willing to sacrifice himself for me.

How had I ever doubted that?

I couldn't fight the tears that were welling up any longer. "I didn't know, Pallo. I didn't know."

"Try to relax now. We shall discuss this another time." Pallo's voice was so soothing. I wanted to listen to whatever he told me to do. I wanted to obey his every command. I shook my head slightly. That didn't sound like me at all. I was definitely not a follower. "Come, we need to get you to bed before the sun comes up."

He was right. Once the sun came up they would all be too tired to do anything. I didn't know why it drained their energy but it did. I didn't fight Pallo when he picked me up and carried me up the stairs. I didn't fight him when he lay next to me in the bed, or when he gently pulled the covers over us.

I reached for him and laced my fingers in his. "I'm so sorry. I should have never doubted you. I should have followed my heart. It told me to love you and trust you, but my head...Pallo, please forgive me. I didn't mean to say all those hurtful things to you...and I...I love you so much that it hurts."

Pallo wrapped his large frame around me and kissed my forehead. "I love you too, Gwyneth, but you have agreed to be another man's wife. I think it is best if you rest now."

Instantly, my eyes grew heavy. Was this Pallo's doing? I clung tight to him afraid that if I feel asleep, he'd leave. I fought the urge to rest and touched his cheek lightly. "The only man I want to spend my life with is you. It's always been you."

He sighed. "Things are different now, *fata mia*. The Fates paired Caleb with you this time around and even I cannot fight fate. To do so would only cause you pain, because you yourself admitted to sharing power with him already, forever tying the two of you together. As romantic as having you all to myself sounds, it cannot be. You belong to another now. The bond between the two of you will only grow stronger each passing day. Do not fight it, Gwyneth, or it will destroy you." He kissed my forehead and pulled me closer to him. "Try to rest."

I was hit again with the need to sleep. Pallo was using his vampire mojo on me and I wasn't strong enough to fight it. "No...you, Pallo...I belong to..." Darkness surrounded me before I was able to finish speaking.

I couldn't have been asleep very long before I heard the sound of the robed men chanting. I didn't have the energy to be doing this again. My body had been so run down lately that I needed to get a good night's rest. These guys were just plain old pissing me off.

I found myself naked and in the room with the altar again. Candles had been lit all around the floor, along the circular walls. I walked towards them and looked up at the paintings. Something touched my shoulder and I jerked around to find Pallo standing behind me.

Immediately, I checked Pallo's eyes. The last time I'd dreamt about him here he went all demonic on me during sex. I didn't want that happening again. His eyes were perfectly brown. He put his hand out to me and I took it. It felt warm against my freezing skin. He pulled me close to him. Our bodies fit together so perfectly. His tall muscular frame seemed to be molded perfectly for my five foot five self.

Suddenly, the robed men appeared all around us. Pallo pulled me tighter to him and hissed out at them. I didn't want to see his face. His voice scared me enough. If I was them I would have run like hell. They didn't. They chanted more. *"She is the vessel, you are the master...the time is near."*

Pallo growled again but they didn't stop. They began to say something in a language I couldn't understand. Pallo's body stiffened. His hands slid down my back slowly. His breathing increased. When he looked down at me, his eyes were pits as dark as coal. Screaming, I tried to break free of his grip. He held tight to me and brought his other hand up and touched my breast. I didn't know why my mind was letting this dream go on. I didn't want to have sex with Pallo when he was like this and I certainly didn't want to do it with an audience--again.

"Pallo, NO!" One of his fingernails scraped across the top of my breast. I pulled back a bit from him and glanced down. Blood trickled from the cut. I shook my head violently. "Wake up damn you, Gwen, wake up!" I shouted at myself but it was useless.

The crazy chanting robed men closed in on us. I didn't know which was worse, the thought of these guys touching me or Pallo's vampire side being in control of him. *"Feed the seed, feed the seed, take her...feed the seed."* Their chanting grew louder and louder. Pallo pulled me closer to him and bent down towards me. I slapped at his face and only hurt my hand in the process. His tongue flickered over the cut on my breast.

I gave up on waking myself up and decided to take another approach. "I love you, Pallo...please stop this." I whispered softly in his ear. He stopped licking my chest and stood very still with his head down. "Pallo, I love you. Please, Pallo, can you hear me? Don't do this!"

He remained still.

Closing my eyes for a moment, I attempted to will my self away. "Wake up, Gwen, wake up! No part of you wants Pallo like this. Not when you have the real, non-demonic version in your bed. Wake the fuck up!" I screamed at myself, but I was obviously too stubborn to listen because I didn't wake up. "Pallo!"

I cracked my eyes open and found myself still in the circular room with the monks. The only good thing was that Pallo no longer looked like he wanted to rip me limb from limb. No trace of his demon was left.

"Gwyneth?"

I grabbed him to me tight. "Make this stop, please make this end. I can't do this anymore. Please...Pallo, I just want to wake up."

"I am sorry, Gwyneth." He sighed and I knew it was bad. "I love you."

"Make it end. Make it all end. I love you too, but not like this." Tears rolled down my cheeks. It was hard to find my voice again, but when it came I used it to say all that I wished to say to him in real life. "The night with Talia...you were right, we are soul mates and I will love you until I die."

"You are immortal."

"I know."

"That is a long time to carry love for someone you cannot have," he said, his voice hollow. He kissed the top of my forehead gently and I felt every emotion in him as though he'd been stripped bare. "Trust me, Gwyneth. I know full well what it means to love someone for centuries only to see them chose another."

I held tight to him and tried to will our conversation to end. Making up romantic versions of how much he loved me was foolish.

"No, not foolish, Gwyneth...nothing about my love for you is foolish." He stroked the back of my hair and rocked me gently.

"Oh, this is just fucking great!" Caleb's voice boomed all around us. That was a first in the crazy monk dreams. Geesh, even my friggin' dreams had issues keeping Pallo and Caleb separate.

Pallo and I looked at each other quickly. Something tugged at us, pulling us backwards into nothingness. "PALLO!"

I woke, still screaming his name. It took me a few seconds to adjust to the room. Someone had turned the bedroom lights all on. I had to squint to keep from going temporarily blind.

"This is just fucking great!" I heard Caleb's voice plain as day and thought I might still be dreaming. I turned and sat up quickly. A sharp pain shot across my left breast. I pulled the front of my shirt open and saw that my breast was bleeding in the same spot where Pallo had scratched me in my dream. I gasped and looked up.

Caleb stood at the foot of the bed. His long white-blond hair was flowing all around him. He had on a brown shirt and a pair of dark blue jeans and he looked amazing. His face, on the other hand, looked livid. He caught my gaze with his green eyes and held it. An icy rage came over them. I didn't understand what was going on. Why was he mad?

Pallo.

Turning to my left, I found Pallo lying next to me. We were both fully clothed. He sat up slowly, looking sore. I didn't think he ever got achy. He glanced at me and wiped the corner of his mouth, coming away with blood on his hand.

I looked up at Caleb and searched for the right words to tell him what had transpired while he was away. As I stared into his green eyes, I knew that Pallo was right, Caleb and I had forged a bond, one that was growing stronger. It wasn't what I had with Pallo--at least not yet, but it was headed that way, fast. "Caleb...I need to...this *here* isn't what it looks like...not this…."

"So you two weren't just having sex."

"No," Pallo said. "We did not *just* have sex."

Granted, Pallo was right, we didn't *just* have sex, we had it hours ago. I was about to tell Caleb this when his head fell back and he laughed loud and hard. "This is fucking fabulous, Gwen, really, you've outdone yourself!" He glared at Pallo. "I come home early worried about you, and I find you in *our* bed with *him*. Tell me, how many times in the last two months have you done this to me? Huh? Do you wait until I'm at least down the road before you start fucking him, or does he 'poof' in the second I climb into my truck?"

"No, Caleb, it's not like that. I've never had him sneaking in here while you're gone. Don't do this. Don't say things that you can't take back." It was ridiculous of me to deny the charges that Caleb was making, yet I did. He was right, not about it happening at the moment, but it had happened--in the very bed we still were laying in.

Pallo stood and looked a little shaky. Was it still daylight out? I didn't know. "Caleb, she speaks the truth. I merely laid next to her to keep an eye on her. Something is off, shall we say, and she required constant supervision."

Caleb walked up to him. "God, Pallo, I really thought we had an understanding. I thought we agreed to be honest with one another. This is low, even for you. And with the shit I've seen you do over the years, that's not saying much!"

I'd had enough of this. "Caleb! We were just sleeping that's all." Great, Pallo's literal translations were rubbing off on me. Hey, if they'd get me off on a technicality I'd go with it.

Caleb laughed wickedly. "Hmm, I would've thought it'd be hard to sleep while you were professing your undying love for one another."

I looked over at Pallo. His eyes were wide, too. Had he had the same dream as me? Glancing down at my breast, I noticed it was still bleeding and covered it quickly with my hand. Pallo's gaze darted to my breast as well. His eyes widened and he looked down in slow motion at the blood on his hand. He shook his head slightly before backing away from me. From the look on his face, he was as shocked as I was.

"Oh, now you don't want to be near her. Should that make me feel better?" Caleb showed no signs of slowing on his verbal assault.

"Something is very wrong here," Pallo said.

"You bet your ass something is wrong here."

"Guard your anger old friend…."

Caleb clenched his fists and narrowed his gaze on Pallo. "*Dún do bheal!*"

"No, old friend, I will speak. Now is not the time for jealousy. Gwyneth is…."

"*D'anam don diabhal!*" Caleb said, spitting each word out while he glared at Pallo. I sat there staring at Caleb as if he were a stranger. In many ways, he was.

Pallo laughed slightly and I wondered if he'd finally snapped. "You are a bit too late on that request, faerie. The Devil has owned my soul for centuries. You are already aware of that, are you not? Correct me if I am wrong, but when I was newly made, was is not you I found fucking the woman I loved...the woman I was to wed...the woman who carried my child within her womb?"

My heart went to my throat. I was the woman Pallo was talking about. In my first life, we had been lovers and when he disappeared, I found out I was pregnant. Caleb cared for me and after six months had passed, we had assumed that Pallo was dead. We weren't far off--he was a vampire. I'd had random visions from my past life and knew that Pallo had walked in on Caleb and me while we were having sex. He'd assumed the child I carried was Caleb's. It wasn't until two months ago that he finally learned the truth. It had been his.

I closed my eyes a moment, trying to keep the memories at bay. The men before me seemed to have great difficulty separating my two lives. To them, the lives blurred into one. They were immortal and had been first-hand witnesses to the events that unfolded centuries before. I, on the other hand, gained my knowledge through them or through random visions. Buying a ticket and watching it at a movie theater would have explained more to me then I knew now, but they couldn't seem to understand that.

"Guys, please stop. This is ridiculous. Let me go put some coffee on and we can discuss this like the adults we all hope to be someday." They looked at me like I'd sprouted a second head. Hey, maybe if I was lucky, I'd sprout a second body too and then they could each get one.

"No, Gwen, I'll deal with you in a minute. This is between the *vampire* and me now."

My mouth dropped. "Excuse me, but did you just say that you'd 'deal' with me in a minute?"

The air around me heated quickly and I recognized the sensation for what it was--Caleb's magic. He wasn't one who pulled his magic out often and now certainly wasn't the time I wanted him to start. His emotions were too high right now. I knew firsthand what it was like to lose control of your power. That wasn't something I wanted to see happen with Caleb.

I tried to bring my power up, but with not feeling very well, I had little to no control over it. "Caleb, stop...please."

He lashed out with his power and moved me backwards on the bed. I screamed as heat surrounded me. Surprisingly, it didn't burn me. Caleb could have incinerated me on the spot, he didn't. Instead, he lashed out, but still maintained control of himself.

"Gwyneth!" Pallo shouted.

Caleb went charging at him. I could feel Caleb's magic building up again. He was planning on using it against Pallo. I knew that Pallo was stronger than any human was, but I didn't know how he'd stack up against Caleb's magic. Caleb was old and his magic was powerful. Digging deep within me, I found the core of my magic and seized hold of it, using it to push Caleb's energy off me. It worked.

I scrambled to get out of the bed. With being sick and having to expend that amount of energy, I could barely keep my eyes open let alone stand. It didn't matter how shitty I felt, I wouldn't let Caleb do anything stupid. "Caleb, no!"

He ignored me as I struggled to get up. I didn't have enough strength in my stomach muscles to pull myself up. I glanced down and it looked like I was smuggling a grapefruit in my lower abdomen. *What the hell?* Pallo and Caleb exchanged more harsh words, but I sounded them out. I just kept staring at my stomach.

Something was wrong--very wrong with me, and it sure the hell wasn't a common cold.

Pushing myself off the edge of the bed, I looked towards Pallo and Caleb. They had each other by the shirts and were nose to nose shouting at each other. Half of their words were mixes of the languages they'd learned over the centuries. I caught the highlights in English and those were bad enough. I really didn't want to know what else they were saying.

"You can't stand the fact that I'm the one who has her." Caleb was practically spitting in Pallo's face as he spoke. "It must just kill you that I've known the pleasure of her company and you haven't."

Instantly, I panicked. Caleb hadn't let me finish when I tried to tell him that Pallo and I had slept together. He had no idea that I'd slept with Pallo let alone only hours ago. I hadn't thought past the moment with Pallo, now I needed to do something. It was about to come out now. Pallo wouldn't pass up the opportunity to hurt Caleb. He seemed to live for moments like this.

"You are right, old friend. I am jealous of you and I am sorry. I have not known her touch in this life and never will." Pallo's words left me standing there speechless. He lied to Caleb. We had been intimate together more than once, but he lied.

Caleb eased his grip on Pallo's shirt. "I knew it. I knew that you wouldn't be able to stand it. She'll never touch you now--you know that right? Things are different now. This time around, she isn't the same naïve girl and you're not human. You're a vampire...you're one of the walking dead and Gwen doesn't let demons in her bed anymore!"

Caleb's words stung me. I couldn't imagine how Pallo must be feeling. I couldn't take it anymore. I tried to push myself between them. "Enough!"

They both stopped and dropped their hands to their sides slowly. They looked like two children who'd been scolded. My gaze met Caleb's--I had to tell him the truth. He had to know that I'd not only slept with Pallo, I'd also made my mind up. "Caleb, I think you should sit down. There's something I need to tell you. Promise me that you'll keep your power under control."

His face went slack. Pallo walked around behind me and put his hand on my shoulder in a show of support. I took a deep breath and continued on. "Caleb, there's something that I need to tell you about Pallo and me."

"No, Gwen...no." Caleb looked like he was going to be sick.

"I'm in love with...what I mean to say is that I...we…" The right words seemed to escape me. I took a deep, calming breath and tried again. "You know that I have *strong* feelings for Pallo--that I care deeply for him. Ah hell, you know that I love him too, right?" Caleb grimaced and turned his head. This wasn't going as well as I'd hoped it would.

Pallo's grip tightened on my shoulder. "What Gwyneth is trying to tell you is that she has informed me that the two of you are to be wed and she has been concerned about how I would take the news. I am happy for you both, of course." I flung around and stared at him with wide eyes. He could have told Caleb or at least let me do it. Caleb deserved to know the truth. Why the hell was Pallo doing this?

Caleb ran to me. "You told him?"

I looked at Pallo, trying to figure out what he was doing. His big brown eyes blinked twice at me slowly. I turned to Caleb and nodded. His arms flew around me, and he pulled me tight to his chest. The sweet smell of morning dew filled my head as he wrapped his magic around us, letting it tug at the piece that now resided in me. "I thought you were going to tell me that you two had...that you'd had…" He couldn't bring himself to finish his sentence. "What made you decide to tell him? I thought we were going to do it together."

I closed my eyes. I couldn't do this. I couldn't lie to his face. Regardless how strong my feelings for Pallo were, I loved Caleb too and he deserved more than this. My stomach grew tight. It cramped up so hard that I doubled over from the pain. Both Caleb and Pallo were at my sides in an instant.

"Gwen?" Caleb touched my arm.

The pain in my stomach tripled and I screamed out, falling to the floor. I lay there curled in the fetal position crying out in pain. Caleb tried to pick me up, but every time that he touched me, the cramps worsened. Pallo put his hand on my shoulder and the pain eased up a little. I reached for his hand and pulled him closer to me. He seemed to understand that I wanted him near me. He sat on his knees and put his entire body next to mine on the floor.

"What's wrong with her?" Caleb asked. The sound of his voice made me sick to my stomach. I was as in the dark as he was.

Having Pallo near me definitely helped with the pain. I straightened my body out to stand up. Pallo slid his arms around me to help me up. "I do not know…" Pallo stopped in mid-sentence, as his hand skimmed over my lower stomach. "Go and retrieve the *Si* doctor in town."

"What's wrong?" He moved towards us and pain crashed back into me. I winced and Caleb stopped dead in his tracks. "I'm not leaving her like this. Maybe I can…."

Pallo put his hand up and Caleb shut-up. "I cannot go, the sun has not set as of yet. She needs to be seen immediately. Go, I will stay with her."

Caleb fell to his knees next to me, and snatched me up in his arms. The minute that I lost contact with Pallo I felt sick again. My body cramped to the point that I thought I'd vomit. "Put me down."

He did, slowly.

"Gwen, honey, I knew I shouldn't have left you alone. I knew that you were getting sick, but I had no idea it was this bad." His concern warmed my heart.

"Go, Caleb, Pallo's right. You need to drive into town. I can't go in like this. It would draw too much attention." The pain in my stomach was threatening to rip me in two. I screamed out again, reaching for anything to help ground me. Pallo's arms came around me quickly and the pain receded.

"My friend, you are wasting precious time. Now go and get the help she needs." Pallo's voice was calm, yet stern. Caleb leaned over and kissed my forehead before he raced out of the room. I knew that it would take him a least an hour to get there and back. I didn't think I could hold out that long.

Pallo helped me back into the bed and sat down next to me. I kept my hand on his thigh. His pants were soft and smooth. I had always loved his choices in clothes. He was very New York--very metrosexual. His hand brushed past mine on the way to my stomach.

"Gwyneth?"

I looked up into his well-defined face. His chestnut brown eyes held much concern. "Gwyneth, have you dreamt of me?"

Under normal circumstances I would have laughed, I mean, come on, how full of yourself can you get? But now, with the freaky chanting men dreams and the cut on my breast I didn't think it was the least bit funny. I nodded my head slowly.

Pallo's head dropped slightly. "In these dreams, did I, did we…."

I'd never heard him at a loss for words before. It wasn't helping me remain calm. I knew full well what he was getting at. He wanted to know if I'd dreamt of having sex with him. I wasn't sure how much of the dream I wanted to reveal to him yet, so I took a more subtle approach. "They keep chanting over and over again. They keep saying I'm the vessel. Then you show up and everything is fine for a little bit, before you…."

He slid his hand under my shirt. I didn't push him away. His touch was the only thing keeping me from doubling over in pain. Lifting my shirt up gently, he looked at the cut over my left breast. He closed his eyes as he sighed. That was not a good sign.

"Pallo, what's wrong?"

"Nothing is wrong, but if you should have another one of these dreams of the chanting men try to wake yourself up. If you are unable to wake, and if I take you to the altar again--and you cannot reach me through my demon, then kill me...do you understand? In the dream if I should try to harm you, then you are to slay me." I couldn't believe my ears. I tried to sit up on the bed. "Do not fear, Gwyneth. It is only a dream. I will be fine. Just promise that you will do as I ask."

What in the hell was he talking about? I had no intention of hurting him, asleep or not. Then it hit me. He had been the one to mention me reaching him through his demon, and he had been the one to bring up the altar. I never told him that part. He had been there with me! I sat up quickly, pulling my legs under me and looked straight into his face. "Don't you dare sit there and pretend like this is no big deal, and don't tell me to kill you!"

"It is only a dream, it is not real."

"Bullshit! You were there, weren't you?"

He pushed gently on my shoulders to get me to lie down. It wasn't going to work. I could've told him that. "Do not be silly, Gwyneth. How could I possibly be there with you? It is your dream."

Before I could think, my hand flew up and smacked him across the face. "Liar!" He made no motion to move away or protect himself from me. He just sat next to me on the bed. "Don't try to lie this away! I never mentioned the altar or you turning all vampire-demon-boy on me. You brought that up, not me!"

He stiffened. I had him and he knew it.

"I am sorry. I should not have tried to deceive you. Yes, I too have been having the same bizarre dreams." He moved closer to me, and touched the sides of my arms. "That does not change the fact that you must protect yourself at all costs. You must be willing to...."

I'd had enough of this. "I must be willing to what? Kill a man that I've loved since the moment I met him? I couldn't do that, even if it is just a friggin' dream."

"You would not hurt me. I would be fine when we woke."

Would he really be okay? I remembered him sinking his teeth into me during sex and waking up with the bite marks on my neck. I touched the cut on my breast and panicked. "No, Pallo! No! It would kill you here, too."

Pallo let out another long sigh. He'd known that if he died in the dream, he would die here, too. That bastard! "I can't believe that you would try to get me to hurt you when you know exactly what will happen to you. Do you think I could live with that?"

I wanted to shake him violently. I wanted to smack his stubborn head against a wall to try to knock some sense into him. Instead, I let my lips touch his. His face softened under mine. I reached my hands up and pulled gently on his long brown curls. His hands danced up my back slowly. Turning my head a little, I pushed my tongue into his mouth.

Kissing Pallo made all the tension in my low abdomen fade away. I pulled at his face to keep him near me. I didn't want this to ever end. I had my Pallo back with me. This was how things were meant to be. He took extra time to savor our kiss before he pulled away from me. I reached out for him. My balance was off because I'd leaned forward so fast and I almost fell right onto the floor. I caught myself and looked up at him. "Pallo?"

"No, this cannot happen again, Gwyneth. You are to be Caleb's wife."

He was right. The only problem was that I wasn't sure if I'd been wrong to accept Caleb's proposal or wrong for sleeping with Pallo. I couldn't help the way I felt about him. I loved him with all my heart. Asking him to come back to the bed had crossed my mind, but I knew that it would only end badly. I lay back down on the bed and Pallo headed towards the door.

"Pallo, stay here with me please."

"That I cannot do...I am sorry." I heard the bedroom door close softy behind him. I had successfully managed to screw everything up again. I was becoming a real pro. I didn't have the energy to try to fix it all now. I hadn't slept well in days and this flu was seriously taking it out of me. I let my head rest on the pillow and crossed my fingers to just sleep peacefully.

Chapter 9

"No, she should be feeling better in a day or two."

I didn't recognize that voice. The room was dark. I had let my eyes adjust and tried to sit up. My body was feeling much better. I wasn't near as achy as I had been before I got some rest.

"So, how often should she take these?" Caleb stood near the door to our room. A tall-thin man who looked to be in his late thirties or early forties stood directly in front of him. The man held a tiny brown bottle out to Caleb. "Have her take these twice a day."

"Should she stop taking the birth control pills?" Caleb asked.

"No! No, she should remain on those. These will help her rest and let her body fight the infection." Infection? Who the hell was this guy? What kind of infection did this to someone?

"Caleb?"

He turned quickly towards me and smiled. "Hey you...How are you feeling?"

Actually, I felt pretty silly. There was no pain in my abdomen and aside from being a little cold I felt fine. "Who are you?" I asked the tall thin man with the pills.

"I'm sorry. I should have better manners than this. I'm Gideon Matthews. I'm filling in for Dr. Brown while she's away." I didn't know that Dr. Brown was going anywhere. I'd just been in to see her last week and she never mentioned a thing. We weren't really close, though. She was a witch and also a licensed physician. That was the reason I'd picked her as my doctor. The general public had no idea about her being in the local coven. Nana, Ken's grandmother, had introduced her to me a few years back. I had been looking into the possibility of having children and Nana knew that Dr. Brown would be the one to talk to.

"Well, it's nice to meet you Dr. Matthews."

He smiled and walked closer to me. He'd looked tall in the doorway, but now that he was getting closer to me I got the full picture. The guy had to be pushing seven feet tall. I should have realized how tall he was when I saw him standing near Caleb. Caleb was above average height-wise himself--making him look small was hard to do. This guy had to be asked if he played basketball at least a hundred times a day.

He put his hand out to me. "Everyone just calls me Dr. Gideon."

I shook his large hand. I couldn't help but notice how red his hair was. I hadn't been able to make it out when he was across the room. I'd always thought that redheads had tons of freckles, but Dr. Gideon had none. His skin was flawless and light. He was almost as pale as Caleb and I were.

"Are you *Si*?"

He smiled, drawing attention to his blue eyes. "No, I'm not magical. My father was a cryptologist and my mother had some Fey blood in her but none filtered down to me. I guess you could say that I was born to understand more than just humans."

I liked the way he avoided calling me supernatural or paranormal. I never really took to those terms, and calling me a fairytale creature or a fantasy hardly seemed true. I was more screwed up than anyone I knew. How would that make me a fantasy?

"Well, it's nice to meet you, Doctor, now if you don't mind me asking, what did you do? I feel a ton better."

Dr. Gideon smiled down at me. "I gave you a hefty dose of an antibiotic laced with magic, closed my eyes tight and wished really hard. Do you think it worked or should we head off to see the wizard?" I laughed. He winked. "Now, Caleb, you said that you had to head out on business again. I think it best Gwen not be left alone. The man who was here earlier, Pallo, I think it's best if you see if he can remain here with her."

Caleb's face tightened. He wanted to argue, I could tell. He looked over at me and back at the doctor. "No, Pallo's a very busy man. I don't think he'll be able to stay for long. Gwen can come with me, I guess."

I suddenly found it hard to swallow. I couldn't believe he was inviting me along. I'd never once been allowed near him when he was working. It hit me then, just how much he didn't trust Pallo with me. If he only knew how warranted his fears were then I wouldn't have to worry about going with him, he'd just leave me.

"Gwen may be feeling better for the moment, but it may not last. If you take her gallivanting all over the countryside and she has another attack, she might not make it back here in time. This isn't a normal human infection, its mystical and I can't guarantee what it will do in the next five minutes, let alone five days. Do you want to see something bad happen to her? Is that what you want?"

"No," Caleb said so softly I barely heard him.

"Then perhaps you should ask your friends to stay with her."

"I really don't want to impose on my...*friends.*"

"You do not want to ask your friends to do what?" Pallo's voice came from behind Dr. Gideon.

"Ah...there you are." Dr. Gideon seemed pleased to see Pallo. "I was just telling Caleb that Gwen shouldn't be left alone, at least not until we know what it is we're dealing with. I suggested that maybe you and your friends, the rather odd gentleman and the one with the blue hair, would be able to stay with her."

Pallo looked to Caleb. I could see the question in his eyes. "If it is for the best, then I can stay as long as I am needed."

Dr. Gideon clapped his hands together. "Great! It's all settled then. Gwen." He turned to me. "I'll be back in a day or two to check on you. I've left my number with the blue-haired vampire, so don't hesitate to call if you need me."

He patted the foot of the bed and headed out the door. All of us watched him leave. It was better than watching each other. I wasn't up for another fight. I was pretty sure Caleb would be calling Mark and telling him he couldn't make it back in. I let my head fall back onto the pillow and prepared for World War Three.

Caleb broke the silence. "Well, I guess I could call every day to check on her. You could send Caradoc or James to get me if I'm needed...and, Gwen is probably going to want to start planning."

Planning? I arched an eyebrow at Caleb. He smiled. "I'll ask James to get you some bridal books. If that's all right with you," he said, looking at Pallo. Pallo nodded.

"Then it's settled. I've got to get back out. The Enchantress struck again. This time, we think she managed to get the guy to murder his girlfriend. Can you imagine killing the woman you love?"

Pallo and I looked at him. What do you say to that? I was still in shock that Caleb was actually going to leave Pallo here with me. I didn't really have the energy to explore his last comment too closely.

"Can we have a minute?" Caleb asked, glancing over at Pallo.

Pallo nodded and headed out of the room. I did the mental psyche up in preparation for a fight. Caleb came and sat by me on the bed. He took my hand in his and placed a gentle kiss on it. His power enclosed me, immediately going straight to the bit of his that would always reside in me. My magic grabbed his and the mixing caused my breath to catch in my throat.

Caleb laughed. "*A mhuirnín*, I don't want to leave you. I'm worried sick something will happen to you when I'm gone."

My brow furrowed. "You seemed fine with it a minute ago."

"Yeah, you'd have taken my dropping everything and staying home with you well."

"What's that supposed to mean?"

He sighed. "Gwen, you would have thrown a fit and pushed me out the door anyways."

The more I thought about it, the more I realized he had a point. I squeezed his hand gently and smiled up at him. There was so much I'd wanted to say to him. I'd been so close to telling him that I wanted to end our relationship, so close to throwing what we had away. Having Caleb this close to me wreaked havoc on my senses. Part of me wanted to pull him close. Another part wanted him away. I was beyond fucked up--they'd have to invent an entire new word for me.

"I want to stay with you but I understand you better than you think. The Enchantress is running loose and while that's important--it pales compared to you."

God, the man could make me melt in an instant. "Promise that you'll be careful. I don't want anything to happen to you."

"Now you know how I feel. I lost you once already. I can't go through that again." He snatched me up and held me close to him, rocking me gently in his arms. Guilt washed over me. I'd done the unthinkable to him. I'd betrayed him with the one person he worried the most about--Pallo. Tears tried to flow, but I choked them back. Caleb looked down at me and pulled my chin up. "Baby, don't cry. I'll be back soon and we'll get to spend time planning our wedding. I've dreamt of the moment you'd be my wife for centuries."

I hugged him tighter, afraid of letting go, afraid of keeping him. How had I gotten to this point? Where did it all go wrong? And, why couldn't I fix it? Someone would be hurt in the end. My only hope was that it would just be me. Somehow, I didn't think it would work out that way though.

Chapter 10

I had no plans on sleeping. I waited for Caleb to leave and the guys to settle in. The sun was still up which meant that I had some time to get away. My head was jumbled mess and being in the thick of the situation wasn't helping. It was moments like this that my age really showed. Regardless how they viewed me, I was still a woman in my twenties trying desperately to figure life out. I dressed quickly and quietly, settling on a pair of jeans and a sweater.

I tiptoed down the stairs, holding my breath out of fear that the men still remaining in the house would somehow hear me. The last thing I needed was to have three vampires barricading the door and making me go back to bed. They meant well, but they were a bit over protective at times. I reached for the front door.

"Going somewhere?" I jumped and turned to see Pallo sitting on the sofa.

"I'll be back in a little bit. I just need some air." I headed out the door. I sensed him before I saw him, and knew he was right behind me. "Pallo, I'm fine, really."

"Did you miss what the good doctor said? He wants you to rest."

"Yes, but don't you think that I'd feel better faster if I was out in the open, breathing in the glorious air?"

Yes, I said glorious--I wasn't twirling on a mountain top singing at the top of my lungs so there was still hope.

Pallo's jaw tightened. I wasn't sure if it was out of annoyance with me, or if was trying not to laugh. Okay, so the whole "fresh air" thing wasn't working out. Onto plan B--the "mature" approach. I walked out onto the front porch and into the light.

Pallo stopped a foot or two inside the door. He couldn't follow me out and I knew it. The sun would still be up for a bit, leaving him a prisoner in the house.

"Gwyneth, please...do not do this."

"I need a break from it all, Pallo. I can't think straight. I can't do this anymore...you tell me that you love me and then reject me over and over again." Reaching up, I wiped away the tears that were threatening to fall away. "Don't you understand that I'd give up everything for you--including Caleb." My words shocked me.

"Gwyneth, you are to be his wife soon. Do not talk this way. What happened between us should not have been allowed to happen. It was a…."

I didn't let him finish. "A mistake? Yeah, I seem to make a lot of those since I met you. Coincidental don't you think?" I let out a loud laugh. The urge to cry had been replaced with the urge to smack Pallo. "I can't do this anymore. I'm tired and this can't continue."

He sighed and put his hand on the door. "I understand but something is wrong with you and I do not want any harm to come to you. Stay home and I will go as soon as you are feeling better."

I turned, expecting him to add more to that. He didn't. That wasn't enough for me. It looked as though nothing Pallo was willing to offer would ever be enough. There were things I could live with and then there was that. I blew him a kiss and headed towards the black car that had been a gift from Pallo.

"Gwyneth."

Don't look back...don't look back.

Glancing in the car's window, I saw the keys laying on the driver's seat. It was my lucky day. I opened the door and got in.

Don't look back...don't look….

I glanced up and Pallo looked livid. As much as I hated pissing him off, I hated the idea of continuing with this inner turmoil more. Rolling the window down, I leaned my head out a bit. "I'll be back before dark."

I didn't wait for a response. There was nothing short of "run away with me" that I wanted to hear from him. I drove down the stone lane and checked the time. I had just under an hour to clear my head. That should just about do it. I peeled out, turned right, and headed down over the bridge.

Fifteen minutes later, I pulled up in front of Nana's house. Nana was Ken's grandmother, not mine, but I loved her as if she were my own. She was a witch and that meant she understood what I was going through. Coming into my powers was scary and Nana had been there for me every step of the way.

I pulled into her single car driveway and parked. I had to laugh when I thought of all the times Ken had tried to get his grandmother to move to a condo or a residential home. She flat out refused to go. I suspected strongly that her ties to the witching world and her love for her deceased husband kept her there. I knew something Ken didn't. I knew that his grandfather still made frequent visits to the house. I knew, not because his grandmother had told me, but because I'd seen him one day while I helped her harvest herbs. He'd been the first and only ghost I'd ever seen. He'd scared the hell out of me. Turns out, he was harmless. In fact, he was rather comical.

Ken's grandfather had sat in the living room on the day I met him and made a countless jokes about Ken being too uptight and how now that he was dead he could look in on Ken anytime he wanted. He then proceeded to tell me that he'd peeked in on Ken while we were engaged and how that was the most "excitement" he'd had in a long time. Nana had thrown a book at him--it passed right through him.

"Are ya' gonna' sit out there on your arse all day or are ya' comin' in?"

Glancing up, I saw Ken's grandmother standing in her doorway. Her four foot ten inch tall body barely took up half of the space. I jumped out of the car and ran to her.

"Nana!"

She opened the door and I embraced her. She had a strong, uncharacteristic smell to her. I pulled back and looked in the house.

"Nana, what are you doing? The place smells like a cross between a skunk and licorice."

She waved her plump hand in the air. "Oh, that's just the anise hyssop I pulled out of the garden a few minutes ago. Come see."

She pulled me towards her kitchen. I walked in and found the counters covered in fresh herbs. She already had herbs, in various stages of drying hung throughout the house. I didn't see how she could possibly need more. I walked over and found the source of the smell--anise hyssop. It was lying on the edge of the sink in a basket. She'd cut it into lengths of six inches. A few of them had sprouted tiny purple flowers. I picked one up and brought it to my nose. Saying it smelled strong didn't even cover it, saying it reeked pretty much summed it up.

"What's it for? Are you trying to ward off the entire world?"

Nana came up next to me. "It's the base for a purifyin' liquid I'm workin' on."

"You have a spell that tastes like black licorice?"

She patted my hand and summoned me to the table. "No, don't be silly, Shorty." She called everyone Shorty. "I didn't intend to get that variety, I ordered plain hyssop, but Betty showed up with this instead. That's just as well, the other smells like a skunk."

I knew Nana's friend Betty, they both belonged to the same coven. I also knew how flaky Betty could be. I looked over at the hyssop and laughed. Yes, bringing a flavored one seemed like a very Betty thing to do.

"Do you want some tea?"

"Yeah, sounds great. So, what exactly are you trying to cleanse?"

She ignored me and poured us both a cup of tea. I watched her grab some ground honeysuckle from her jars on the counter and toss it into my cup. She'd been doing that since the day I met her.

"Nana, the honeysuckle isn't going to make Ken and I get back together. He has somebody else now. We both do."

She turned and smiled, her blue-gray eyes sparkling. "Here you go...I know that the two of ya' have found others, but I do it all the same. Besides, I kind of like that blond boy, although he has hair like a girl. His backside is nice and well...when I caught him out in your yard workin' with his shirt off...well, Shorty, ya' don't need me to tell ya'...he's a fine boy indeed."

I laughed, she was right. Caleb did have hair like a woman. In fact, his hair was better than most women's. And, he was a fine man indeed.

Nana's tea was always wonderful. I took a few sips and enjoyed the moment. "So, what exactly does honeysuckle do?"

"Why it makes ya' dream of your true love, of course."

I fought to keep from spitting the tea across the table, instantly thinking about my dreams of having sex with Pallo. Nana gave me the *"something's up, spill the beans"* look, and I did. I told her about the robed men chanting around the altar. I told her about Pallo being there. I even told her that we'd had intercourse in the dreams. That should have embarrassed me, it didn't. I knew Nana too well to think she'd be judgmental. When I got to the part about Pallo having identical dreams, she stopped sipping her tea and stared hard at me.

"How ya been feelin' lately? You look a little pale?"

"Not well. I've been having stomach cramps, headaches, nausea, fever, chills. Plus, I'm gaining weight at an alarming rate. It's weird because I was told that my faerie blood prevented me from gaining too much weight. Anyway, you name it, I've got it. At first, I thought I had the flu then a doctor came out to see me and thought it was sort of a mystical infection. He gave me some magic-laced antibiotics. I don't know though."

Nana nodded. "I'll call the girls."

Chapter 11

By the time I left Nana's every member of her coven had been alerted to the dreams that Pallo and I were having. It was very odd knowing that many women knew that I'd dreamt of having sex with Pallo and he'd returned the favor.

I drove as fast as I could without going over the speed limit. It had been dark out for almost two hours already by the time I left Nana's. I'd lost track of time retelling the story to each woman on the phone. I knew Pallo was going to be pissed. I just hoped he'd get over it quickly--I doubted it.

I'd left my purse at home and in it, my cell phone. I knew that it would be best to call home. I wanted to try to ease the tension before I got there. I'm a chicken, what can I say?

I pulled over at a gas station and got out to use the pay phone. I thought about every communicable disease known to man as I put the receiver up to my mouth and was thankful that I was immortal. Death by way of a telephone infection didn't sound fun at all. I had to make a collect call to my own house, which seemed silly, but without my purse, I had no money.

James was the one who accepted it. He spoke in a hushed tone, "Where the bloody hell are you?"

"I'm fine. I'm at a gas station just outside the city limits. I'll be home in like ten minutes. I just wanted to make sure Pallo knows I'm fine."

I noticed a man in a brown car pulling up. The man got out and began filling his tank. I did a polite smile as he glanced over at me.

"Pallo's been pacing at the end of the lane since the sun went down. He stood at the door like a damn statue for an hour prior to that. I half thought the bloke was going to walk out into the damn daylight for you. Why the hell did you take off?"

"James, I'm sorry. I needed a break, I needed to…."

Some people were raising their voices near the cashier and I was having a hard time hearing James. I had to stop and turn my body in towards the phone.

"Gwen, you should have waited for one of us to go with you. Pallo's been a…."

A loud bang came from behind me. A woman screamed and someone shouted. I turned and looked. The man from the brown car was holding a gun. There was a body of a man on the ground and the gunman was aiming at the cashier. She was backing up slowly with tears in her eyes.

"Gwen? Gwen?" I heard James' voice through the phone.

"Oh my God!" I pulled the phone away from my ear still shocked by the events unfolding before me.

The man from the brown car turned his attention to me and then back to the cashier. I took a step forward. I didn't know what else to do. I wasn't sure how much damage a bullet would do to me, but I stood a hell of a lot better chance of surviving a gunshot then a mortal. I healed fast I knew that much. I was guessing that I wouldn't be able to heal a shot to the head or heart, but I wasn't positive. The man's hand shook and if I had to take a stab, I would have said he was struggling to put the gun down.

I picked up on the faintest sound--it was a female's voice, singing in a high-pitched tone. I thought I'd been the only one to hear it, but the man looked up into the night sky, closing his eyes as he rocked back and forth to it. He looked as though he was dancing, but there was no music. There was only the eerie sound of the woman singing.

The man's head jerked up and I watched his finger pull back on the trigger. I put my hand out and called on my power faster than I'd ever done before. I heard myself speaking, but I didn't recognize the language. My power thrust the cashier out of harms way, but drew the man's attention back to me. I put my other hand up and lashed enough power out at the man to send the man airborne, but not before he fired off another shot, this one directed at me. I watched, in what seemed like slow motion, as the bullet headed towards me. Unable to move fast enough, I braced for impact. Something struck from the side, sending me flying to the ground. My head bounced off the cement and I bit down hard. Blood poured from my lips and I pulled my head up as quickly as I could.

I looked back towards the pay phone. A man dressed head to toe in black was there, bent over, with his back to me. His head came up and I saw the dyed blue hair.

"James!"

He fell forward. Screaming, I scrambled to my feet. The cashier was bent over the unconscious gunman. "No! You killed him! No! God, no!"

I looked at her like she'd sprouted a third eye-ball. The guy had just tried to blow her away and she was pissed at me?

"You killed him, you killed my husband!"

Ungrateful bitch!

Shaking my head, I dropped to my knees next to James. I turned his body over to survey the damage. I sucked my breath in. The bullet had gone into his chest. I was by no means an expert, but it looked like it had been a blow to the heart. His hand came up, I thought he was going for his chest wound, I was wrong, he was going for my hand. I took it and leaned over him, caressing his check with my other hand.

"Tell me what to do, James. Tell me what to do…."

He opened his mouth but no sound came out. I heard sirens coming in our direction. Under normal circumstances that would have been a blessing but I had a vampire dying on the ground before me and humans were not allowed to find out they existed. I'd worked for the Paranormal Regulators, Ken's firm, long enough to know how this went down. They would "dispose" of James. They'd make no effort to heal him. A shot to the heart meant death to a vampire, so they wouldn't waste time or resources on him, and they would most likely hurt the only remaining witness, the cashier. They would cause damage that would affect her short-term memory. That, of course, would be a last resort. First, they'd bring in a witch to try to wipe her memory clean and those of any responding officers that had shown up. It would be a mess.

My power rose up again. I didn't fight it. I found that it generally handled stress better than me. Magic poured out of me and over the area. The cashier froze in mid-movement. I glanced down at James and watched as his body lifted off the ground. Getting to my feet, I ran to open the car door without any more thought on my part and watched as my power eased James into the back seat. I kept forgetting it was me, it was my mind that did this, even if it was on a subconscious level. I slammed the door shut and started the car.

I pulled out and headed down the road. I looked back at the gas station, from what I could tell the cashier wasn't moving yet. I hoped my magic would wear off soon. At least I hoped it would. The responding officers would be pretty freaked out by a petrified female and a dead body.

James made a small noise and I tried to reach over the seat to touch him while I drove. My arm wasn't long enough. "James, hang on...I'm taking you to Pallo, he can fix this. I know he can...hang on James...don't you dare give up!"

I pulled onto my road, and I mean my road, I was the only house on it. James touched my hand and I grabbed hold of his, giving it a squeeze. He gave a weak one in return and then his arm went limp. Slamming on the brakes, I put the car in park and climbed into the back seat. James' blue eyes were glassy and staring at up at the interior roof of the car.

"JAMES!"

I slammed on his chest, he didn't respond. "JAMES!" I hit him again. Something grabbed me from behind and yanked me out of the vehicle. I kicked and carried on, until I saw the long white blond hair blow past me.

Ceasing to struggle, I turned and looked up at Caradoc. He set me down gently.

"Are you hurt?" he asked, seemingly unfazed by my blows.

"No, James...James is hurt." I looked into the back seat. It was empty and the other door was open. I saw Pallo putting James down on the ground. I climbed through the back seat as fast as I could.

I know, I know, walking around the car would have been faster, I wasn't thinking clearly.

I dropped down next to them. Pallo looked at James then at me. "Go back to the house with Caradoc."

Shaking my head no, I did my best to shield my thoughts from him. It wasn't easy to do and I knew that it wouldn't last long, but I wasn't about to leave James' side. "Did the bullet hit his heart?"

Pallo reached towards me. "It is still in his heart, I cannot heal him with it lodged in there. I am afraid that your *dear* James will not...."

My dear James? What the hell?

This was no time for jealousy. I smacked his hand away and thought about sending enough power into him to launch his ass back to his house. I refrained. "Don't do this, Pallo! He saved my life...do you understand me? I won't let him go like this, not if we can help him!"

"Gwyneth, you cannot save all your *precious* men all the time," Pallo said dryly.

I glared up at him. "If you're not willing to help then get the hell away from him so I can try!"

Placing my hand over James' chest, I sensed his pain and visualized the bullet in his heart. I thought about it as being on a rope, I tugged the magical string in my mind, and felt it give. I yanked harder and the bullet flew out and through my hand.

"Ahh...ouch!" I screamed out.

Pallo grabbed my hand and turned it over. The bullet had gone all the way through it, leaving a gapping hole in my hand.

"Hey, beautiful," James said.

Shocked, I stared down at him and he smiled. "James?"

"Look," Pallo said, pointing at the blood dripping from my hand. It was falling into James' open chest wound. I bent over him and watched as he healed himself. James lifted his head up and looked down at his chest.

"The woman went straight to my heart," James said, grabbing himself and doing a lame country boy accent. I pushed him hard.

"Jerk!"

He grabbed my bloody hand and pain shot through it. Something demonic crossed over his face. I'd never seen James shift into full vamp-mode and it scared me. His blue eyes grew dark and his nose widened. Fangs came out as his head lunged at my hand. I thought he was going to sink his teeth into my hand, but he didn't. He tongued the wound, lapping up the blood. The feel of his tongue pressing into my open flesh should have repulsed me. I didn't. Instead, I felt drawn to James, as if we were sharing more than simply my blood. I knew he would never hurt me and even though his demon had surfaced, he still had hold of it enough to be gentle with me.

Pallo seized James by the throat. James dropped my hand and changed back to normal. James' eyes widened, but he made no attempt to free himself from Pallo's clutches. He could play the role of subordinate vampire all friggin' night, but I wouldn't. I grabbed hold of Pallo's hand and tried to pry it off James' neck.

"Pallo, no!"

"He calls himself your friend, yet he feeds off you like you are nothing to him."

James tried to talk, but Pallo's grip didn't allow any air to pass through his windpipe. His blue gaze locked on me, pleading with me to forgive him. In my mind, there was nothing to forgive. He was a vampire, he drank blood, it happened. It was gross but it happened and he hadn't hurt me.

"Pallo, let him go this instant or you will never be welcome in my home or my life again. Do you understand? Read my thoughts now and know that I am NOT exaggerating!"

Pallo's eyes grew dark. "You would choose him over me?"

"Don't make me. Let him go." I touched his arm and ran my hand up it.

He let go of James' throat and stood. James coughed and I glanced over at Caradoc, who was still on the other side of the car. *Smart man.* I motioned for him to deal with James and I went after Pallo.

Pallo was storming off down the street. I knew that he could have got away much faster but he didn't, he wanted me to come after him. It was a test, and if I didn't go then I would fail. I wasn't one who liked to fail so I ran after him.

"Pallo!"

He didn't stop. I continued to run after him until white-hot pain shot through my stomach. "Pallo, help, oh…" I flipped over in mid-stride and hit the ground hard. I curled up into myself. The pain was so great that I couldn't even cry out. Again and again the cramps came, each one lasting longer than the one before. This wasn't normal, it felt as though my insides were being laid open with a dull knife.

My body grew cold and I began to shake on top of the vicious cramps.

"Gwen!"

I felt hands on me and opened my eyes to see James next to me. "Gwen, what's wrong? Shit, you're freezing."

He picked me up as if I weighed nothing and spun me around. I knew vampires could fly, I just never got used to it. We moved up and off the ground. I closed my eyes and put my head against James' healed chest.

Chapter 12

"Don't go!" I said, grabbing James' arm and pulling him back to me.

He closed his eyes slightly and I could see the struggle within him all over his face. "Pallo wants to come in and check on you, love, and I think it's time you let him."

I glanced over at my bedroom door and knew that somewhere in my house Pallo was listening to every word we said. "I don't care if he wants to come in. He was going to let you die!"

"He'd've been a bit late on that one, 'cause I'm already dead. It would have been better all around if you'd have left well enough alone, Gwen."

I touched his soft cheek and shook my head. "Don't say that. Don't even think that! You may not give a damn what happens to you, but I do."

James narrowed his eyes, searching my expression for something. I pulled him closer and his muscles tensed. It was clear that he didn't want to be close to me, but I didn't care. I needed to hug him, needed to be sure he was safe and that he knew he was loved. "Jameson, you have two seconds to wrap those pale ass arms around me before I give you a good dose of faerie power."

He chuckled and relaxed. Slowly, he eased himself over me. It was odd to hug him while lying down. It felt so much more intimate. When I pulled him close, he was left no choice but to place his body on mine. For the fist time since I'd known James, I took in his sweet scent and felt my body responding to him in ways it shouldn't. We were just friends, yet moisture began to build between my legs and my nipples hardened against his hard chest.

James stiffened and began to pull back from me. I held tight to him. My eyelids fluttered closed as I drew in another breath, taking in his scent. My body tingled and without thought, I rubbed against him and kissed the side of his neck softly. Before I knew it, his lips had found mine. We opened our eyes at the same time and jerked away from one another. We sat up fast.

Awkward silence followed. James still sat next to me on the bed and it took a moment for me to realize that my hand was resting in his lap. Mortified beyond belief, I cringed. James burst into laugher. My mouth dropped open.

"How is this funny?"

He bit his lip and nodded, suddenly looking very series. It was forced, I could tell. "I think the real question you ought to be asking yourself is--how the hell is it not funny?" That did it, he feel forward, laughing even harder.

It was official, he finally snapped. The blue hair dye must have been a cry for help. "James? Care to share?"

"Oh...you...ha...Like you don't have enough issues!"

"Hey!" Okay, he had a point. I was neck deep in emotional baggage as it was. I closed my eyes and shook my head. How the hell did I always manage to get myself into these messes?

"Whatcha thinkin' about, love?"

I peeked out at him and let my forehead crinkle up. "Can't you just read my mind and figure it out? That's what Pallo and Caradoc do to me." I meant it as a joke. James didn't take it that way.

"Gwen, I'm not like them. I'd never do it on purpose, you know that. Occasionally a random thought or feeling you're havin' comes to me, but I do my best to block it out. Hell, I'm not even sure I'd read you if you asked me. You kind of scare me. Plus, I know who your father is and I'm a wee bit concerned about what kind of sick shit might be goin' on in that noggin of yours."

That was bold to admit on his part. He was cementing the groundwork for our friendship and that meant a lot to me. It was good to hear that one of them wouldn't take advantage of being able to read my thoughts. I'd always assumed that James did it, too. He seemed to always know what to say to me, or when to offer his support. I'd always assumed that our friendship was based off his vampire skills of perception. I didn't realize it was just him being a good friend.

He laid his hand against my cheek. I turned my face into his palm and kissed it gently. "Thank you."

James jerked his hand away like I'd scalded him and then tried to play it off. "Right, then...well, how's your hand feeling?" He picked it up and looked and examined it closely. It was completely healed. "Sorry about makin' a snack of you."

I laughed softly. "No worries! I'm fine, and thanks for saving my life tonight. How the heck did you manage to find me so fast?"

He shifted on the bed slightly. I got the distinct impression that he didn't want to tell me. I touched his face lightly, turning his attention to me. "James, how did you find me so fast?"

His gaze darted downward. "I, umm...I can sense when you're hurt or scared."

I shrugged. It seemed like most vampires had some sort of power, so I wasn't too surprised. From the way James was acting, I got the distinct feeling that there was more to the story. "James, full disclosure buddy."

"A vampire should only be able to sense a person with the intensity I sense you if they've had intercourse or use 'em as an all you can suck buffet."

And here I thought that I was confused before. Now, I was now shocked. "But, James, we haven't had...and you don't suck...."

He shook his head fast. "Yeah, I know its friggin' weird. I try to block you out, but still sense you." He stroked my cheek lightly. "I can't say for sure, but I think I may have a closer bond to you then Pallo has. And I don't know why. That's not even the worst part."

"There's more?" I really didn't want to hear the rest of this.

"Oh, there's more! I...umm...before I figured out what was happenin'...I sort of sensed you while you were havin' sex."

"What do you mean, sort of sensed me?" Now I knew that I did not want to hear the rest of this.

He took a deep breath. "I thought I was dreamin'--I had no idea they were real."

"They?"

James gave me a sheepish smile. "It happened quite a bit for in the beginning...I just thought they were dreams, my fantasy about you," he averted his gaze for a moment, "but when you walked into Necro World a couple of months ago, I realized you were alive and that dreams weren't dreams at all."

It took a moment for all that he'd said to sink in. Prior to going to Necro's Magik World & Supernatural Theme Park, I'd had no recollection of a past life and no knowledge of my biological birth parents. Once Caradoc had opened the door and let me in, my life changed completely. Prior to that, I'd been nursing a broken heart from my break-up with Ken and hadn't even entertained dating again.

Another thought came to mind. "James, who did you 'sense' me having sex with?"

"Ken and Caleb," he put his hands up quick, "but just the first time with him! Honest! And it was only a portion of it...not the whole thing."

Tipping my head, I stared into his blue eyes, hoping beyond hopes that he wasn't lying to me. From day one, I felt comfortable with James--I could trust him with anything. No, he wasn't lying. If anything, he was the most honest man in my life, next to Caleb that is.

I sat up and rubbed my temples. Whatever was happening to me had left me feeling like I'd been hit by a freight train. I twisted slightly on the bed and my knee brushed past James' leg. Heat flared through my leg and James dropped his hand down on it. Closing his eyes, he looked strained for a moment before the heat vanished.

"James, what's happening to us?"

"I'm not exactly sure."

"Could we ask…?" I stopped short of saying Pallo's name.

"Pallo doesn't know about any of this, Gwen, and you can't tell him."

I glanced at the door, wondering how close Pallo really was to us. "He does now. I'm betting he's listening to every word we say! I've all but given up on private thoughts around him."

James shook his head and touched my chin. "I'm blockin' him from hearin' this. I'm not strong enough to hold him out long so listen carefully. Somehow, you and I have bonded enough for my vampire senses to perceive you as a lover...as my *mate*."

"Your mate?" There was no way to hide my astonishment. He could have told me he really wasn't a vampire at all, but rather a shapeshifting were-cockroach and I'd have taken the news better than this.

He smiled and patted my leg gently. "I expect nothin' from you and I can't even begin to understand how the hell it happened. I shouldn't be tellin' you all of this, but you've a right to know. You've been manipulated enough by the men in your life. I'll not do that to you, love. Just promise that you won't say anything to Pallo and Caleb."

"I promise," I said, a little too fast.

James shook his head again. "You can't ever tell them. This isn't something that they'd take lightly. Pallo would kill me before he risked us becoming more than friends, Gwen. Caleb would help him, you know it's true. You've got to swear it and mean it."

My thoughts ran to Caleb and Pallo and to how odd they'd been acting in regards to James. "Oh God, I think they already suspect something."

"What makes you say that?"

"Because, they've been acting strange about me spending time with you. And then...err...there's the whole thing about Pallo refusing to heal you."

"They most likely do sense something, but they've no clue what it is yet."

"But how do you know for sure?"

"I'm not ashes."

The reality of his statement sunk in. If Pallo would've had his way, James wouldn't be sitting with me now. I wasn't sure what to say that would prove I'd never betray James' trust. I meant it when I said I wouldn't tell Pallo. Short of writing it in blood, I wasn't sure what I should do. I let my instincts guide me, leaned forward, grabbed the back of James' head and pulled his face to me. My mouth slammed down on his before he had a chance to protest. I pushed my tongue and my magic through him, letting him have a tiny bit of my power.

Sharing magic wasn't something to be taken lightly. He would forever have a piece of me, a link to me.

I drew away from him slowly and stared into his blue eyes. "I promise."

"Well, now that you put it that way," he said, laughing.

Chapter 13

I woke to find the sun out. It was a refreshing change after the last few nights. It was also refreshing to not have horrendous pains. I'd spent the greater part of the night doubled over with James stroking my hair and holding me like a child. I didn't want Pallo near me. I was too tired of the emotional roller coaster we put each other on to want to deal with him.

Deciding to make the most of my day, I dressed quickly and set out to get things done. I needed to call Caleb and I desperately needed to clean my effects out of my office.

I crept down the stairs softly and headed for the phone. I dialed Caleb's number and waited for him to pick up. I was redirected to his voice mail and listened to his pre-recorded voice greeting me. "Caleb, it's me. I miss you. I've been thinking about the wedding. Maybe we should do it soon. I don't want to wait. The sooner the better. I need to talk to you about some things first. If you still want to marry then I say let's just do it! I don't need or want a big wedding. I just need stability--I need you." Relieved, I let out a sigh. "I love you and I miss you." I hung up the phone and tried to keep the burning in my chest to a minimum.

"Care to fill me in on what goin' on?"

Spinning around, I found James lurking in the shadows of the hallway. I'd learned that vampires didn't have to sleep during the day, they could still function, but they were a great deal weaker when the sun came up. I put the phone down and looked past him for any signs of Pallo or Caradoc.

"Caleb asked me to marry him."

James looked like I'd just told him that I was really a five headed Jack-in-Irons posing as a female faerie. It took him a minute or two to say anything.

"Okay, so what does this mean? Now, you're not actually entertaining marrying him are you? I mean, you've got to be 'shagged-out,' you didn't get much sleep last night, so you're not thinkin' clear this morning."

"Don't sound so surprised, he's a great guy, and I know he'll always be good to me, and I said yes and I meant it. And...."

James took a seat on the bottom step. He looked so out of place at the foot of the staircase in an old farmhouse, but it felt right to have him with me. "And what, Gwen?"

"And...Caleb and I could start a family together. Not right away, of course."

"Of course," he said, dryly.

I sat next to him and put my arm around him, pulling him close to me. "I need a friend right now James. For everything else, I have Pallo. He hates me enough for a hundred men."

"Gwen, that's not true and you know it."

"Do I?"

"Why do you think he goes full-on every time he's around you? Sure the guy walks around half-cocked as it is, but the minute you step into the picture, he's back to having rage issues. You don't fuckin' act like that over people you could give a damn about. No, you do that over people you love."

I laughed slightly. "And when did you become such an expert?"

He stared at me, his expression unreadable. I waited for a sign, a glimpse into what he was thinking. I got none.

"James?"

"The very fact that you don't know the answer to that tells me there's no point in explainin' it." With that, he got up and walked away, leaving me to sit by myself to think over what he'd just said.

Chapter 14

I pulled into the parking lot outside of the Paranormal Regulator Department for our district. Of, course to the everyday average civilian the place was just a building that housed several floors of law offices, a private investigation team, and other run-of-the-mill businesses. No one would ever guess what really went on behind the scenes. The place had more supernatural juice flowing through it than hell itself.

The paranormal convicted offenders were held in various levels underground. It was way more high-tech than a normal prison and guarded more securely as well. If you wanted to go down there you needed level one clearance. Ken had it, and that meant as his assistant I did too. I'd only been down there once and had no intention of ever returning. It gave me the creeps.

I pulled my ID badge out and flashed it at the guard at the front desk. He motioned for me to scan it and I did. Once I got the green light, I headed to the elevators. I waited for one of the mail boys to exit then climbed in and pressed the sixth floor button.

"Gwen!" Judy yelled as the elevator doors opened. I braced for impact and watched her tiny frame come running at me from behind her desk. I gave her a hug and tried not to breathe too deep. She had a tendency to go a little heavy on the perfume.

"I'm so happy to see you. I keep asking Ken about you, and...oh, dear, I guess I don't need to tell you how he is. So, how have you been? Are you back for good?"

Judy's questions seemed never-ending. I looked over her head of dyed red hair down the hall to Ken's office. His door was shut. Either he wasn't in or he was with a client. I answered as many of Judy's questions as I could before excusing myself and heading down to my office.

My office was adjacent to Ken's so my door was next to his. I stopped just short of touching his door and listened. I didn't hear him and normally you could hear Ken just fine, even through two-inch thick wood.

Opening my office door slowly, I looked around. Someone had closed my blinds and it didn't smell like Ken had opened the place up since I began working from my house eight weeks earlier. I walked over and pulled opened the blinds. Soft rays of sunlight filled the room. Tiny particles of dust floated about in the light. I smiled. It felt good to be back. Even if it was only to clean out my desk.

A thin layer of dust was on my oversized cherry desk. I ran my hand across and wiped the dust onto my pant leg before walking over to my closet. I rummaged around and found what I was looking for, an empty box. I started with the bookshelves. Most of the books I'd collected had been gifts from Ken about supernatural creatures. Whomever he hired for his assistant after me would probably need them, so I decided to leave them. I picked up the framed picture of the two of us meeting the Governor. Ken looked pleased and I looked lost--typical of our relationship.

My fingers ran over a framed copy of the Nocturnal Journal, a publication put out by the supernatural underground, and I couldn't help but get sentimental. Ken had made the cover for busting up a ghoul-fighting ring. The interviewer had asked Ken some serious questions about the case and then broke into questions about his personal life. At the time the issue was released, we had been engaged. Ken told the reporter that I was his "rock, his supporting assistant, love interest, and soon to be wife." I'd been shocked to see that they'd printed a picture of the two of us that had been taken at a charity dinner. We were locked arm and arm, looking into each other's eyes with so much love that it brought tears to my eyes.

How could I have let it all go so wrong?

I put the journal and the framed picture in the box and moved on. By the time I'd reached the end of the bookshelves, I had over half the box full. I set it on my dusty desk and plopped down in one of the navy wing back chairs that clients used. I heard someone shuffling about in Ken's office and turned to see the door that went between our offices open.

"Gwen?"

Ken stood there in his dark gray pants and white shirt looking at me. I had almost forgotten how massive his body was. He damn near filled the doorway. He was built like a lineman. His above average height helped to keep him from looking awkward, and his love of exercise and health food kept him trim.

"Hey," I said.

His eyes darted to the box on my desk. He came in and shut the door behind him. "Gwen, no...didn't you get my message? I didn't mean it. I don't want you to leave."

He came within a foot of touching me and stopped. The last time we'd touched had been very intimate and very much in the presence of a third party. I'd had sex with Ken and Caleb at the same time.

Hey, I know, I know, I should really pace myself.

"Gwen, come on, cut me some slack. I've been getting a lot of pressure to move on and I thought by telling you not to come back that I'd be doing just that. I was wrong. You belong here."

"Pressure from whom?" I didn't need to wait for his answer. I already knew it, Beth. He'd been dating her for two months now and was already getting pressured to sever all ties with his ex. It was clear, she and I were going to tangle. My guess was I'd win.

"I know I was wrong. I don't want you to go anywhere and that's all that's important."

I stood up and walked to the other side of my desk. I reached into my upper left-hand drawer and pulled out some more pictures and my address book. I tossed them in the box and headed over to the wall. I took one of my paintings off the wall and set it aside. I'd always hated the thing. Ken had picked it out. I didn't see the point of having a huge painting with nothing but two blue lines down the center of it. He called it abstract. I called it a waste of canvas.

I turned the dial on the wall safe and popped it open. A large manila envelope was stuffed in it. I already knew the contents of it without having to look. Ken required me to keep a set of papers on hand in the event that I'd need to get away quickly. Apparently, it was standard operating procedure for persons working in the world of the supernatural to maintain cash, credit cards, IDs, and charms against being located on hand. Ken had a similar one in his safe. I moved it aside and pushed the Beretta out of the way. Ken had also insisted I have that as well. I never used it. I wasn't too crazy about guns.

I had to stand on my tiptoes to reach the back of the safe. Finally, I found what I was looking for. I felt the tiny box under my fingertips and pulled it out slowly.

"Gwen, did you hear me? I don't want you to go...not just because I'm still in...umm...I still care about you." In my own sick way, I found it funny that he couldn't even bring himself to say he still loved me. "I want you to stay because you're the best person for this job. Where else am I going to find a faerie willing to put up with me?"

He did have a point. He had one of those personalities that you either loved or hated. At the moment, I was up in the air on which way I was leaning. I pulled the tiny black box out and turned towards him.

"Here," I said, thrusting my hand towards him. "Sounds like you'll be needing this and please don't try to deny that the pressure to get me out of here isn't coming from *her*." I couldn't bring myself to say Beth's name. I barely knew her but I was positive that I didn't like her.

Ken glanced down at the box and put his hand over mine. Feeling his warm skin touching mine should have calmed me down. It didn't. "I gave this to you, I don't want it back--I don't ever want it back." He opened it up and the diamond ring inside sparkled. "Why do you have to do this, Gwen? Why do you have to push me away so hard?"

"Me push you away? That's a good one! Did I call you at home telling you not to come back to work?" I pushed his hand off mine. The ring box fell to the floor.

"No...no, you didn't, instead you just show up here and try to leave without so much as a heads-up or a good-bye, then you go out of your way to make sure I know that you're done with me." Ken came at me. I could see the hurt in his eyes. He was fighting back tears and crying was not something Ken did openly. "Gwen, we fucked up, okay...I can admit I was wrong, can you?"

"Caleb and I are engaged."

Ken took a step back and put his hand onto the desk. He reached up and loosened his tie. I'd never seen him so pale. I was afraid that he might pass out. His brown eyes narrowed as he ran his hand through his sandy blond hair. "Gwen, you can't be serious. You hardly know him. Sure somehow you knew him once, like two hundred years ago, but you know as well as I do that it's not the same, it's not real. What we had was real...it was based off who you are now, not someone they wish you still were. Don't do this, it's a mistake."

Screaming in his face sounded wonderful, or at the very least kicking the ring box across the floor. I did neither. He was right. We had both been at fault for things not working out between us. In the beginning, it was because of Talia, the psycho biker bitch who was dubbed as the keeper of the hounds on her really demonic days. She had seduced Ken into bed with her and I happened to walk in on it. That had turned out not be his fault. It was hard to fight a vampire's pull. I knew that first-hand. I could have forgiven him and we could have moved on, but two other factors had come into play--Pallo and Caleb. Once they entered my life, I wasn't able to find room for Ken in that mix so he'd pulled away. I never tried to stop him. No, instead I'd hidden away at the farmhouse not wanting to confront my feelings for him.

Looking at him now, I knew that he'd hit the nail on the head. He knew the real me. The me that Caleb and Pallo had only known for two months. He'd been the one that I'd shared my desires with, the one who helped me get some sort of a hold over my powers. Without him, I'd still be hearing others thoughts and would most likely be insane. It was Ken's love and support that allowed me to function among humans during a time when I was not only a danger to myself, but to others as well. That wasn't the only thing he did for me. He'd been the one who loved me based solely on the woman that stood before him now--just plain me. No hidden agendas, no ties from a past life, just him, just me.

Suddenly, the hair on the back of my neck rose and it felt like we weren't alone. I glanced around the room fully expecting to find someone but found nothing. Ken's gaze was locked on me. He didn't seem to notice the odd fluctuation in the temperature around us or he probably just assumed it was my doing. I went to say something to him, but he interrupted me.

"What? You're awfully quiet. I tell you that you're making the biggest mistake of your life and you don't say a word?" He snorted and shook his head.

The air around us lit with energy--energy that wasn't mine. I searched around for the source of it but nothing was there. The energy pushed against my skin and I caught the faint sound of a woman. She was singing. I'd heard that before. Where had I heard it before? I racked my brain and came up empty.

"No snappy comebacks, Gwen. No hitting below the belt? That's not like you Gwen." His face was so close to mine now that I could feel his warm breath on my cool skin. For a split second, I thought he might actually hit me and then his lips met mine. My body reacted wildly. I threw my arms around his neck and pulled him close to me. Ken tasted of fruit juice and mints. Slowly, we bit at each other's lips. His tongue pushed into my mouth and I playfully pushed it back out. This continued as our hands moved to touch anything accessible.

Ken pulled back slightly. "Gwen, we can't do this...I can't...we have to stop."

"I know."

The energy in the room pushed harder on us. Ken grabbed the back of my hair and fastened his mouth over mine.

I couldn't shake the feeling that something was in the room with us, watching us--wanting us to ravish one another. I tried to fight against its pull, but I couldn't. Part of me still wanted Ken and I knew that I always would.

I backed up until the large desk pressed against the back of my legs. Ken's body weight increased on me and left me leaning over the desk. The box was in the way and I had to push it aside to be able to lie across the top of the desk. We'd done this before when we were engaged. We'd made love in his office or mine at least once a day. We had perfected the art of having sex on office furniture.

Reaching up, I loosened his tie. I managed to get the first three buttons of his white dress shirt undone before I was hit with the scent of his Dolce & Gabbana. I had always loved the slightly fruity smell of it on him. I nuzzled my face into his upper chest and took a deep breath. Ken's soft fuzzy chest hair warmed my face. I licked him. He yanked his tie off and unbuttoned his shirt more. I helped him with the last few and laid back for him to start on mine.

He dropped his face to just above my pant line and bit the edge of the sweatshirt I'd thrown on. He pulled it up and his chin scraped over my stomach. I whimpered. It wasn't even lunch time yet and he had a five o'clock shadow already. *God, I'd missed him.*

He moved my sweatshirt up and left one of the tiny tunics I loved so much between us. I untied the string holding it up, and pulled it from beneath my sweatshirt.

Ken's mouth met my exposed, erect nipple. I moaned softly, running my fingers through his sandy-blond hair. My body was starved for his touch and I pulled at him as he explored my exposed stomach and breasts. He undid my pants and I arched my head back with anticipation. He eased them down over my hips and off my legs.

"Gwen?" He ran his fingers over my slightly swollen abdomen. "Is there something I should know?"

"Don't ask...just fuck me hard, Ken. Take me and fuck me until neither of us can walk. Take me like an animal. Punish me for misbehaving." It was my voice, but it wasn't something I'd say. Something was off, something was wrong. I tried to concentrate hard on why I shouldn't be doing this with Ken, but I drew a blank. I could hear the faint sound of the woman singing. It was so soft, yet high, all at the same time. How odd. It pulled at me and Ken seemed to respond to it, too.

"Gwen," he said, tenderly as he buried his face deep between my legs. He moved his tongue into the crevice of my slit and found my swollen clit. My body jerked with each lick and my fingers fought anything to grab instead of him. I didn't want to claw his face. I settled on grabbing the edge of the desk and used it to try to pull my body up and away from him. I didn't really want to get away but he was causing my legs to twitch involuntarily leaving me with a ticklish, burning sensation deep within me.

Ken moved his hands up, grabbed my waist, and yanked me back down towards his face. "Yes, Gwen, I'll punish you." The promise of that sent spine tingling chills throughout me. *What's going on?* Ken wasn't one who acted this way in the bedroom, or in this case the office. My mind clouded as I tried to focus.

He rammed his fingers in to meet my wetness. "Ahh, Ken." I jolted upright, only to be pushed back down by his other hand as cream eased out of me and aided in his entrance. I contracted my skillfully trained muscles around him as he pulled his fingers out of me. I felt hollow without him, without his touch.

"Ken." I grabbed a handful of his hair, lifting his head up. His eyes were glassy as he stared up at me. "Together," was all I said to him. He knew what I meant by that. He knew I was close to hitting a full-blown orgasm, the kind that curls your toes, leaves you breathless, and I wanted to share it with him. He stood slowly. I stayed lying down, he'd made me lightheaded and I was positive I couldn't stand.

He pushed his long fingers into me again, seeking my moisture to rub over his cock. Ken stood tall with his white shirt unbuttoned--his hand caressing his glistening shaft and his eyes fixed on me. "I'm going to fuck you so hard, Gwen. So unbelievably hard."

I nearly came from his words alone. "Take me!"

I put my arms out to him and he thrust himself into me, so hard that I almost fell off the desk. I screamed out, unprepared for such a forceful entry. Quickly, Ken took my sensitive nipple into his mouth and sucked on it, allowing pleasure to chase away the pain. He pulled my hips hard towards him, causing the head of his cock to strike the back of my cervix with each blow. An odd, warm, soothing sensation hit me with each movement he made.

Ken moved his upper body over mine and his chest hair tickled the tips of my nipples. I pulled his face to me, pushed my tongue into his mouth and let a small moan escape my throat in the process. My abdomen tightened and he tried to talk. I didn't let go of his face. I kept moving my tongue around his. I knew he wanted to tell me that he needed to take a break. He didn't want to finish yet, but I wanted him to share this with me. Grabbing his ass, I massaged it with my hands, encouraging him to come in me.

He began a series of rapid thrusts that drove the air from my lungs, leaving me panting and clinging to him. "No, more, Ken...please let me come."

He let out a very uncharacteristic snarl and his voice sounded deeper than normal when he spoke, "You'll take everything I give you. You'll take and you'll love it." He slammed into me hard, pushing me closer to the edge of my climax. His gaze locked on mine. "Tell me how much you want me to give it to you, Gwen. How much do you want me to bring you and come all over inside you?"

That was so far from something Ken would say that I began to pull back into myself, only to have the energy in the room wrap around me fast--clouding my mind again.

Ken thrust into me again. "Say it, Gwen. Tell me how you want it."

"God yes, Ken! I want it. I want it!" My body tightened and my thighs began to shake. He shoved his cock into me and grunted--spilling forth semen. It was odd how I felt every last drop of it. It was so warm and so buried deep within me. He fell on top of me and covered me with kisses while my body soaked up all that he had to offer.

The fog that had been my mind cleared and I took a deep breath in.

Ohmygod, what did we do?

He had Beth and I had--well, I had a whole string of other issues. I pushed on his chest, but he didn't move. The temperature returned to normal and I no longer sensed the presence of something foreign around us. I opened my mouth to tell him about the magical presence, but he spoke first.

"Gwen, I'm still in love...."

He was interrupted by a knock on the outer door. He stood up quickly and pulled his pants up from his knees. He put his hand out and helped me sit up. I dove down onto the floor and gathered my clothes up. We both were only half dressed, when he asked who it was.

"It's me," Judy said. "Beth is on line three for you. I sent it to your office, but you didn't pick up. This is her second time trying to get you."

I looked at my phone. Sure enough, line three was lit up. Ken moved in and kissed me again with so much passion that I almost whimpered when he pulled his lips away. I caught his scruffy face in my hands and laughed. It was a matter of laugh or go insane. As fun as a straight jacket sounded, I opted for option one.

"Hey, I've still got it," he said.

"Still got what?"

He kissed at my earlobe. "The ability to make you...," his hands slid over my jeans and brushed between my legs briefly, "laugh."

I laughed again before motioning to the phone. "Yeah, I'm sure that's what you meant. Ken...she's waiting for you."

He looked at the phone and turned his head. "What in the hell am I going to tell her?"

"Nothing," I said matter-of-factly. His face went blank. I knew my suggestion was wrong, but I didn't really expect Beth to believe that some crazy unknown energy rode in on some chick's voice and caused Ken and I to fuck each other's brains out. Hell, Ken dealt with the paranormal on a daily basis and he wouldn't even believe me. Ms. Perky Realtor Lady would never understand. "Don't tell her about this. Just talk to her, see what she wants, but do *not* bring this up. Don't jeopardize what you might have with her over us."

"You regret it already, don't you?"

I concentrated on the floor. It seemed less threatening than Ken. "Do you?"

He was quiet for a moment. "No, I'm not sorry we did it."

"We can't do it again."

"Maybe we could go back to the way things were. We're still hot together, Gwen. Even you can't deny that."

"It was parting sex and that's all Ken, even you know that." The lies I'd just spewed forth made my head hurt, but I didn't have a choice. Ken had a shot at happiness with Beth and I refused to see him lose it.

I seemed to have a running theme going with the sexual good-byes. Thankfully, I didn't have anyone left on my list.

"So, it was a pity fuck that you no doubt regret," he said, his voice cold.

As much as I wanted to deny what he was claiming, I couldn't. It was true--I did regret it. I hadn't intended on letting this happen. I'd come here with the idea that I'd clean my stuff out and be done with the place. Now I'd managed to successfully add even more skeletons to my already overflowing closet. The damn thing was threatening to consume me.

My obvious failure to come up with the appropriate response quick enough was an answer in itself. Ken didn't look at me when he picked up the phone. I couldn't blame him. I'd hurt him again without meaning to. That seemed to be the only constant in my life.

The office suddenly felt very crowded and I didn't want to linger around listening in on his conversation with Beth. I headed towards the box sitting on the desk. Ken put his hand on it and gave me a stern look. He mouthed the word "no," and pulled the box to him. He wasn't about to accept my resignation, not even after I'd hurt him yet again. I gave up and nodded my head. He was right. No one else would put up with his shit and the fact that he still wanted me to work for him, said he was the perfect man to put up with mine.

Chapter 15

I made my way down to the Paranormal Regulators Research Department. I scanned my ID and waited for the door to open. I expected to see Kyle, a shaggy haired over-achieving teenager who, by the luck of the genetic gene pool, was not only a genius but also a werewolf. He'd been with us for a little over a year. His dad worked up in accounting and shared his full-moon issues.

Kyle didn't greet me. Instead, a tall slender man with a head of short black hair stood there. His blue eyes screamed familiarity and I tried my best to place where I knew him.

He extended his large hand out and flashed me a devilishly handsome smile. "Justin Wilson."

I accepted his handshake and stared up at him. So, this was Rick's oldest son? Rick Wilson and I had been co-workers up until he'd been murdered. Talia, the same woman who managed to break up Ken and I, had also managed to infiltrate Rick's family and win over his youngest two boys, Jonathon and Jacob. They killed their father as a sign of loyalty to their new master, Talia. She in turn gave them the curse, in my opinion, of being shapeshifters. They'd tried two months ago to kill me in both their forms, human and hellhound--and paid for it with their lives.

"It's okay, I don't bite," he said, winking at me.

I looked at him, horrified. His own brothers had literally mauled his father and left nothing but a mutilated torso behind. How could he joke like that?

Justin took a step toward me and I backed up into the hallway. I caught sight of the sides of his hair and saw the tiny flecks of white creeping up through the black near his ears. His father had had the same salt and pepper hair and the same blue eyes. I had to admit--Justin looked a hell of a lot more like his dad than his demonic siblings did.

"Are you all right...Ms.?"

I tried to focus on the here and now. Rick's death had been so hard on me that I hadn't been able to attend his funeral. I was still struggling with the fact he was gone, I wasn't sure I could stand looking at a younger version of him.

Justin took another step towards me and it took everything in me not to bolt and run. "Miss, are you all right? Do you need me to call someone for you?" He reached out, took hold of my ID card and stopped moving. His crisp blue eyes scanned my body. I felt like the newest exhibit at the zoo.

"What?" I asked, unable to stand the fishbowl feeling any longer.

"I...umm...err...you caught me off guard. I wasn't expecting to meet the woman who killed my brothers."

Every instinct in my body urged me to take flight. I checked the hallway to see what my options were. They were surprisingly bleak. The research library was tucked neatly away to keep curious employees at bay. If Justin was anything like his brothers then I would be fighting for my life all by my lonesome.

"I didn't expect to see you here either. I better be going, I have to…" I had to get away from him, but I didn't think sharing that with him would be wise.

"I would have thought that Ken would have told you I started here."

Ken knew about this? Of course he did, he was basically the head guy now. "No, he didn't mention it to me. Well, it was nice to meet you, but I'd better be going."

He stepped back and looked at the door. "Five minutes ago you needed to come in, now you're trying not to break into a full-blown run. Is it me?"

I didn't know what to say, he'd caught me. How do you tell someone that you're leery of them because their brothers were murdering hellhounds? I couldn't come up with anything clinically proven to work, so I just winged it. "I wanted to look up some information on Enchantresses but I think that it may too awkward for us both if I'm here. I can come back another time when Kyle is here."

The right side of Justin's thin lips pulled upwards. I noticed that he had the very same smile as Rick and this helped to let some of the tension in my shoulders out. "I suppose that if you left, you would spare us the initial weird phase of the game, but you'd only actually be delaying it. I'm not the research guy. I'm with the investigation department. I'm their newest detective, so I'm guessing that we'll be seeing each other quite a bit. So, really it's up to you, now or later?"

I looked over his shoulder. "Where's Kyle?" I really didn't want to go in there with just him.

"I'm sorry, but shouldn't I be the one who's worried about being alone with you? You've got quite the reputation around here now."

"Listen, I did what I had to do to stay alive. I'm not sorry about it and the only thing I would change if I could is I'd bring Rick back." I couldn't believe that I was saying all of this aloud. I had called upon the element of fire and used it to melt one of his twin brothers. The other had tried his best to seek revenge on me and ended up being torn in two by Giovanni and his people. No, I didn't feel bad about Jacob and Jonathon at all, but I did miss Rick.

"Ms. Stevens, I'm not sure you'll believe me when I say this, but I'm happy that you did what you did. It saved me the trouble of having to hunt them down and kill them myself. I'm not sure I could have done it, and they sure the hell deserved it."

I relaxed a little. The guy had a point. His brothers would have needed to be brought to justice and an elite group of cleaners would have been sent out to eradicate the hellhound problem. In essence, that's what Ken, the vampires and I did. In fact, Ken had been promoted to the head of the Paranormal Regulators shortly after that. Now, we officially were the group that handled ugly matters. That meant that Justin was now part of that group. He was now one of us.

Justin looked so much like Rick that he took my breath away. He even managed to dress like his father. His khaki pants and long sleeved blue dress shirt looked like something Rick would have shown up in. They both had that casual dress thing down pat. He was so normal compared to the men in my life. I could still remember only three months ago, Rick trying to persuade me to let him fix me up with Justin. At the time Justin was living in Miami, but was considering moving back. I hadn't had a chance to take Rick up on his offer--he died before I could.

I walked past Justin and into the library. "There are some books out on the table in the back. I...umm...was already looking up information about Enchantresses."

I gave him a very suspicious look. *"Really?"*

"Yeah, an old friend of mine called me. He's been tracking one in the area and needed a little more information about her."

I stopped in front of the piles upon piles of books and journals on the furthest table wondering what was going on. He wasn't kidding, the guy looked like he'd been at it a while. I wondered what, if any, headway he'd made and I also wondered who else was looking for information on the Enchantress.

I was well aware that Caleb wasn't the only bounty hunter who specialized in hunting the supernatural. He was one of the only ones who was now permanently in the area, thanks to me. Prior to dating me, Caleb just moved around as needed. He lived his life out of hotel rooms, but didn't have to. He made an obscene amount of money doing his job, but he wasn't flashy--he was just Caleb.

Thinking about Caleb made my heart hurt. I dreaded telling him about what happened with Ken and Pallo. He'd told me once that he could share me with Ken without a problem, but he couldn't share me with Pallo. Caleb was the most open-minded person I'd ever met when it came to sex, but he was extremely limited when it came to Pallo.

I sat down in front of a stack of handwritten books. The Paranormal Regulators keep a group of scholars on retainer who create and maintain all of their documents. These men and women went to great pains to research and record events. I'd asked Ken once why we didn't just put everything on computers. He looked at me and smiled. "Gwen, so many Internet sites that people assume are run by nuts are run by us. We give them the information they need to know, under the disguise of being fiction, of course, and then they maintain the databases. As for our permanent records, the people in charge think its best to put out only what it necessary."

He was right, if the public knew what was going on in the world--they'd riot and most likely never come out of their homes again. I glanced over the material and saw that it made reference to mermaids and sirens. Even though I was a faerie, I didn't know near enough about the creatures of the world.

You'd think I'd be an expert. I was, after all, fucking enough of them.

I'd begun taking classes and seminars, per Ken's request, with famous cryptozoologists and had a decent little library of my own in my office, but I didn't know jack about Enchantresses. Hey, I'm not perfect!

Justin sat down beside me and pulled his notepad out. It was full of sketches and notes. I leaned over his shoulder. "I think you missed your calling, you should have been an artist."

Our faces touched briefly when he turned to me. "Yeah right, my dad would have just loved that. No, I'm doing what would have made him proud."

"You mean what DID make him proud. He talked about you all the time. He hardly ever mentioned the other…" I didn't even want to talk about the devilment twins. "Anyways, you were…are, the apple of your dad's eye."

"Thanks," he said, pulling another book closer. "You know, Dad talked about you, too."

"Did he?"

"Yeah, he seemed to think that the two of us would hit it off."

We both laughed a little, but neither one commented on that any further. Instead, we focused on research. I read about the Enchantresses' ability to sing a song that only males respond to and how they were siren-like in their behavior. I wondered where I could order a clone of Orpheus from at this hour. I didn't think it was too likely that the all night discount store would be stocking those types of things, so I continued on with my research.

After a half hour of looking over basically the same information in twenty different formats, I decided to take a break. I put my head down on the first volume of exotic sea creatures and let the leather cover press hard into my forehead. Maybe I could soak the information up through osmosis. It was a thought.

Justin's cell phone rang and I surprised myself by not jumping out of my skin. After the attempts on my life, I'd grown to be quite the little paranoid faerie. I don't think anyone could blame me, but still, it was embarrassing.

"Yeah?" Justin said. He turned his notebook pages back and skimmed through them. "Listen, once these guys have been exposed to her song, they can't fight her. They can never fight her. There's mention of 'truth through the pain of love,' but it's not clear…yeah…Damn cryptic phrases that I can't make heads or tails out of…what? No, I'm not finding any tested methods of extermination…hmm, as fun as that sounds, I'm sure they'd rather have her alive…No…Yes…Okay, but be careful, I don't think you're immune to her either." Justin glanced over at me. "Well, my new assistant and I will keep on it." He winked at me. "Yes," he said and blushed. "That will be enough of that." He turned away from me. I didn't doubt that he was getting teased about working with a woman. Men seemed to like to do that to each other. "Yeah, I can meet you in about an hour…All right, see ya then. Bye."

Justin put his phone back in his pocket and looked at me. "Would you like to come with me? I'm going to drop off some notes to my buddy and then grab a bite to eat."

"Umm…" I didn't want him to get the wrong idea. I didn't need any more men in my life right now. "I'm not really dressed for meeting clients." This was such a lame cop out. I had a change of clothes in my office. There was no way I was going back up there to get into them, but I did have them if needed.

"Hey, Gwen, I'm not trying to trick ya' into a date. Besides, I heard you were dating someone. If you'd like to come along, I'd enjoy talking shop with you. If you don't want to come, I'll understand that, too. It's your call."

Wow, no strings, it seemed too easy, but that's what I needed--I needed things simplified for me. I still didn't know what I was going to do about Ken. I'd just had sex with him and walked out. I didn't even bother to say good-bye. The worst part of the whole thing is that I still had to figure out how best to tell Caleb about what I'd been up to.

I took a deep breath. I couldn't even begin to think about my Pallo problem.

Chapter 16

I helped Justin gather up a folder full of Enchantress information. I did manage to convince him to let me make two copies of everything after I told him that my fiancé was looking into the case as well.

Justin hadn't said too much since we'd been in the car. He'd gotten quiet after I had brought up Caleb. I kept checking the time and staring out the window. Dusk was less than an hour away and I was sure that Pallo would be up soon. I hadn't left a note or anything to tell any of them where I was. I really hadn't expected to be gone the entire day. I guess that attempting to clean out my office, screwing my ex, and digging up information on some crazy Enchantress takes more time than I thought. Go figure!

"So, do you want to tell me anything about this friend of yours we're meeting?" I asked.

Justin shot me a wide smile. "Let's see, his name is Balec. I've known him for close to ten years, and he's got a thing for the ladies."

That caught my attention. "A thing for the ladies? Do tell."

Justin chuckled and changed lanes to avoid being stuck behind the slowest driver in the world. I had half a mind to use my power to move the car off the road, but I was a good girl and didn't.

"I think Balec will be into you. You are exactly his type of woman. Tailor made, even." Justin must have sensed my disapproval with his statement because he immediately tried to clarify his meaning. "You see, he's always been *good* with women. I met him while I was in college. He'd show up every now and then at a bar close to the campus. The ladies were into him, still are I'm sure. I haven't seen him for about a year. I've talked to him, but since he'd relocated up here and I was still in Miami it made it hard to get together."

Justin went on to tell me about Balec's natural gift with women. Apparently, he was quite the gigolo. He had girls throwing themselves at him every time Justin had ever gone out with him. Justin admitted something that most men wouldn't do in front of a woman. He admitted to being jealous of Balec in that respect.

"I'm positive that he'll try to hit on you and if you're like the rest of the girls he's had, you'll fall for it. I'm just warning you...take it or leave it, but I'll tell you this, the guy's a looker and he's got a thing for girls with long black hair, milky-white skin, lush lips, dark lashes and fit little bodies. Girls *exactly* like you."

I sat upright and tried not to look embarrassed. I don't think I was very successful. "Thanks for the tip."

We pulled up outside a small bar. The place was an absolute dive. I gave Justin a look of disgust. Why in the heck were we meeting Balec down here? The place had bars on all the windows and enough posters of naked women on the windows to make a man blush.

I followed close behind Justin, carrying the folder full of information. Justin pulled the door open for me and I went to walk in. My cell phone rang and I had to fish it out of my pocket. I backed up onto the street to make sure not to lose the signal.

"Hello?"

"Hey babe's, how's it going?" Caleb said. It warmed my soul to hear his sweet voice.

"I'm fine, how's everything going for you? Did you guys find anything yet?"

"Yeah, we've got some great leads. I'm following up on one tonight. I just wanted to check in with you. I miss you."

"Caleb, if you get a chance--can you come home, I need to talk with you."

I was answered with silence before he let out a long sigh. "What's going on, Gwen?"

"We need to talk. I need to tell you some things and let you decide if you want to go through with the wedding. Caleb, I love you." I closed my phone and shut it off. I didn't want to get into it with him over the phone. I'd said too much already. I'd see him soon enough and we could duke it out then.

Pushing the door to the bar open, I looked for Justin. He was waving at me from across the cramped bar. I never realized that bars got packed before nightfall. I assumed all the heavy partying and drinking went on after hours. I was wrong. These heathens did it anytime.

I could barely squeeze through the mass of people. I bumped into a blonde who looked like she wanted to spit nails in my face for being within a foot of her. The feeling was mutual so I gave her a daring smile. Most of the crowd here looked rough. I was beginning to wonder about this Balec guy and Justin.

I slid into the seat across from Justin in the dark brown booth. The seat was cold even through my thick jeans. I lifted my butt off the cold seat and hovered above it, hoping it would warm itself. When Justin saw the look on my face he burst into laughter. I didn't find my ass freezing to be funny, but then again.

A middle-aged woman approached us and asked if we wanted any drinks. I said no, but Justin said yes. He ordered a beer and I went with ice water.

"I didn't think they let you drink on the job."

"Gwen, we don't have a normal job, nobody gives a rat's ass what you do, so long as you do it quietly and you do it well."

I couldn't argue with him. He was right.

Chapter 17

It was strange for me sitting there with Justin. We talked about everything and nothing at all. We talked about his father and psychotic brothers. We talked about how hard and dangerous our job is and how we receive absolutely no recognition by the public. Most of all, we talked about the people that are important in our lives. He told me about his ex-fiancée, who still lived in Miami. She'd broken his heart and it didn't seem like he was going to be healing that any time soon.

He ordered shots for us both after I finished telling him the story of my life. He was good with the part about me being brought back by my mother for a second chance at life. He was cool with my father being King of the Dark Realm. I hadn't even told my closest girl friend, Sharon, that much. When I got to the part about juggling three men at one time, his mouth dropped open.

"So, do I know any of these guys?" he asked, before he licked the salt off his wrist. I watched him down another shot of tequila and followed suit myself. Yes, I succumbed to peer pressure, I'm a loser. I didn't want to drop Ken's name into the mix. He was now in charge at the Paranormal Regulators office and I didn't need one of his subordinates having that much information about him. It was common knowledge that we'd been engaged up until eight months ago. It was not common knowledge that we were still sleeping together.

"No, I don't think so. Why?"

Justin leaned forward and tossed me another one of his father's smiles. "I just wanted to size up my competition."

I threw a lemon wedge at him. "Shit, I've got enough baggage, and after talking to you I realized that you may have more than me. We'd spend more money in therapy than we make. It'd be doomed from the get go."

We both sat there laughing. "I think you might be on to something there," he said. "Yeah, I'm already lugging around enough of my own shit. I've been with a woman who broke my heart. I guess I should thank you for the warning." He laughed softly. He looked past me, back towards the entrance, and then down at his watch.

"What time is it?"

"He was supposed to be here an hour ago. He's usually pretty good about being on time. If he doesn't show up soon we can head out." Justin looked down at the table full of empty glasses. "We might need to call for a ride."

I couldn't believe how late it was. I knew that the vampires would be up by now and that Pallo would be either gone or ready to kill me. Caradoc would do whatever Pallo told him to. James, on the other hand, would worry about me. He would defy Pallo's orders in a heartbeat for me, and that could cost him his life. I felt bad for not checking in with him. The place was way too loud for me to call James in there, so I decided to head out to the sidewalk.

"Justin, I need to call home and check in. I'm sure that they're going to be worried about me."

"Okay, I'll come with you."

I tried to argue with him that I really didn't require a chaperone to walk out front. He wouldn't hear any of it. I tried to stand up but he grabbed my wrist.

"He's here," Justin said. I followed Justin's gaze. I saw a swarm of girls surrounding someone in a black cowboy hat. Balec's back was to me and the crowd of women around him made it impossible to make him out. His head was moving around oddly and it took me a minute to realize that he was kissing some brunette.

"Balec!" Justin called out.

The tall man turned reluctantly away from the woman he was kissing and looked in our direction. I caught sight of a black t-shirt and that was all before another woman threw herself on him. My eyebrows rose as I turned to Justin.

"You weren't kidding, he is an honest-to-God chick magnet."

Justin laughed. "See why a guy could get a complex around him."

I did. I leaned back in my seat. My bladder was overflowing from all the drinks we'd had and the alcohol began to go to my head. Balec needed to get his ass in gear or I was going to wet my pants and that would not make him very appealing in my opinion.

The group of people around us parted. I looked up to see two people walking straight at us. One was a tall brunette, with the biggest set of breasts money could buy. Her face was nuzzled into the neck of the man in the black hat and he had his hand planted on one of her breasts. He shifted a bit. My jaw dropped and my pulse sped as I sat there looking up at Caleb.

He was too into returning her kisses to notice me. She slid her hand into the front of Caleb's jeans and grabbed hold of his erection. He let out a throaty laugh and continued going at her mouth. They were about to do each other on the friggin' table.

My blood boiled and worse yet, my power started to rise. I got that tingling sensation that begins in my elbows and moves to my hands. I could have made a tornado appear in the middle of the bar and whisk Caleb away. Instead, I glared at him and let my power build. I had been feeling horrible about what I'd done to him and he was whoring around, too. He'd made such a big deal about getting married, settling down together, being monogamous, yet here he was leading some sick double-life.

"You okay?" Justin asked.

I turned my cold stare on him. He pulled himself backwards and looked stunned. "This is your friend Balec?"

Justin nodded. I lifted my head slowly and watched Caleb's tongue dive into the busty girl's parted mouth. She stroked his cock as best she could in his jeans. I cleared my throat.

"I don't mean to interrupt, but I think you might want this...Balec!" I let his name roll off my tongue slowly. I tossed the folder onto the table and stared up at Caleb. He pulled himself away from his little pet-slut and looked at me. His green eyes widened, and he pushed the girl away from him quickly.

"I...umm...," was all he got out before I picked up my glass and threw my drink at his groin. He backed up as I rose from my seat. Justin mirrored me. He didn't have a clue why I was so pissed off, but Caleb did. The tall brunette stepped up to me ready to go to blows.

I would eat her for lunch. Poor girl, she was too stupid to see it coming.

"Who the hell do you think you are?" she asked as she tried to smack me. I grabbed her wrist and twisted it, hard enough to hurt her but not hard enough to break it. She gasped and I laughed. How sick is that?

"I'm his..." I didn't know what I was to him. "Correction, I *was* his fiancée."

Justin coughed apparently choking on his drink. The brunette looked up at Caleb and then to me. Caleb just stared at me wide-eyed. The bar suddenly felt way too small for us to be standing in. I needed fresh air. I went to walk past Caleb and he grabbed my arm. That was the dumbest thing he could have done. My power lashed out at him and set him flying backwards towards the bar.

I watched as his body slammed into two big guys on bar stools. Caleb wasn't hurt, but he'd managed to get some of the natives restless. They came up at him swinging. I smiled and stormed out towards the door.

Gotta love the power of pissed off gal!

As the door swung shut behind me, it drowned out the sounds of the entire bar erupting into a brawl. I smiled and stormed off down the street. I didn't have a clue as to where I was going but I knew that I wanted to get away from Caleb. I had no ground to stand on with him about his cheating, but that didn't mean it hurt any less. What got me the most was that I had been beating myself up all day about what had happened with Ken and Pallo, all the while Caleb had a harem of women at his beck and call.

Caleb averaged being gone three days away a week. Had he been seeing women the entire time he was away from me? Had I really been naïve enough to believe I was important to him? No wonder he was so accommodating about leaving to hunt for the Enchantress even though I was sick. Gawd, he'd even had the nerve to ask me to marry him. I suddenly felt very cold and clammy, and I knew that I was in no position to be jealous. But I still was.

My stomach cramped. I'd thought that my case of the flu had subsided since it hadn't acted up all day. Guess I was wrong. The cold night air wasn't helping any. I still felt like crap and I wanted to get as far away from Caleb as physically possible. I pulled my cell phone out and called home.

Chapter 18

Twenty minutes later, I watched as Pallo's black car pulled up in front of me. The lights shut off and James stepped out of the driver's side. He walked over to me and hugged me tight to his chest. I knew when I called home and he answered that he'd come in an instant no questions asked.

I told him I'd left Pallo's car parked down at the Paranormal Regulators and I told him that my keys were in the office. I'm assuming he called Ken because a vampire wouldn't get very far into the building without setting off every mystical alarm there was.

I stood there hugging James tight. I wanted to cry, and it would have been the perfect time to do it, but I couldn't. I was too damn cold to do anything. James' long dead body felt so warm to me. I snuggled in tighter to him.

"James."

"Yes."

"Thanks for coming," I said as he kissed the top of my head lightly and led me around to the passenger side of the car. I climbed in and waited for him to get back in. I told him about the events of the day. He drove along silently and never passed any judgment on me when I told him about sleeping with Ken. In fact, he never said anything at all.

"Pull the car over."

James never questioned my orders, he just did. I looked over at him. His dyed blue hair caught some of the light from the moon. He looked like a rock star--a very quiet rock star.

"James...just say it, tell me what you're thinking."

His jaw tightened and he looked out his side window, away from me. He was quiet for a few minutes before he finally spoke. "Why do you surround yourself with men that are destined to hurt you?"

"What?"

He turned and looked straight at me. "Come on Gwen. First you pick Ken, its obvious the guy's a prick. Sure, maybe he was good to you, but that doesn't make him any less of an asshole. Then you find Pallo again. Yeah, you two have a history together, but that history was different, he was human when you loved him once. I've known the man for over two hundred years. He hasn't had a normal, healthy relationship once in that time frame, and then there's Caleb. You push him away and keep him at arm's length. The guy's spent four hundred years on this earth pining after you. That in itself screams issues. Then you're pissed off when you find him shaggin' gals that look just like you...And for the record, I have to touch on Giovanni! I know what you're going to say-- you don't have feelings for him. Bullshit, I've been privy to your feelings long enough to know better."

I sat there and let everything he'd said soak in. James was right and he'd only ventured a tiny bit into the Giovanni territory. I wasn't too sure about my history with Giovanni either, but I knew that the relationship was dysfunctional at best. James had valid points. I did seem to flock towards needy men. I didn't know what the hell my problem was.

"What do you think I should do? You seem to be an expert on me now."

"For fuck sake, Gwen open your eyes and see what's right in front."

"What's right in front of me, James?"

"Forget it. The fact that you have to ask tells me that you don't get it, and you never will."

"That's the second time tonight you've said something like that. Just tell me what it is that's on your mind."

"I can't."

I stared at him and couldn't help but reach up and touch his smooth cheek. He flinched and that cut me deep. "Why can't you tell me?"

"Because you'll take it the wrong way and assume I'm pressing you into something," he said, his voice barely above a whisper.

"How do you know I'll take it the wrong way?"

He gave a droll look and rolled his eyes. "Please Gwen, don't try an' sit there and tell me that you'd be fine hearin' about how much it tears what's left of my heart out to watch you throw yourself at men who've had centuries to get their acts together, yet they never did. And you'd love knowin' how confused I am when you're near me. I don't want to lose your friendship and I will if I tell you why I'm upset."

I sat there for a minute, too stunned to speak. I especially didn't want to be the one to point out that he'd just confessed everything to me.

James jerked away from my touch. "Bloody hell, I fuckin' just spit it all out. Didn't I?" He hit the steering wheel and I was surprised that he didn't break it. "See, Gwen, I told you I'm confused when I'm around you. This better fuckin' wear off."

"What better wear off?"

"This whole mate, bonding thing."

I shook my head slightly. "We're not even sure how or why it happened. What makes you think it will wear off?"

The look in his blue eyes would haunt me for the rest of my life. "Because I'm damned if I do and damned if I don't. Giving into the way I feel would enhance the way you felt about me, but it would never work out. Caleb and Pallo will destroy anyone or anything that gets in their path. Hell, we're lucky the two dumbasses haven't killed each other yet."

I bit back a laugh. He was right, they were dumbasses. "Hey, what do you mean by 'enhance the way I feel about you'?"

He shifted slightly in the seat. "You know earlier, in your room...I wasn't guarding my feelings enough and the next thing I know, we were neckin' like...like…."

"We were in love." I finished his thought for him. I had felt something wash over me in my room. There was no woman singing, no weird buzzing energy. There was just James and I. "So, are you telling me that your vampire mojo-stuff is making us feel that way?"

The muscles in his neck tightened. "No, Gwen. My 'vampire mojo-stuff' is the only thing holding the feelings at bay."

My jaw dropped. "What? If you let your powers down we'll be all over each other again?" That thought was both terrifying and exhilarating. Awe, all nutty and wrapped up in one neat lil' package. How sweet.

James cocked an eyebrow at me. "You want proof?"

"Yes...no. NO! We don't need that right now."

"Tell me about it."

A gut wrenching thought hit me. I grabbed James' hand, not caring if we lost control or not. "You're not going to leave now and stay away from me are you? James, we can go talk with Nana...or even Giovanni." The minute I said his name I cringed. Last time I'd said his name out loud, he'd shown up within minutes.

Instantly, I felt his presence. He wrapped his cool energy around me and surprisingly enough, it radiated peace. *Bella, are you hurt?*

"No."

James narrowed his gaze on me. "No what?"

I ignored him and concentrated on Giovanni. *I'm fine...err...thanks for checking though.*

Thanks for checking though? What the hell was that? I'd officially lost my mind--again.

The sound of Giovanni's soft laughter filled my head. It wasn't in malice. It was soothing and genuine. I couldn't help but smile.

This situation with James is most curious, bella. Most curious indeed. He sighed. *You have but to call and I will come to you.*

Thank you.

With that, Giovanni pulled his energy away.

"Gwen, haven't lost your marbles on me now have you?"

"What? Umm, no...sorry, it's been a long day. Where were we...right, you leaving. Are you going to distance yourself from me?"

"Do you want me too?" He looked series, so unlike my James.

I turned and looked out the window, biting back tears. I'd no right to guilt him into staying. He was my best friend. He'd replaced people who'd known me for years and he'd only known me a short while. The thought of losing him, his laughter, his stupid jokes, his odd phrases--his everything scared the hell out of me.

He put the car in gear and from the sudden tension in the air, perceived my silence as a yes. It was then that I faced him, not bothering to hide my tears any longer. "No, James. I don't want you to walk out of my life. You're the ONLY thing in it I trust and...not only that...I want...no, I don't want you to go."

"That's good to know, 'cause if you'd have said yes I'd of lifted my 'vamp mojo-stuff' and made you change your mind," he said, with a smile on his handsome face. The odd tone in his voice that told me he wasn't joking. I should have been mad. I wasn't.

"Where should we go now? I'm thinking that sittin' out here all night is fun and all, but come mornin' you'll have your vampire well-done if you know what I mean."

"I don't want to go home."

"I know."

I put my head back on the seat and closed my eyes.

Chapter 19

James found a little motel on the outskirts of town. Its neon blue sign was partially burnt out. It now read *Stark*, instead of *Star Dusk*. I didn't care. I didn't want to go home, not after hearing that Pallo hadn't left yet. James didn't think Pallo had any intention of leaving me. I wasn't too sure about that.

The motel room was small, but cozy. It had two double beds and a tiny bathroom. The manager gave us a discount because the television wasn't working properly. Apparently, it wasn't picking up all the pay-per-view movies correctly. James laughed and claimed that his night would be ruined--no porn. The manager took him seriously and gave us a discount.

The room was done in several different shades of pink. I couldn't be certain, but after staring at the pattern on the wallpaper long enough, it looked like it was moving. I had to tear my eyes away from it--it was making me nauseous. I plopped down on the bed closest to the bathroom. James walked over to me.

"Are you goin' to take a shower?"

"Is it that obvious that I need one?"

He shifted his weight back and forth a bit. "It's just that...well, I saw Ken earlier and I suspected, but when I hugged you I knew." He took a deep breath before he continued. "I knew that you'd had sex with Ken before you told me. I can smell him all over you."

I'd forgotten how keen a vampire's senses were. I rolled my eyes at him as I climbed out of the bed. He had unintentionally made me feel like a tramp, not that I hadn't acted like one. James would never hurt me outright, and I appreciated his heads up. If he could smell it, then Pallo would, too.

I stepped into the tiny stand-up shower and unwrapped the bar of soap. The motel only had a tiny bottle of shampoo conditioner mix in there. The bottle wouldn't wash all my hair. Having hair that hangs to your butt takes a hell of a lot more than a half an ounce of shampoo, it would take at least four of those. Even if I could get away with using it, I'd never get a brush through my hair when I was done. I had to use a ton of conditioner every time I washed my hair. I wrapped my hair into a French twist to keep it dry.

The warm water felt great against my cool skin. I noticed that my lower abdomen and breasts were extremely tender. James was right, I was getting chubby. It only seemed to be my stomach, but I noticed it. I had developed the tiniest of pooches. I'd never really had to put much effort into working out, but I had a feeling that I was going to have to start.

When I came out, James was sitting on the edge of the bed by the door. He looked up at me, saw me wrapped in the white hotel towel and smiled. "That's a nice look for you, love."

"Thanks, I thought I might wear it more often. Maybe I could start a new trend."

I climbed under the covers, still wrapped in just a towel. I had a sneaky suspicion that my clothes carried the scent of sex with Ken. I didn't want to come right out and ask James. It was a little weird for even me. See, even I have my limits.

James turned the lights off and lay back on the other bed. He leaned over and turned the volume down on the television set. I always wondered what possessed the people who owned motels to secure the remote to the bedside table. It was in no way more convenient than using the knobs on the TV and I didn't know of many people who had use for a remote that wouldn't work with any other TV.

"Thanks for doing this for me, James."

"You don't have to thank me, Gwen. That's what I'm here for."

"No, you're here for so much more than that." I wanted to reach out and hold his hand, but I knew better.

Chapter 20

The sounds of chanting men surrounded me as I stood in the circle room. The altar was lit up by hundreds of candles. I backed up and bumped into Pallo. He was so quiet that I hadn't heard him. I'd seen the way this dream had ended and didn't want to have a repeat performance.

I reached up and stroked a piece of his brown hair from his face. Tucking it behind his ear, I looked into his chocolate brown eyes. His hand came up and met my naked waist and I pushed it away from me. As much as I craved his touch, I knew that my mind would betray me. I knew that I would twist the dream around and it would end badly.

"Gwyneth?"

"I'm sorry. I'm afraid of you now...here." I motioned to the surrounding room.

"I would never purposely hurt you. Remember what we discussed. You know what you must do if I...."

I shook my head. I wouldn't hurt him. It didn't matter what he turned in to. I'd never kill him. I took another step back and felt arms grab hold of me. I looked up at Pallo. He was suddenly surrounded by robed men as well. He tossed some of them off like they were flies while trying to get to me.

I hit one of the robed men in the gut and tried to strike out at another one. I missed and ended up with four of them pinning me back against the wall. The cool touch of metal clamped over my wrists as they chained my arms to the wall. I tried to kick out at them and then stopped. It was my dream and fighting it seemed silly. I knew I was dreaming. I could get control over this-- eventually we'd wake up and be fine, right?

I heard the muffled sound of someone calling my name. I knew that voice. It was James. I knew he was near me.

"JAMES! James wake me up! Now! Wake me up!"

The men's chants grew louder and turned into a language that I could no longer recognize. Pallo cried out and threw his head back. His body twisted and a growl emanated from deep within his throat. I knew what I'd see when he looked at me. I knew that he had just crossed that line between himself and his demon.

The faceless monks gathered around Pallo. He moved towards me. I felt like the fly and he the spider. I struggled to free myself. It was pointless.

"Feed the seed...feed the seed...," they chanted over and over again as Pallo stood before me.

Reaching up, he touched my exposed breasts. Under normal circumstances I would have been elated, now I was just terrified. As hard as I tried to fight it my body was excited by the idea of having him touching me. The louder the chants became the more I wanted sex. Then it was there, the faint sound of a woman singing. The odd buzzing energy filled the cavern.

Pallo moved his hands down over my butt, to the back of my legs. He lifted me to him. It took everything in me to keep from kissing his now distorted face. I didn't want to do this with him when he was like this, not when he was in full out vamp-mode. I wanted my Pallo back.

"Pallo?"

He snarled at me. I screamed and this seemed to excite him more. He pulled my legs around his waist and I fought to put them back down. He prepared to enter me. He aligned his cock with me and seized hold of my hair.

"JAMES!"

"Gwen! Gwen, wake up!"

My eyes opened and James held me upright. My cheek stung-- someone had slapped me. I grabbed it and centered my gaze on him.

"Sorry about that, you..." He looked over at the bed and back to me. I was in the center of the room, naked with James' arms wrapped tight around me. "You levitated, Gwen. Your body lifted up off the bloody bed. I tried to wake you. I heard you say Pallo's name and you sounded terrified, then you called for me. I didn't know what to do. I had to wake you up, so I...."

I touched my hot cheek. He had smacked me! Amazingly enough I wasn't mad at all. I was grateful. I wrapped my arms around his neck and hugged him tight. Doing this put his face directly in my naked breasts. My nipples went erect as my body reacted to him. The buzzing energy that I'd come to recognize as a bad thing surrounded us. And, I heard the faint sound of chants all around us.

"Do you hear that?" I asked.

James said something that sounded muffled. I realized that I still had his face stuffed between my bosoms. I let go of his neck and he set me down.

"Not that I'm complainin', love, but what the hell was that about?"

I didn't answer him. The sound of drums beat loudly in my head as the buzzing grew. My heartbeat matched the steady rhythm. My muscles contracted and my palms burned--itched to touch flesh.

Take the vampire into you. Take him into you now, a woman's voice said in my mind. I tried to push her out, keep her at bay, but she thrust her power at me. *Take him now!*

"Gwen?"

I put my lips up to meet James'. I had to force my tongue into his closed mouth. He pushed me back softly. The chanting began again. I reached down and grabbed James between his legs. His black jeans couldn't hide the fact he was interested in me. His erect cock fought to get out of the top of his pants and I wanted nothing more than to free it. He wanted to do this as much as I did, at least physically.

James pushed back on my shoulders. "Gwen, what the hell's come over you? Have you gone mad? What the hell is that friggin' buzzin' noise? Are you doing that? Damn woman, I'm working my arse off to keep shit under control for us and you go and do some sort funky faerie thing!"

I didn't know or care what he was talking about. I made another attempt to grab him. The drums beat harder in my head. He dodged out of my way and looked off into the distance.

"Pallo's callin' me."

"What?"

"Pallo is summonin' me. He wants me to return and he knows I'm with you."

I looked around. I couldn't hear anything but the beating of drums in my ears. Each pound made my body ache more for sex. I spun around fast and hit the wall hard, accidentally driving my fingernails through the palm of my hand. The blood welled up under my finger. Slowly, I turned to face James. His eyes flickered to black and then back to blue. The blood had caught his attention.

"Gwen, no...I can't fight you and my demon. *Please.*"

I put my blood soaked fingers out to him and moaned as his cool tongue flickered over them. "You don't have to fight me, James."

He turned his head away from me, leaving my wet fingers to fall from his lips and put his hands up in air. "Gwen, I thought we talked about this. We can make our friendship work, but not if were fuckin'."

"Oh, but weren't you the one trying to tell me how I keep picking the wrong men. Now, James, are you telling me that you're not interested in what I have to offer?" I heard myself speaking and knew that it wasn't me controlling my words.

I made another attempt at touching James. He grabbed hold of my arm and twisted it behind my back. He turned my body away from him and herded me towards the bathroom door. I dug my heels into the carpet. I may not have the strength of a vampire, but I did have the strength of a faerie. James had to relieve some of the pressure he was putting on my arm or he'd break it. I knew he wouldn't hurt me so I didn't let up.

The chanting and rhythmic sound of the drums made my head sway slightly with the beat. It was matched by a pounding on our room door. The manager's voice greeted us. He wanted to check in on us, our neighbors had reported a disturbance. James let go of me and I looked at the door.

James walked to the door and opened it slightly. He explained that we had just gotten a little 'carried away'. He explained that we were still newlyweds and it happened. The man must have tried to look into the room because James pulled the door tight into him and explained that I wasn't decent.

I moved up behind him and ran my fingers over his butt and back. I could hear the middle-aged, balding manager telling James and I to tone it down or he'd be back. I had an overwhelming need to speak to James. I leaned into James' ear and whispered, "I can use him for sex if you won't let me use you." I was implying that I'd do the manager if need be, but I didn't know why I said it. The man was repulsive.

James shut the door and looked at me. His blue eyes were wide and confused. "Gwen, somethin' isn't right with you." The sound of the woman singing grew louder and James jerked. He spun around, checking ever corner of the room. The singing voice reached new levels. "Holy bloody fucking shit...that's the song of a Siren."

A Siren? Didn't they bind people to them with their songs? Aside from Orpheus, I'd never heard of anyone escaping their clutches. "James, no...it can't be a Siren."

"Did ya' not listen to yourself, you just suggested you'd bang that *wanker.*"

Putting my body against his, I put my leg up. I kissed at his neck and pulled at his t-shirt. He tried to pry me off him but I wasn't about to give up. I needed to be touched and somewhere deep inside him, he wanted to touch me. I knew it.

"Gwen, please fight this. Come on, love. For me, please."

I slid my hand down the front of his pants and encountered a wealth of tight curly pubic hair. I moved my fingers downward and gripped his hard shaft in my hand. He, like Pallo, was not circumcised. James gasped.

"Call your master then, vampire. Let him know she will have someone tonight. Let him decide if it is you or a stranger. Tell the vampire that it need not be him but she will have someone." It was my mouth that spoke, but that wasn't my voice. I looked at James with wide, scared eyes.

"Gwen, if your head starts spinning 'round, can I slap you again?"

I knew he was attempting to lighten the situation with humor, but I couldn't bring myself to laugh. "Go away, James! Go now, before…."

James pulled me closer to him. "I'm not about to leave you in the hands," he looked around, "okay, air of a Siren. No way in hell!"

"Ple-ase," I whispered.

"I can't believe that I'm about to say this but I'm actually hurt that you don't want me."

I struggled against the energy in the room. "That's not it...can't lose you, too...I ruin every man I touch...can't ruin you, James...love you too much."

"Fucking hell, Gwen. You can't say things like that! I'm doin' everythin' I can here to keep myself under control. Help me out here."

I grabbed the back of James' head and pushed my mouth against his. I let every bit of my need for sex come through. I tried to share the rhythm of the drums and chants with him. The sound intensified. I had no desire to fight it.

James' eyes swirled to black quickly. He grabbed both of my wrists and pushed me towards the wall. I bit at him, trying to get him to come at me with his mouth. He didn't.

"James, please…."

He growled and it excited me. "I have to try and keep you under control until Pallo arrives."

The moisture between my legs increased. I wasn't going to make it. I could feel something pulling me. I tried to fight it but I didn't understand it enough to know how to combat it.

"James." I looked at him, trying hard to regain my composure. "James, I'm not going to make it. Just go."

"I told you already that I'll not leave you and I meant it." James brought his face down slowly towards mine. I moaned as his lips touched mine voluntarily. He was kissing me without passion. He was holding back and I knew why--Pallo.

A spark of energy flew out of my hand. It struck the TV and started changing the channels. James looked down at me and he understood. We were in deep shit.

His kisses became firmer after that and he gave himself over to me. His body relaxed and he stopped pinning my arms to the wall. He didn't let go of my wrists yet, but at least we were making progress.

I could feel a different energy rising up through me. This wasn't my magic, at least not as I knew it to be. I watched as a shudder ran through James. He'd let down his guard, his control. He'd warned me about what would happen, but I had no idea it would be this severe. The emotions that ran through me left me clawing at him, to get him closer to me, to fuck me, to love me.

His mouth came down hard on me. His hands moved towards my breasts. The feel of his fingers brushing past them sent me into an uncontrollable fit. I ripped his shirt off and yanked his pants open. He didn't stop me.

The next thing I knew, James was grinding his body against me. His hips were perfectly aligned with mine. I struggled to get him free of his pants and almost had him out when someone knocked on the door again. James didn't stop pushing against me and I ate at his mouth--drinking his passion down. Was it meant to be this way between us or was this the Siren's doing? At the moment, I couldn't focus enough to care.

"Gwen?" I heard Caleb's voice. "Gwen, are you in there?"

James pulled his head back and looked like he'd been struck. He thought I would send him away now that Caleb had arrived. He was wrong. I pulled James back to me and he wrapped his arms around him. He picked me up and spun me around. He edged us towards the bed. I kissed at his face, his neck, his shoulders, anything I could reach.

The pounding on the door increased. "Gwen, open the fucking door. Pallo called me. He said you'd be here. He's on his way. What's going on?"

I ignored him and felt my excitement grow as James laid me down on the bed. I heard Caleb yell for me again. The pounding on the door sounded faint. "Drop your magic and open the Goddamn door, Gwen, let me in."

I hadn't put a spell on the door, or at least I didn't think I had. Warding spells were beyond me. I could feel Caleb's hot energy pushing against mine. He was powerful, probably more than me, and somehow I was keeping him out.

"Gwen?" I heard Justin's voice. "Gwen, let us in. I know you're pissed at him, and it's not like he doesn't deserve it, but…."

I heard Caleb yelling at him. Justin began talking again. "Like we don't all know that she's pissed at you! Gwen, he was working undercover. I never thought to give you his real name. I thought I was protecting his identity. Gwen, I never realized you guys knew each other…I didn't know he was with you now or I wouldn't have told you about all the other women."

"What the hell did you tell her?" Caleb demanded.

"The truth."

Apparently, that answer scared the hell of Caleb because he began thrusting power at me in an attempt to break my "hold" on the door.

I laughed as James' body moved over mine. His eyes held hunger--hunger for me and for sex. I loved every minute of it.

Caleb's pounding continued. "Gwen, please let me explain, it's not what you think. Gwen, nothing happened…please I was following leads and the girls. They're in league with the Enchantress, I know it, please, Gwen. I'm sorry…please." He moved to pound on the window. It should have broken easily for him, it didn't. Some sort of magic was keeping him out.

"Let me try," Justin said. The door flew open and I heard him entering the room as James' mouth found mine. "What the…?"

I looked over James' shoulder as he moved his mouth down on mine. I saw Justin trying to get Caleb away. Caleb wasn't having any of it. He looked like he'd been through the wringer. The bar fight must have been a doozie. He made an attempt to step into the room and was thrust backwards.

The cold energy rose up and off me. Justin turned and looked at me. His eyes met mine and I knew that whatever had captured

James now had Justin as well. He moved towards me. The sexual energy in the room was so thick that it was getting hard to breathe.

"Gwyneth, pull your magic back," Pallo said. I hadn't realized that he'd arrived. He was standing next to Caleb looking at the three of us.

Justin moved towards me, he looked flushed. His blue eyes locked on me and I knew that he was about to join us. My hand reached out to him. I hadn't moved it, something else had. The chanting returned louder than before and I had to close my eyes to try to steady myself. When I opened them again I looked up at James, his black eyes faded back to blue. Abruptly, he stopped kissing me and stood slowly.

"James, don't go!"

He looked down at me with so much love in his face that it managed to nick some of the Siren's hold on me. I reached for him and he closed his eyes, shaking his head slightly. "If we cross the line--we can never go back. I could never go back."

Justin made a move to come to me. James grabbed him and pushed him towards the door. I sat up on my knees on the bed and pulled the sheets up to try to cover myself. I hoped that it would cause the burning desire to stop, it didn't. James stopped things from going further and I appreciated that.

Caleb and Pallo tried to enter the room. The magic surrounding us wavered. Pallo entered but Caleb was held at bay. I looked over at him, his green eyes hardened. He was angry with me. He assumed I was the one keeping him out. Maybe I was.

James whispered something to Caleb. Caleb turned and looked in at Pallo. "Get her out of there, something else is in there with her! That's not just Gwen!"

James said something else to Caleb that I couldn't make out and Caleb's face went white. "Pallo, it's a Siren! A Siren is using its call on her!"

The chanting boomed around me once more. Pallo spun around in a circle looking for the source. His eyes locked on mine. He heard them, too. The TV's volume increased. The bedside table's drawer opened and the phone book came flying out. Pages ripped out on their own and flew around us.

"Stay away from the light..." I said half under my breath, in a bad attempt at humor.

"What?" Pallo asked as he made a move towards me. He stopped and glanced at Caleb.

Pallo had been put in this position before. He'd been forced to watch as a lust spell, that my well-meaning father put on fruit, consumed me. It hurt him more than he'd ever let on, I was sure of that. He put his hand out to me and said something. I couldn't hear him above the beating of the drums, the wind, and the television.

I shook my head and looked around the room. The lights began to flicker. I pulled the sheet around me tighter in a protective manner. The door to the room slammed shut and the room fell silent.

"Pallo?"

He looked around and back at me. "I know even less than you, *fata mia*. You are sure that you did not do this?"

"Yes."

He took a step towards me. This was the first time I'd ever seen him in a bright red shirt. It was such a contrast to his pale white skin and brown hair that I wasn't sure how much I cared for it on him. I'd gotten used to Pallo's grays and blacks. Thankfully, he'd stuck with what worked on the lower half. His black jeans fit him snugly and accented his muscular thighs. Even without some horny supernatural force pushing me I'd want to have sex with him.

Pallo walked over to the edge of the bed. He looked down at me, and put his hand out. I took it. His hand engulfed mine. Pallo had a way of making me feel extra small. I was petite to begin with, being next to Mr. Muscle made me seem downright minuscule.

"You are cold."

"So are you," I said.

He looked at the door. "They are still trying to get in."

"I don't hear anything."

"Nor do I but James is still in direct contact with me."

I pulled the sheet off the bed and wrapped it around me. Pallo helped me stand. I was freezing and had developed a nice case of the shakes. My body no longer craved sex. All I wanted was some food and some rest.

Pallo got my clothes out of the bathroom, hesitated, and then handed them to me. "And how is our *good friend* Ken doing?"

Shit, I'd forgotten that my clothes smelled of the aftermath of my and Ken's romp on the office desk. I avoided making eye contact with Pallo. I didn't need him making me feel ashamed of that, too. It happened and I couldn't take it back. I wasn't even sure I wanted to take it back. Pallo's temper and Caleb's double life made Ken look downright plain. Maybe, plain was just what I needed.

I dressed quickly and did my best to focus on my feet--not Pallo. When I was finished he walked over to the door.

"Any ideas on how we can remove the spell?"

"I'm not sure I want the door open," I said. Pallo seemed to understand my meaning. What did I have waiting for me on the other side? I knew I had at least one irate--lying faerie, one of my best friends that I'd forced to almost cross that line, and a guy I just met that I was sure I'd have had sex with if James hadn't have intervened.

No, opening the door sounded less and less appealing.

"Gwyneth," Pallo said lightly.

I put my hand out and tried the door. It opened.

Chapter 21

I rode home with Caleb. Pallo forced me to. I tried to get in the car with James, but Pallo lifted me out and put me in the back of Caleb's SUV. Thankfully, I hadn't had to look at Justin when I came out. He'd gotten a call and had to leave. At least one thing went my way.

Caleb had tried to give me a hug when I first came out. I couldn't do it. I wasn't sure what I was feeling but I knew hugging him wasn't what I wanted to be doing. He didn't say anything when Pallo tossed me in the back of his Explorer. He just started it up and pulled out of the Star Dusk Motel parking lot. Pallo and James stayed behind to handle the manager.

Boy, was that guy in for a surprise. I wondered if they had a poltergeist clause--probably not.

Caleb adjusted the rearview mirror. Green eyes stared back at me from time to time.

"What else do you want me to say, Gwen? I explained it all to you. God, even Justin explained it to you."

"Yeah, *Balec*...he explained everything about you. I don't know you at all. I let some fucking faerie pull one over on me! I am so stupid! This entire relationship was built on lies." I hardened my face. "I want out of it, now!"

Caleb slammed on the brakes. The cars behind us followed suit. If we weren't both immortal I would have been pissed. Caleb pulled over to the side of the road and cut the engine.

"Gwen, I had a life before you...after you I mean. What was I supposed to do, sit around for the rest of eternity in mourning? How the hell was I to know you'd show up one day? I should have lived like a monk, is that what you expected of me? Should I have held out for centuries in the hopes that my dead lover would return?"

The outburst wasn't what I expected of him and he knew it. I'd thought that Caleb was the one person in this world that I could trust most, no matter what. Now, I knew I'd been wrong.

"Gwen, look at me. I didn't do anything I swear."

"Every time you left for nights on end, supposedly working, were you doing 'nothing' then, too?"

Caleb slammed his hands on the dashboard. "GWEN, I didn't do anything. I haven't been with anyone but you since you came back into my life. Can you say the same?" The trump card had been tossed into the mix. He knew I'd slept with Ken at least once since I'd met him. He was with me when I did it. Hurting me to protect himself was a valid response to the situation. That being said, it didn't piss me off any less. If he wanted to throw stones-- I'd throw stones!

"No, I can't say the same. In fact, I've got a surprise for you too, *Balec.*"

"Gwen, don't do this. My name is Caleb and you know it. I just moved the letters of my name around and use that when meeting with informants or...."

I put my hand up. I didn't care how or why he used the name Balec. I would have cared to know ahead of time, that was all. "Well, Caleb the Saint. That is what the history books will remember you by, and I will get to say I knew you...and I was one of the lucky ones who you fucked, because I knew your *real* name." He tried to reach out to me. I kicked the back of his seat. "You bastard! You ask me to marry you and put so much pressure on me that I couldn't think. You made me feel like I was about to lose you if I didn't make up my mind then and there, then you run off and have a harem of chicks waiting in the wings." I slapped my forehead. "Damnit, Caleb we shared power, exchanged magic. You fucking tied me to you even though you didn't want me. Was this all to get back at Pallo? Was winning this time around really that important to you? If you didn't want me, you should have said something. I would have done you a favor and played along--no need to bind me to you then. This is just great, Caleb." I glared at him. "You really are your mother's son."

I was beyond disgusted. I opened the door and climbed out. There was nothing for miles around us. The freeway had remained sterile and undeveloped all these years. I didn't care. I walked across the dark field. I just wanted to get away from Caleb before we said any more hurtful things to each other.

I heard his truck door slam and then my name as he shouted it. I ignored him and kept walking. I felt the hot sensation of his power as he struck me with it. It felt like a rope was being wrapped tightly around me. There, of course, was nothing there when I looked down but I could feel it. He was going to hold me still until he was done talking to me.

The wind caught hold of his black hat and blew it off his head. His quick reflexes let him snatch it before it blew out onto the highway. He looked at me and his eyes burned with rage.

"Let me go, Caleb...drop the magic."

"No, I'm like my mother after all, and she's the head sorceress. Why shouldn't I use it then I could be just like her?" He came up to me and had to stoop down to put his face in my face. "Gwen, you've had things your way long enough. It'd serve you right if I did fuck other women. You are hardly one to talk, *Gwyneth*. I know you still have feelings for Pallo. I worry every time I walk out the door that you won't be there when I get back. I don't understand you. It's like you do everything you can to push people away. Oh, men are good for sex and that's it. Gods forbid one of them loves you and wants to spend his life with you. No, you like a good fuck, but no commitment. That makes you a...."

I was so mad at him that I wanted to push him out into the center of the busy road. Maybe getting hit by a semi would knock some sense into him. "I'm a what? A whore? Is that what you wanted to call me, Caleb?" He looked away. I pushed against his magic with my own but had no luck lifting it. "Answer me, Balec...oh, I mean, Caleb. I'm interested in hearing your perspective. After all, you did have a women's hand in your fucking pants tonight. The phrase takes one to know one seems fitting here."

He raked his hand through his long blond hair and shook his head. "You're pushing me away--again! Why don't you want to let me in, Gwen? *Táim i ngrá leat*--yet you don't care!" His green eyes narrowed on me. "My mother was right. You are a faerie whore who doesn't care about anyone but herself."

My jaw tightened. Caleb had officially removed the gloves. This was about to get ugly--okay, uglier. My nostrils flared as I let my rage build.

Caleb clenched his fists before his face softened a bit. "I didn't mean that, Gwen. I'm hurt, confused, and...."

I laughed. "No, you said exactly what you meant, Caleb. I'm a whore. A whore who up until two months ago hadn't had sex in half a year--the man prior to you was my fucking fiancé! Never once did I stray from him. Never once did I ever entertain sleeping around. No that began when you and Pallo came on the scene. I was happy before you! I didn't feel any burning need, any holes in my heart. I was content not knowing about my past. I was fine not loving you! You show up, out of the blue, with vampires, crazy sorceress mothers and all your other supernatural bullshit and then am shocked to find out I'm conflicted. You and Pallo expect me to be something I'm not--the Gwyneth you both knew died. The only thing here is the whore you both made me.

And while we're on the subject, here's one for you...this afternoon Ken fucked me on my desk, and..." Caleb's face jerked back to me. "Oh, and let me nail the lid in the coffin while I'm at it, no pun intended...You know you're little fear about Pallo and I? Well, it was oh so warranted! I fucked Pallo, more than once. Hey, imagine the coincidence, I was fucking him--again while you were running around doing your Enchantress whores. Yep, looks like you're right. I am a whore. Happy that you held me here now? Are you pleased that you shared your power with me? You've bound yourself to a whore who you hate. How's it feel, Caleb?"

Caleb and his power dropped to the ground. I took a step back from him. I should have felt victorious. I'd won the verbal sparring match. I felt the exact opposite, I felt like a piece of crap.

I dropped to my knees and pulled him to me. His body shook and mine followed suit. I'd said such horrible things to him. Things that were twisted and laced with hate. He was right. It was my way of keeping him at bay and avoiding commitment. "Caleb, baby, I'm sorry. This isn't what I want. I didn't want to hurt you. We both said things that were ugly...I'm sorry."

"Were you ever going to tell me?" he asked, quietly.

I stroked his hair and put my head against his shoulder. He didn't touch me. "That I slept with Ken? Yes, that's what I wanted to talk to you about."

He kept his head down. "No, I don't give a shit about Ken, he's not a threat...I mean Pallo. Would you have ever told me about you and Pallo?"

I went to say yes, but stopped and thought about it. "No."

He pulled away from me and covered his face with his hands. I should have made a move to touch him, to comfort him, but I just sat there. I was sick, both literally and figuratively, and tired. I couldn't fix this. No one could. I didn't single-handedly bring us down, but I sure played the larger role in our demise. Walking away wasn't an option. At least not anymore. We'd shared magic, cemented a bond that between faeries was unbreakable. Above that, as much as I wanted to pretend like I didn't care about him, that I didn't love him the same as Pallo, I knew I was wrong.

"Caleb?"

He ignored me. I couldn't blame him but it still hurt. So much had been laid on the line, the wounds so fresh--there was nowhere to go with my feelings. Normally, I would have cried in his arms and then made love to him, but that wasn't going to happen. He couldn't even stomach looking at me.

Caleb's cell phone rang. He didn't answer it.

"You'd better get that, you don't want to keep the honeys waiting for their hunk of burning *Balec*."

He shook his head. "Don't do this to us, Gwen."

"Me? This is all my fault? I'll take the majority of the blame, but not all of it. Besides, what else could I possibly do? I'm a horrible person, remember? Oh, I know the wedding is off, not that I needed to verbalize it. I'm sure you gathered as much on your own. So, consider this my final attempt at pushing you away."

My insides twisted and turned. Why was I like this? Why did I say such ugly things to him? All I really wanted to say was that I loved him and I was sorry, yet those were the very words that escaped me.

Caleb rose slowly from the ground and looked at me. His green eyes were swollen and tears stained his cheeks. I couldn't breathe. I'd done this to him. I'd hurt him, no one else. Disgusted with myself, I turned and walked away from him.

"Gwen, did you ever love me or was I just a substitute until you and Pallo could work out your differences?"

What the hell was he talking about? I wanted to marry him. Was he insane? "Caleb, you know the answer to that already."

"Do I, Gwen? Because that's what I feel like. I feel like your relief batter. A nice warm dick to keep around until Pallo comes to his senses and opens his arms to you. That's exactly the way you make me feel."

Spinning around, I glared at him. "No, Ken was the substitute! You were just good for free labor...well, maybe not free. I did pay you with sex." I didn't mean a word of it but I was hurt. I loved him more than life itself but my pride prevented me from telling him.

Suddenly, the air around me felt hot, too hot. The hairs on my arms stood on end. Caleb was losing control of his power. His fists clenched tightly at his sides. He was trying to get a hold on his power, but the ever-climbing temperature surrounding us told me it wasn't working. He had enough power to destroy us both if he wasn't careful.

"I'm sorry, Caleb." The air around me thickened, I put my hand out to him. "I didn't mean that...I love you, and I was just hurt that you weren't honest with me. It's not just that...I hate myself for hurting you. There's no excuse for my behavior, but you should know that I do love you. I did want to be your wife and start a family."

The earth beneath my feet shook. I staggered backwards and just missed falling. "Caleb?" It was too late. He had no control over his power and if I tried to fight him with my magic, I'd risk killing him. He stared down at his hands and then looked up at me with pain filled eyes.

"I'm sorry too, Gwen. I love you and I wanted to be your husband." He held his hands out. "Pallo will take care of you now...I love you."

Oh, God!

He was going to take his power into himself--draw his magic into his body. He would not survive that. I did the only thing I could think of. "I love you and I picked you. Always remember that in the end I wanted you and only you...not Pallo. I loved him, but wanted a life with you! I wanted to start a family with you, Caleb. I wanted it to be you walking through that door every night and *our* children running up to greet you. I'm sorry I hurt you." Choking back tears, I used my power to draw his away from him and to me.

"GWEN...NO!" He lunged for me. It was too late. The scalding hot blow of his magic sent me airborne. I felt like I was being burned from the inside out and probably was. The last thing I remembered hearing before the darkness surrounded me was the sound of Caleb screaming for me.

Chapter 22

I had brief moments of alertness. Pallo's face greeted me each time. I would wake to find him tipping cups of broth to my lips. Once, he was washing my arms down with something cold. I tried to reach out and touch him but my arms weren't working for me. I closed my eyes and let sleep come.

I couldn't be sure how long I'd slept, but by the looks of Pallo it'd been a long time. When I opened my eyes, I found him sitting with his head back in a chair next to my bed. My arms finally cooperated with me and I reached out and touched his hand. He sprang into action and was next to me in a flash. He kissed my forehead.

I squeezed his hand gently. "How long have I been asleep?"

"You have been here for over a week."

Over a week? I pulled his hand to me and kissed it. "You were here the whole time. I could sense you by me." I didn't say it aloud but I had also sensed that Caleb had not been around me.

Pallo moved my hair out of my face and sat on the bed next to me. "When we found the two of you on the side of the road Caleb assumed he had killed you. Taking his power into you was foolish, Gwyneth, very foolish. He was right about you being dead. I had to share my blood with you and that was not even enough to bring you back." He touched my shoulder and ran his finger down the length of my arm. "I had to sink my fangs into your flesh. To do that while one is dead, and to share blood as well means..." He touched my neck lightly.

My fingers traced up his arm and found the spot he was touching. My eyes widened. "Am I...a...am I one you guys now?"

Pallo smiled. "There is something in your faerie blood that prevented you from turning. Part of me hoped that would be the case, you had lived with Giovanni for many years and he can be a wicked man. If he treated you anything like he treated everyone else then I would have to guess he tried to turn you as well and you were not a vampire when I met you."

Pallo was trying to justify saving my life. That was unnecessary. "Pallo, it's okay. I understand. You did what you had to do. I know that, and you stayed with me."

Tears came to my eyes and I was powerless to stop them. I cried because of Pallo's concern and care, and I cried for the events of the last few weeks, but most of all I cried because I'd lost Caleb. Pallo leaned down and kissed my forehead.

"Gwyneth, he blames himself for this." To Pallo, reading my thoughts was second nature. I was used to it. "We found him holding your dead body to his chest. James had to physically drag him off you because he did not want to let you go. His love for you is great and his hate for himself is equally as strong. He did not come here because I do not think he could face what he'd done. For the first few days you were...unrecognizable."

I tried to sit up. My body ached. Pallo helped me to get into a semi-comfortable seated position. He retrieved my light yellow robe and brought it over to me. I tried to stand up but my body wasn't ready for that just yet.

Someone knocked softly on the door. I looked up to see James standing there. He glanced at Pallo and then at me. He flashed his legendary shit-head grin at me and came running towards me. I thought for a minute that he might try to pick me up and I *so* wasn't up for that. Pallo moved away and let James sit next to me on the bed. He put his hand out and touched my back.

"How ya' doin', kiddo?" James leaned in and squeezed me gently. "You bloody-hell better never think of pulling a stunt like that again."

"Which stunt is that? Damn near getting you killed by your boss?" I looked at Pallo. I hated referring to him as James' master and he knew it. "Or dying?"

James laughed, "Don't worry, 'the boss' over there went easy on me. But, you, what the hell were you thinkin' absorbin' all Caleb's mystical magic into you? Are you daft? Doing 'at is suicide."

"James, I love it when you get worked up, you can tell you're not from around here. You go all British on me."

"God save the Queen," Pallo said, laughing softly.

James and I sat there staring at him, stunned. He wasn't a comedian normally so hearing him crack a joke took us both by surprise.

James laughed and nodded towards Pallo. "Hmm...Gwen, maybe you should die more often. It lets him flex his Florence Nightingale muscles. I couldn't get him to wear the sexy nurse's uniform. Though I did try."

Pallo appeared confused by James' comment and that made me laugh so hard that my sides hurt.

Chapter 23

It took another two days for me to feel up to leaving my room. I was thankful that they had stayed to help me. James turned out to be quite the little household helper. He'd taken over cooking and laundry duties. His food was surprisingly good. Maybe he and I could swap recipes.

Caradoc was left in charge of commuting back and forth between my house and Pallo's businesses. Pallo owned and operated Necro's Magik World and Supernatural Theme Park and a host of other money making attractions. It was only about a half an hour away but Pallo wouldn't dream of leaving me. I didn't think he wanted to admit it but he enjoyed being in the country. He'd spent the last two hundred and fifty years of his life as a vampire and he had an image to maintain. I could see it in his face, which was normally full of that dark-brooding kind of emotion. As of late, he'd been a wise cracking, almost normal guy.

He'd spent the greater part of the night before explaining how I might have some odd side effects from his bite. He was already concerned because my body temperature was lower than normal to start with from me being sick. I assured him that I understood why he did what he had to do and wouldn't hold anything that might crop up against him.

The only real side effect I'd noticed was that my days and nights had gotten all jumbled around. I think that was due to the fact that nighttime was when the vampires were up so I naturally didn't want to be lying in bed alone all day. Other than that I seemed normal, well, as normal as I could get.

I put on some clothes that James had left out for me. He'd made a fine choice in clothing for me. I pulled the blue jeans on and white t-shirt. The pants were a little hard to get buttoned. I looked down at my abs and wondered what was happening. Faeries bodies don't change after a certain age. Yes, we age, but it's at a pace so slow that it takes close to a thousand years for us to appear to be in our forties. I made a mental note to call my father soon. He might be able to shed some light on my problem.

Pallo appeared in my doorway with a white rose. I looked around my room. It had morphed into the land-of-all-things-pretty-and-scented some time over the course of the week and a half I'd spent down and out. Pallo kept me in a steady stream of fresh flowers, James baked every sweet thing he could think of, and Caradoc had given up and brought me a stack of magazines. I think he must have grabbed one of every one on the shelf because the stack was almost two feet high and included car and men's fitness magazines. He'd tried and that's what counted.

"Are you all set?" Pallo asked.

I let out a small laugh when I saw that he was wearing a long sleeved tapered waist blue jean shirt. There were no buttons on it until mid-chest. This left most of his massive upper body exposed. I wasn't complaining one bit. I loved looking at his pale chest. He had on a dark pair of fitted jeans and a pair of black boots. He looked amazing but it wasn't his normal dark and brooding look.

"So, the fresh air helping you break down and go country?" I asked with a smile.

Pallo looked himself over and gave me a wicked little grin. "I have it on good authority that you like a man like this. I have to admit it is rather comfortable."

He was right, I did, and I knew what, or should I say who, he was basing his decision off of, Caleb. I tried my best not to think of Caleb but I was failing miserably. Ugly words had been exchanged between us, things that we could never take back and so many of them were true.

Caleb was right when he said that Ken wasn't a threat. I couldn't picture myself spending the rest of my life married to Ken. I looked over at Pallo. He was adding water to one of the vases full of flowers he'd had delivered. I thought about having him around me every day. He'd risen to the challenge of taking care of me and not once pulled any moody vampire shit on me. The only problem with him was that I'd be destined to spend eternity in the darkness with him, and as for a family, I wasn't sure, but I didn't think he was able to offer me that. I'd never heard of a vampire having a child before and someday I wanted to be a mother. Not any time soon, but someday. I thought of asking him, but I didn't.

"I have wondered that myself," Pallo said quietly.

I turned and looked at him. I wasn't sure what he was talking about. "Wondered what?"

"Everything you were just thinking of--a life with you in the dark and whether or not I am able to produce a child again with you now that I am a creature of the night. It does not matter now anyway."

I didn't know what to say to him. I should have been angry with him for reading my thoughts again but I didn't think he did it on purpose. We seemed connected in some strange way.

He came to me, put his arm under mine and steadied me. His sweet smell enveloped me. I loved that about him. He always smelled fresh and sweet, almost like a woman, but was one hundred percent male.

My arm fit nicely into his and I had to pull on him to get my body up and standing. I thought about what he had said, about fathering a child with me again now that he was a vampire. My chest constricted. I knew from being told and having more and more flashbacks of my past life that I'd been pregnant with his child when I died. I wondered how our lives would have been different if I'd just run away with him when he had asked me. Instead, I ran from him, trying to protect him from Giovanni. He disappeared after that and I ended up in Caleb's bed. Pallo, I later learned, had ended up at the mercy of Giovanni. A part of him had to hate me for my poor decision. I hated myself and in truth it wasn't even me that made it--it was the old me.

Pallo turned to me and pulled me into his exposed chest. "Gwyneth, all things happen for a reason. I have never, nor will I ever, blame you for what I am. Giovanni and his people took your life and the life of our child away. He gave me eternal life. I am able to be here with you now because of that. I would have died long ago, and nothing in your faerie world of magic could have prevented that. So, do not ever feel guilty about events that transpired hundreds of years ago and that you have only broken memories of. You are not the same person you once were, you are stronger now."

I let him hold me. I tried to keep myself together but I couldn't. I let the emotions that had been threatening to eat me alive out. Pallo pulled my hair back and tipped my face up to him. I wanted to erase all the negativity from my past and start over again. I wanted more than anything to leave and never look back, to run as far away from my troubles as I could. How did that make me a stronger person? How could he claim I'd changed when I all wanted to do was to run?

I thought about heading into my office, getting the manila envelope out of the safe and assuming another identity, one with less baggage. Maybe I'd be able to fit in with normal people, the kind of people that didn't have magic or a thirst for blood. I looked into Pallo's dark brown eyes and knew I couldn't leave him behind. I wanted to take him with me. It was silly. He'd never leave his money and his power behind. He'd spent centuries carving his niche out in the society of the undead. I hated myself for thinking of running away and I was angry with him for thinking I'd changed. I was a coward.

He pulled my chin up harder and straightened my face to look directly at his. "The very fact you wanted to take me with you proves you are different, and if you feel you have no other choice, then you have but to ask me and I shall leave with you, *fata mia.*"

"Could you please try to stop doing that?"

"What?"

"Could you at least wait until I've verbalized my thoughts clearly?"

"Gwyneth, even as an immortal I do not have that kind of time," he said. I laughed through my tears.

I leaned up to give him a hug and found his lips touching mine. My head grew light and I closed my eyes. I waited for more but he pulled away from me. He backed up and left me standing alone.

"Pallo?"

"I am sorry. I did not intend to take advantage of you. I am sorry. I will send James up to take you out for some fresh air." Pallo turned and headed for the door.

"Stop right there, mister!" He obeyed, but didn't turn around. "You're the one preaching about how much stronger I am now. How can I be strong and vulnerable all at the same time?"

"I wish I knew the answer to that."

"Don't go, please."

"You and Caleb have much to discuss. I sensed...something in you when I brought you back. It is important that the two of you work out your differences."

I didn't bother expressing my displeasure with him or asking him what he was talking about. I had the feeling his antenna was in full mind-reading mode. I couldn't believe he'd be the one to pull away again. I didn't want to lose him, yet I felt powerless to keep him near me. He'd spent the last two months distancing himself from me, for reasons all his own, and just when I finally thought that he'd come around he pulled away again. Caleb had walked out and given up on me. Now Pallo was, too. I knew if he walked out that door it'd be over between us before it ever had a chance to get started again. It was for the best. He deserved better than me, an indecisive female who looked like someone he once loved.

Let him go, Gwen. Let him go back to his life. He was happy before you. Let him go.

Pallo glanced over his shoulder at me and walked out of the door. He had made his choice. I would be a big girl and learn to live with it. A sharp pain shot through my stomach. Doubling over, I grabbed for the bed. I hit the night stand instead and sent a vase full of yellow daisies crashing to the floor. The pain was so great that I couldn't scream out. I could only clutch myself tightly and claw at the floor to try to alleviate the pain. Whatever this was--it was tearing me apart.

I gasped, as the pain eased for a moment. The thought of calling out for help occurred to me, but I didn't do it. Dying seemed like a better option than forcing Pallo to help me yet again. Pain seized hold of me again and I bit down hard on my lower lip.

God, make it end...just make it end.

I'm not sure if I was praying for relief or death. Somehow, I think it was the latter of the two. Suddenly, strong arms wrapped around me and I looked up to see Pallo holding me. He put gently into the bed.

His touch made the pain ease up. I pulled him to me, leaving him no choice but to climb into the bed with me. Turning my back to him, I let him spoon me while he ran his hands over my stomach. He jerked his hand back and leaned over to look at my stomach. I looked down too, it had gotten bigger. The faint sound of the chanting monks began again and I pulled Pallo tighter to me.

"They're coming, Pallo. I can feel it."

"Rest now and do not forget what I told you about the dreams...do not let me take you to the altar, no matter what."

"I'm not planning on going to sleep."

Pallo's cool energy rose up around me. "Yes, you are." It slammed into me as sleep swallowed me whole.

Chapter 24

Reaching out, I touched the cave wall. I waited to see the robed men again. They didn't show. I looked in at the circle altar room and waited for Pallo to show up. He wasn't there either. I turned and walked down one of the halls. It narrowed and I had to turn sideways to make it through.

"Gwyneth!" I heard Pallo's voice behind me. I turned to face him.

"Pallo? What's happening? Why do we keep having these dreams? Why the hell did you force me to sleep?"

"Something else took hold of my power. I did not mean to do that to you. Please…" He spun around fast. From my vantage point all I could see was his body, but he must have seen someone coming. His eyes widened as he looked back at me.

"Run. Do not look back...do not let me touch you. Run!"

What? Why did he want me to run and where was I supposed to run to? Just then a breeze tickled my neck. I turned and glanced behind me. There was an opening in the cave. I could see the night sky out it. I looked back at Pallo and heard the chanting men approaching.

"Go, Gwyneth!"

"No, I'm not leaving you here with them. I know that you were walking out of my life for good, but I'm not willing to walk out on you. I won't let anything happen to you!"

His eyes flashed black. "Go!" His voice was deeper than normal and had a hint of a snarl in it. It didn't matter how he spoke to me I wouldn't leave him here with those men.

"Go ahead and eat me. I'm not going anywhere." I folded my arms in protest.

His hand shot out at me, narrowly missing me. "Go now! They want me to take you. Gwyneth, they are calling my demon to the surface, they are controlling it...not me...if they will it to kill you, then it will." I watched flecks of red spin into his eyes. He jerked his head back and cried out.

That did it for me. I turned and ran. I hit the opening and the cold night air smacked me in the face. The ground was freezing beneath my bare feet. At least I wasn't naked this time, thank God.

This time I was wearing an off-white gown that hung almost to the ground.

"Wake up, Gwen. Wake up!" I pushed my way through the dense forest brush and ran. Something swished and landed behind me. I knew it was Pallo. I ran faster and stepped down hard on something. Pain radiated up my foot and into my leg. I fell to my knees, and closed my eyes to focus, trying my best to block out how much my foot hurt. I felt it then. The power looming around me.

I turned my head slowly and saw Pallo standing there in black loose pants and no shirt. The night breeze blew his wavy brown hair around. He looked like a Greek god, all except for his black eyes and fangs. He'd wanted me to kill him if he came to me like this again, but I knew I couldn't. I wondered if he attacked me now, even though this was a dream, would I die? I thought about my bleeding breast and knew the answer to that was yes.

Pallo took a step towards me. I scrambled backwards to get away from him. My foot caught in my long gown and I ended up getting twisted in it. I fell flat onto the ground. Pallo knelt down in front of me, slowly.

I pulled at the gown trying to get it untwisted. My hands brushed across my stomach. It was bigger now. My lower abdomen was now rounded out at least four inches from its normal flat position. I managed to get the gown down just as Pallo's fingers touched my legs. I hadn't noticed how long his fingernails got when he did his vampire thing before, but I did now.

"Pallo?"

He snarled at me. *Nope, Pallo wasn't home right now.* I tried to pull my power up but nothing came. Whoever was responsible for these dreams had seen to it that I was bound, unable to use my magic.

Pallo leaned over me. His fingers moved slowly up my leg and inner thigh. He pushed his face down between my legs, burying his face deep into me. I tensed up, expecting him to sink his teeth in one of my most vulnerable spots. He kept his head there but made no move to hurt me.

My hand skimmed across something hard and jagged. It was a rock. That must have been what I'd stepped on. I cupped it in my hand and waited for him to get closer. He moved his fingers up more, over my mound. He stopped on my abdomen. I cramped up and cried out. I brought the rock against the side of his head, hard. I had to control myself--I too, possessed strength stronger than a human did and I didn't want to kill Pallo. I just wanted to knock him out for a minute.

I brought the rock up fast and came into direct contact with the side of his head.

"Wake up!" I screamed.

Chapter 25

I woke screaming. I was outside. For a moment I thought that I was still dreaming but when I looked down at myself I didn't see the off-white gown. I was back in my clothes again, although, they were a great deal tighter. I reached down and unbuttoned my jeans. My belly popped out of them. I just stared at it. It was huge.

Something moved towards me, rustling branches as it went. My night vision was better than it used to be but not nearly good enough to see what was headed my way. My senses were keener, most likely one of the permanent side effects Pallo had talked about.

Scrambling to my feet, I looked around. I tried hard to get a sense of where I was. I could smell wood burning. I hoped that was the direction of my house but the sound was coming from that way. I made a split second decision and ran in the opposite direction.

I bit my lip hard to keep from crying out as a branch sliced my upper arm open. I grabbed the cut with my other hand and kept moving forward. My stomach got tighter as the cramps came and went. I fought against the urge to stop and throw-up. Stopping while something was chasing me would be very bad so I pushed deeper into the woods.

Living on over two hundred acres of woods seemed like a good idea when I moved out here. No nosy neighbors, no noise, and no one to help me if I needed it. I ran until I caught sight of a small brown structure.

I knew where I was now. I was about a mile away from the house. The structure was an old maple sugar shack. It had been built almost a hundred years before to help with the harvest of the maple from the trees. I'd been fascinated with it as a child. Then my adoptive parents died and left me the land it came with it.

I ran up to it and pushed an old piece of wood up to open the door. It stuck for a minute and I pushed harder. It gave and I ran in. The floor was dirt and the shack had nothing but an old table and fireplace in it. I looked around. There were no windows. I was thankful for that--to a point. No windows meant no moonlight and that equaled pitch black. I moved to the center of the shack and stood very still.

Something stepped on a twig outside the door. I drew in a deep breath and waited. I tried to call upon my magic, but it wasn't cooperating with me. It was fickle like that. I managed to only get a tiny bit of it to rise up.

Hey, I'd take it.

The door burst open and I lashed out. "Gwyneth?" I heard Pallo's voice.

I ran towards him, expecting to find him lying on the ground unconscious. He wasn't. He was standing to the side of the door staring behind him. His eyes widened as he watched a large branch from a tree snap off and fly to the ground. Good thing he was a fast mover. I turned and looked at him. I wanted to see his face. I had to know if he was still in his demon form.

"Look at me!" I screamed.

He reached his hands out to me and I took a step back. "No, it is fine...see." He came closer and I saw that indeed he was telling the truth.

Pallo opened his arms to me and I fell into them. He held me tight for a long time before he finally spoke. "I thought I made it clear that you were to kill me if I came at you in demon form in the dreams again."

I pulled back from him. The moonlight caught the side of his face and I saw the dried blood on his temple. I reached out to touch it and he winced.

"I'm so sorry, I...I just wanted you to wake up, I didn't mean to hurt you that bad."

Pallo grabbed my wrist. "Gwyneth, I told you to kill me. I am not mad at you for hitting me, I am mad that *all* you did was hit me."

My stomach cramped again. I leaned forward and put my hand on Pallo's shoulder to steady myself. His hand moved around my waist and brushed past my stomach. He lifted my shirt up and looked at it.

"Gwyneth!"

Glancing down, I saw it was moving! Pallo put his hand on it and it settled down, then his gaze fell onto mine.

"James told me that you and Caleb were using protection."

What the hell? Like I wanted to discuss my contraceptive choices with him.

Heat rose to my face. "Oh, he did, did he?" I wanted to smack James. I confided in him and he ran tattling to Pallo. I don't know why it surprised me, but it did. I knew Pallo was his Master, but I never thought he'd betray my friendship.

"We are...were...I am," I said, coldly.

"What about when you were with Ken?"

I thought back to the day on the desk. No, Ken and I never used protection. I wasn't able to contract any STDs and pregnancy wasn't an option with Ken. He wasn't a match for me.

Pallo ran his hands over my stomach. "You are with child. I have known since I found you in Caleb's arms on the side of the road." His voice was flat.

I pulled back and looked at him. Was he was joking. I reached down and touched my stomach. Butterflies crept into my belly. He was right, Oh my God, he was right!

"This can't be...I take birth control pills everyday, I take them, and I've felt sick ever since I started them, but I still take them."

Pallo touched my arm. "What do you mean, you feel sick?"

"Cold, the shakes, I thought it was the flu or a nasty side effect of the pills. I can't be pregnant. Caleb didn't..." I went to say that Caleb didn't glow the last time we'd had sex but stopped. When a faerie was ready to fertilize an egg their eyes swirl and change color. It is a built in birth control. Caleb was having problems controlling his and mine at first, but lately he'd been doing just fine.

Pallo reached out to me. "Caleb didn't what?"

I shook my head. I didn't want to talk about this with him. I wouldn't talk about our sex life with him. It would hurt Caleb too much. Not that Caleb's feelings should concern me. I hadn't seen or heard from him since my near death experience on the side of the highway. "Gwen, listen to me, you need to tell me what it is that you are thinking."

He never called me Gwen--this was serious. "I...can't be pregnant." I looked down at my stomach. Dr. Brown had explained how a *Si's* gestation period worked to me. I would grow at faster rate than a human woman would, but not this fast! Judging by my size I was guessing that I was far, but not that far along. Caleb and I had spent the day making love before he left to hunt the Enchantress, but I never noticed his eyes changing colors. Ken wasn't a match for me and Pallo was a vampire. As far as I knew they didn't produce children. It had to be Caleb's.

"Caleb," I said quickly. "He's going to want to know. He'll want to start planning, he'll want to...."

Pallo touched my arm. "I think the child is mine."

I stared at him and knew that my mouth had fallen open. "What?"

"I had to ask you about the others to be sure. Partly because I do not believe it myself." He looked away as he spoke to me. "When I found you in the dream, I sensed something different about you...I..." His head slumped downwards. "I could smell you, you smelled of me, of my..." He didn't finish.

I wanted to hit him for saying such lies but I could feel the truth in his words. I thought back to the first dream I'd had with him on the altar. They had called me the vessel as he'd spilled his semen in me. I thought about his black eyes as he bit down on my neck. My mind raced to our lovemaking during waking hours and how my eyes had burned.

My knees grew weak and I collapsed down onto the ground. Pallo was next to me in an instant trying to pick me up. I batted at him to get away from me. Reaching down, I touched my stomach.

"Is it a demon? Will it come out a vampire?"

I waited for him to say no, to tell me that what grew inside of me was a beautiful human child, but he didn't. He touched my stomach softly. "I do not know."

I cried and Pallo pulled me close to him. I let him. I didn't want to fight with him. It wasn't his fault this was happening to me. Whatever was going on was happening to us both.

Chapter 26

I clung to Pallo for the longest time. He finally had to pull me off him. He glanced up at the sky. I knew what he was thinking. Dawn was coming. I wanted to stay where we were until the events of the last few weeks made sense but Pallo didn't have that kind of time. I took his hand and let him guide me.

The walk back up to the house was quiet. Pallo and I held hands the entire time. We got back up to the porch and I stopped.

"I have to tell Caleb."

His grip on my hand tightened. "*We* have to tell Caleb." I didn't agree with that, but I didn't want to fight with him.

"Will you still marry him?" Pallo asked.

"What? I highly doubt that he's still going to want to get married. Besides, I never had a chance to tell you, I called the whole thing off. That's what set Caleb off that night. Even if that hadn't happened, I'm sure this would be too much, even for Caleb. Not many men are willing to marry a woman pregnant with another man's child."

Pallo smiled but it didn't look friendly. "Ah, I forget sometimes that you have little to no memories of your past with us."

I thought about what he was saying and then it hit me. This had happened before. I had lived with Giovanni for many years. He was the tall black haired vamp with tons of attitude. It's because of Giovanni that I met Pallo. He was the son of a wealthy vineyard owner and still very human. He and I fell in love at first sight. We spent many months together before he asked me to marry him and run away from Giovanni. I'd taken great pains to keep Pallo a secret from Giovanni because I knew what a monster he could be. I knew Giovanni would kill him and I refused to allow that to happen. I ran away and left Pallo, in an attempt to keep him safe. The saddest part of it all was that I knew I was with his child. Apparently, guilt had gotten the best of me, because I'd gone back to look for him. He was gone. I had nowhere left to go. Giovanni would kill me and the child for betraying him and Pallo was missing. So, I did the only thing I could think of, I went back to Caleb.

Caleb and I had been lovers at one time but I'd left him for Giovanni. He had every right to refuse me but he didn't. It started out as friendship. He helped me plan for the child and look for Pallo. After months of waiting, rumors came back that Pallo was dead. I sought comfort in Caleb's arms. The love that had once been between us returned. Shortly after that, Pallo walked in on Caleb and me making love. He was furious and a monster. He'd gone looking for me at Giovanni's when I disappeared. All he found was an angry master vampire.

Giovanni sired Pallo to get back at me. He knew I'd grown to hate his dark side and knew I would hate Pallo's as well. When Pallo returned to find Caleb and me, he took one look at my swollen belly and assumed the child was Caleb's. A fight broke out and I ended up being chased down a hall and then pinned to a wall by him. In the end, Pallo sent me fleeing from him to avoid hurting me. Somehow, I fell into the clutches of Giovanni again. My life and the child's life ended shortly after that.

I looked at Pallo and understood fully what he was talking about. Caleb had taken me into his bed and planned on marrying me once before, even though he knew full well the child I carried was Pallo's. However, last time around Caleb and I hadn't been matches. We were incapable of creating life together and he knew that. This time around, we were very capable of it and I knew he would be devastated if this child was Pallo's and not his.

"Gwyneth, do not look so sad. Once you were very happy to be with my child."

"It may not be your child. In fact, odds are pretty damn good it's not. Vampires don't produce children. The dead can't create life." I wanted to hit him. I wanted to hit anyone. I wasn't sure about the last part. I'd never looked into vampire fertility rates.

"You are correct, I have no doubt that your *little* Caleb has had ample opportunity to give you this." He reached out and touched my stomach. I pushed his hand off me and opened the front door.

Caradoc and James were sitting in the living room staring at us as we walked in. I didn't need to ask if they overhead, they were vampires they had amazingly good hearing. Caradoc stared at Pallo and James stared at me with shock in his eyes. I thought I saw a flash of anger in them but I didn't stop to ask how he was taking it. At the moment, I didn't care.

I headed up the stairs. Pallo followed close behind me. I walked into my room and closed the door behind me. I'd hoped he'd take it for the sign that it was--I wanted to be alone. I pulled my jeans off. There was no way I was going to make it in those. I searched around my closet and decided on a long navy blue skirt and a white sweater. I grabbed my knee high black boots out of the closet and put them on.

Standing back, I looked at myself sideways in the mirror. My swollen belly stuck out enough to tell I was expecting and I looked horrible. My skin was so much paler than usual, and that wasn't saying much.

I headed towards the door and stopped before I opened it. I took a deep breath and went out. Pallo was leaning against the hallway wall. His gaze raked over me.

"Going somewhere?" he asked.

"Yeah, as a matter of fact I am. I'm going for a drive to clear my head."

He stood in front of me. "No, you are staying here. You have not been dealing well with this pregnancy, you have been very sick. Driving around by yourself is not a wise decision, and it is not going to happen. Should I bring James up to remind you what your last drive around town nearly cost him?"

I began to argue and then stopped. It wasn't like me to back down from a fight. "You're right," I said. He looked shocked. "I won't go alone, I'll take Caradoc."

"No, I will go with you."

"You're the reason I need to think." I walked away from him and he grabbed my arm. I sucked my lip in because the arm he grabbed was the one I'd cut on the tree branch. He pushed me, softly, back against the wall and put his face in front of mine.

"I will go with you." His mouth came down on mine. At first I kept my lips closed. My body grew warm from his touch. My inner thighs tightened. I parted my lips and kissed him back. My body reacted to him. I wanted him, I'd always want him, and he knew it. I put my hand on his chest and pushed him back from me.

"We can't do this," I said. His hand slid down to my stomach. It was a very subtle way of saying we already did. "Pallo, I'll take Caradoc."

"No, I will accompany you or you will not go!"

My temper flared. "Who the hell do you think you are? You don't own me. I will come and go as I please."

I slapped his face and headed off down the hall. I saw a black blur pass me. I headed down the stairs and ran right into Pallo. I'd forgotten how fast he could be when he wanted. He grabbed my shoulders and pushed me back towards my room. "Get out of my way!" He picked me up. I tried kicking my feet in protest but it was useless. "I won't spend the rest of my life with a sadistic-dictating-vampire!"

He didn't put me down but he did stop. "I will not watch you walk out on me again. I drove you away to your death with our child in your womb once already. I will not let that happen again. I could not live with myself if something happened to you." He glanced down at my stomach. A wave of guilt swept over me. Pallo wasn't trying to hold me hostage. He was trying to protect me. The last time he'd watched me leave pregnant I never came back.

I touched his cheek. He pulled away from me. I'd hurt his feelings saying those nasty things to him. "I'm sorry, Pallo. I was just angry and I wanted to hurt you."

He carried me through my bedroom door. I tried to turn his head towards me, but it wouldn't budge. "Pallo, please, I'm sorry…."

"I am not angry with you."

"Could've fooled me."

He set me down on the edge of the bed and took two steps back from me. I was hurt. "I do not trust myself around you." The sexy expression on his face told me exactly what he didn't trust about himself.

That made me smile.

"So, if you don't trust yourself why bring me in here?" I lifted my arms and motioned around the bedroom.

Pallo's face twisted into a wicked little grin. "I am a hopeless fool." He let out a long sigh. "I will make you a deal, you stay up here and rest and I will go down and have James fix you something to eat, then if you still want to go out for a drive I will take you myself, anywhere you want to go."

I looked up at him. "Sounds good, all except the part about sleeping...the psycho chanting robed guys show up every time I shut my eyes."

"No, they show up every time *we* shut our eyes. I will stay awake while you rest. I will send Caradoc up to watch over you as you sleep. When I return, I will sit with you myself. I will wake you if there are any signs of trouble."

"Why can't you just stay here with me now? I know that you can call the boys without leaving this room or opening your mouth."

A devilish smile played across his face. "Ah, I have been caught. I want to make some calls regarding our dreams but I am very pleased to hear that you want me to stay with you."

I opened my mouth and then closed it again. What could I say? He was right. I moved up onto the bed and took my boots off. I slid under the covers and waited to hear Caradoc come in before I got too comfortable.

Chapter 27

I woke to the smell of chicken. Opening my eyes, I found James standing near the edge of my bed with a tray of food. He gave me a big white grin and looked down at the tray.

"Chicken soup, crackers, and milk, for the mommy-to-be."

"Mmm...smells great, and it's not from a can. I'm jealous."

James nodded his head to the side. "Boss-man thought you'd like it."

I turned quickly. Pallo was sitting on the bed next to me. "I didn't hear you come back in."

"You were very tired. Did you rest well?"

I reached up and took a cracker from the tray James was holding. "Yes, I did. In fact, I don't remember dreaming at all." I glanced out the window. It was still dark. I knew Pallo hadn't slept much during the day hours today. He'd been up and worried about me or worse yet, dreaming the same crazy dream as me.

"Why don't you get some sleep? I could watch over you, too," I said.

Pallo looked at James and then to me. "No, no you go and eat. James is becoming quite the domesticated one. Let him try out his skills on you." He leaned back on the bed. "On second thought, I think that I may rest for a bit. I am drained."

"But, Pallo, I think one of us should watch you, just in case." He ignored my comment. I grabbed his hand and placed it over my stomach. "If you believe what you told me, then you need to make sure you're safe, and here."

Pallo's gaze darted down to my belly and then back up to me. He knew full well that I was telling him that if he planned on being a father, then he'd better damn well start taking care of himself. He nodded his head.

"Very well, James, send Caradoc in, and when you are done stuffing her full of your cooking, take her for a drive, if she wishes to go."

My heart skipped a beat. He trusted me enough to come back to him. That meant a lot to me. He wasn't one who was prone to trusting people. I wouldn't let him down. I bent over and kissed his cheek.

Chapter 28

"So, do you think its Pallo's baby?" James asked.

I pushed my foot into his leg hard. He picked it up and continued rubbing it. We'd been lying on the couch watching movies for a few hours. He'd offered to rub my feet and I'd taken him up on it. I didn't really feel like having a heart to heart, but if I was going to do it, I was glad it was him.

"I don't know what to think."

"Yes, you do."

I wanted to kick him for being right. He knew me well. "Damn you."

"You're too late, try another one."

I sat up. "Shut-up!"

"Right then, I just wanted to know if I was going to be an uncle or not." I punched him in the arm and he fake sobbed. His face turned serious, fast. "You know, it *could* have been mine."

I thought about our night in the motel room. He was right. We'd come so close to having sex. "James, I haven't said thank you yet for what you did that night."

"There's no need to thank me."

The room was silent for a moment. My thoughts went back to his original comment. He could have easily been the father of my child if he wouldn't have stopped us. I weighed the options in my head. "I should have slept with James. He'd make a great daddy, he's my best friend, he's adorable in the want to lick every inch of his sexy body kind of way, he's caring, he can cook, he's the only 'mate' I have that isn't a demanding jerk the majority of the time, he's funny and sexy...wait, I already mentioned that...huh...must be because he's super sexy, he's thoughtful, he's hung like a horse, he's...."

"Sprouting an erection listenin' to you go on and on."

I froze. *Tell me I didn't say that all out loud. Tell me I didn't say that all out loud.* Hell, I'd said it all out loud. I closed my eyes tight, wishing myself away. I cracked one eye open. My wish didn't come true. I was still on the couch. Sure, where's a little faerie power when you need it.

I was embarrassed beyond belief. I moved to get up and James grabbed hold of my legs tightly. I looked at him, expecting him to lecture me on all the reasons why we could never be. He didn't.

"I'd have liked to be the one--to share this with you." He touched my stomach lightly and nodded.

"You are sharing it with me, James." I took his hand in mine and squeezed it. I rubbed the back of his hand with my thumb and concentrated on not crying. "You share more with me than anyone else in my life. Don't ever doubt that."

He dropped his head down, nodding slightly. I squeezed his hand harder. It was odd being around him. I didn't "think" about it. I didn't worry about every little thing. I was just me and he seemed to like me, quirks and all. Hell, he was weirder than me by a long shot and that's part of what attracted me to him.

"All in favor of a change of subject say aye," James said.

I rolled my eyes and laughed. He wasn't right in the head, then again, I wasn't holding a full deck either. I put my hand up. "Aye!"

"Great that's settled then." He rubbed my legs gently. "At least I got one bit of information out of our little roadside motel experience."

"What's that?"

"I got a rather nice peek at your *jack and danny* and was pleased to see you don't have a *bucket fanny*."

I laughed. "Speak English...jerk."

"Come on, Gwen. You know what a *jack and danny* is."

"Nope."

"It's your fanny."

I giggled. "Why the hell are you calling my ass a *jack and danny*?"

James covered his mouth, but I could still see him smiling--extra wide. Great, I'd missed something big. "Love, here in America fanny means arse, but were I'm from, it means something entirely different."

From the look on his face, I knew this had to be a doozie. "Okay, hit me with it. What's fanny mean to you?"

He ran his hand up my leg and cupped my mound. I drew in a sharp breath as I felt his power lifting, allowing the feelings he held back for us to peek out. He crawled up the couch and kept his hand on my sex. He nuzzled my cheek with his face and caressed me. "It's another word for...quim."

I moaned softly as he stimulated my clit through my clothes. My body tightened under his touch.

"You know what quim means, don't you?" He ground his hips against me as his tongue darted out and over my ear. "It means cunt."

James sat up fast and returned to his end of the couch as though nothing had ever happened. I couldn't feel his energy around me anymore. He must have gotten control of it. That was great and all, but what the hell just happened? "James?"

"Yeah?"

"Nothing," I said, as I stared down at him. "Hey, wait a minute. What does bucket fanny mean then?"

"I'm not sure I can demonstrate that one." He put his hands together forming a circle, then expanded the size of it considerably. The smile that spread across his face was priceless. I could get used to seeing him like that. "It suggests one has a large...umm...hell, a large hole to put the pole in."

"Are you saying I'm loose?"

He chuckled. "Not literally!"

I jabbed my foot back and caught his groin on accident. The smile left his face and was replaced by a rather painful expression. "Shit James, I'm sorry. I didn't mean to...."

"It's all right, love. I've no need of 'em at the moment anyway."

"Again, you wonder why it is that you don't have a steady girlfriend?"

"I think we both know why I don't have a steady gal." He winked at me and laughed. I went to jab him again but he sat straight up, tossing my legs on the floor in the process.

"Hey!"

"Pallo!" he said, flying off the couch and up the stairs. I followed close behind him.

James burst through the bedroom door a fraction of a second before me. He gasped. I came in behind him and he caught my body with his arm so I couldn't go any further. I looked up.

"Sweet Jesus!" was all I could get out. My mind had a hard time registering what I was seeing. Pallo was upright, a few feet to the right of the bed. He wasn't standing. He was levitating, at least ten inches off the floor with his arms were outstretched, and his head thrown backwards. Caradoc was holding a black cloth in his hand. It took me a minute to compute it was Pallo's shirt, or had been his shirt. It was a tattered mess. Pallo's upper body was bare.

Pallo hissed as if in pain with his head still back. Caradoc was blocking my full view of him and from where I stood it looked like he was cutting Pallo's chest open.

I made a move towards him. James stepped in front of me. "No."

"What the hell is he doing to him?"

Caradoc turned and looked at me, before he took a step back. My eyes widened as I watched a huge laceration appear across Pallo's chest. No one had touched him! Blood splattered across the room. Caradoc moved back in to try to stop the bleeding. I heard the sound of the robed men chanting. James stared at me and nodded--this time, he'd heard it, too.

James put his arm down and let me pass. I reached Pallo's levitating body and stopped just short of touching him. The chanting grew louder. Two more cuts ripped open across his chest. There was now only a small portion of him not cut up. I put my hand on his chest and called his name. His head flicked forward but his eyes stayed closed. I tried calling his name again. He didn't respond.

"Stop! Stop hurting him!"

The buzzing energy surrounded me, tugging on me ,wanting me to follow it. I glanced back at James. He was already shaking his head no and coming towards me. Pallo hissed again.

"I'll come, I'll come, don't hurt him anymore...please...I'll come."

Pallo's body lowered to the ground. Caradoc caught him before he hit the floor and put him on the bed. I pushed past him to check on Pallo and then realized how foolish that was. He had a heartbeat when he wanted to have a heartbeat I wouldn't be able to tell if he was okay.

"Is he dead?"

"If you mean dead in the literal form then yes."

I felt sick to my stomach and instantly broke down into tears. I reached for Pallo and wanted to wrap my arms around him.

James rushed over to me. "No Gwen! Caradoc doesn't understand what you mean. Pallo's not dead...well...not any more dead than he was before this. Caradoc didn't understand what you meant."

I shot Caradoc a nasty look. He bowed his head apologetically. "Caradoc, go and get blood for Pallo. James, you work on dressing his wounds."

"What are you plannin'?" James asked.

"I'm planning on going in after him."

"No, you are not goin' in. I don't know what the fuck is goin' on here, but that's no dream. Whatever the bloody-hell it is, it's deadly," James said, practically spitting on me.

"I know." I pushed past him and climbed on the bed next to Pallo.

James came around to yank me off. I called up enough power to knock someone out and waited for him to get close enough to me.

"James, if this doesn't work out...."

He looked at me puzzled as I raised my hand out. I brought it back down quickly on my own chest and released my magic. It felt like someone hit me in the chest with a brick wall. Darkness swept in around me.

Instantly, I found myself standing in the cave with the altar. I heard the murmured voices of the monks. They were clearing away from the center of the room. I screamed and ran forward when I saw what they were surrounding. They had Pallo's wrists and ankles shackled outward with chains. His body was stretched tight and off the ground. One of the robed men held a whip. I pushed past him and to Pallo.

His head was slumped down and I lifted it gently in my hands. Briefly, his eyes flickered opened and he lifted his head slowly.

"Gwyneth?"

"I'm here, Pallo, I'm here."

"No," he said softy.

I turned and glared at the robed men. My power burned to get out, to be free, to punish all that hurt him. I wanted to unleash it out. Incinerating all these bastards sounded like fun to me. "Fix him and take him down. Now!"

They gathered together, and grew silent.

"You will take him down and fix him or I will ward myself against dream invasions and you will NOT get me in here again."

I don't know what possessed me to threaten that, and I didn't think I had the power to do that, but I was betting I could find someone who did. They murmured amongst themselves before one of them stepped forward towards Pallo. He put his hands out, letting them linger just above Pallo's skin. I watched as the wounds pulled closed and sealed over. Pallo's pale perfect skin was all that was left. Two more men moved in and began to unchain Pallo.

"Now, we *will* leave this room. I can't wake for some time. I saw to that before I came in. You'll have us here in your...whatever the hell it is...for longer than normal. We will not...I repeat...we will not stay in this room."

Pallo dropped to floor. I bent down and helped him to stand. I took a step towards the exit. The man with the whip stepped in to my path. I let go of Pallo long enough to reach my hands out to the man. I almost touched him. He jumped back and let us past. I didn't look back.

Pallo was doing better by the time we made it out of the cave. He stood on his own and giving me a very nasty look. "Gwyneth, you should not have come."

I walked forward through the brush. "Right, you wanted me to stand there and watch you die?"

"Yes...that is exactly what I wanted you to do." He followed close behind me. "I can not believe that they let you come here. *Madonna!* If you want something done right, do it yourself."

"They didn't let me fall asleep. In fact, James was in the process of trying to stop me when I showed up here to get you."

"What did you do?"

Whistling and pretending to be innocent crossed my mind, for like a millisecond. "I used magic to knock myself out."

He grabbed hold of my shoulders and spun me around. "NO!"

"Too late now...besides, I couldn't watch that, Pallo, I had to stop it. I had to come. I couldn't let anything happen to you. You may not feel the same for me, but...."

"That is why they did it. That is why they tortured me. They did it so you would come. I refused to summon you. They tried to make me change, force my demon to the surface. They knew you would come, Gwyneth."

"Well, I guess they're smarter than you and what do you mean *summon* me to you?"

We walked more. Pallo tipped his head back and rolled it around, stretching. He looked a little uncomfortable with what he was about to tell me. "You know that I can summon my people."

"Yes, but I'm not..." I reached down and touched my swollen belly. "The baby, they wanted you to contact me through the baby. Can you do that?"

"Theoretically, if the child is mine, yes."

I put my hand out and stopped him. "Do it."

"No, Gwyneth, I do not wish to know. I would rather live in ignorant bliss than to know the child was not mine."

I glared at him. "Do it!"

He sighed, then gave me the quickest of kisses on my cheek before he vanished into thin air. I spun around in a circle looking for him. He was gone. Walking to my right, I stopped in mid-motion as my stomach cramped up. I backed up and headed the other way. The cramps eased and I felt compelled to run.

I ran until I came to a large dark oak tree. I knew to turn left there. I did and continued running. I pushed through a large bush and into a grass clearing. I didn't see any sign of Pallo but I knew he was there.

"Stop lurking and come out, I can feel you near me," I said.

Pallo touched my shoulder. My entire body reacted to him. I felt alive, free, and in need of him. I put my hand on his, letting him turn me around. I buried my head into his shoulder and cried.

"You cry because I am the father." His voice was low.

I pulled back from him a little and looked up into his brown eyes. "I'm crying because I should be upset that it's you and I'm not. What does that say about me?"

He exhaled out slowly and relaxed. He kissed my forehead, and wrapped his arms around me tighter. "I am the wrong person to ask, I am biased."

I laughed and pulled him close to me. "What did they do to us?"

"They helped us create a child together."

"But why?"

"That, I do not know."

Pallo ran his hand over my stomach. The baby kicked and Pallo felt it. He leaned down to put his head closer to the baby. I leaned in and met his lips with mine. His hands moved up around my back. We pulled close to each other with our lips still locked together. He reached around and slid his hand under my sweater. His hands were warm on my skin. He traced tiny circles on my stomach. Taking a step back from him, I pulled my sweater over my head. This left me nude from the waist up. I hadn't been able to wear a bra because my breasts were enlarged and were sore.

Pallo glanced down at me. "What about Caleb?"

"He left me, remember, and the engagement is off. Besides dream sex doesn't count, right?" A nervous laugh escaped my throat.

He rubbed my stomach. "What are you thinking?"

"I think that I need you right now."

"You are feeling this way because I called you to me. You will regret this when you wake."

"I haven't ever regretted sleeping with you. My only regret is that we always end up fighting. Were we always this way?"

Pressing my body against his, I moved my hands over his lower abdomen. I let my fingers dance along the edges of his black pants. I moved my fingers into the tiny line of hair that started just below his navel. I undid his pants and slid my hand in. His cock was thick and hard, ready for me. I wrapped my fingers around him and stroked him gently. He gasped.

"*Fata mia--anima mia.*"

"I never know what the heck you're saying to me. For all I know you could be calling me a six breasted seal maiden.

Pallo's face lit up as a sly grin washed over it. "Six breasts? Hmm, that would be something to see."

I couldn't hide my shock. Here we were, trapped in some fucked up dream state and he managed to be funny and sexy. Maybe they had training for that when he was young--how to woo the ladies, Italian style.

"No, it was more on the lines of winning the love of your immortal mate than wooing, but if you would prefer to think of it as such, then who am I to stop you?" His grin turned wolfish and the strangest feeling of Déjà vu came over me. "Gwyneth?"

I closed my eyes and leaned into him. The feel of his hard chest under my cheek made my body quake with need. It didn't help that my hand was still down the front of his pants. The minute he began to run his fingers through the back of my hair I knew--this was how it used to be between us. Pallo had been happy, full of life and excited about his future.

"No, Gwyneth...I was excited about *our* future." He began to grind his hips against me, leaving my hand working over him, stroking him. He seemed to grow even bigger as we went. It was clear--he wanted to do this as much as I did, maybe more. I pulled his cock out of his pants and held him tight in my hand.

"You want me, too."

"*Voglio fare l'amore con te,*" he whispered sweetly as he lowered our bodies to the ground. Pallo grabbed my arms as I went to lay back and pulled me to him, laying himself down on the hard ground. I looked into his brown eyes and put my lips to his. I knew he was lying down to keep me off the cold, damp, night grass.

I sat up to slide my panties off. I was no longer graceful at it. Now with my slightly rounded belly I was having problems. I managed to get them off. Pallo never said a word. He just smiled at me and pulled me towards him. I kissed him tenderly and moved my head down--finding his erect cock waiting for me. His skin tasted salty, warm, delicious. It was the first time I could ever remember it being anything but cool. I licked around the base of his cock, taking in his sweet scent. A small moan escaped his throat. I moved my lips over the head of him and took it into my mouth, allowing my tongue play with him as I moved my head up and down. I used one hand to help steady myself. I used my other hand to work his pants down a little further.

"Gwyneth..." He tugged gently on my shoulders and eased me back towards his face. Straddling him, I pulled my long blue skirt up. His cock sought me out, seeming to know exactly where I would be. As he neared the opening of my pussy, I leaned forward to kiss him. My belly was too big to get to his lips. He laughed softly and moved my hips ever so slightly so he could slip the rounded head of his shaft into me. He eased in slowly. I drew in a deep breath and put my hands on his chest to balance. I let the weight of my body come down thus driving him deep within me. I rode him gently at first and then I increased my pace.

Pallo's hands moved to my hips. He helped to direct my body to move in the most stimulating way for the both of us. Numbness swept upwards from my toes. It moved into my calves, inner thighs, before finally settling in between my legs, causing me to cry his name out and lean forward. His hands found mine. He laced his fingers tightly in mine and pulled me to him. Our mouths met and he pushed his hips up hard causing his cock to thrust even deeper into me. My body was still tingling from my own orgasm when his struck. His cock throbbed deep within me, filling me with his essence. The idea of spending eternity soaking him up sounded perfect to me.

I tried to lean down and kiss him again but it was too uncomfortable for me. The look on his face screamed contentment. I entertained telling him how much I loved him but it didn't seem like enough--it never seemed like enough with Pallo. Telling him that I couldn't breathe without him was more appropriate but I didn't have the nerve.

I slid off him slowly and moved down to lie next to him. I lay there with my leg up over his naked body and my head tucked neatly into the crook of his arm. He turned and kissed my forehead as he brought his other hand around to touch my arm. Holding onto him like this felt perfect.

The baby kicked. Pallo moved his hand down to touch my stomach.

"Did you feel that?"

Sadness filled his eyes. "Yes Gwyneth, but I do not sense a child so much as my own power within you. I cannot explain it..." His arm stiffened and he leaned over and whispered in my ear. "Cover yourself and move to my other side."

I didn't question him. I grabbed my sweater and slid it back on. I pulled my skirt down and slid across him, pulling his pants up as I went. He kept a hand on my chin the whole time to look as though he was only paying attention to me. I knew better, I could see it in his eyes. He'd sensed someone or something near us and he wanted me out of the line of fire.

I moved to the other side of him and tried to stand. It wasn't as easy as it used to be. Getting off the ground now took a great deal more effort. Pallo rose to his feet and put his hand out to me. I took it. He pulled me to him and put his face into my neck like he was kissing me.

"Whoever lurks there waits for permission to come forward. Stay behind me and if I should change again here, do what you must to keep me at bay. You have the child to protect now."

I appreciated him letting up on the whole kill him thing but was nervous about the person hanging around watching us. I wondered how much of the show they'd been privy to. My guess was the entire show.

Pallo looked out into the darkness. "Come."

He pulled me completely behind him. I couldn't see anything there. It was like trying to see past a linebacker! I poked my head around the left of him to see who our visitor was. The very fact that we had a visitor didn't surprise me in the least. I knew we were in some sort of magically charged dream. I had a feeling that every move we made was under close surveillance.

My stomach cramped tightly and I had to grab Pallo's shoulder to keep from falling over. His hands moved to steady me but he continued to look out into the darkness.

"I can help her," a familiar voice said.

Pallo never took his eyes away from the direction the voice had come from. The pain gripped me again. This time it was so intense that I screamed out with it and clawed at Pallo's arm. He didn't seem to mind.

"Come," Pallo said.

I watched a figure come out of the darkness at us. He wore a robe, but instead of brown like the others, his was dark red. He seemed much taller than the others did. I wasn't planning to line them up side by side for a comparison, so I didn't dwell on it too much. He came within ten feet of us and Pallo told him that was far enough. He nodded. I tried to catch a glimpse of a face beneath the robe but all I saw was darkness.

The red-robed man put his hands up in a manner that suggested he was harmless. I let out a small snort. *About as harmless as a starving crocodile!* Pallo turned to me and frowned. I couldn't help myself. From my viewpoint, these guys were the reason we were neck deep in trouble.

"I've only come to help." I knew that voice. Somehow, it was familiar to me, yet I couldn't come up with a reason why.

Pallo moved his body in front of mine. "Who are you?"

"That is not important. What is important is the fact that she is dying."

Pallo reached back and grabbed my hand. I held tight to him as he caressed me with the lightest of touches.

"I'm sure you have noticed her growing colder, acting stranger and then there is the obvious…" He gestured towards his stomach. "The power that grows within her is draining her life force. She cannot sustain it much longer. My mistress hoped the faerie would be strong enough to bring it to term, but it is plain to see she is not."

I doubled over in pain again. The red-robed man took a step forward. "Her body craves blood and her senses are turning more vampiric by the minute. She shares your power and your strength each time you enter her body, but she needs more. She needs another power source. I can offer her that. Let me enter her--allow me to give her my seed, my power, and I can give her my magic as well."

Chanting voices sounded from all around us. The red man took another step forward. *"Feed the seed, feed the seed."*

"Leave us! You will not harm her or our child," Pallo said, his voice deeper than normal.

Shit, a shift was on the horizon if he didn't calm down. As much fun as standing behind a "daddy demon" sounded, I'd have to pass.

The red-robed man let out a maniacal laugh. "Do you really believe a child is in her? No, you know better than that, Vampire!

She is carrying part of your power in her and that of another, but no child will come of it. She is empty, merely a vessel."

No child? Merely a vessel?

"What the fuck is in me?" I tried to step towards the man but Pallo grabbed me and refused to let me move.

The chants grew louder. "That is something only you can answer. Look within."

"Great, I get an OB-red-robed-asshole for a spiritual adviser."

"Gwyneth," Pallo said, his voice stern.

"No, I need to know. If I'm not carrying a baby...our baby, then what am I carrying?"

The "fountain of wisdom." He lifted his arms. "Look within, faerie."

I closed my eyes to block some of the pain and a sad reality hit me. "It's raw power! Ohmygod! It's evil, full of hate and rage and...I won't survive the birth...will I?"

"No," the man said, and disappeared. The chanting stopped.

Pallo turned to me and pulled me close. He began to say something comforting. I put my finger on his lips. "No, there's nothing you can do to fix this. Don't tell me it will be okay. I want to be brave and tackle this head on, Pallo, but I'm scared."

"So am I, Gwyneth."

Chapter 29

Something touched my stomach. I opened my eyes, saw the familiar contents of my room and breathed a sigh of relief. I turned to see who was touching me hoping that it was Pallo. It was Dr. Gideon Matthews. Pallo was pressed against the far wall, carefully watching every move the doctor made.

"How far along is she?" Pallo asked.

Dr. Gideon looked down at me and shook his head. "I've never seen anything like this and I've seen a lot. I don't have the right equipment here, but I would guess somewhere around the fifth month, according to a human cycle. The heartbeats...or whatever they are, are strong."

We both stared at him. "Heartbeats?"

"Yes, I hear more than one, but it's strange, unlike any heartbeat I've ever heard before." He stood up and pulled my sweater back down over my stomach. "Gwen, I can't tell without the proper equipment, but this doesn't seem normal--well, as normal as you would be pregnant. I'm concerned with the fact that you were taking massive doses of what you were told were birth control pills. When Pallo called me and told me about your situation, I immediately began running tests on the pills Dr. Brown left for you. The pills weren't for preventing pregnancy at all."

I sat up fast, a little too fast. "What?"

"They were actually more of a fertility drug. It's the strangest thing I've ever seen. I know that a spell had to have been put on them. I just don't have the background to know what kind it is. I'm sending some over to the local coven...Don't worry, I'll keep everything very hush, hush."

Pallo walked closer to us. If I didn't know better, I'd say he seemed hesitant to come near me. "Can you tell what grows inside her?"

Dr. Gideon scratched his chin and shook his shaggy head of red hair. "No, I think we should look into doing an ultrasound on her soon. I do know that it's not human, but then again neither are either of you."

I nodded and another wave of pain hit me. Dr. Gideon ran to me. The pain worsened. Pallo touched my hand and it let up. They exchanged looks, nodded, and headed out into the hall together. Pallo pulled the door closed behind them. I listened and was surprised to find that I could hear them, even through the thick door.

Vampirism has its perks.

"This thing, it told her that she would not survive the birth, do you agree? Will Gwyneth die attempting to bring this to term?"

I heard the hushed voice of Dr. Gideon next. "I'll be amazed if she makes it through the pregnancy...let alone to term. These things in her are not normal. They are draining her at an alarming rate. Bring her in to my office tomorrow. I'll take a look at her there. I can't make any promises. I'm going to go make some phone calls about this. Oh, Pallo...make your peace with her now. At this rate she'll deliver within a week, and well...you know."

"Thank you, Doctor."

The door opened and Pallo stepped back in. He forced a smile onto his face. I looked towards the wall. I didn't need his false smiles to soothe me. I needed the truth.

He walked towards me. "Are you hungry?"

I shook my head no. He came and sat on the edge of the bed. I heard a movement downstairs and then I heard James cursing silently under his breath about dropping the bread on the floor.

"I don't want to eat anything he's sending up right now. My luck the sandwich will be hairy."

Pallo appeared shocked. "You heard that?"

I nodded. He put his head down. He knew what that meant--I'd heard every word he and the good doctor had said. I faced the wall again. Pallo moved up and touched my shoulder. I jerked away from him. I didn't want to be touched right now. I just wanted to be alone. He bent down, kissed me and left the room.

Chapter 30

"Come on Gwen, get up," James said as he sat next to me on the bed with his hand on my thigh.

"Why did Pallo send you in here? I told him and I'll tell you...leave me alone!"

"You can't lie 'round forever, besides you're getting a bit gamey." He nudged me slightly. I put my knee up and pushed him off the bed.

"Hey!"

"Hey, hell! I'm not getting up. End of discussion."

James stood up and gave me a dirty look before storming out of the room. The door slammed shut behind him. That was fine by me. I didn't want anyone near me. I was perfectly happy to lie in bed and feel sorry for myself. I didn't need a support system right now. No, now I just needed a Do Not Disturb sign on the door.

The door opened again. "Go away."

"No, I am afraid we cannot do that," Pallo said.

I looked up to see him standing in the entrance way with Caradoc and James. They looked like they could be male strippers--Vampire Chippendales. Caradoc had on dark black jeans and a white loose silk shirt. James was wearing his signature all black ensemble and his hair was back to normal, well, if you consider bleached blond and spiked normal, then yeah it was back. Pallo caught my eye. He was wearing a dark brown tight shirt with a scoop neck and a pair of light tan pants. I'd never seen him look that way. The shades of browns were amazing on him. They pulled out the highlights in his brown hair and his eyes, leaving me breathless. A knowing grin spread over all three of their faces.

"What's so funny?"

"You are getting cleaned up and going out with us tonight, like it or not."

They all swept around me. Caradoc picked me up. James held the door and Pallo waved at me. I tried to kick him. He dodged out of the way and laughed. Caradoc carried me down the hall to the bathroom. James opened the door and I saw that they had drawn a bath for me. I waited for Caradoc to set me down, he didn't. He walked me right up to the bathtub.

I looked up into his slender face and checked his green eyes for signs that he was about to dump me into the tub fully clothed. He was unreadable, as usual. "You wouldn't?"

He nodded and smiled. "I would."

Taking on three hardheaded vampires was stupid. I gave up. "You win. Put me down, I'll get cleaned up."

Caradoc set me down and walked towards the door. I called out to him. "Hey, tell Pallo that he's gonna get it when I get a hold of him."

Caradoc's gaze went to my stomach, which was now huge. Two days had passed since Dr. Gideon had come by, but my body looked like I was in the final month. I'd refused to go and get an ultrasound done. What was the point? I wasn't going to survive the birth, and even if I did, I wasn't even sure what I was giving birth to. Would it help me to have an image to go off of? No, I didn't need to see what kinds of demonic powers were alive in me--I could feel them.

Shutting the door behind him, Caradoc left me to get cleaned up. I pulled off my clothes and climbed in the tub the warm bath water. I slid under and wet my hair down. Pallo had been kind enough to make sure my shampoo and conditioner were within arm's reach for me. That saved his life, a little, with me. I put a small dollop of lavender scented shampoo in my hand and worked it through my hair.

When I was all done in the tub I stood slowly and stepped out. I heard the door crack open. Pallo poked his head in. "Is it safe?"

"If you're wondering if I still want to kill you, then the answer is no. If you want to know if I'm upset with you, then the answer is yes." I tried unsuccessfully to wrap the towel around me. I needed at least two towels to make it around my stomach now.

How embarrassing.

I looked down at myself. The only things on my body that had changed were my breasts and my stomach. My breasts were large to begin with, now they were downright obscene. My stomach was campaigning for second place in that department as well.

"I think you look lovely."

"I look like a beached whale. I'm going to have to wrap a sheet around me to go out in public."

Pallo smiled and stepped back out into the hall. I brushed my hair and teeth. The door opened again and Pallo stepped in carrying bags. I looked down at the logos. He'd been maternity clothes shopping!

"Not me, James and Caradoc," he said. I was used to his ability to read my thoughts, it no longer creeped me out.

There was a ton of bags. "Good heavens, how much did they buy?"

"I think they got one of everything. I am not a hundred percent sure, though."

"Pallo, I'll be dead before I can wear all that."

He stepped past the bags and grabbed my shoulders. "That is not funny, Gwyneth."

"I wasn't joking."

We both knew the hard truth. I would not survive the delivery. There was no use pretending like everything was fine, it wasn't. I'd gotten pregnant with the assistance of fertility drugs that I thought were birth control, chanting crazy monk guys, and a dead guy in demon form.

Yeah, I was screwed.

I bent down, grabbed some undergarments, which looked to be industrial strength, and a pair of jeans. I put them on and frowned.

"I'm wearing jeans that have an elastic panel built into them."

"I can see that."

I growled at him and he laughed. He bent down and pulled out a navy blue long-sleeved acrylic sweater. He handed it to me and smiled. "I am guessing James picked this out. It matches your eyes."

I took it from him, a bit puzzled. "Why do you think James picked it?"

"Oh, my naïve little faerie, I do love you."

I tried to hide my excitement, but I don't think I did a very good job. He'd said that he loved me. Was I reading too much into his comment?

"Why do you always refuse to ask what is on your mind?"

I rolled my eyes and took the top from him. "Maybe because I know you'll save me the time and just pluck the thoughts out of my head."

"Do you wish for me to address your concern?"

Address my concern? Oh, that was just the way I wanted him to handle our situation. Men!

"Gwyneth, you may be even more stubborn than me."

"Don't make me hurt you," I said, laughing slightly.

"Your concerns are unnecessary. I said what I meant, Gwyneth. I am not a man who casually offers his love. I have only loved two women in over two hundred years."

Hearing that he'd loved someone else hurt. The guy had been alive a hell of a long time to only have feelings for one person, I was being ridiculous again. Must have been the non-pregnancy, pregnancy hormones.

His laugh was warm as it ran over me. "*Fata mia*, do you not see that you are both women I have loved. I understand you are you, yet you are different. It is wrong to lump you into one entity."

Damn, when the hell did he become Casanova? Perhaps it was in his genes--his very, very sexy genes.

Neither one of us commented further. Besides, what was I supposed to say? Thanks for loving the two of me? Yeah, see my dilemma.

I headed toward the door. Pallo stopped me and handed me a pair of black slip-on shoes. I took them, but had to hand them back to him to help me get them on. Humiliation in the form of footwear, always fun.

Pallo stood and wrapped his arms around me tight. "What if I were to ask you to marry me instead?"

"Why, you looking for a short-term commitment? I'll be dead in a few days."

"Gwen," he said, his voice stern.

I pulled back and looked at his face. He was serious. "Pallo, vampires don't get married. They don't do the *commitment thing*...James told me that...."

"James?" Pallo looked disgusted.

I put my hand on his cheek. "Stop! I asked him about it once and he told me. Don't go getting all pissy with him about it."

"You asked him about vampires making commitments? Why?"

"Now who's being naïve?"

His face softened. He leaned in and kissed me. I didn't push him away. "So, what is your answer?"

My eyebrows went up. "What was the question?" He looked angry. Then it hit me, the marriage thing. "Well, you didn't come right out and ask me and I don't think it's in your nature, as a vampire, to settle down with one woman for all eternity. You seem to enjoy letting me in for brief moments and then shutting me out."

I turned to head out of the bathroom. Pallo's hands shot up and pushed the door closed. He pinned me back against it. He wasn't hurting me so I didn't make a big deal about it.

"Do not presume to know my nature, Gwyneth. You have no idea how many years my heart ached to have you back. I did horrible things to try to forget you...to forget the pain. Gwyneth, I do not think you should be so quick to assume that I would not want to be with you forever, when in fact I have spent forever wanting you."

I didn't know what to say. Of course I would commit to him. I'd wanted him to ask me since the moment I'd walked into Necro's Magik World two months ago and first laid eyes on him. If I'd felt this way in my last life about him then I could see why I would leave two immortals to be by his human side.

I searched for the right words for the moment and came up empty handed. The best I could do was cry tears of joy and triumph that my dreams of being loved by him were coming true-- even if only for a few short days.

I touched Pallo's cheek. He turned his face into my palm and closed his eyes. He kissed my thumb and brought his hand to mine. He leaned into me and our mouths found one another and we savored every second of the other's touch.

Someone knocked on the door. I jumped and banged heads with Pallo. "Sorry," I said reaching up to rub my head.

He smiled down at me and looked at the closed door. "What is it Caradoc?"

"Excuse me, Master, but Gwen has an important call. I attempted to take a message but they wished only to speak to her."

Pallo stepped back and I opened the door. We headed down the hall to my room. I picked up the phone.

"Gwen?"

I didn't recognize the voice on the other end. "Yes?"

"Gwen, this is Mark." I sat down on the bed and instantly felt like I was going to throw up. The only Mark I'd ever heard of was Caleb's partner. If he was calling me then something was wrong with Caleb. "I work with Caleb."

"I know who you are, Mark, what's wrong. Is Caleb...?"

He cleared his throat. "Caleb and I were hot on the trail of our latest bounty, and we lost contact with each other, and...well...that was three days ago. I haven't spoke to him since then and...well...we kind of made a promise to each other that if anything should ever go wrong, we'd contact the other one's family...and...well...."

"And, you're calling me because you promised him you would." As I said it, my throat went dry.

"Yes."

"Mark, I'm going to give the phone to a close friend of mine. Tell him everything that happened the last time you saw Caleb. No, come to think of it, tell him everything you know about this case."

"I'm sorry but I can't discuss this with...."

I cut him off. "Mark, I'm sure you're a great guy. Caleb trusts you, so I should as well, but know this, I am 'just' like Caleb, I posses the same gifts he does and you know what gifts I'm talking about. Do not make me come after you."

"Is that a threat, lady? I hunt evil shit down for a living, babes."

"No, Mark, that's a promise. And, as far as you hunting 'evil shit down for a living'...ha...honey, I was born to rule the Dark Realm. 'Evil shit' gets nervous when I'm around. I will hunt you down and peel the skin from your body inch by inch, keeping you alive so I can enjoy every moment of it. Don't think for one minute that I'm joking. I don't joke when it comes to people I love and if you give me enough time I will think of a more creative punishment for you. I'm surrounded by men who have had hundreds of years worth of practice. Now, are you willing to talk to my friend or not?"

"Yes," he said, his voice small.

I handed the phone to Caradoc and ran to the bathroom. Pallo came rushing in behind me. I sat on the closed toilet seat, with my head bent down, splashing water on my neck from the sink.

"I'm being punished," I said, still looking at the floor.

"For what?"

I touched my stomach and looked up at Pallo. "This."

"Be honest with yourself. There has been outside, mystical interference."

"No, Pallo, you want honesty, then you should know that this happened with Caleb, not only because of this..." I said, touching my stomach again, "but, because I wanted what you asked me to be true. I wanted you to really want to spend eternity with me. When Caleb asked me, I felt pressured--almost obligated to. It's not that I don't love him, but it's not the same as with you...damn you! Damn you for being you! You're like a drug, a dangerous drug that I can't kick, that I don't even want to kick." I put my head down and let the tears come out. It felt good to cry. It's what I spent most of my days doing anymore. I was weak and just as foolish as I'd been the last time I was on this earth--maybe more so.

"Gwyneth, I think it will make you happy to know the promise you made to Mark proves you have changed and that you are stronger this time. The Gwyneth of old would have never been so bold as to threaten a man."

"I meant every word of it," I said, referring to my promise of peeling Mark alive if he didn't help me.

"I know."

Pallo left me alone. I appreciated that. I didn't need his comfort right now. Besides, I knew that it wouldn't be sincere. He and Caleb were not exactly friends but not exactly enemies either.

Chapter 31

I heard the guys banging around down in the kitchen and went to see what was going on. Rounding the corner, I saw them all leaning over a trunk on the table. The black trunk was from the basement. It was Caleb's. I never opened it. He told me it was some old tools. I suggested he put them out in one of the barns with the rest of the tools, he said he would rather just store them in the basement. As I watched James pull a long shiny silver sword from the trunk, I knew why Caleb wanted them in the house.

"When do we leave?" I asked.

All three of them turned and looked at me. Pallo motioned for me to follow him into the living room. He tried to get me to have a seat on the couch. I refused. I knew what he was getting at. He wasn't going to let me go.

"I already know...I can't go."

"No, you cannot come along. We are meeting this Mark shortly after dark, and I do not want to have to worry about you along with Caleb. Besides, I think that you would make Mark nervous. If I were him, I would be very concerned about being around you right now." Pallo smiled. If I had to put a label on it I'd say that he looked pleased that I had it in me to be a sociopath. "Now, you are not staying here alone. I tried to get a hold of Sharon first, but I have not, as of yet, been able to reach her, so I...."

Someone knocked on the door. Pallo glanced at me and then to the door. He seemed a little uneasy. I knew that he'd been trying to brace me for whoever was behind the door. James poked his head around the corner and pointed at Pallo. I knew he meant it was Pallo's fault not his.

"Where's Gwen?" I heard Ken say.

Monty, can I have door number two, please?

I shot a nasty look at Pallo. He knew damn well that Ken and I weren't talking. Pallo turned his back on me and looked towards the front foyer.

"Ken, how nice of you to come on such short notice," Pallo said.

"Sure, you said it was important. Any leads on Caleb's whereabouts?" He stepped in and looked over in my direction. "I called around on this guy, Mark, and he seems legit...Holy fucking hell! Gwen? What the fuck?"

I sat there with my hands on my now gigantic stomach and smiled up at Ken. I was happy to see James standing behind him, because for a minute there I thought Ken would faint. He didn't. He did come in and sat down on the chair next to me. He just kept staring at me. Pallo steered James out of the room and left Ken and I alone.

"I thought they said it would be hard for you to get pregnant, almost impossible?"

"They did, but I told you about finding a match with Caleb," I said trying my best to break it to him gently that a human could never have given me this--that he could never have given me it.

He leaned forward and put his hand out to touch me. I let him. "So, we really need to find Caleb...not that it wasn't important before, but now..." He patted me gently on the belly.

"Well, no...he's not the father."

"Me?" he asked and moved closer to me. He sounded almost hopeful.

"No."

Pallo entered the room again and walked over to me. He was carrying a glass of ice water for me. I took it. He bent down, kissed me and then whispered something sexy in Italian in my ear. I knew a show when I saw one and he was putting on a doozie of a show for Ken.

Ken stood up quickly. "Jesus H. Christ! What do you think you're...you let him in you? What does Caleb think? When did this happen?"

"Ken, sit down. It's not what you think."

"It's not what I think? Well, seems to me that you let a dead guy fuck you and somehow knock you up...all while you were engaged to Caleb, but fucking me on the side."

Maybe it was what he thought, not exactly, but close. I finally managed to convince Ken to have a seat. I watched him do his nervous hand-through-the-sandy-blond-hair-thing, and fidget. Trust me, watching a six foot two inch man fidget is funny. Pallo kept his hand firmly on my shoulder as I told Ken about the events of the last week. Ken stood and paced the room during the robed monk part. He got a drink during the part about me not making it through the birth and I most certainly did not leave out the best part which was that I was most likely giving birth to some sort of demonic force or a demon for all we knew--however you wanted to look at it.

The room was quiet. Pallo rubbed my shoulders gently as Ken sat upright in the chair. He kept shaking his head no. I wasn't sure if he thought this would solve everything or not. It was annoying the hell out me that was for sure! Finally, his brown eyes tore away from me long enough to look at Pallo.

"We have to figure out what's inside her."

"Yes, I was hoping you would be able to persuade her to go into town and see the doctor. I also think it might be beneficial for her to see a witch. A witch might be able to tell us what magic was involved in these dreams."

I tried to try to stand up. I had to accept Pallo's hand to get out of the cushy chair. There is nothing more humbling then needing help out of a chair because your belly is too big. "I already beat you to that part." I looked at Ken.

"You told my grandmother about this?"

"No, just the dreams, I didn't know I was pregnant at the time."

Ken looked at me and shook his head again. "I need another drink."

"Have one for me while you at it."

Pallo laughed. "Me, too."

Chapter 32

We agreed that Ken would stay and watch me while the three vampires went to meet with Caleb's partner, Mark. I watched as Ken tried to explain how to fire a gun to Caradoc. He was an old school vamp who preferred swords to guns. The two of them went out towards the back barn where the old haystacks were to try it out. James thought the moment was too good to miss so he went along for shits and giggles. The thought of sending a camera out with him had crossed my mind.

I went out into the kitchen to find Pallo. He was holding a long silver sword with a red handle. I walked up and put my arms around his waist. "Are you planning on needing that?"

His brown curls tickled my face. Since he'd been staying with me, he began smelling like the lavender scented soaps and shampoos I used. I had others to choose from but he had gravitated towards them. I wasn't sure if I should be flattered or nervous that one of the men in my life liked to smell nice, too. *Men-plural.* Yeah, the more I thought about it, the more I realized it was true. I had two men that I was extremely serious about in my life, maybe even more depending how you looked at it. I was a mess and I knew it.

Pallo pulled out a silver handgun and popped the clip out. He pushed it back in and handed it to me handle first. I didn't want to take it. Ken had taken me to the range on several occasions but I'd never been left in charge of a firearm before.

"Pallo?"

"Gwyneth, it is loaded with silver-tipped, hollow point ammunition. In layman's terms, Caleb hunts the supernatural, so his bullets are modified to kill them--kill us. Aim for the heart and that should be enough to kill anything that you may run into, even something like me."

"I'm not the one going out into the night to hunt down some crazy bitch who's managed to get men all over the city shooting at their loved ones." A shudder ran through me as I thought back to the gas station incident. I was positive that the Enchantress was behind that, somehow. In fact, the more I thought about the odd events of the last few nights, the more convinced I was that she was behind it all.

"Be careful, Pallo...I can't lose you."

He touched my cheek and came away with a tear. I hadn't realized I was crying. I'd been doing that a lot since I met him. I took the gun and laid it on the table, hoping there wouldn't be a point that I needed to use it. I watched in silence as Pallo armed himself. I'd never seen him carry a weapon and was surprised at how adept he was at it. I had a tendency to forget he was over two hundred years old and into some seriously dark shit.

Great, the love of my life was the Don of the supernatural Mafia. If he started paling around with anyone named Guido then we were going to need to have a very lengthy discussion. Right after I hid all the baseball bats in the house.

Pallo chuckled as he picked up the sword again and turned it in his hand slowly. He looked at home with it. I silently wondered how many times in his life he'd been required to use one. He glanced back at me and I shook my head to indicate I really didn't want an answer to that question.

Pallo and I were so different and Caleb and I were so alike. I tried to stop thinking about Caleb, but I couldn't. I was sure Pallo knew, he seemed to be a permanent fixture in my mind. Another great side-effect of his life saving bite!

"Why do you put up with me?" I asked.

Pallo put the sword down and turned. "The same reason you put up with me, *Il nostro amore è eterno*--our love is eternal."

As much as I wanted to melt into his sweet words of love, I couldn't. Reality had bitten me in the ass more times than I cared to remember. The truth of the matter was that Caleb and I, regardless of our differences, had a strong history too. "What happens when Caleb comes home? Do we all go back to fighting?"

"Ah, you are confident in my abilities to bring him back? How can you be sure I will? I mean, I do stand to gain quite a bit with him out of the picture, permanently."

I looked up at him. He was right. I should question his motives for going, but I didn't. No part of me felt like he wouldn't give it his all. I knew the history between Caleb and Pallo. I knew that Caleb had stepped up to the plate when Pallo was gone to take care of his family--to take care of me. Pallo couldn't deny he owed Caleb for that, and maybe more. "You'll bring him home, or die trying, and that's what scares me."

Pallo moved into me. I put my hand in the back of his hair and pulled him closer to me. I brought his lips to mine and pushed my tongue into his mouth. His body was pressed so tightly against mine that I could feel just how pleased he was to see me through his tan pants. His thick erection seemed grow the longer we held each other. I tried to pull him tighter to me but I had to turn sideways to do it. My enormous belly was getting in the way.

Damn demon pregnancy.

I was about to tell Pallo to be careful, when I was hit with a sharp pain in my back that radiated down to between my legs. I cried out and bent down--gripping at my lower stomach. Pallo tried to help, but I pushed him away as another round of pains shot through me.

"Gwyneth, what is wrong?"

I knew what the problem was but I wasn't about to tell him. I was in labor, and if he found out, he would not go help find Caleb. He would stay with me and be a first-hand witness to my demise. I wouldn't put him through that, I couldn't. I also couldn't lie outright to him. He could sense a lie, all vampires could. Pallo also had the gift now of being able to scan my mind without thought. I fought to keep my head clear and to keep him out of it. I tried to think of something wonderful to say to him, nothing came to me.

I moved to sit down. Pallo's hands never left my body. The pain subsided and I did my best to compose myself. He could not watch me die giving birth to something he was a part of. He'd spent the last twenty-six years behaving himself, at least according to most vampires' ethics, prior to that he'd been a ruthless killer. I knew that losing me so very long ago had triggered the monster within Pallo and I would do everything in my power to prevent him from going down that path again.

"Gwen?" Pallo very rarely called me Gwen and whenever he did it was serious. He was calling me Gwen more and more as of late and that wasn't a good sign. I took his cool pale hand in mine and patted it. "I think we should rethink the whole, who goes and who stays arrangement."

"Yes, I think you are right. I will stay with you, and…."

"No, Pallo. You need to go, but I think Ken should go, too."

He stood. I knew he was getting ready to argue with me. "Wait, I know I can't be alone right now and I know how important it is that you help with the search. Your powers are greater than both James' and Caradoc's put together. As for Ken...you'll need a shooter on board. I saw Caradoc's face when Ken tried to show him how to use a gun. He didn't want to understand it. He's an old-school vamp who doesn't want to use new toys..." Pallo tried to speak but I put my hand up. "*Taci!*" I smiled as the surprise of me picking up on his native language hit him.

His eyes widened. "*Fata mia*, you just told me to shut-up."

"Hmm, James told me that meant listen."

Pallo bit back a smile. "Did he?"

"Should I even ask what *scopami più forte* means?"

Pallo tossed his head back and laughed from the gut. "Ask me again, when we have more time together and I shall give you a demonstration on its meaning." Something passed quickly over his face. "Why would James tell you this?"

"Hey, I don't even know what that means."

His lips narrowed. "Why did he teach you that?"

I shrugged. "Because I asked him to. I wanted...I wanted to learn to say romantic things back to you."

If you make fun of me for saying romantic I'll stake you through the heart. I knew he was listening in on my thoughts.

A sly smile graced his face. "Perhaps you should avoid taking his advice."

"You're not planning on telling me what it means, are you?"

His smile widened. "I promised to demonstrate for you later."

"Okay, back to the topic at hand--Ken going with you. The way I see it, Caradoc is stronger than James when it comes to hand-to-hand combat, am I right?" Pallo nodded. "Great, and you need a shooter...Ken. So, that leaves James. He can stay with me. Before you start going all 'jealous' on me, think about how fast James is when it comes to flying and think about how easily he fits in with humans. If I need to go to the hospital, do you think Caradoc will blend in?"

He turned away and walked to the front window. The shutters were still closed. I was sure that the sun had already set because Caradoc and James went out, but no one had gotten around to opening them. Pallo was silent for a few minutes and then he looked at me.

"Do you promise to have James contact me if any changes in your condition occur?"

"Yes." *Don't sense my lie, don't sense my lie.*

"Very well, I will go and tell him the news. I am sure he will be *more* than pleased with his new responsibility."

I gave him a nasty look as he walked out. I didn't care for his jealousy of James and he knew it.

Chapter 33

I crawled on the bathroom floor, trying to reach the edge of the tub to pull myself up. Another pain shot through my lower body. It felt like someone was pounding my lower back with a sledgehammer. After Pallo and the others had left to meet Mark, I told James I wanted to soak in the tub and relax awhile. He offered to help me, and after I socked him in the arm, I gave him a job. I sent him on a blood run. I knew that would keep him gone for a little while. I knew the vampires' blood supply was running low at my house and the last thing I wanted running around was hungry vampires. So sending James to the blood bank seemed like a good idea. I had no idea how bad the contractions would get or I would have rethought it.

I tried to pull myself up again and failed. I lay on the bathroom floor screaming out in pain until I heard the bathroom door burst open.

"Hey Shorty, you weren't thinkin' of tryin' to do this all by yourself now, were ya'?

"Nana?" I lifted my head to see Ken's tiny grandmother standing beside me. "How'd you know?"

"Oh child, I've known since you came to my house for tea. You had that look about ya', it wasn't exactly a new momma' glow, but it was somethin'."

I tried to sit up to see her but another pain hit me. My forehead hit the floor with a thud.

"Now, why don't ya' just lie still. Let me help ya'...the girls and I took a look at those pills the doctor sent over. He was right about them havin' a spell on them and he was right about them havin' some type of fertility drug in them, but he was wrong about them doing nothin' to stop you from getting' pregnant."

Intelligent conversations were beyond me with the contractions coming closer and closer, so I just listened to her talk. She told me about pills being used to help something grow and have life, but not necessarily a baby. The spell that was used on them allowed me to act as a succubus, a female vampire that can become pregnant. This explained my blood cravings and my falling body temperature.

I listened as Nana went on about sensing that I was carrying something deep within me when I came to see her the other day. She also made it very clear that it was not a child in me. I knew that but hearing it said aloud again only served to confirm it. She had talked to Dr. Gideon about it and he agreed. He hadn't wanted to worry me, but the two beats that he heard were not heartbeats, they were something else. Betty, one of Nana's sisters in the coven, figured out that I was acting as a vessel for the merger of two magics, two powers, and that when it came time for them to be released, they would kill me--or consume me. The women in Nana's coven had spent the last day making large amounts of banishing and purifying potions.

I watched as Nana filled the tub with water and added jelly jars full of thick liquid. The smell of anise hyssop and lemon verbena filled the room. She looked down at me and smiled.

"Do you understand what I'm about to do?"

"Yes," I said between gritted teeth. "Banish the evil spell that holds the...power...oww...in me."

"Very good, now let's get you up and in the tub."

She put her plump hands under my armpits and tugged on me. At four foot ten inches tall and pushing only eighty pounds, she wasn't going to budge me. Another contraction ripped through me. I screamed out.

A gust of wind hit us. "Gwen?" I heard James' voice. "Who the hell are you?"

"Don't take that tone with me, Shorty!" Nana said. She rubbed something on my stomach. The pain intensified and I screamed out. I felt something warm running from my nose. James was next to me in an instant. His hand came to my face. He pulled it back and showed me that it was blood.

"What the bloody-hell are you doing to her?" James made a sudden move towards Nana. I heard her giggle and saw James land on his butt on the floor. Messing with a witch was never pretty. James looked at me with his blue eyes wide. "Get a load of the ol' nasty nana."

"James, its okay...help her do...what needs to be done." I struggled to get the words out. Our gazes locked and he nodded.

"Great, now that that's settled, let's get her in the tub," Nana said, still laughing at James. James picked my body up and set me fully clothed in the tub. My skin felt as though it was singeing off. I screamed as smoke rose up from my arms. Nana grabbed me.

"Help hold her still, boy!"

I could hear my heart pounding in my ears. I wanted out of the water. I wanted away from the room, the house, my body. I clawed out, fighting to run, I caught James' arm and he winced but did not let go. Nana began to chant and throw salts and oils in the water with me.

Something clawed at my stomach from the inside--digging up, trying to get out. I reached down and pulled my shirt up high to see what was causing the excruciating pain. Hundreds of tiny mounds rose up under my skin. I heard screams and cries and the sound of heavy breathing. I realized the screams were coming from me and also James. He held me down, staring wide eyed at my now grossly disfigured stomach.

Nana repeated a low chant over and over again. The pain increased. I grabbed James' hand and squeezed it as hard as I could. I screamed and fell backwards into the tub full of oils and water. Water covered my face. I screamed out again as pain riddled through my body and took in a huge gulp of water. It burned on the way down. James yanked my head out of the water and I coughed as he hit my back. Water flew out of my mouth and nose at him. He didn't move away, he moved closer. At this rate, he'd be in the tub with me any minute.

"Good, you're here." I heard Nana say.

I screamed again and didn't look behind me to see who'd come in. I didn't care if they let the whole city in. They could charge admission to see the faerie giving birth to the demonic power for all I cared. I just wanted whatever was in me out.

"Let me in there," Dr. Gideon said. His head of red hair swept down next to me. He began to check my vital signs. He glanced at James and I saw James' eyes widen. They didn't need to tell me how bad it was. I was living it.

The clawing in my stomach returned. Gideon glanced down and caught sight of the ripples. "Oh, my God!" He backed up slowly.

When your own doctor is freaked out by you, you know you're screwed.

"Do it, Sive," he said, backing away from me more.

Sive was Nana's real name. I looked at her and nodded my head. I needed her to know I trusted her and that if my end was near, I was happy that she was here, too. Gideon began to walk towards me. Nana put her hand up and stopped him.

"Nothing alive can be near her when this happens. You boy, make a circle of salt around her, and then get out fast, if you value your life."

James looked at her and then at me. He grabbed the bag of salt Nana was holding and did as he was told. When the circle closed I suddenly felt like I was suffocating. I pulled at my throat trying to get air in. My fingers dug into my skin and I knew that I was drawing blood but I didn't care--I wanted air.

"GWEN!" James screamed.

"Don't go in there child, you won't survive it."

James stared at me, his eyes full of pain. "I'm dead already...I'm a vampire."

Nana shrugged her shoulders. "Well, that's a bit unnervin' but good in the sense that it can't harm you. Go on now, boy...and whatever you do, do not let her past the circle till' I say so."

James agreed and rushed over to me. I couldn't get air into my lungs and my chest was pinching tight like it was about to explode. My body shot up out of the water and I screamed out. Hot air moved down and filled my lungs. Something jerked my body backwards and I hit the wall. James grabbed me to him, and my hands went around his throat.

I didn't want to hurt him but something else was controlling me. Pushing him backwards, I knew that if I made it over the salt line I'd be free of this pain. I'd be dead but definitely free of the pain.

"Gwen!"

I looked into James' blue eyes. I struggled with the power within me and let go of his neck. He pulled me into his arms. My stomach and breasts were exposed to Dr. Gideon and Nana. It was embarrassing, but I really didn't want to die so I lived with it. Nana picked up a small purple glass bottle with a cork in it and threw it at me. It hit my stomach and exploded in a cloud of smoke. It felt like someone had run something the size of a telephone pole through me. I heard screams and screeches, then the chants of the robed men, and finally a fading sweet sounding song of a siren--of the Enchantress.

The smoke cleared and I fell forward.

"Gwen?" James was on me in an instant. He rolled me over. His eyes scanned my half naked body. "Gwen, look!"

I looked down and saw what had surprised him. My stomach was normal. It was flat, and my breasts had returned to their normal size. "You're warm," he said. He was right. He leaned over me and pulled my ripped maternity shirt up, trying his best to cover me, then looked back at Nana. "Can I bring her out now?"

"I think that'd be fine, Shorty."

Chapter 34

I snuggled closer to James' back. Snuggling against him felt good, right. He hadn't left my side since the banishing took place. He'd been the one to help me get cleaned up, dressed and he'd insisted I eat. Nana had tried but James was too pushy even for her. Now, as I looked at him, I was extremely happy with my decision to keep him here with me. He'd proved himself to be most valuable--a true friend indeed.

His weight shifted a little. "How are you feeling?"

"Better, and you?"

He turned towards me slowly. "I feel like I got a leg over last night."

I smiled at him. "Jameson." I reached up and ruffled his perfectly spiked hair. "I don't understand half of what you say. Are all Brits like you?"

"'Tis' better to be daft, than dodgy," James said, giving me a huge grin. The man had an incredible smile. "Sorry, just toying with you, love. No, I try not to do it. Pallo likes us to blend in and all."

I touched his shockingly blond hair again. "So, how's the blending in thing working out for ya'?"

"It's going well, thanks. So, are you hungry?" By his tone, I got the impression that something wasn't right.

"James, you okay?"

He smiled and appeared fine, but the strangest thing happened--I heard his thoughts as he stared into my eyes. *No, I'm not okay. I held you in my arms, terrified that if I loosened my grip, even a bit, I'd lose you.*

I touched his cool cheek. "But you didn't let go of me, James. You held tight and I made it through because of your strength, because of...."

He lifted his head a bit and cocked an eyebrow up. *Tell me you can't read my thoughts.*

"Uhh, okay...I can't read your thoughts. Happy now?"

"Fucking hell," he said, under his breath.

"What's wrong?"

*What's wrong? What's wrong? She can't be serious! I'm fuckin'
bonded to my best friend, who doesn't seem to understand that
that means my power, hell, my body perceives her to be my fuckin'
wife--like its easy tryin' to shag another chick when your fuckin'
willy's developed a sudden case of monogamy! If that's not bad
enough, she also happens to be my master's girlfriend and she
asks what's wrong! Shit....*

James narrowed his eyes. *You heard all that, didn't ya?"*

I nodded and ran my thumb over his smooth cheek.

*I don't suppose you'd be willin' to push me out into the sunlight
come morning? It'd be a right bit better than havin' to look you in
the face.*

"That's not funny, Jameson!" I cupped his face with both hands.
"We'll figure this out and once we do...."

He grabbed my wrists. "You won't have to put up with my
lovesick ramblin'. I try to keep it to myself, Gwen. I do, because I
know you don't feel the same way. I get it and I'm fine with it.
Hell, it's probably some cockamamie magic-thing gone bonkers
that'll wear off and we won't even be able to stand the sight of
each other."

"Maybe we should rethink the whole 'you not reading me'
thing."

James looked puzzled. "Why?"

"Because if you read my thoughts, you'd know the real reason
why I want to figure out what's happening with us."

"Gwen."

I pressed my finger to his soft lips. "Go ahead, do it."

He hesitated for a moment before I felt the slightest of tickles in
my head. Peace washed over me and I could have sworn that my
hair lifted slightly. James was a hell of a lot more powerful then he
let on. I barely had a chance to think about what that meant before
James pulled back from me as though he'd been struck.

Shaking his head, he stared at me with wide eyes. "Gwen?"

James didn't need to verbalize what he'd found in my inner most
thoughts. The ones I had somehow been able to keep from Pallo, I
already knew them. I just didn't want to admit it.

He leaned forward and kissed my forehead gently. "I feel the
same way." With that, he turned and climbed out the bed. He
didn't look back as he headed out the door and I knew why. We
would have crossed "that line," the one we barely managed to stay
off as it was. The one that would mean his death. There was no
way in hell I'd risk his life over something we didn't understand. It

made no sense. Caleb and Pallo, they made sense. I had a history with them. James made no sense at all.

I think the Fates have a personal grudge against me.

I sat on the edge of my bed and stared out the window at the night sky. The continued need to run my fingers over my stomach to assure it was back to normal consumed me. So much so, that I didn't hear Nana come in. "You look a hell of a lot more comfy now."

I felt a thousand times better. She and Dr. Gideon had discovered I was acting as an incubator for some sort of a magical presence. It fed off the power of others, so it was draining me along with whomever else I came into contact with, in the biblical sense of the word, of course. Gideon had narrowed the cause of it to the pills that Dr. Brown had given me. From all he could figure, someone had wanted me to act as the vessel for this rising power, and I had. Nana said she could feel both faerie and vampire magic in it, and that was more than likely the cause of the two heartbeat-like sounds.

I thought of Pallo and how disappointed he'd been when we found out it wasn't a child in me, but rather someone's sick attempt at harvesting, creating, unleashing a hellish power. Thinking of him made me think of his sweet smell, the feel of his hard body as it pumped into mine and the brief glimpses I had of him truly happy.

Suddenly, Pallo seemed to be all around me, like he was tugging an undetectable string. He was calling me. We'd thought that meant that the child, or magic, I was carrying was his, and in part it was, but as his pull on me grew I knew that it was another one of the side effects of him bringing me back to life with his bite.

James rushed into my room and looked down at me. "I have to go."

"So do I."

He gave me an odd look.

"I felt his pull, too!"

"*Bloody hell*! Oh, he's gonna love knowin' he's got power over you," he said. There was no hiding the hurt in his voice. He took a deep breath in before continuing. "Pallo's near water, a larger body of it. A woman's with him. I get the sense she's the one who's havin' Pallo call us...his summons are normally more forceful...this is different...still his power, but different."

"Did we get the summons, 'cause I didn't pick up on any of that? All I got was the shit scared out of me." I sat up and he reached for me.

"You're not a vampire, love. I am." Lifting my hand to his lips, he laid the gentlest of kisses on it before turning and heading out of the room. "I'll meet you downstairs."

I found my thick soled black boots, tossed them on then met James at the bottom of the stairs. We looked like we were attending a Goth get together or a funeral. I sincerely hoped it would be the Enchantress'. I had a sneaky suspicion that she was behind all of this.

"I'll be right back," James said, heading towards the kitchen. He returned quickly with the Caleb's weapons chest.

James picked a Beretta Tomcat and I went with the Sig Sauer P232 silver handgun that Pallo had left out for me. My knowledge of weapons had been forced upon me by Ken. He'd go on and on about them. The only way to shut him up was to pay attention. Now, maybe I could put that knowledge to good use. I put it in the back of my pants and sifted through the endless supply of weapons that Caleb had. I grabbed two wooden stakes and a Bowie knife. It had an arm sheath already, and I had James help me with it. I felt a little like a female Rambo--hmm, perhaps a faeriebo?

Gideon met us at the front door on our way out. "All set?"

"You're not going," I said, straining my neck to make eye contact with him.

"Yes, I am."

I didn't feel like wasting time arguing. I looked at James and felt our bond surge. *Do you care if he comes?*

Nope.

"Great, let's go!" I said out loud.

We headed out the door, and Nana came up behind us, calling my name.

"Here," she said and handed me a vial of ointment and small herb stuffed cloth doll. I gave her a puzzled look and she laughed. "These might come in handy. One's a banishin' potion and the other's a poppet...used for bindin' if you need it."

I grabbed my black leather coat and put them in the pocket as I slid it on. Nana pulled James' head down towards her and put a pouch on a cord around his neck, then did the same for Gideon.

"Now, those talisman's should help with the problem of gettin' all caught up in her singin' lies," Nana said and then looked over at me. "Bring my grandson home safely."

I nodded, gave her a hug, and promised that I would bring Ken back to her safely. I hoped that I could make good on that promise.

Chapter 35

We pulled up to the boat docks about forty minutes later. Gideon cut the engine and turned to look back at James and me. "You know that you two look like hit men."

I glanced at James and he smiled. Gideon shook his head. I couldn't help but laugh. "Tonight, I think that's exactly what we are."

I followed James out of the car and surveyed the area. The docks were poorly lit and there was no light from the moon to help us. Two large freighters were docked near us. They only served to add to an already dark situation. Their size alone was menacing and seemed to set the tone for the night.

James looked slightly purple in the odd night lighting. I laughed softly at the sight of him looking like a grape. I glanced around for oompa loompas but found none. Just as well, James would have gotten a kick out of being rolled by little men, I was sure of that.

James tipped his head to the side as he looked past the ships to a large warehouse. He was sensing something, and I was sensing him. We were a fine pare. I moved up closer to him and Pallo's pull grew stronger. Something moved in the darkness near us. I knew that it wasn't friendly before it bothered to show itself, so did James. Gideon, on the other hand did not. He walked up behind me. Pushing him out of the way, I threw one of my stakes past his head.

"What the...?" Gideon's voice was strained. He thought I'd just tried to impale him. Men, save their life and they still assume the worst of you.

James bent over the slumped robed figure and gave me a "we are so very fucked" look. Another robed man appeared behind James and saw me. The man's focus went to my stomach and he gasped. *Shit*, they still thought I was pregnant.

James, behind you!

James stood quickly. He spun around and delivered a blow to man's upper chest. The man collapsed on the ground and it hit me then. They were human. They seemed so mysterious in my dreams, so untouchable. Now they seemed fragile, and that was good for us and bad for them.

"I have an idea," I said.

A shit-assed grin spread across James' face. "You don't say."

"It's been known to happen for time to time." I blew him a kiss and he laughed. "You two, grab their robes and put them on."

They did as I told them to and came up behind me. Great, they'd get in without a problem, now for me. They all thought I was still pregnant. Looks like I had to give them a big belly. Glancing up at James, I winked. I closed my eyes and ran my hands over my stomach, remembering how large and swollen it had been only hours earlier. I let my energy flow through me and let my power work its shifter magic.

"Gwen," James said softly.

I looked down at my now huge belly. Gideon stood there with his mouth open. I reached up and pushed his bottom jaw closed. "I'm able to shift--morph my appearance. I guess it's a faerie thing."

"That is no ordinary faerie thing." Gideon didn't move. He just stood there staring at my swollen belly. Like it was the first time he'd ever seen me this way. I didn't really need a doctor who looked more like a deer caught in headlights than a trained professional, but he was with us so he needed to come along. I patted him on the arm and edged him forward.

"Okay gentlemen, its time to hand the helpless lil' pregnant woman over to the Enchantress' minions.

You, helpless, that'll be the day, James' voice pushed through my mind.

We entered the large white door and were immediately hit with the scents of Jasmine and Lily of the Valley. One was used to stimulate attraction and lust, the other, the Lily of the Valley, was used to lure faeries. Both seemed to be doing a bang up job.

Mental note: Avoid Lily of the Valley in the future, only leads to trouble.

James went in first. He thought it might look odd if the prisoner was leading the captors. Tipping them off that we weren't what we appeared to be was low on the wants list at the moment. Kicking the crap out of the Enchantress was moving up rapidly.

Gideon had his hand on my shoulder. His size alone made him look intimating, the robe only added to it. I was thankful he kept his head down. His worried eyes would give him away.

The inside of the warehouse looked more like a luxury hotel than a shipyard's storage unit. Granted it had a lovely eerie quality going for it, but some people paid big bucks for that. It just seemed to follow me free of charge. I'd make a joke about being a tourist attraction, but it would only lead to the obvious "everyone *rides* for free."

The place was covered in huge throw pillows and rugs. All looked to be made of soft, deep colored velvet. Candles stood on stands and hung from the ceilings all over the place. They acted as the only light source. The soft sounds of the waves crashing against the pier outside filled the building. The overall effect was almost dreamlike, in a spooky get you knocked up with demon power kind of way.

Chants began to sound around us. We walked further in and found a large opening. In the center sat an oversized bed done in deep burgundy. Smack dab in the middle of it lay a naked woman. She had a body that Venus would envy. My gaze followed the curve of her hipbone upwards to her rounded white breasts. I moved up her smooth neck and to her face. I took a step back when I realized I knew her.

"Dr. Brown?"

She laughed, running her fingers through her long soft brown hair. "Most people call me Mira, but you, the surrogate mother of my child--my power, may call me whatever you like."

Her child? Dr. Brown was the Enchantress? My hand ran down over my stomach. I had a couple of choice things to call her, none of which were her name. I bit my lip and refrained. Kudos for me!

She extended her arms and let out a high-pitched sound. Robed men came flocking in by the pairs. I waited for the start of forty days worth of rain, but it didn't come. Gideon tightened his grip on my shoulder. He wasn't digging the idea of being surrounded either. Who could blame him?

Dr. Brown, Mira, motioned to James and Gideon to step aside. She looked to her left and two men appeared. They took their hoods down and I gasped. Ken and Caradoc stood by her side. Caradoc bent down and kissed her hand, moving up her arm. He took his time, savoring every moment of her soft skin beneath his lips. I wanted throw something at him and wake him from his trance. He was consorting with the enemy and that was not tolerable. I tried not to scream out or shoot Mira. I wanted to strike at the right moment and it wasn't quite perfect yet.

"My dear, Gwen, how do you like my boys?" She ran her hand across Ken's backside. I had to take a deep breath and let it out slowly to keep from lunging at her. "I have more toys, would you like to see?"

She motioned again and two more robed men stepped out. One was wearing a black robe and the other a red one. I knew that red-monk, or sort of, he'd been the one to come to Pallo and me in our dream. He'd been the one who had wanted to plant his seed in me. I shuddered at the thought of that.

"Come, boys, let her see you. She has earned it. Let her look at the power that fills my power in her body. Let her see what will destroy her."

The two men pulled their hoods down and I fell to my knees. I couldn't breathe, couldn't think, couldn't move. How? How had she managed this? Pallo stood there in the black robe looking past me, his eyes void. To his left was Caleb in the red robe. She'd turned them both.

"Oh, come now, Gwen. I shall let you keep one of them, that is, if you survive the birth." Mira let out a long sultry laugh. "The other I shall keep as a token reminder of my time here."

"Why? Why us?" I wanted to know--needed to know what we'd done to deserve this. We had a big enough mess of our own. We didn't need her added interference.

"Oh, that's easy. I needed to find a female who could withstand the gestation period for my power to grow to its full strength. An ordinary human girl would have died at conception. But, when you and Ken came into my office, I knew I'd found the right girl. And, when the handsome faerie lover came into your life, I knew that the time had come. I gave you the pills that contained my essence and told you to take them every day. Your faerie lover was a match to you, which was needed to make it work, he fertilized it...he set your womb in motion. Then," she put her hand out to Pallo, "I discovered that you had a mate from your past that still lived. The two of you were not so easy to get into the bedroom as you and the blond-faerie were, so I had to think of a more creative way."

"The dreams," I said, softly. Not wanting to believe what Mira was telling me but knowing it was the truth.

She smiled and turned her dark blue eyes on Pallo. "I was so happy to find out that I could call his demon. When his semen entered you in his demon form, it was guaranteed that all was to be successful. I had to find a way to keep the blond one from interfering, so I lured him away from you, and gave him the urge to find other companions. It was hard. His love for you was strong. His work was done, he had planted the seed--ripened the womb, and it was the vampire who needed to feed it."

I looked at Pallo and Caleb and tried to reach them with my eyes. I pleaded, fighting back tears the entire time. I didn't want to believe that I'd lost them both, I couldn't believe it. Neither one responded to me. They were gone.

"Oh, Gwen, you were so predictable. I remember you coming to see me after you'd broken off your engagement to this one." She pointed to Ken. I cringed. "Yes, you could not handle his betrayal. So, I sent some of my sirens ashore as normal women and had them seduce your faerie. I have to admit it took much energy for my sirens to lure him from you, and even then they could not get him to submit. He kept calling your name and coming back to his senses. They almost had him that night in the bar, when you and the police officer showed up. I was very disappointed but I knew that you'd seen enough to push him out of your life. You are so very predictable."

I tried to make sense of it all. My head was spinning. How could this have happened to us? Hadn't we been through enough already? I stared at Mira, willing her to burst into flames. It didn't happen. Instead, she summoned Ken over to her.

"Go, my love, and bring her to me. I want to assure the power is strong within her before I release it." She clapped her hands and hundreds of monks appeared. "You shall all take turns fucking her."

My heart leapt into my throat and I got to my feet quickly.

"Like hell they will!" James shouted out.

Mira looked like someone had slapped her senseless. Too bad it wasn't me. She seemed delusional to begin with so I'm betting it wouldn't take much to toss that one over the edge of sanity. I just hoped I'd get to be the one to do it for real. She stared at James and then at Gideon. She threw her hand up and their robes fell away from their bodies.

"Oh, you have been a bad girl, Gwen, a very bad girl." She turned to Pallo and Caleb. "Kill everyone but her...hold her down for the others to have her. We must increase the power within her womb before it arrives. I need it. My time is nearing an end. GO!"

Pallo and Caleb nodded and rushed towards us. Ken followed close behind them. Gideon pushed up next to me. "Now what?"

"You run and don't stop, some will follow you. Get in the car and go! Call Sive...she'll know how to get in touch with Justin at the PR-Dept. Tell him that we're going to need a really big clean-up crew here tonight." I looked up at Mira and smiled. She'd fucked with the wrong faerie. "Now, I'm going to kill that bitch."

Gideon began to argue. I lashed power out at him and sent him flying out towards the door. I couldn't worry about him, too. James was capable of handling himself, Gideon wasn't. He was a healer not a fighter.

I tried to throw a wad of my power at the guys to slow them down. Caleb put his hand up and absorbed it into him. Pallo rushed at James and sent him pummeling into the wall. Caleb grabbed hold of my arm and flung me around. Pallo came up behind me and snatched me by my hair. I kicked out and caught Caleb in the arm. He seized hold of my foot and threw it down.

Ken came out of nowhere and pulled at my shirt. I managed to free one of my hands from Pallo's grip and I slashed out and got the side of Ken's neck with my fingernail. He jerked back from me, staring at me with wide eyes.

"Gwen?" he said, blinking.

"Ken!" I'd managed to reach him. I remembered what Justin had told Caleb on the phone, the pain of love could break her hold--that was it. If someone they loved caused them pain, they could be reached.

Ken grabbed hold of Caleb and tried to pull him away from me. Somehow, he managed it and was left facing an expert in hand-to-hand combat with powers that could kill even me. Caleb would annihilate Ken. I had to stop it. Reaching up, I freed the knife from my arm sheath. I pulled it across Pallo's arm. It didn't faze him. I made a mental note to self, that Pallo didn't think getting his arm sliced open hurt. As much as I wanted to be freaked out by that, now wasn't the time. I'd have to do better--inflict more pain. He yanked my hair hard and pulled me to the ground. I tried to pry his hand from my hair, but couldn't.

Pallo had me pinned down. His body pressed firmly against mine. Black pushed through his brown eyes. His demon had surfaced and I really didn't want his demon on me. I held tight to my knife. "Pallo, please don't make me do this! Please."

He snarled and lunged his head down at me, brining the full weight of his body down on me. It all happened so fast. One minute he was attacking me, and the next he was laying next to me, clutching his stomach. Blood poured from his wound that still had my knife embedded deep in it. Oh God, I'd stabbed him in the stomach!

"Pallo!"

"Gwyneth?"

Joy ripped through me, giving me the energy I needed to get to my feet fast. Mira screamed and hordes of robed men ran towards me. I pulled the gun out and fired a warning shot. They kept coming--idiots.

"MIRA!" I screamed out.

She put her hand up and the men stopped. She smiled wickedly as she spoke to me, "What is it that you want from me?"

"Two things really...One, I want to let you know that I am going to kill you before this night is over, and two..." I let my magic drop, allowing my stomach to go back to normal. A look of horror came over her. "Yeah, about that vessel thing...it ain't happening, hon', I don't give birth to demonic-magical-cocktails. I date weird enough things. I sure the hell don't want to give birth to more."

"KILL HER!" she screamed out.

Caleb turned and fixed his green gaze on me. I could feel his hot power creeping up. I knew that I couldn't survive the full force of his magic twice. I turned the gun on him and pointed it at him. My hand shook part of fear of having to hurt Caleb and partly because the gun was heavier than it looked. I had to bring my other hand up to steady it.

"Stop, Caleb!"

He took another step towards me and smiled. The temperature in the room shot up.

"Caleb no! Don't do this!"

The air around me grew hotter.

"*Gráim thú.*" Telling him that I loved him didn't even seem to faze him. I shot past him at first but he kept coming, the air around me was hard to breathe. I was so hot, too hot. Caleb could blow us all up if wanted to, and it looked like that was exactly what he had in mind. I aimed the gun directly at him. I couldn't do it--I couldn't pull the trigger and hurt him. I eased up on the trigger and heard Pallo shout my name.

Something struck me in the back of the head and I heard Mira's voice loud in my ear. Pain shot through my neck and radiated into my head. My vision blurred for a second and it was enough for her to get the upper hand. She hit me again and then went for the gun. It discharged, and then I dropped it. I brought my extra-thick boot up and hit the side of Mira's head. She staggered backwards and I used the opportunity to kick her again, this time in the stomach.

"How do you like it...bitch?" I was referring to the horrendous stomach pains I'd experienced being her guinea pig, but I didn't give a damn if she understood what I meant or not. I wasn't above causing her pain without reason.

I made another move this time to hit her, she dodged and looked past me. "Shame on you, Gwen, shame on you."

I turned and saw what she was talking about. Caleb was lying in a pool of blood on the floor. It was clear to see that he'd been shot in the chest. Ken was holding his hand against Caleb's wound, attempting to stop the blood from flowing out of him.

Rage consumed me. Suddenly, my skin crawled with power and I could think of only one thing--killing Mira. Pulling the other stake out of my pocket, I spun it in my hand. Mira looked at me and laughed. I drove the stake into her chest so far that my hand hit her breast. She fell to the floor and I rode her all the way down. I kept my hand pushed against her chest until the stake stopped moving. Her heart had stopped. It was my turn to laugh, and laugh I did.

Someone grabbed me by my shoulders and called my name. It took a minute for the fog in my head to clear but when it did I found James shaking me.

"Gwen, you all right?"

"James?"

"I'm here, love. It's over."

I placed my hand over his and nodded. He pulled me to him and held me tight. I pulled away from him and checked on the others. Pallo was slumped down on the floor with the knife still in his stomach. I ran to him and dropped to my knees.

"What do I do?"

He gave me a goofy grin. It wasn't something he did so it caught me by surprise. "Well, for starters you could pull the knife out of me. I am not able to remove it. It can only be removed by you."

"Why only me?"

"Because it is your *Si* magic that holds it there."

I took a step back and he grabbed my hand. "I can't...Pallo...I didn't mean to hurt you...I can't do it again, Pallo."

"Gwyneth, it will heal, I promise."

James moved down next to me and yanked the knife out of Pallo.

Pallo narrowed his eyes and stared at James. "How were you able to remove it when I was not?"

Oh shit! This was not good. "I must have let my power…."

Pallo put his hand up. "No, Gwen, he will tell me. Not you."

Great, he'd Gwen-ed me. This was definitely not good.

"You smell different, James. You smell," Pallo looked up at me, his eye went cold, "of faerie power."

"It's my fault!" I said, a little too fast. "I did it. I pushed my magic into him while he was saving my life. It just spilled out."

"Gwen, I'll not have you...."

Shut-up! He'll kill you without a second thought, James. He'll at least think a bit on it before he kills me.

Gwen.

My gaze went to Pallo. He sat there, stoic, building the walls he used to keep me out once more. I would have commented, but something else moved over me. A strange power that wasn't my own, yet wasn't completely foreign to me.

Bella, do have need of my services? Giovanni's thickly accented, deep voice moved through me.

"Giovanni?"

Pallo and James jumped to their feet. Pallo moved towards me, but stopped as he encountered the power. "His magic surrounds her."

Bella, are you hurt?

No, I'm fine.

"He's talkin' to her...using telepathy," James said, sounding less than pleased.

"And you know this how?" Pallo asked.

What of your faerie? I sense that he is injured.

My faerie? Oh God, Caleb!

Spinning around fast, I found Caleb's lifeless body spread out on the ground. Ken had given up and was sitting on his butt covered in blood. I ran to Caleb's side, followed closely by Pallo and James. I touched Caleb's arm and knew that he was dead. For a second, I couldn't think. He couldn't be gone, not my Caleb. Not the man who'd spent weeks digging a whole in the ground just to make me happy. *No!*

I grabbed the knife from James' hand and slid it across my arm. Blood fell quickly into Caleb's wound. Nothing happened. My faerie blood was the same as his but not near as strong. I couldn't help him but Pallo could.

"Pallo, help him...please!"

He put his hand on my shoulder and tried to pull me away. "Gwyneth, you and I both know that *our* Caleb would not wish to live his life tied to me. You yourself have felt the aftermath of what happens when I interfere. Do you think Caleb would welcome being at my beck and call?"

I rounded on him and grabbed his torn shirt. "Damn you! You can help him--you helped me. Help him!" Pallo avoided my gaze. "Or, don't you want to help him?"

"Gwen, Pallo's right. There's no way in hell that Caleb would want to be part of our world. You know Pallo can summon you. Do you really think Caleb would be okay with that?"

I looked up at the ceiling because I couldn't think of a better place. "Giovanni, help him please! I'll do anything...anything you ask, no strings, no tricks. Please!"

"Gwyneth NO!"

I glared at Pallo. It was only when I looked into James' blue eyes that I felt remorse. I'd managed to hurt him again.

"Giovanni, please!" I should have been terrified, calling out to a man whom everyone feared so much, but I wasn't. My gut trusted him, so I'd follow it.

Bella, it will take me a bit to arrive there and there is no time to spare. I can sense his separable soul beginning the exit process. If it is not held by magic then he will die. I do not posses that ability. Ask Pallo again. Perhaps for you, he will make an exception.

"Pallo, please."

"I cannot, Gwyneth. He would not wish this it to be."

I shook my head. My eyes blurred as unshed tears filled then and my lip quivered. "Pallo, I will never forgive you for this--ever!"

He put his hand on my shoulder and I pushed it off. I didn't want him to touch me. I didn't want him near me.

"Gwen, please," James said.

"GO!" I screamed out, lashing power out, sending them flying backwards. I hadn't meant to include Ken in it, but it happened.

Caleb was unbelievably pale. I cupped his face and put my forehead against his. "I'm so sorry. Baby, please don't go. Hang on for me. Please, just a little bit."

I felt it then, the piece of his power that I carried deep within me. It struggled to break free. The only way our bond would be broken was if one of us died. As the power tried to leave again, I knew that Giovanni had been right--Caleb's separable soul was trying to leave.

"Hang on for me, Caleb! Hang on! This can't be our end. I sure the fuck didn't come back after two hundred years to lose you this soon." Tears ran down my face, and onto his.

Giovanni's power brushed back over me. I had an overwhelming urge to reach into my pocket. I found the vial of ointment that Nana had given me. Opening it, I brought it to my nose.

"Honeysuckle and Lily of the Valley."

Yes! Thank you, Giovanni.

I smeared it on my hands and rubbed it onto to Caleb's face. I let every ounce of my power pour through me. I wasn't strong enough yet to heal him. But I knew someone who was.

"Sorcha, I call you forth to the mortal realm," I whispered into Caleb's ear. The words didn't just come to me out of the blue, I'd felt compelled to say them--compelled by a force that felt oddly like Giovanni. He'd help in the best way he knew how, by bringing in the big boys. The air around me crackled. Yep, something powerful was coming.

Thank you.

It was the least I could do, bella.

The ground shook and the candles near me blew out. I sensed someone hovering over me. I didn't need to turn around to know who was there.

"Help him please," I said, breathless and not bothering to hide the desperation from my voice.

Sorcha gasped and rushed to my side. "What have you done to my son?"

"It was an accident...I...it was his gun...and she knocked it..." I looked over in the direction of the very dead body of the Enchantress, and back to Sorcha. I had summoned her from somewhere important. She was dressed in a full-length hunter green gown. It brought out the color of her eyes. Caleb had inherited the same eyes and the same white-blond hair that his mother had. He hadn't gotten her evil spirit, thankfully.

"He was shot with one of his own ammunition?"

"Yes," I said.

"Caleb not only uses silver...he uses *sanguid-niric* in each one."

I had no clue what the hell she was going on about. But from the sound of her voice, it was bad.

"It is fatal to supernaturals if delivered through the heart," Pallo said softly.

"Everyone who lost their right to read my mind please raise your hand. There better be two vampires with their hands in the air." I didn't turn around.

Sorcha looked down at Caleb, choked back a sob, and placed her hand over mine. This was a serious matter for her. I knew that touching me was the last thing she wanted to do. She hated me with a white-hot passion and wanted me dead. The feeling was mutual so it didn't bother me. She drew on my energy and used her own to call Caleb's essence, his separable soul, back into his body. I watched as his chest wound closed. I held my breath until I saw his chest move up and down, slowly and steadily.

Sorcha turned and looked at me. "I will take him back with me. I'll need to watch over him. You will come, too."

"Gwyneth, no!" Pallo shouted.

I didn't bother to turn around and look at him. I'd meant what I'd said. I'd never forgive him for not helping Caleb.

"Why do you need me?" I asked Sorcha.

"I don't, but if I return without you, your father will assume I did something to you. He was with me when you summoned me. He will want to make sure you are safe."

"Forgive my pessimistic nature, Sorcha, but why the hell are you suddenly worried about pleasing my father?"

She set her green eyes on me and shook her head. "You really don't know him at all, do you?"

"How do I know I can trust you?"

She waved her hand in the air to dismiss my silly little claims. The lady was a pit-bull in wolf's clothing. I knew better than to assume her harmless. "Bring the vampire if you must."

I turned to Pallo, he stepped forward and I shot him a nasty look. "Sorcha, I'd rather take my chances with you. I never want him near me again!"

The hurt showed on Pallo's face and I was happy for it. Sorcha threw her head back and laughed. "Oh, how I would love to hear what made you have a change of heart, but we do not have time. I need to get Caleb back soon. I'll need to call on your father for assistance with him. If you are taking anyone with us, do so now."

I looked at Pallo. His refusal to help Caleb survive was too fresh in my mind to want to have him near me. Ken would never survive the trip to the Dark Realm and back. He didn't posses enough magical blood to protect him. That left James. He had also tried to convince me that Caleb should just die. I decided to go it alone.

"Gwyneth, please take James with you. Do not trust her. She played a part in your death the last time. Do not forget that."

I turned away from him and looked at Sorcha. "Let's go!"

The earth shook again and then I felt it slip away. I bent down and touched Caleb to make sure he was all right. I heard the distant cries of Pallo and James and closed my eyes.

Chapter 36

Sorcha had remained true to her promise. She took me back to my father's castle with her. We situated Caleb in what used to be his room and a wizard was tending to him. Sorcha had one of the guards show me to the room I'd be staying in.

The room was bigger than my whole house. It had a massive, deep cherry-colored wood bed in the center of it, and enough seating to throw a colossal get-together. The dark navy walls offset the stone bottom and gave the room a sort of old world charm. My favorite thing about the room was the bathroom. It was as big as my bedroom at home. It had a raised tub that was big enough to fit at least six people in it. It was a room that would make Pallo proud.

Thinking of Pallo made me sick to my stomach. I believed he would do anything to bring Caleb back to me safely. I was wrong. He let me down when I most needed him and that was unforgivable in my book. I'd thought that we'd finally made it through all of our issues. Instead, we'd managed to create more.

"Excuse me."

I spun around and found myself looking at an incredibly thin young girl with a head of sandy-blonde hair. She was holding a gown in her arms and bowing down to me.

"Lady Sorcha wishes for you to dress for dinner. The King will be joining you shortly."

I thanked her and took the dress from her. I laid it out on the bed and took a good look at it. It was one piece but looked like two. The top portion was a corset that was gold and navy blue. Tiny leaf patterns were pressed into it. The bottom portion of the dress was the same color navy blue that was in the top, minus the gold leaf impressions.

I went into the bathroom and took the quickest bath ever. It felt weird being there, but I didn't have a choice. I was covered in Enchantress blood, and I'm pretty sure everyone else's, too. I needed a minute to regroup. It'd been a long night and I wasn't sure how much more my body could take. I'd already managed to give birth to evil magic, stab one of my boyfriends, kill the Enchantress, and shoot Caleb in the chest.

Yeah, it'd been a long night.

I looked up at the row of circular mirrors that lined the bathroom. For a second, I could have sworn they moved. I put my hand out and touched one. The image that was reflected back at me changed. It was still me but with full make-up on.

I looked like a gothic streetwalker. I touched the mirror again and another less colorful version of me with make-up came up. That one wasn't too bad. I normally lined my navy eyes with black liner and the lipstick was just a shade darker than I normally wore.

"That should do," I said aloud.

My face tingled for just a minute and the mirror image faded away. I looked up to find my make-up done and my hair pulled into two sections on the top of my head. It left the back of my neck exposed, but forced my long black hair to spill forward, over my shoulders and down past my breasts.

I *so* needed one of those at home. Visions of James asking it who the fairest one of all was popped into my head and I laughed out loud.

I turned and walked back into the bedroom. My gown was laid out nicer than the way I'd left it and a pair of matching navy high heels sat on the floor at the foot of the bed.

I did my best to try to get into the dress. It wasn't working out for me. I'd never worn anything even remotely close to it, at least not in this lifetime. I gave up and tossed it onto the bed. I walked over to the massive balcony door and looked out into the night. Caleb had told me that it was always night in the Dark Realm. I didn't know how anyone could get used to living this way.

The street below was crowded. I'd say people were walking up and down it but that would be a lie, nothing down there really resembled anything human. The few that did were obviously vampires or witches. I backed up into the room and closed the door. I turned back to the bed to try to tackle my dress problem again.

A light tapping noise came from behind me. I turned and saw James standing out on the balcony. I walked over, opened the door, and stepped out.

"How in the hell did you get here?"

He rolled his eyes at me. "Gwen, I'm a vampire, the Dark Realm is like a second home to me. Sort of like how the mall is to you." He looked down at the street full of things and back to me. "Right then, maybe not a second home, but I do get unlimited access to it."

I shook my head and backed into the room. James stood out on the balcony looking in at me. "Umm...do you mind?"

He wasn't attempting to come in and then it hit me. "This isn't my house." I knew a vampire had to be asked into your home and this was not my home.

"I hate to argue with you, love, but the place is yours. It's your father's, and he apparently is a firm believer in what's his is yours, 'cause I can't come in."

"Fine, James, *you* can come in."

He walked in and dusted himself off. He took one look at the dress on the bed and busted out laughing. "Nice outfit."

"Yeah, it'd be great if I knew how to get the damn thing on." Flipping it over, I looked at all the ties in the back. It would take an army to get me in it. James walked over and took it from me.

"Drop your towel and I'll help you."

I gave him a sideways look with a questioning look. "James, if you wanted me naked, all you had to do was ask." I laughed, he didn't. "What the hell's your problem?"

"It's hard enough to keep control of our bond thing, but offerin' a bit of the muff up isn't helpin', even if you are just joshing me."

"You're the only person to have full access to my mind, James. You tell me if I'm joking or not."

He swallowed hard and closed his eyes for a moment. "Do you want help with the dress or not?"

He was pretty damn old and he did, more than likely have some experience when it came to this sort of garment. "Do I even want to know how many of these dresses you helped women into in your day?"

James stepped closer to me with a lecherous grin. *Gwen, it's not the puttin' it on that I'm an expert at.*

A clear image of James, pumping himself into another woman came to me. I did my best to squelch the jealousy I felt. It flashed before me again, this time so real that I knew it was James' doing.

Knock it off!

He wagged his eyebrows and smiled. *Awe, was it somthin' I said?*

I really don't want to see you screwing other people.

He drew in a sharp breath. *Yeah, well now you know how I feel.* James grabbed my towel and pulled me close to him. I thought he was going to kiss me, but he didn't. He turned me around and ran his hands over my shoulders. He worked his hand into my towel and yanked it away from me.

He disappeared for a moment but the minute I went to turn around, he reappeared behind me. James ran his hands down my legs, slowly. When he reached my foot, he tapped it lightly. "Lift it up, love."

I did. I tried to turn around and face James, but he grabbed my hips and held me firm. He tapped my foot again and I lifted it for him. He slid a pair of black panties up my legs, letting his fingers splayed over my hips. The feel of his hands on me was almost too much. It was best I stay facing forward and we both knew it. No sense setting ourselves up for disaster. Besides, we still had to face each other once the screwy vamp-mojo thing was fixed and I really didn't want to lose my best friend. "So," I said, softly. "How's the weather?"

James snickered. "And you call me odd."

I was about to comment further when he snatched my towel up and pulled it around me quickly. I yelped as he jerked me around to face him. His blue eyes held a bit of sadness in them. Compelled to touch him, I did. I smiled and stroked his cheek lightly. "Thank you for being you, James."

"Gwyneth!"

I looked up and saw Pallo standing on the balcony, glaring at the two of us. I kept my hand on James' cheek.

"You didn't mention he was coming, too," I said, a bit peeved at James.

James tried to look innocent. He failed miserably. Pallo pressed his body against the open door, but couldn't enter. I glared at James, daring him to invite Pallo in. He knew better. He grabbed the dress and dropped down before me. He tapped my leg again. I lifted it and stepped into the dress. He pulled it up my legs, stopping only when he got to the towel he'd wrapped back around me.

"Gwen, you need to ditch the towel, as lovely as it is, it doesn't go with the outfit."

James, are you insane? He'll rip you limb for limb.

His eyes widened. *Gee, good to know you have all the faith in the world in me.*

Pallo growled. I didn't need to see his face to know he was livid.
Just let him in, Gwen.
No.

Have it your way then. James pulled the towel from my body. I stood before him, nude from the waist up. That was "different" to say the least. He pulled the dress up and over my breasts, spending way too much time there, and winked at me. *Let him in, or I'll get him so 'effing pissed off that he'll kill me for sure. You need to talk to him...work out your differences. The man loves you, Gwen. Don't doubt it for minute.*

I opened my mouth to yell at him but remembered that Pallo didn't know about our newfound ability. "Just help me get this damn thing on."

"Okay, I'll do ya'," he said. It was a loaded statement, I knew it and so did Pallo. He growled out again and my chest tightened. It was wrong to do this to him.

James stepped forward, adjusted the corset up over my breasts and walked behind me. He tugged and pulled on the back of the corset. For a minute or two I fully expected my head to pop off, the thing was downright uncomfortable. James reached the top of it and leaned into me. His fingers slid over my bare shoulders.

"Let him in now, Gwen, please."

The please on the end that did it for me. "Fine, Pallo, you may enter."

Pallo came flooding into the room. I could feel the anger rolling off him. He went towards James. I stepped in his path. "Don't even think about it. If you touch one over-processed hair on his head, I will revoke my invitation. ALL my invitations! Do you understand?"

That stopped him dead in his tracks. He turned to me and looked down at me. The corset pushed my already large breasts up and out towards him. I wasn't sure how my nipples weren't hanging out. Fabulous, if I popped a "berry" in the middle of dinner with my father, I would slit my wrists. Too bad I was immortal or it would have been a dramatic statement.

"Okay, shoes." I put my hand out. James took it to steady me as I slipped the heels on.

Pallo's gaze raked over my body, soaking me in, before coming to a stop on my stomach. Something akin to pain flickered through his dark brown eyes. "James told me," he said. I was happy to hear that I wouldn't have to go into detail about the non-baby, baby-thing. I touched my stomach and noticed Pallo take a tiny step forward. I wanted to run to him and throw my arms around him. It took all my will power to remind me I was still mad at him. His full lips curved into a tiny, half smile and I knew he'd been in my head again.

I growled at him and he broke out with a full smile. Glad to know someone found this all amusing.

Pallo glanced over at the door. I turned but heard nothing. A second later, I heard a knock. I looked at Pallo and he shrugged. He didn't know who it was either.

"Only one way to find out," James said, as he walked towards the door. He reached out and flung it open.

"Kerrigan!" I shouted out and ran to him. I tossed my arms around him, and give him a hug.

He laughed and hugged me tight. "It is good to know I am missed. I can assure you that you are."

My father stood as tall as Caleb but had even more mass to him. He was not fat, by no means, just chalked full of muscle. Like Pallo, but taller. He looked like he could rip your head off and serve it to you for dinner if you weren't careful. With him being the King of the Dark Realm and all, I thought it best not to dwell on that. He was dressed in a long set of white robes. I'd never seen him wear that color--it looked nice, but different. His hair was the same raven black as my own and I'd gotten my navy blue eyes from him as well. The white robes screamed special occasion and I wondered what was going on.

My father spun me around and looked at my dress. His brow furrowed a bit. "My little girl is all grown up. You are beautiful, don't you agree?" he asked looking over at James and Pallo.

James dropped to his knee and Pallo leaned forward. "King Kerrigan, it is good to see you again," Pallo said.

"Stand, we are like family now. Speaking of which, let us go down to the common room, I have an announcement to make. It is one that concerns us all."

He took my hand in his arm and led me out the door. Pallo and James followed closely behind us.

Chapter 37

The common room was anything but common. A set of massive chairs, I assume thrones, sat on a raised platform at the head of the room. Tables lined the sides of the basketball court sized room. Each table was decorated with black tablecloths and red roses. The center of the floor was clear of tables. It looked like it was set up for a dance. I looked up at the ceiling and did a double take, huge black spiders hung down from silver webs. I backed up and hit Pallo. "Are they real?"

My father looked up at the spiders. "You don't like them?"

I shook my head no. He waved his hand and they all disappeared. "Hmm...now I will have to think of something else to decorate the room with."

"What exactly are you decorating for?"

From the looks of it, a massive funeral--oh, joy we'd come jut in time for a faerie wake. Yippie, never can have too many dead people in a room.

Pallo laughed and quickly covered it under the guise of a cough. He was eavesdropping in my noggin again. Ignoring him, I investigated the room some more. A huge cage of bats sat in the upper left hand corner of the room. I tried to back up more but Pallo wouldn't move.

"Uhh...Kerrigan...I mean...dad?" It was still odd to call him dad. I hadn't really known him that long.

"Yes?"

"What kind of party is this?"

"Gwyneth, I would have thought you would know. It is for your engagement party this evening."

Seeing Pallo walk in the sunlight would have shocked me less than that statement. Was he on faerie-dust? I glanced back at James, he was trying not to laugh. Pallo looked lethal--what else was new. I put my hand out to my father, and touched his arm. "This is really nice and all, in a horror picture show kind of way, but I'm not sure why you did it."

He squeezed my hand gently. "I think it is time to introduce you to my kingdom. Speculation has been circling about a child of mine existing. It is best to lay the rumors to rest and what better way than the announcement of your coming marriage to Caleb."

"Didn't you get the memo?"

Kerrigan stared hard at me. No, I guess he didn't get it. He didn't know the engagement was off. I wasn't even sure how he knew the damn thing was even on. One look around the "common room" told me he was proud of me that was comforting. I think.

"Kerrigan...err...dad, Caleb isn't well. He's not up for all of this."

"Nonsense, I just left him." He looked off towards the far end of the room and the door opened. I couldn't believe my eyes. Caleb walked through wearing a white set of robes like my father. His long blond hair hung loose to his waist. He generally kept it tied back and only rarely let it down. His gaze met mine and he looked away.

My father sensed the tension between us. He asked Pallo and James to accompany him down to the kitchen to oversee the food preparation. It was a lame excuse to give Caleb and me some privacy but it worked. He was the friggin' king of the dark creatures. He could have said, "Let's go stare at a toilet bowl for an hour" and they would have agreed.

Caleb came to a stop in front of me and stared down at my dress. "That looks like something my mother picked out. Sorry."

I smiled up at him and put my arms around him. He didn't hug back. "I'm sorry I said all those hurtful things to you. I didn't mean them."

"So, you didn't really sleep with Pallo?"

I let go of him and refused to meet his gaze. He grunted. "Yeah, that's what I thought." For a moment, I thought he'd offer something else up, but he didn't. There was dead silence between us for a bit. "Gwen, I never meant to hurt you. I tried to turn my power into myself, but you absorbed it all into you...you died in my arms." He put his hand out to me and I took it. "My power ripped your life force away and I was powerless to stop it! Pallo and James came, and I watched them bring you back from a death I caused. I couldn't face you after that, I tried...I swear I did...I tried to come and see you, but I couldn't bring myself to enter the room."

"I don't blame you for what happened, Caleb. I'm fine now. Besides, I was the reason you got shot."

He touched his chest and looked at me. "You shot me?"

I explained about how the Enchantress used him to attack me and how he tried to unleash the full force of his magic against me again. I also told him that I couldn't bring myself to hurt him but the gun had accidentally gone off during my struggle with the Enchantress. He bent his head down and looked away.

"It's a damn good thing she did cause the gun to go off. I had no control over myself. I would have destroyed you. You should have done it sooner."

I touched his face and he looked up at me. My magic flared and immediately sought his out. For one moment, we stood locked together by magic alone. "I could never hurt you, Caleb. It wasn't even you--you were like her puppet."

"Gwen, I think I had sex with her...I'm not sure, but I think I did. I shouldn't be telling you this but you have a right to know."

My stomach tightened. It hurt to hear him say that. I respected his honesty but it still hurt. "Did all of you have sex with her?"

Caleb's jaw tightened. "Ken did, so did Caradoc, but Pallo didn't."

The Enchantress had said that Caleb had put up a good fight against her sirens. I closed my eyes and thought about him being inside of her. I shuddered and felt sick to my stomach. I remembered her words then--her sirens had almost gotten him while he was at the bar. "Caleb, I don't think you did. When I saw you at the bar, I think that broke her hold over you for a bit."

"Yeah, for a bit, Gwen. But I spent three days with her after that. It's foggy, but I'm fairly sure something happened."

Caleb was making an effort to be honest with me. He'd learned from his mistake. I owed him the same respect. "Caleb...."

I took his hand in mine and led him over to one of the round tables with roses on it. I motioned for him to sit down and I did the same.

"This is going to be bad, isn't it?" he asked his soft face full of concern.

I nodded my head yes and proceeded to tell him about the events that had happened while he'd been hunting the Enchantress. I told him about the dreams with Pallo, the altar--and how I ended up being a vessel for the Enchantress' evil magic.

"So, you were carrying some sort of mixed-magic?"

"Yes."

He looked away. "Before you knew that it wasn't a baby, what were you planning on doing?"

"I was going to tell you, but I got the call from Mark shortly after I found out."

"Gwen, did you think it was mine?"

"Yes, at first I did." He stood up and walked away. I chased after him. "Caleb, wait."

He spun around. "Did you at least want it to be mine?"

My silence spoke volumes and he slammed his hand down on the nearest table. A dozen roses tipped over, sending water running everywhere. I grabbed his arm. His power prickled upwards, making me feel like tiny spiders were crawling all over my body.

"Caleb, stop, I've seen firsthand what happens when you let your magic overrun your emotions." As soon as I said it, I regretted it. His eyes welled up.

"You don't have to remind me. I held you in my arms and felt you fight for your last breath, Gwen. The whole time I had you, I knew I'd done that to you, that I had caused you pain. No, you don't have to remind me what *I'm* capable of, I know full-well what happens when I let my magic *overrun me*."

I heard my father and the guys approaching. James was watching my father like he expected him to grow horns any minute. Pallo was watching me. Caleb looked down at me and gave me a nasty look.

"Well, I see that you've made your decision finally."

"Don't talk about things you don't understand, Caleb."

He took a step towards me. "What the hell is that supposed to mean?"

Another voice interjected and saved me from having to defend myself. "It means that she told the vampire where to go. He refused to save your life and she refused to forgive him for it," Sorcha said from behind Caleb. He turned towards his mother. "She summoned me to help save your life and she came here *alone* with me."

Caleb turned and stared at me. "Are you crazy, Gwen? My mother hates you and even when she likes someone, she's scary!"

"Caleb!" Sorcha said in disbelief.

"Mother, please...you've made your feelings for Gwen very clear." He looked over at me and shook his head. "Why the hell would you go anywhere with her?"

"Caleb, really, I am standing right here," Sorcha said, stamping her foot down hard on the floor.

"Great, then you can tell her that she was insane to go with you."

Sorcha tossed her hands up and smiled at me. I took a deep breath before talking. "Caleb, your mother never tried to hurt me.

She brought me back with her and let me help get you situated, then sent a dress up for tonight. She's been on her best behavior."

Caleb stepped closer to his mother. "Is this true?" Sorcha nodded her head. "Why are you behaving yourself?"

Her answer took us all by surprise. "When you told me she had accepted your proposal, I told Kerrigan and we were both very excited for the two of you. I would never deny my son his life-mate...I could not do that to you, Caleb. Although I would prefer that it was anyone other than...."

"Sorcha," my father said sternly. She laughed as she walked up to Caleb and gave him a hug. I'd never pictured her as the maternal type, hmm, go figure.

"Come." My father motioned for us.

We stood and followed him to the front of the not so common, common room. He instructed Caleb and me to have a seat. He looked over at James and Pallo. He waved his hand out and my eyes widened. He'd dressed them in all black suits with matching capes. They looked like textbook vampires. I smiled when I saw how much Pallo disliked it. James seemed to think it was cool, why was I not surprised.

The doors to the hall burst open and the place filled to the brim with people, for lack of a better word. I watched as every creature imaginable wondered in. Some looked like they'd just crawled from the grave, while others looked completely normal. I noticed quite a few faeries arriving, along with numerous vampires. A group of people walked in that were dressed up but lacked that mysterious vampire quality. I leaned over to Sorcha who was on my right and asked what they were. She laughed and told me that they were a clan of werewolves--lycans.

Guests continued to flood in for the next twenty minutes. Soon they all found their seats. My father rose to his feet and the room fell silent. All eyes were on him. "Welcome, and I thank you for attending this most glorious of celebrations on such short notice. As you can see, several guests accompany me this evening. I'm sure you all recognize Sorcha." I couldn't be sure but I though I heard a boo. My father pretended as if he didn't hear it and continued on, "You all know Caleb." The room burst into applause. "And, I am sure that you have all heard of the great Master Vampire Pallo." The applause continued. My father skipped James but James didn't seem to notice or care. He was still admiring his Dracula ensemble. "Now, the young woman sitting before you is Gwyneth, my daughter...Princess Gwyneth to you all."

You could hear a pin drop. No one spoke. They all stared at my father and then at me. He put his hands above his head and a large bubble appeared. In it, I saw a picture of the most beautiful woman I'd ever seen. Her hair was golden and hung almost to her ankles, her skin was tanned, and her eyes were a light shade of green. A collective murmur went through the guests.

"I am sure you all remember Lydia," Kerrigan said.

I did a bubble double take. That woman was Lydia, my biological mother? I'd never seen her before. The image changed to Kerrigan and Lydia kissing. I should have felt sick to my stomach seeing my dad make out but it was beautiful. They were so in love and it showed. The next image that flashed was of Lydia very, very pregnant with me. Images continued to flash of the events of my life. My father had paid me frequent visits as a child. Each time he came he collected a memory of me and displayed it for all to see. He portrayed me in the most loving light and I was proud to be his daughter. When all was done the bubble vanished.

A tiny man with green skin and a forked tongue stood up and yelled. "All hail, Princess Gwyneth!" Everyone in the room began chanting my name. I looked at Sorcha. She nodded her head in approval. I didn't know what to do so I just sat really still.

My father put his hands up and the commotion stopped instantaneously. "Now, I would like to share even more good news with you. Caleb has asked for my daughter's hand in marriage. I have agreed to allow him to have it, and since you are all well aware of modern day woman's feelings, he asked her as well and she accepted."

We received a standing ovation. The room shook. My father motioned for Caleb and me to come forward. We did. I reached my hand to Caleb and he took it reluctantly. My father put his hands up again. The room fell silent.

"Now, does anyone here object to this promised union?"

I opened my mouth and Caleb leaned over to me. "We no longer get a say...or *I* would object myself." His grip tightened on my hand.

Great, my soon-to-be groom hated me.

My attention went to Pallo. He was fixated on my hand in Caleb's. James tried to speak, but Pallo yanked him back down to his chair. James' blue eyes found mine and they didn't look pleased. *I'm sorry, Gwen.*

It's okay. I'll be fine.

It's not okay and it's not fine.

James, it's fine, really.

He shook his head slightly. *But Gwen....*

Pallo's voice boomed through my head, causing me to jump slightly. *I believe she said she was fine, Jameson.*

My eyes met Pallo's and I saw his hurt, his confusion, his anger. There was nothing I could do at the moment.

Kerrigan's voice caught my attention. "Very well then...we shall meet back here six full moons from now for a wedding. Eat, drink, and enjoy."

Servers came out carrying trays full of foods. An uncooked pig went to the werewolf table and I almost threw up. Caleb let go of my hand and walked away from me. My father beckoned for me to join him and I did. A large table appeared before us, already full of food and wine. Pallo and James stood and walked over to two empty seats on the far end of it. They had apparently done this sort of thing before. It was all new to me.

I looked down at the place setting and gave up counting the utensils after I got to five. I was raised in a middle class suburban home, you got a fork, a spoon, and a knife if need be. Caleb came and sat on the right hand side of me that put him smack in the middle of Pallo and me. His back stiffened and he held his head high. To the average person, the one who didn't know him, he looked like my father, he looked like royalty. To me, he looked like he was having to work overtime to be close to me.

I sat there staring at the red mystery food before me. It was covered in some sort of sauce, and had a side of some oddly greenish colored goop. I put my hand over a fork and went to pick it up. It didn't budge. I tried another and it didn't move either. I looked down the table at Pallo and James. They were both sipping large goblets of dark red liquid. James stuck his tongue out at me again and I snickered. Caleb looked over at me and his lips drew in tight. He pressed a smile out and put his hand on mine. He squeezed so tight that I thought for sure that I'd have a bruise later.

"If you don't mind, this is after all our engagement party. If you could refrain from flirting with *him*, I would appreciate it."

I leaned in and whispered to him. "I wasn't flirting with Pallo. I was laughing at James."

Caleb gave my hand another squeeze. "I know."

"Ouch!" I yanked away from him and rubbed my hand. I looked at one of my four forks and thought about using one to stab his robe sleeve to the table. I wondered how good that would look to the guests. I made another attempt at picking up something to eat with and gave up. Sorcha, who was sitting to the left of my father leaned forward and looked down at me. She nodded her head and I saw the tiniest fork option rise up gently. I grabbed it and stared back at her. She winked and I smiled softly.

"Caleb, I think your mother's caught onto the fact that you hate me and want me dead. Hey, you're lucky in the sense that she'll have no problem offing your fiancée. Just say the word and I'm dead--*again*."

He stopped moving his food around his plate. "Gwen, I don't want you dead."

I let out a small sound indicating he could have fooled me, and noted he did not mention that he didn't hate me. Interesting what you can learn over the first course of a meal. I looked down at my food and followed Caleb's lead. I pushed it around and pretended to be eating it. I had no appetite and just wanted to go home.

Home was an interesting concept all unto itself. I'd grown used to having Caleb and Pallo around, now it would be just me. I didn't need a huge farmhouse all to myself. It had been built with the idea that it would house a family and I'd never have one of those. I seemed destined to push away everyone I loved. Caleb was right. I was self-destructive.

The next course came out. It didn't look any more appealing than the last. I'd decided that wine would be my dinner for the night. I'm sure somewhere that was considered a food group. I looked over at Caleb. His eyes were fixed on his plate. He wasn't touching his food either and I knew that he'd rather be doing anything than sitting next to me.

"Caleb, what happens now?"

"They'll keep bringing food out for a while and then we'll be expected to mingle together and greet the guests."

I was happy he'd spoken to me without the tone of disgust but that hadn't been exactly what I'd meant. "No, Caleb, what happens to us when we leave...when we go home."

He snorted. "We don't have a home...you did a *bang up* job of seeing to that."

My lip quivered and my eyes wanted to shed more tears. I didn't want to break down in front of the entire Dark Realm so I did my best to keep it together. I deserved everything I was getting and more. Karma was a bitch and it'd been chasing after me for over three hundred years. It was time to make some serious changes-- time to pull myself together and get on with my life. I'd managed just fine, or at least close to fine, on my own before I'd been re-introduced to Pallo and Caleb. I would do fine again but I wouldn't do it here in the Dark Realm. No, too many memories were here, too many ghosts. If I stayed I would still have to deal with Ken every day at work and live in the house where so many wonderful moments had taken place. Pallo told me I was stronger this time around but I knew I wasn't strong enough to deal with all of this as a whole. No, I would leave first thing in the morning.

I planned every detail out in my head. I would go to my office and get a new identity out of the manila envelope. I could withdraw enough funds to sustain me for awhile and just disappear. Somewhere warm and sunny sounded perfect. I'd have less of a chance of running into things that go bump in the night in a tropical location or at least I hoped that was true.

Finally, the food stopped coming. My father and Sorcha had been neck deep in making plans for a wedding that would not be taking place if Caleb and I had anything to say about it. The room filled with the sound of classical music. My father stood and all eyes went to him. He looked at me and then to Caleb. Caleb stood and put his hand out to me. I took it and he pulled me to my feet gracefully. He led me out to the open floor.

Hundreds of eyes were upon us. Reaching his hand out, he took my chin, and pulled it up to him. He brought his lips down to mine softly. An eruption of clapping and praise sounded all around us. To them we looked very much in love. They weren't the one on the receiving end of his coldness. He drew back from me and led me on to the dance floor. He moved his right hand beneath my left arm. He lifted my left hand with his free one and stepped into me. I moved back and then forward in direct opposition to whatever he was doing. We matched beautifully and wowed everyone. I never realized I could waltz. It must have been some residual effect from my prior time here. Somehow, my body remembered doing this with Caleb. I knew he preferred the common box step over other forms of waltz and I knew he liked to pull me into him at various times and come close to kissing me. Our lips barely missed each other each time he did this and I could see the tiny spark of surprise in his eyes that I knew to blow gently outward to arouse him.

Almost all of my memories had been of Pallo and our brief time together. These were some of the first feelings of moments between Caleb and me and they in no way revolved around drama associated with my love of Pallo. My only regret was that it had taken so much longer to have a breakthrough about him. Maybe that could have prevented so much pain and heartbreak, or maybe not.

Instantly, I was his with a vision of the two of us, our naked bodies tangled together. His long hair spilled all around us and he held himself propped up above me. I twisted my head to the side and found that we were lying in field of purple and yellow flowers. It was beautiful. I knew this was special and I knew why. It was the day we lost our virginity to one another. The day we'd done what we'd longed to do--love each other fully. The memory pulled away, leaving me breathless and clutching onto Caleb's hand.

The song ended and other couples joined us on the floor. I thought for a moment that Caleb was going to push me away, he didn't. He leaned in close to me. I knew it looked like he was just hugging me but in truth he was moving in to not be overheard.

"Remembering times of innocence?"

"I remembered times with you," I said softly back to him.

He let out a small laugh. "As I said, times of innocence."

I moved my face into his hair. "I don't want to fight with you anymore, Caleb, please."

He tightened his grip on my waist and turned me to match the music. "Well, Gwen, you're a little late on that, don't ya' think?" He spun me faster and his arm began to hurt my waist. "Don't come running back to me when your world falls apart. I'm done cleaning up your messes." His fingers dug deep into my hip. I tried to wriggle free of him, but he wasn't letting go. He was hurt and angry and he'd had these feelings building for four-hundred years. I was going to hear about it even if I had no memory of ninety percent of it.

Caleb tugged on the power that he'd shared with me when I'd agreed to marry him. "It's my turn to make you hurt, Gwen. It's my turn to be the one who controls our destiny. I hope that you are capable of feeling guilt and remorse, because I know you can't love anyone, not with all your heart."

He turned us into another couple and continued on, never apologizing. He was moving faster than the beat, fueled not by the song but by pain. "I thought we were making a life for ourselves this time. I thought that because Pallo was no longer human he'd lose his appeal. I was wrong." My heel twisted and I would have fallen if Caleb hadn't been holding so tight that I could barely breathe.

"Gwen, do you even understand how much you've hurt me? I watched you leave me for Giovanni, who was dark and twisted. I tried to warn you and you went anyway. I thought when you discovered what he really was that you'd come back to me but you didn't. You found a mortal. You found Pallo." My dress tore from his fingers digging into it. I hoped it would hold up. I really didn't want my unveiling to be literal.

"Gwen, when you showed up pregnant and scared, I opened my arms to you. I never questioned you and I never made you apologize for leaving me. That was a mistake. One of many that I made last time and I will not repeat them."

I was getting sick to my stomach from him moving us around so fast. I patted his shoulder gently. "Please, let's go somewhere and talk."

He let out a small laugh. "You have nothing to say that I want to hear."

The song came to a stop and he let me go. I fell backwards and struck the table full of werewolves in human form. One of the men grabbed my arm and kept me from falling over the top of the table. He looked at me and then at Caleb.

Caleb stormed away. The man helped me to my feet and I thanked him. He was nice enough not to comment on what he'd seen.

"Thank you...umm?"

"Mikhail," he said. I only had a second to look into his face, because I found myself being pulled away. I wanted to remember to tell my father about the man who'd been so kind.

Someone pulled me out a side door into a narrow dark hallway. I screamed and a cool hand covered my mouth quickly. "It is I," Pallo said. I wasn't sure if that was supposed to be comforting or not. He let go of my mouth and stood before me. He looked like everyone's idea of a vampire. He'd have been a shoe in for Dracula himself if his hair was black.

"I know what you are planning to do," he said as he pushed me towards the wall. "You think you can run away and forget all of this. You tried that before and failed miserably. Learn from history, Gwyneth, or you are doomed to repeat it."

He'd been in my head again during dinner. He'd listened in as I made my plans to leave. I brought my hand up fast and struck the side of his face. He never even flinched.

"Stay out of my head, Pallo...and, you know what, I'm sick and tired of everyone blaming me for shit that happened over two hundred years ago. If you ask me, you guys are the problem. I was fine before I met any of you!"

"Our destinies are intertwined, we are all linked...you, Caleb, myself, and others. It is a sad truth and I am sorry for that. It does not change the fact that you cannot run away from all of this. Two hundred years of being gone did not solve a thing, what makes you think now is any different?"

"Because, last time around I didn't think I could survive on my own. Hell, in those days a woman didn't stand a chance, but now, you said it yourself, I'm stronger. I'm not asking for your permission to go anywhere. I'm a grown woman. I'll do whatever hell I want to. You two can go back to whatever it is you did before I showed back up."

He was about to say something else, but we were interrupted by the sound of someone laughing. Pallo backed away from me and Caleb came into view. He looked past Pallo at me. Normally, he tried to take his anger out on Pallo, now he was going for the source. Apparently, he'd changed, too.

"You couldn't even make it through our engagement party before you were in his arms again," he said, his jaw clenched tight.

Pallo moved towards him and Caleb's hot energy filtered up. Pallo must have felt it as well, because his cold static essence flew up around us. Caleb moved forward.

"Don't think you can fight me, vampire. I kill your kind for a living."

Caleb sounded dark and that was not like him. I made a move to go to him and Pallo's arm came out to stop me. He was right, at the moment Caleb shouldn't be approached.

"Old friend, if you wish to try to kill me, then it saddens me but I will accept your challenge. I think you are letting your emotions be your guide this fine evening. You should be celebrating the announcement of your coming wedding. It is one you have been waiting for, for many, many years," Pallo said in the calmest voice I'd ever heard him use.

Caleb nodded at me. "She'll never commit to anyone. She wants everything, but gives noting in return. She's a selfish bitch and a lying whore." He looked directly at me, and his eyes went cold.

"You like to get in men's minds, in their hearts and fuck with them. You've always been that way. The minute you open your fucking legs, men loose their minds, their will. I'm thinking it would have better for everyone if you'd never come back, Gwen. Really, what greater good have you served? You've ripped my heart out. Hell, I don't even know if Pallo has a heart, if he does then I'm sure you did the same to his. Oh, let's not forget dear ol' James. 'He's just my friend, Caleb...you're being silly, Caleb,' yeah, right. Have you fucked him yet?" He put his hand up and I flinched. "Wait, don't' answer that. Let's guess. Pallo you go first."

I took a step back as hate radiated off him. I would not stick around and take this abuse. If he wanted free of me, then fine, he'd be free of me. They could all be free of me. I was sick of being pulled in two different directions by men who were at least ten times older than me. They'd had centuries to dwell on the past, to think of what should have been different. I had a few fragmented memories and twenty-five years under my belt. They'd turned me into a whiny indecisive shell of a woman, and I'd had enough.

Pallo turned his head back towards me, but kept his eyes on Caleb. "You earned my respect and I am forever in your debt for caring for her and my unborn child while I was...away. Because of this I tell you now to think with your head, Caleb. I can sense you do not mean the words that are coming from your mouth. You are hurt, it is understandable, yet you must set these feelings aside."

When hotheaded Pallo is the voice of reason, you know we have problems.

Caleb pushed against Pallo's energy with enough magic to show that he didn't care what words of wisdom Pallo had to offer. "How can you stand there and tell me to calm down? She's hurt you, too. Hell, she's hurt you worse. You're no longer alive because of her. Don't stand there and try to make me see a light that you can't even walk out into. She didn't just run off with your baby--she ran off with your soul!"

"Say what you must, Caleb. However, when morning comes and you realize you were harsh and want to take it all back, Gwyneth will be gone."

Caleb looked past Pallo at me. He thrust a hefty dose of hot magic my way and it pushed me back into the wall. "Go, then Gwen...leave now...save time and energy. It wouldn't be your first time running out on me. You're good at that. I hope I don't draw the short stick again and be the one who stumbles upon your dead fucking body. Get the hell out of here! Do me a favor and go straight to Giovanni. I'm curious as to what creative way he'll come up with to kill you again. I've got a few suggestions."

"CALEB, consider this your last warning," Pallo said, growling slightly.

Caleb ignored Pallo and glared at me. "Run Gwen, heaven forbid you face your problems head on. Go, off with you!" He thrust another does of magic at me and I cried out.

I turned and ran down the long hall. I had to kick the heels off to keep from falling on my face. I ran, not because I couldn't stand to hear the nasty things Caleb was saying, I ran because somewhere in my past I'd known that type of hatred--that hatred that causes men to go blind with jealousy and rage and to do something so unforgivable that it is never mentioned again. Yes, I knew that, and my body recognized it for what it was--a warning. I ran for my life. The hallway felt as though it was closing in on me. So many times I'd dreamed about an event so similar to this that the lines between my past life and this one blurred.

Pallo shouted at Caleb, "Enough!"

"Let the bitch go, Pallo."

"This is the same...think about it Caleb, this is how we lost her before. This is exactly how we lost her. She is not separating the two. To her, the fear is real--death is coming."

"Are you telling me that she's reliving the last few moments of...fuck! Gwen, stop! Damnit Gwen, stop! I was hurt and angry…."

I rounded the corner and recognized the hallway. I ran down to my bedroom door. I ran full force into the room and slammed the door shut. I let my forehead fall against the door as I locked it. My magic flared through me and knew enough to guard the door. Great, autopilot worked for me. My breathing was heavy and my chest was tight.

"*Bella*, you didn't seem to enjoy the announcement of your own engagement. Trouble in paradise so soon?"

I screamed and spun around to find Giovanni standing on the balcony. His long straight black hair hung to his mid-back and caught the eternal night's glow. He was dressed in a black tuxedo and even had on a top hat. He was the only vampire I'd ever met whose skin wasn't pale. I looked at his black eyes and wondered what brought him here to me.

"Did you come to try and kill me again? That's getting old. Besides, you'd have to get in line. Caleb has first dibs this time around." My words sounded brave but on the inside I was scare beyond belief. I just wanted to start over, never go to Necro's World and never meet any of them.

"No, *bella*, I have not come to harm you. No one knows I am here. The King wishes me dead now, and Sorcha was not pleased with my refusal to kill you a second time, though, she was not the sole instigator in that," he said. His Italian accent was thick. "I only came because I sensed your fear and your confusion. I've no wish to cause you any further pain. I simply could not rest knowing you were in need of comfort."

"May I come in?"

"No."

"I give you my word that no harm will come to you."

I thought about Pallo and Caleb, they both hated me right now and I couldn't say that I blamed them. It was obvious Caleb would rather stick a hot poker in his eye than marry me and Pallo had his chance to voice his objection to the engagement but he didn't. I was tired of living in turmoil. Tired of it all.

"*Bella*, allow me to comfort you. I would leave you be, but we are connected and when you are in pain, I feel it. And, I cannot bear it."

I heard Pallo's voice from the other side of my door. "Gwyneth, who are you talking to?"

"Go away, Pallo."

Giovanni raised a jet black eyebrow at me and glanced towards the door. "Now, may I come in?"

"No, Giovanni, you can't come in, but I'll come out." I walked towards him. Something slammed against the door. The castle was built for things with super-human strength. It would take a couple more slams to get in. I walked to the edge of the balcony door and stopped for a minute. Once I crossed that line that there would be no turning back. Both Pallo and Caleb liked to throw the past in my face when it suited them, why shouldn't I throw it back in theirs?

I heard Caleb tell Pallo to move. The temperature in the room jacked up fast and the door burst open. Pallo stopped in mid-stride when he saw Giovanni standing there. Caleb just stared at me. The hate in his eyes had been replaced by fear.

"Gwen?"

The two of them stood side by side. My soul mates together at last and for once in agreement. I'd no longer sit around and try to struggle with fate. It had dealt me two matches, two mates for a reason, and that was clearly to make me insane. It had to stop.

"Are you ready?" Giovanni asked. I nodded my head slowly, slightly scared of what was to come.

"Gwyneth, no," Pallo said, his voice full of pain. "We can fix this, Caleb and I can come to terms...do not do this."

"I didn't ask to be brought back and I didn't ask to be reunited with the two of you. I'm sorry for all the pain I've caused you both and I promise to stay out of your lives for good this time. Do me a favor and stay out of mine."

I stepped towards Giovanni on the balcony. He took my hand in his and pulled me close to him. My stomach dropped when we left the ground but I think it was more out of relief than fear of heights.

He held me close to his chest and for the first time in months I didn't feel conflicted or confused--I felt safe.

Epilogue

Flying for an extended period with a master vampire was definitely an experience a person remembers. When we stopped I thought we'd gone only a few miles, in truth we'd gone thousands. Giovanni had explained to me how the portals from the Dark Realm work. They are set up much like a subway with various on and off points, however, they do not operate in real time. You can open one door and be in Michigan, open another and be in Australia. We'd picked the one that led back to Giovanni's house, or excuse me, his castle--his villa.

He was tucked safely away in his room because the sun was rising. That left me free to roam about his home. Big, big, and big basically summed the place up. I felt like I'd stepped into the pages of a magazine. Everything had a place and everything jived. When we'd first arrived Giovanni had made an attempt to offer me something to eat. It was a good thing that I wasn't hungry because the man only had blood in his refrigerator. I laughed and I could tell that he felt badly about it. There was no way he could have foreseen me joining him so it was fine that he wasn't prepared.

Giovanni also kept trying to apologize for the state in which his house was in. There was only a thin layer of dust on everything but by the way he acted you'd have thought that he was asking me to make do in a city dump.

I headed up the curved staircase to the room he'd told me was mine. I opened the door and walked over to the large French doors that opened onto a massive balcony. The balcony overlooked the backyard. A huge in-ground pool was there, a tennis court, and several large gardens. I especially liked the box hedge maze, from my viewpoint it looked amazing. I had to laugh, Giovanni couldn't go out into the daylight yet his home was equipped with endless daytime activities.

I sat out on the iron chair with a matching table and watched the sun come up. I closed my eyes and let the first morning virginal rays touch my skin. I savored every second of it. My mind wandered for the first time since I'd arrived. I fully expected my thoughts to go to Caleb and Pallo instead I thought of James. I would miss him most. We'd become extremely close friends--and a friend was what I needed most right now.

* * * *

Giovanni and I have been living together for close to two months now. I think that surprised him as much as it surprised me. We aren't sleeping together. I'm positive he wants to but I have no interest in starting another relationship. So far, he's been fine with that. I was quick to let him know that if he got out of line with me I'd kill him. He thought that sounded fair, since I warned him and all.

I sometimes think of the engagement party. I haven't tried to contact anyone. I need a break from Pallo and Caleb. I've felt so free of guilt and responsibility with Giovanni--I don't want to go home. He doesn't judge me or ask me to make a choice, and he's never once brought up our past together. He seems perfectly content to just be in the same room as me, and that's what I need most right now.

I do find myself missing James more and more. It's funny how you can miss your friends more than your lovers. An old friend of mine once told me that intimacy is a vital part of a healthy relationship. I hadn't understood what that meant until now. I've been thinking about calling James but he'd be forced to tip Pallo off on my whereabouts.

As far as I know, the wedding is still set to take place four months from now. I don't see it happening. The groom can't stand me and I'm not sure how I feel about him. I wish it was cut and dry. I wish I could say that our situation can be summed up fast and wrapped up with a neat little bow--that I have no feelings for Pallo or Caleb, but they would both be lies, and we've already had more than enough of those.

THE END

Printed in the United States
41677LVS00001B/19-33

9 781586 087197